THE HEARTLESS AND THE WICKED

BOOK ONE

THE RUINS OF THE HEARTLESS FAE

MAHAM FATEMI

For my family,
always and forever

ROSAIN AND ITS SURROUNDING LANDS
???
???
???
THE NORTHERN SHORES
FROST ISLANDS
THE NORTH
THE POISON ISLES
THE MISTLANDS
???
???
???
ROSAIN
SKARLLAND
THE FOREST OF GREAT DIVIDE
EVENTYRSLOT RUINS
CAPITAL
THE LINE OF NO RETURN
THE SOUTHERN WALL
UNIFIED TRIBES OF KRIGER
THE ICE SHORES

1

Rumor had it the heartless fae ate the hearts of children and stole the souls of the innocent in order to satiate their wicked hunger for chaos and evil. Kolfinna thought that was rubbish because she never once wanted to do either of those things. The only thing she wanted was to stay hidden, like she was doing now. Instead of traipsing through enchanted forests and kidnapping children, she was scrubbing dried bird poop off the windows of the prestigious Hiskal academy.

The summer heat blazed around her in a thick, humid blanket and rivulets of sweat slid down her back, dampening her clothes. Kolfinna's fingers hummed with the familiar twinge of mana as grass tickled her ankles. If she wanted to, she could manipulate them to grow tall, or she could call forth the roots of the nearby willow trees to do her bidding. But doing so would reveal her true nature because only the fae could manipulate nature itself.

So she quelled the feeling of wanting to connect with the trees, the grass, and the plants surrounding her, just like how the blazing heat dried the cleaning rag in her hand. One small slipup and everyone would hunt her down. She couldn't allow that. Never again.

Kolfinna dipped her rag into the bucket of warm water and dragged it across the opaque glass windows once more. The ancient building had a crumbling foundation with the occasional renovation littered across it like a patchwork quilt. Even with all the wealth it brought in, all she had to do was run her hand along the aging walls and flecks of yellowed paint would chip away. She wasn't sure if she was supposed to clean off the peeling paint to reveal the natural gray stones underneath it, so she pretended she didn't notice. Just like how she pretended not to notice the students running laps on the school training grounds a hundred feet behind her.

The school had once been legendary for training powerful hunters, but now that the number of fae was sparse in the world, it shifted its attention to raising soldiers. She regarded them warily. Was she close to their level, or was she worse? She couldn't tell.

"*Inga!*" Dalla called out sharply.

Kolfinna jumped when Dalla poked her ribcage. Dalla raised a graying eyebrow and placed one hand on her hip while the other held a bucket of dirty, brown water. "I've been calling your name for a while now," her boss said, undertones of annoyance coloring her nasally voice. "We're moving to the next section of the building."

"Ah, right. Sorry." Kolfinna still wasn't used to her new name.

She dropped her rag in her own bucket of grimy water and hoisted it up by the wire handle, which bent at the weight. Tepid water sloshed over the rim and splashed against her feet. Dalla lurched back, face twisting.

"Watch where you're moving that thing!" She huffed in exasperation. "Let's go. You too, Jofurr."

Jofurr was hunkered over a bench, scrubbing it with a thick bristle brush. The afternoon sun reflected off his balding head as he jumped to his feet, all too eager to move on. "I was waiting to move to the next part," he said with a laugh as he gathered his cleaning supplies.

Kolfinna's bucket hit her leg with every step she took. Even after a year, her leg was still stiff, the muscles resisting the movement as she walked forward and a sharp pain shooting up her ankle and shin. She felt like all the students and teachers were watching her limp forward, possibly whispering among themselves about why she had such a broken gait.

They shuffled along the side of the building until they reached another section of it, this time closer to the students. Some of them wrestled each other while teachers overlooked them, and another group threw daggers at a dozen threadbare dummies with targets on their chests. Their uniforms were drenched in sweat and their faces were red in the scalding heat.

Jofurr watched them silently, a faraway look in his

eyes. Maybe that was the life he wanted, Kolfinna thought. Most people wanted to go to a prestigious military school.

"I used to want to be a student," he confided with a sigh, confirming her suspicions. He turned back to cleaning the windows running along the side of the building. "I was born an Elemental, but my powers were too weak for me to have been accepted in any military school."

Before Kolfinna could ask what type of Elemental he was—fire, water, air, lightning, or ice—he answered her unasked question by raising his hands over her bucket. A trickle of water rose in a straight line until he waved his hand and it streaked back in.

"Everyone wants to be in the military." Dalla wiped down the window carefully. "Those kids are going to make way more money than the three of us combined. You're lucky you were born an Elemental. At least you had a chance to become something."

His cheeks tinted red. "It's embarrassing I wasn't able to become anything."

Kolfinna quickly dunked her hands in the water to hide how she trembled. In the past, she would've thought she could defeat everyone in her immediate vicinity—the students and the teachers alike, regardless of the yellow or purple shiny badges hanging on their breast pockets. But now, if any of them attacked, she would escape into the folds of the city surrounding the academy and never look back. *He* had shown her just how terrifying the military could be.

"You're the same age as them, aren't you, Inga?"

Jofurr's kind eyes searched Kolfinna's face. He lowered his cleaning rag when she didn't answer immediately, and it took her a second to realize he was talking to her.

Kolfinna nodded.

"That's a shame." He sighed again and glanced at the training students. Sweat trickled down the side of his face and stained the collar of his shirt. "You should be in school, don't you think? Instead of working out here."

"She's not gifted," Dalla scoffed. "What's the point of wasting tax money on people who won't contribute?"

"Hey, she's contributing! She cleans—"

"Oh, please. We don't contribute. The military, the soldiers, the Royal Guards—the people who make differences—contribute."

"I think we're just as—"

Kolfinna drowned them out and stared at the window in front of her. She wiped up and down, up and down, over and over until the smudges were gone. A year ago, Dalla's remarks would've sparked her fury and she would've shown her just how much she could contribute, but she had since learned to calm her anger. It had been like a wildfire, burning and raging and smothering everything, but now she kept it like a steady bonfire. Contained.

It was better for everyone when Kolfinna was calm.

Inga, Kolfinna chided herself. Her name was Inga now.

At least it wasn't Astrid or Ophelia or Aslaug anymore. She didn't like those names, but they were common, and common meant people didn't think twice about them. Astrid could blend in with all the other Astrids, but Kolfinna was a name that made people pause and ponder. She hoped she didn't have to become another Ophelia. This time she was Inga, and she liked Inga because it was short and sweet, just like her sister's name, Katla.

"—fae."

Kolfinna flinched. Her attention swiveled to Jofurr and Dalla, who were both still cleaning the windows, seemingly unaware of her stiff posture or bloodless face. Her heart continued to race a million beats a second, but no one was jumping on her and pointing fingers. They were conversing like normal.

They didn't find her out, she told herself. *Relax.*

Jofurr scratched his head. "—they're going to keep wasting resources on—"

"It's not wasted resources if they do it in their free time," Dalla said.

He shrugged. "I guess, but with the powers they have ... don't you think their abilities would be better used in other ways to help people?"

"Hunting fae is for the greater good. I don't know what other task could be more important! My own father was a member of the Hunter's Association," Dalla said, puffing her chest out. A rare smile upturned her thin, peeling lips. "He even helped hunt a few back when he was younger."

Kolfinna's grip on her rag tightened and warm water

squeezed out from the cloth, dripping down her wrist and pooling uncomfortably on her sleeve. The Hunter's Association had been a wing of the military before people realized the hunters weren't doing much. They couldn't hunt fae that didn't exist. Their predecessors had fulfilled their goal: eradicating the fae. Now, it was only a hobby organization to catch stragglers that somehow slipped out from the fine-toothed comb the Hunter's Association filtered through the years. Most fae were dead. All the ones Kolfinna knew were dead.

A year ago, her blood would've boiled at the mention of the Hunter's Association. Her mind would've been filled with hundreds of thoughts of how she would enact brutal, violent retaliation on any hunter she saw. But now, her veins ran with ice at the thought of a hunter. Her mana shriveled and her mouth filled with ash.

Dalla's smile faded and she paused with her cleaning. "Unfortunately, a mission gone wrong and that was that."

"I'm sorry to hear that." Jofurr's voice lowered in sympathy.

"Thank you," she said with a dismissive wave. "But it was ages ago and I've long moved on in life. But it's a shame the association is no longer as funded as it used to be."

"It's a good thing," he said. "Because they've done their job."

"Not really. There are still fae wandering around, kidnapping innocent children and new brides! One thing my father always told me is to never trust the fae. They're evil, deceitful, and manipulative! It's in their nature." Dalla leaned closer to Jofurr as if she was telling him a long-kept secret. "Those monsters have an advantage over us, even with their dwindling numbers. While we have to work incredibly hard to be able to use our magic, it comes easily to them! So, no matter if it's a child fae or a grown one, never trust it, because chances are, it's biding its time before it takes your soul!"

Kolfinna focused on a particular cluster of dead bugs splayed across one of the windows. She scrubbed at it with her rag, watching as their dead bodies swam across the glass with every wave of her hand. Dalla was half right. Magic *did* come easily to the fae. They were more attuned to the mana flowing through their bodies, as if their vessels were made for mana. But the fae didn't kidnap children or brides. Or eat souls. Or whatever outlandish folktales had spread throughout the centuries.

Kolfinna swallowed the bile clawing up her throat. She was Inga, and Inga was *normal*.

"Do we have any jobs after this one?" Kolfinna hoped her smile wasn't strained and awkward. She didn't remember how to smile. Katla used to smile all the time. *Such a pretty face with an evil smile*, Katla used to tell her when they were amicable, but when they fought, she used to say *you're an evil little thing with a pretty smile*. It was all in jest. But Katla was dead, and Kolfinna's smile fell flat.

"No." The frown lines framing Dalla's mouth deepened. "The school didn't book us for the interior cleaning, and our next clients canceled this morning."

"So we're done for the day?" Jofurr's eyes lit up.

Dalla exhaled exasperatedly and gestured towards the windows of the decaying school. "Yes, but only *after* we're done with these windows."

That seemed to invigorate him because he bobbed his head and set to work polishing the windows like his life depended on it. Kolfinna joined him in the monotonous job. Up, down, side to side. She moved the damp cloth over the smears of fingerprints and dead bugs. In the reflection, the students had stopped running laps and sat on the ground. They drank water out of canisters and laughed with their peers. She could imagine herself with them. She would smile and laugh freely like there was no burden on her shoulders. She would wrap her arm around her friend and give her a squeeze. She would pat another one's back as he heaved for air. Maybe they would complain about how hard their teacher was pushing them. But then Kolfinna dragged the rag over the reflection, banishing it from her thoughts.

"Inga, do you have plans after work?" Jofurr asked as he moved to the next window beside her. His blue eyes shot in her direction. "If you're free, my wife is making her famous beef stew for dinner tonight."

She could imagine herself sitting with Jofurr and his wife and kids. She could see it so clearly that she almost said yes, but then the opposite picture took over: Jofurr pointing at her as he told the military officials she was a fae. The thought sent razors down her spine.

"Ah, I have plans," she said with another strained smile.

"Oh, really?"

Time slowed and she swallowed the thick dread building in the pit of her stomach and clawing up her throat. Why did he doubt her? Could he tell she was lying?

"That's a shame," he said with a kind smile. "Maybe next time."

"Yeah ..."

Dalla snapped her fingers and called out to them, "Quit dillydallying and get to work!"

They didn't talk again after that. All three of them worked for another twenty minutes before Dalla dismissed them. As Kolfinna left the school grounds, she could finally breathe again. The military students were everything she could never be, and everything that would bring her downfall. That was the one thing she didn't like about this town, the capital: there were too many academies, too many aspiring soldiers, and too many soldiers and Royal Guards. It was nauseating.

Kolfinna breathed in the aroma of buttery pastries wafting through open bakery doors, the smell of spices lining the market streets, and the sweet scent of regional flowers from the flower shops. A crush of people filled the streets, and even though she hated the feeling of so many people so close to her—close enough to maybe figure out she was a fae—she *liked* the bustling capital, despite that the Royal Guards were headquartered here and that there was a military fortress nearby. It was actually better to be in the thick of the enemy because they least expected her here. She also liked how she could disappear into the crowds of people. She was just one droplet in a large pond. Buzzing towns meant it was easier to hide away.

As if on cue, her leg throbbed, reminding her that she couldn't seamlessly blend in anywhere. Her limp made people stare, whether she liked it or not.

Even now as she left the school grounds and entered the thick of the city, she could feel the eyes on her. They never left her.

The late afternoon spilled rays of honey across the busy streets. Soldiers in their drab gray uniforms filled tiny pockets of the streets, their power ranking—mostly white, but a few grays—stamped on their chests below the Rosain's lion and roses emblem. Poor and middle-class folk wove through the street. The poor either had short clothes that barely fit or clothes that were a size too big— all of which had patches of mismatched cloth to cover the holes and tears. The middle class, on the other hand, wore clothes that were crisp, clean, and free of patches. Kolfinna didn't fit in either category. She wasn't poor, per se, but she was nowhere near middle-class.

She maneuvered the streets carefully, keeping an eye on the soldiers. Her heart rate picked up in pace as one of the soldiers glanced in her direction. She bored holes into the ground, her wavy black hair curtaining her face so they couldn't see her. Her naturally pink eyes were brown due to the medicinal herbal tea she drank every day; it wasn't time for the tea's properties to run out, which would've rendered her eyes back to their natural color, but she still couldn't meet the soldiers' eyes for fear that they could see that she was different. That there was an enchanted, peculiar beauty about her. Or that her eyes showed flecks of pink when the sun waned.

Her leg continued to throb as she pushed forward. She could still feel the icy cold brush of death whispering against her body—against her leg and ankle. She quickened her pace, her feet nearly stumbling over themselves as she wove through the thickets of people. It had been one year since she confronted *him*, but every thought of the military made her body tense with trepidation. He wasn't among them, she repeated to herself like a mantra. There was no way he was here.

She passed a rowdy tavern with patrons hooting and hollering and drinking like the sun wasn't out. A few men hung outside it, their drunk, salacious gazes flitting over every passing woman. Kolfinna's lips curled into a scowl as one of them glanced her way. He ogled her body with a drunk grin but froze when he met her expression. She was sure he could tell she wanted to rip his eyes out of their sockets. Her hands itched to draw blood.

Not today, she told herself, giving him an even darker look as she continued her walk. *Not today.*

Because Kolfinna was Inga now, and Inga didn't get into fights. Inga controlled her anger.

She kept repeating that in her mind as she walked to the outskirts of town. The throng of people thinned until she was at the edge of the city, where there were open dirt roads lined with shrubbery and silver birch trees marked the entrance of the woods.

The cool air of the woods breathed life into her pores, and her fingers twitched to call forth her mana and warp the plants beneath her feet, to draw them up to their full height or twist them to create a canopy. It didn't matter what. She just had to do *something* with it. But she pushed down the feeling and went deeper into the woods. It wasn't until the sun dipped along the horizon that she stopped and sat on the leafy ground.

Every day after work, she liked to relax in nature, whether it was the woods or a tiny patch of grass in the city alleys. She wasn't sure if it was a fae thing or something only she did, but nature had a calming effect on her. It was like a cleansing ritual, washing away her stress until she felt like she could finally breathe. Because only these trees, this grass, and these bushes understood who she was and accepted her.

Kolfinna massaged her right shin slowly. Her foot ached and sent pangs up her leg. It didn't usually hurt unless she walked on it for too long or was on her feet all day, which was every working day. Her fingers ran over the muscles of her thigh, calf, and then her ankle. She hated how *he* had marred her body. She could still feel the icy grips of his magic when it had violently latched onto her leg and shattered it. It didn't set correctly and now she was stuck with a permanent limp.

A distant owl hoot brought her back to reality. Back to the canopy of trees surrounding her, the luscious greenery, and the humid air sticking to her skin. Kolfinna lay on the bumpy, leaf-ridden ground and breathed in the scent of damp moss and wildflowers. She closed her eyes and dug her fingers into the grass and soil, relishing the pulsating life at her fingertips. She breathed in the life force. She so badly wanted to release her mana, the thrumming energy nestled inside every living creature, and turn it into magic. She wanted to use her magic and make the trees dance and drop their leaves over her like a waterfall, and then make the grass grow as thick as a cushion so she could sleep.

Katla's image was burned in the back of her mind. Her distinctive round nose, plump lips, and expressive eyebrows that wiggled in different forms depending on her emotion. Kolfinna pressed the heels of her hands against her eyes. Her sister would've been alive if Kolfinna had been able to use her powers properly. If she hadn't lost control.

2

Kolfinna had chosen the most inconspicuous apartment she could find. It was tiny, dingy, and, best of all, full of the poorest, roughest group of scowl-faced individuals. It was the type of place where whole families jammed into a single-roomed apartment. Noise traveled through the thin walls like it was everyone's business. It was always loud during the day, but eerily silent during the night. As if everyone had something to do with the underworld nightlife. No one asked about the other, and so no one bothered her. It was perfect.

Her apartment had no furniture whatsoever. Every night, she slept on a pile of blankets, the hardwood floor always pressing against her rigid body. She didn't have anything to call her own except the clothes on her back. She didn't allow herself to become attached to many things. She had to travel lightly, especially since she hopped from city to city every few months.

Kolfinna inhaled the steam from the tea cup. Brownish liquid swirled in the chipped ceramic cup; it was uncomfortably hot against her fingers, but Kolfinna preferred discomfort. It was a reminder that she couldn't ever be idle.

Every morning and night she had a cup of hot "weedy" tea with three spoonfuls of honey. The bitter concoction was made with equal parts of dandelions, crabgrass, and creeping thistle; to humans, it was just an array of weeds, but to the fae, it was invaluable. It concealed their true eye color into a muddy brown for around twelve hours. She wouldn't have been able to survive among humans if it wasn't for the tea; it was an old recipe passed down from fae to fae. A secret well-kept from humans.

Kolfinna sipped her morning tea slowly. It warmed her throat and although it was hard to swallow, she continued drinking the dark substance. Katla used to drink tea with buttered bread. She would dunk it in her cup until the bread absorbed the tea, then chomp on it wetly. It grossed Kolfinna out whenever she did it, but she now longed for those quick morning breakfasts they had shared. Now, she ate breakfast alone. Always alone.

She reached for her woven basket and flipped the lid open, only to find a half-eaten loaf of crusty bread and a few dried apricots. Groaning softly, she pushed the basket away from her. She would have to drop by the market and grab a meal or two this afternoon. She hated grocery shopping; hated the way people stared at her and asked questions. Kolfinna wasn't beautiful, per se, but she had the effect all fae had on humans: they were drawn to her for some reason. They themselves probably didn't understand it.

She wasn't like Katla, who had perfectly encompassed all beauty standards and made people gawk at her. Katla, with her thin frame, wide smile, and dazzling green eyes, fit in wherever she went. She had been blessed in every manner: conventional beauty that didn't make one wonder if her attraction was due to fae blood, green eyes that were brighter and more vivid than a human's, but didn't stir suspicion, and an infectious, kind personality. Kolfinna was the exact opposite. In fact, it always surprised everyone to find out they were siblings. That was how much they didn't look alike; if she didn't know any better, she'd say they weren't related at all. Kolfinna was homely, chubby, awkward, and curt to the point of rudeness. She couldn't draw the same attention. She had to remain hidden, or people would realize she wasn't normal.

Kolfinna scarfed the contents of the basket and laid on her pile of blankets. She liked the busy city life, but she'd stayed here for too long. It was time for a change. Jofurr had asked her to stay for dinner yesterday. That was the first step. Next, he would figure out who she was and send her straight to the Hunter's Association. That was always how it played in her head. It had never happened before, but she had some close calls. The last town she was in, her coworker had noted how suspiciously pretty she was despite her features being boring. Another had pointed out her eye color never looked the same—a side effect from the weedy tea wearing off. And once, a young passing boy had said she smelled like nature, like moss and roses and rainwater. She left each of those places the very same day.

Where should she go this time? Maybe somewhere rural? She usually stuck to cities, since it was easier to blend into the crowd, but the rural area had its pros and cons. Cons were that they were more superstitious and wary of newcomers. Pros were that even if she was caught, she could probably defeat whichever officers were there, since the stronger officers—whether the military or Royal Guards—were stationed in busier cities.

An abrupt knock broke her from her reverie. Her body froze on instinct, her eyes darting to the door and then to the window. *No one* knocked on her door. The people in the apartment kept to themselves. So who was it?

She quietly placed the teacup on the floor and sprang to her feet, keeping one eye on the door and another on the window as she slunk toward it.

"Who is it?" She glanced out her window at the alleyway. Two men peered inside the windows on the lower level. Their uniforms were a blur of white and silver, with a shocking red cape. Kolfinna fell to the floor as one of them glanced up. Her stomach dropped—why in the world were the *Royal Guards* here?

"We've come to ask a few questions," came a deep reply from the door.

The walls of the apartment suddenly felt too small—too crowded, too *suffocating*. It would take less than a minute for the room to fill with guards, swords, and charged magic.

They were here for her.

And they weren't normal men. They were the freaking *Royal Guards*. The Royal Guards were too prestigious, too busy, too pretentious to have anything to do with a normal citizen. If they were here in this rundown apartment complex, they were definitely here for her—for a criminal.

Blood pounded in her ears, her chest tightened painfully and her breaths came in shallow inhales. She had to use her magic. It was the only way to escape. The only way to make it out alive, because if the Royal Guards caught her, she was dead.

She squeezed her hands together to keep them from quivering. But what if they weren't here for her? If she used her magic, she would be irrefutably outing herself as a fae.

"Ma'am, we're here to ask some questions," the voice called again, sterner this time.

There was no time to think. Kolfinna unlatched her window and threw it open. Mana pulsed beneath her fingers and she sighed in relief at the familiar feel of life pumping through her veins. Almost automatically, the smell of damp moss and wet tree trunks filled the air, and gnarled, brown roots, infused with her mana, shot through the cobbled streets. The men below yelped in surprise as Kolfinna tangled the roots around them, flicking her wrists to manipulate nature and bring a thick, woody tree root in front of her. She hoisted herself up on the windowsill just as the door behind her burst open. Over her shoulder, two Royal Guards filled the room, their mouths open in a shout and their ornamental swords drawn.

She leapt onto the root and her right foot slipped, the abrupt motion awkward for her stiff ankle. Kolfinna's arms flailed and she almost plummeted down five stories before righting herself by grabbing the windowsill behind her.

"Hey—" one of the Royal Guards inside her room shouted.

Kolfinna released the windowsill and dragged her hand across the stones below it, directing her mana to control it. The Royal Guards in her room drew closer to the window, but before they could reach it, she forced the stone wall to stretch and seal it shut. She then raised the root and latched onto it, controlling it so it brought her closer to the ground, while simultaneously wrapping the two Royal Guards on the lower level with a cage of unrelenting weeds, thorns, and roots. They swung their swords to cut down the plants, but they were quickly engulfed in her nature manipulation.

She could hear their muffled shouts as she lowered herself with the help of the root. Her apartment was located on the top floor, so she weaved more vines to crack through the ground and assist her so she wouldn't fall on the hard cobbled street. They came beneath her feet at her command and she stumbled to the ground, unable to find her balance because of her right leg. The two Royal Guards she had tangled up were now struggling against the vines, but it was only a matter of minutes before they freed themselves. Kolfinna bolted in the opposite direction of them. Were there more? Or only those four? She needed to reach the cusp of the city and disappear into the woods, where her magic was the strongest.

Her leg painfully dragged behind her with every stride she took. Fear lodged into the back of her throat. She had somehow run away from those four, but there was no way she could defeat them in a fair fight. They were the Royal Guards! The Royal Guards never accepted anyone below a yellow ranking.

A water spear whizzed past her cheek and grazed a strand of her pitch-black hair. Over her shoulder, one of the guards she had entangled had freed half of his body and now struggled against the vines, his hand outstretched and his dark brown eyes set on her as water settled around his fingers.

A water elemental user.

It wasn't the worst matchup against her, but he was a Royal Guard, and if he wanted to do damage, he definitely could.

Kolfinna raised her hand and caused the weeds and shrubs to entomb him once more. Her magic came back to her easily, despite being dormant over the past year. Using mana to create magic was like a muscle—the more practice and training one did with it, the stronger it was, and the more time one didn't use it, the rustier and more strained it became. Despite the ease with which it came to her, it drained faster and less efficiently than in the past.

She rounded the corner of the alleyway, only to be met with half a dozen Royal Guards slouching in wooden chairs on the outdoor patio of the neighborhood tavern.

"Hey, it's her!" one of them shouted.

She cursed softly, her mana pervading into the pavement below her as she raised her hands to mold the ground like she saw in her mind. She imagined a wall rising between her and her pursuers, and in a split second, the stones groaned beneath her feet and shot up in uneven blocks to stave them off. Kolfinna's good foot pounded the pavement, broken up by the dragging of her right foot as she took off away from them.

Why were there so many guards?

The early morning citizens pushed away from her as she sprinted down the thickening streets; they clung to the buildings and watched, ashen, at the flurry of motion she created. The city that had once kept her safe and hidden, now shook with her uneven gait, the city-dwellers forming a path for her as they stared in horror.

They knew. Her earth manipulation had shown them what she was—a fae.

A heartless, evil fae.

Would she even be able to run away? Her right foot was killing her and she was slowing down already.

Kolfinna couldn't keep running in the open like this.

She needed to flee into the alleyways and find a way to the edge of the forest. But that would take time, and she most certainly would have to engage in battle. How long could she last against them?

An ear-screeching bang followed behind Kolfinna. Behind her, a woman had punched through her stone wall; the other guards swarmed from the hole she created. *Well, dang*, Kolfinna gritted her teeth. *They've got an Enhancer?* Yellow? Purple? Her power level had to be at purple.

The Royal Guards wouldn't let her step foot into the forest, she realized as she was driven deeper into the heart of the city. People were just starting to enter the early morning streets, and unlike the streets by her apartment, they didn't keep out of her path. In fact, they didn't seem to register what she was, or why she was running, until they noticed the growth of nature behind her. Kolfinna raised vines and walls behind her with every turn to obstruct her pursuers' path, and the people who had just woken up, unaware of the commotion, screamed and lurched out of her way.

"A fae!" someone to her right screamed.

She ducked when someone threw something her way. Their faces blurred together, but she could still feel their fear and hatred for her. *Kill her*, they all seemed to say. She drove her vines to shove the bystanders away. They shouted when her plants lashed them to the ground. The last thing she needed was to get taken out by a bystander by accident. A flying pan to the face would stun anyone.

Kolfinna rounded the corner, gaze roving over the tall buildings and the blur of faces around her. The edge of the forest—where was it again? She couldn't think straight past the adrenaline rush and even though she had walked through the capital streets hundreds of times, her sense of direction was gone. She felt like she was in an unfamiliar town running nowhere.

"Stop resisting!" an angry snarl came to her left, alarmingly close.

She barely had time to look before she heard the hauntingly familiar sound of cracking ice beneath her feet. In seconds, a thin sheet of ice spread across the cobbled street, sunlight gleaming off it in harsh, blinding rays. Her feet slipped from beneath her and she waved her arms to catch herself but she still slammed onto the icy ground. The ice split where she fell and she winced as pain radiated from her bad knee down to her ankle.

The chilling cold made her inhale sharply.

It can't be.

The man to her left walked almost in slow motion, the ice pulling away from the ground beneath his booted feet to keep him from slipping. He raised his hand and ice magic spread around her ankles, rooting her in place as it slowly spread over her body. The icy grips felt like stone.

She would die. She would die. *He* would finally kill her.

Breathe.

The man took a step toward her; she could hear the

shouting of the other Royal Guards—not too far anymore.

Breathe.

Instead of the chilling blue eyes she expected to find peering down at her like she was a half-dead insect clinging to his sturdy boots, she was met with brown eyes. And instead of inky black hair, this man had white-blond hair.

It's not him.

A flood of relief washed over her. So long as it wasn't *him*, she could still run away.

He was only one step away, his hand stretched out to grab her. There was a hard set to his jaw, and he stood at least a foot taller than her, towering over her just like the buildings behind them. His ice tightened around her. Another inch closer. And another.

Her magic exploded around them, stones and vines violently hurtling toward the Royal Guard. Her mana pulsed through her body and she willed it into the icy ground. She imagined a stone spear shooting out from the ground; in seconds, her imagination came to life as she carved the spear out of the stony street, then aimed it at the ice bindings over her chest and legs. The stone spear smashed into the ice encasing her, shattering it and freeing her, but not without scraping the delicate skin of her stomach. She barely registered the pain as she sprang to her feet; ice shards scattered over the ground and glistened like broken glass in the morning sun.

The Royal Guard's eyes widened, and that was all the time Kolfinna needed to bring forth the stones from the street toward her body. Tiny rocks flew toward her, drawn by the magnetic pull of her mana as she employed them to cloak her fists like gauntlets. The ice elemental user reeled back at her display, widening his stance and narrowing his eyes in concentration. He had likely never faced a fae, judging by his alarmed expression, and maybe hadn't known that along with nature manipulation, she could manipulate the earth as well.

Kolfinna pulled the rocks toward her shins as he charged her. She shot her vines out from the ground to wrap around his legs. Ice clung to his fingertips, as if ready to attack the vines, when she punched him in the chest and face. She spun and kicked him with her good shin, equipped with her rock armor, against his head. He slumped forward in a heap and she tightened her grip on him with her ropey vines.

She quickly tied up the guard with her vines, her heart racing a million beats a second; she had defeated him, somehow. A year ago, she would've expected nothing less from herself, but that was back when she was naïve and overconfident.

She didn't have time to think—they were gaining on her.

Half of the Royal Guards were stalled by the vines and roots she had thrown at the civilians; they seemed to be emptying the streets and helping civilians to their feet. A pang of guilt had her hesitating, but she continued her escape; she didn't hurt any of the civilians, only pushed them out of her way. They would've killed her given the chance, she reasoned.

The Royal Guards would reach her in no time; she wasn't fit enough to outrun a Royal Guard, who were trained in combat and endurance, and her only advantage was that they likely didn't have training or real experience fighting a fae who knew how to use her magic. But that advantage was waning; she was using up a lot of mana at a frightening rate.

Heat singed the hairs on her arm and a wave of fire rose to her right. She barely had enough time to raise a shield of plants before stumbling to the ground. A scorched, rotting smell stung her nose and her shield of plants crumbled to charcoal in seconds, the wind carrying their ashes around her.

Impossible!

The only way someone could burn her vines was if their mana was more powerful than her mana coating and controlling the plants—and if there was one thing Kolfinna was proud of, it was the strength of her nature manipulation.

Kolfinna twisted on the ground to face the assailant.

A man in his late twenties stood in the center of the road, a shock of red hair contrasting with his pale skin. Expressionless silver eyes were trained on her and fire burned at his fingertips. He had a calm but terrifying aura around him and he wore the Royal Guard uniform, but instead of the characteristic white uniform with silver accents and buttons, his uniform had gold accents and even the red cape had gold clasps instead of silver. A gold badge shone on his breast pocket.

Rows of apartment buildings and glass storefronts lined the streets, and people poked their heads out from the second and third stories, watching with bated breaths and wide eyes the chaos ensuing on the streets. People ran all around them, trying to get as far away as possible. Kolfinna wanted to slip away from all the attention; all these people knew what she looked like now. She would have to run to the countryside to keep the rumors at bay.

"No need to keep running," the red-haired man said in a velvety voice. The fire in his hands shifted into a shade of purple, then blue. "If you surrender, I won't hurt you."

Kolfinna rose to her feet unsteadily. Her voice came out strangled. "Liar! You're here to capture and kill me!"

Kolfinna jumped back and focused her mana to the ground. Dozens of vines erupted from the stones and headed in the man's direction. They were faster than the ones she had been showcasing earlier; with this man, she couldn't afford to ration her mana. She needed to go all out. He was deadly and strong—she could tell by the blue color of his flames that he wasn't an ordinary fire elemental user. One wrong move and she'd be dead.

Fire shot from the ground in blazing red heat, burning her vines instantly. Uneasiness stirred in the pit of her belly. He shouldn't have been able to burn her vines that quickly.

Kolfinna forced more vines to follow after him while she put more distance between herself and him. He raised his hand and a wave of fire, once again, crisped her vines into dust.

His silver eyes followed her and he stepped forward, but Kolfinna raised two stone walls on either side of him. He glanced at them almost curiously, and she clapped her hands together, bringing the two together to smash him. He leapt forward, escaping the jaws of her trap. The stone walls crashed into one another, but Kolfinna didn't let him escape so easily. She wrought another stone wall in front of him and did the same, attempting to sandwich him between the others. He moved lithely, his gaze darting from wall to wall, taking in his surroundings.

She manipulated a sneaky vine to shoot up and wrap around his ankle tightly, just as two more stone walls came toward him. Kolfinna's heart raced—she got him. He didn't have enough time to escape from both the vines and the walls. But he did something she didn't expect: in seconds, he wielded his sword. Fire caught onto the blade, fierce and melding the silver blade into hot red, but it was too late. The walls crashed into him, a burst of dust filling the air.

Kolfinna breathed out raggedly and tried to set her feet on the crumbled street, her right leg pulsating with overuse. Her mana was dwindling and she was reaching her limit; if she tried to fight every single Royal Guard, she would surely run out of mana and be captured. She could already see the other Royal Guards surrounding the street beyond the hazy smoke that lifted through the air.

She needed to run—

The temperature in the street rose significantly until drops of sweat beaded her forehead. The smoke and clouds of dust thinned to reveal a figure standing between the two shattered pieces of stone walls, which she recognized as the ones she had thrown at him. They lay on the ground, sliced in half, burned and radiating red from the heat. The red-haired man stood in the center of it, soot and debris coloring his white uniform in shades of black and charcoal. A red glow emanated from his surroundings.

Kolfinna stumbled a few feet away.

He was too strong, she realized, but what other choice did she have other than to fight?

She pulled dozens of rocks from the ground with her mana and shot them at him. He raised his sword and with a flash of red steel, deflected them. He ducked, dodged, and slashed. Every time he struck the rocks, they incinerated and sparked, some of them flying a distance and crashing into the apartment buildings. Shattered glass littered the crumbling streets, people screaming in the distance.

Sweat dribbled down Kolfinna's forehead and dampened her neck. Her mana was being depleted even faster now. Her hands trembled, but she wasn't sure if it was from exhaustion or fear. Even as he cut the rocks she sent his way, his focus was on her. The weight of his gaze sent shivers down her back.

He was a monster, and he wasn't even using his blue flames against her. Or even violet ones, or white, or orange. Or any other color than the weakest of them all—red.

Who knew there was another monster other than *him*? But instead of the icy grips she was so fearful of, this man's form of violence was fire.

The Royal Guards were several meters away from the red-haired man. Kolfinna raised a stone wall between them, but one of them broke through it easily.

"Can you really afford to keep your eyes off me?"

A jolt of fear ran through her body as he darted toward her. She had been avoiding close combat; it was her weakness, after all. She wasn't trained in combat to keep up with a Royal Guard, so her only strength was her magic—and that didn't seem to work on him.

Kolfinna infused her mana with the rocks beneath her feet and they sprang up to cling to her body like armor. Her mana threaded over the rocks and held them in place over her body. In seconds, she wore a rock armor and helmet.

The man cleared the distance between them and swung his fiery sword at her neck. She ducked, and he easily shaved the top layer of her rock helmet. He twisted the sword to aim down, but she leapt back, his sword cracking into the ground. The blade hissed against the cobbled street, steam rising from it.

Kolfinna hesitated—how could she beat him?—but sprang into action the next second. She punched his chest, the weight of her rock armor heavy on her body, but he parried and cut her across her chest. Heat scorched her body and she leapt back, stifling a scream. Her armor crackled and snapped in the area where he had slashed her. Fiery pain throbbed her skin and flesh. Her armor had taken the brunt of the attack, but it couldn't completely keep the heat at bay.

She jumped back, but he was onto her again. *Slash, slash, slash*—he kept striking her mercilessly, and she could barely dodge. Her armor had to take whatever she couldn't dodge. Budding bruises and burnt marks scored her body; no matter how much she kept building up her armor and reinforcing it with more layers, he easily cut it down. Her breathing became labored and her movements more sluggish. He, on the other hand, didn't break a sweat. His moves were clear and crisp. Every movement seemed planned and fluid, like he was dancing rather than fighting.

Sweat dampened Kolfinna's breasts, her thighs, her back—every inch of her was drenched in it. Heat singed her feet and before she knew it, the soles of her shoes were burnt and brittle. The temperature in the street kept rising until it was suffocating to even *breathe*. Plants and moss that adorned houses were black crisps, and baskets and stacks of hay caught on fire; it took her a second to realize the other Royal Guards weren't paying attention to their fight. They were taking care of the streets. Water elemental users were splashing water on houses to keep them from burning, their water turning to steam the instant it touched the hot, brick houses. Air elemental users were pushing stray rocks from their battle away from the windows of houses and people. Ice elemental users were creating walls of ice to stop the fires from spreading, and the other Royal Guards were evacuating citizens.

Her eyes widened with that realization. They didn't think she would escape or win. They were just trying to reduce the collateral damage.

"Come on, Kolfinna." The man lowered his blade, and the tip of it kissed the ground. A crackle of fire sparked white at the contact. "There's nowhere for you to run. Give up now, before you get hurt."

He knew her name.

"Get away from me!" she snarled, hating that he was right, that there was nowhere for her to run.

He sighed, and walls of flames rose dozens of feet high, closing around them in a fiery arena. Kolfinna's fists clenched together and she whipped her head left and right. She had nowhere to escape. More sweat collected on her brow, and her clothes stuck to her body.

"The only reason you survived against Blár Vilulf is because he toyed with you." He pointed his sword in her direction and stared at her with a haunting calmness. The surrounding fire made his silver eyes gleam red for a few flickering seconds. "You only escaped him because of his inability to take things seriously."

Kolfinna flinched. *Blár*. The name of the man who defeated her last year. Her leg ached terribly, remembering the way his ice had shattered the bone. Was that revelation supposed to anger her? That Blár had toyed with her? It was something she had already known. Blár had been too monstrously strong for her to face off—just as this man was.

She just needed to escape somehow.

And then it struck her. The man in front of her, with his red cape, gold and white uniform, and characteristic red hair, was distinctive. The silver eyes. The overwhelming fire magic. The way the other Royal Guards left him to fight her. It was all so obvious.

"You're the captain of the Royal Guard," she whispered. "Fenris Asulf."

It made sense. There were four power levels, from weakest to strongest: white, gray, yellow, and purple. There was a tier above that, but it was never worth mentioning since it was so rare—black. And there were only three people in the entire country of Rosain who were considered black ranks: Blár Vilulf, Fenris Asulf, and Hilda Helgadottir.

And standing before her was that same Fenris.

"Indeed, I am," Fenris said. "And you're Kolfinna the fae."

The fire walls grew even higher until all she could see was red. Even with her stone armor—which normally kept her cool—her body was unbearably hot. Her feet stung, and it was hard to keep her eyes open from the heat. Even breathing hurt; every breath seemed as if she were inhaling fire.

She needed to escape. She couldn't face this foe.

Kolfinna raised vines from the ground, but in a matter of seconds, he burned them. She kept gathering more and more vines, but he burned them without a second thought. She backed away, heat radiating against her back as the fire walls closed in, roaring loudly. Her body trembled and she looked for an escape, but there were no gaps in the fire walls.

Fenris was in front of her in an instant. He kicked her in her midsection. Her armor shattered easily and she was flung to the side. She bounced on the burning cobblestones, her body rolling like a rag doll. Bits of burning stone scraped her skin. Her clothes tore at the knees and elbows. Pain and fire exploded all around her. Everything was so *hot*.

Black colored her vision. She could feel herself becoming disoriented, and she tried to blink to clear it. The sky was red. Flecks of black and white sparks flickered in the air. She struggled to push herself up but stopped when the hot, steaming tip of a blade singed her neck.

"Kolfinna the fae." Fenris's voice crackled like a whip. "You are hereby arrested on charges of murder. May the king have mercy on you."

He swung his sword. *Crack.* Her head crashed onto the hard cobbled street. Her vision dimmed and darkness took over.

3

Kolfinna expected to wake up in a prison cell, or maybe in the afterlife, but when her eyes fluttered open, she was in a modest bedroom with lilac wallpaper and clean, crisp, and starkly white bedsheets beneath her. Even the sheets smelled like lilacs. And she was dressed in a soft, pale-yellow dress. It was all too bizarre.

She cringed when she moved, her temple throbbing, but she was able to sit upright without her vision dancing with black. Her injuries weren't as debilitating as she had thought they would be. Especially after facing off against Fenris Asulf, one of the strongest men in the country.

Why am I still alive?

"You're awake."

Kolfinna lurched back until she smacked into the lilac wall, her hands raised to attack.

A man sat at the end of the room with a thick, yellow-paged book pinched between his fingers. He regarded her with an unreadable expression and snapped his book shut. He wore the attire of a Royal Guard: red cape, militaristic styled white and silver-accented uniform. His dark hair was slicked back, revealing his equally dark, but kind, eyes. A hint of a smile graced his lips.

"I won't hurt you."

As if she would believe that.

She shoved the blanket off and bolted toward the door, but water immediately slammed her to the ground. Pain jolted down her body as she continued to squirm under the cold torrent. It was relentless, and it kept her down. Water magic was supposed to be weaker than the other elements in combat, since all it did was hose you, but she had never met anyone who could pressurize their magic to make their water strong enough to *keep* someone down.

"No need to run," he said as he placed the book on the side table beside him and rose to his feet. "I'm really sorry about this—"

Stomping filled the room and was a constant *thud, thud, thud* to her eardrums before it stopped. She tried to turn her head to look at who had entered, but the water continued to blast on her back, nearly drilling a hole in her spine. From what she could see from her peripheral vision, half a dozen people filled the room.

The water pressure eased and stopped altogether, prompting her to slowly push herself on her elbows. Water sopped and dripped from her braided hair, which now resembled a knotted rope. She ran a wet hand over her drenched face, water clinging to her lashes and eyebrows heavily. As she pulled herself into a sitting position, she realized the water made her dress cling to her body like a second skin. She probably looked like a wet rag doll.

Half a dozen Royal Guards filled the tiny room. All of them practically bared their fangs at her, ready to pounce. One had fire raging on his fingertips while another had a sword with lightning sparking off the edge.

"Her eyes ... they're pink," one of them hissed to the other. "She's a fae all right."

"I wouldn't mind carving them out of her skull," another mumbled.

"No worries, I've got her," the water elemental user said, raising his hands to placate them. "She's not going anywhere."

"She's a murderer. We don't know that." An older, clean-shaven guard narrowed his eyes at her. "She's a fae."

"Yes, yes, we're quite aware of that," the water elemental user said with an impatient nod. "Someone call Captain Asulf. The rest of you can leave."

When no one made a move to leave, the man sighed. "Look, she's not going anywhere. I've got her under control."

"She's a fae," one of them said. "She defeated Torsten this morning and he said she can use stones to fight—"

"The fae are able to use nature-based magic," the water elemental user said with an impatient wave. "That *includes* earth magic."

"My point is that we can't take her lightly," the other man pressed, shooting a glare at her. "Who knows what else she can do?"

"I've got it under control." The water elemental user snapped his fingers. "Magni, stay with me. Eyfura, please call Captain Asulf. As for the rest of you, please leave and guard the hallway."

Hesitation brewed between the guards and the water elemental man raised an eyebrow. "Is that understood?"

"Yes, sir," they said simultaneously before dispersing.

Another dark-haired man, Magni, she assumed, stood beside the first man. He towered over her and peered at her with a distasteful look in his sharp green eyes, a scowl twisting his pretty face. His hands were bunched together to his side and if Kolfinna didn't know any better, she'd say he was itching to swing at her.

The water elemental user kneeled beside Kolfinna until they were almost at the same level. His brown eyes, which reminded her of tree bark and soil, were kind but stern. She recognized him as one of the men she had fought in the streets earlier that day.

His voice softened. "We can either talk like this, or you can cooperate and sit. Which will it be, Miss Kolfinna?"

Kolfinna chewed on her lower lip. He was a liar. What cooperation?

All fae were meant to die. Brutally.

And now that they had her, they would kill her. Or would they throw her in a dungeon and toss the key? Let her rot until her remains were found centuries later? It wasn't uncommon for fae to be killed in horrific manners. She had even heard that a few decades ago, there was a doctor who performed experiments on fae, dead and alive. She didn't have any proof, but surely the rumors had come from somewhere.

There were no exits. If the others had listened to the water elemental man, the door was flanked by Royal Guards, and here in her room there were no windows. The small, modern room now reminded her of a prison cell with pretty, purple wallpaper.

"Just kill me already," she whispered, her fingernails digging into the wooden floorboards.

"Gladly," the other man, Magni, snapped. He unfurled his fists but clenched them again when the water elemental man shot him a hard look. "But we have business with you."

"We would like your cooperation."

"Cooperation?" Kolfinna looked up between the two men. She was no longer Inga, who controlled her anger and her tongue, who remained silent to blend into the background. She was now Kolfinna, the fae. The murderer. So she laughed. It came out soft at first, but then grew shrill. "You guys want me to cooperate with you? You're just here to imprison me and then kill me! Or will you humiliate me first?"

Kolfinna would die a tragic death just like Katla. Just like all the other fae. Her laughter faded into the peeling lilac wallpapers. Emptiness cored her innards.

"We're not here to hurt you," the water-wielder said.

"It's true. My name is Mímir Thorbjorsson. I'm one of the lieutenant captains of the Royal Guards."

The Royal Guards were supposed to be gallant, honest, and prestigious in every sense, but she couldn't believe his words because he was meant to protect *humans* in Rosain—not fae.

Kolfinna inched away from him on the floor, her skirts clinging to her body immodestly and creating a pool of water around her on the wooden floors, which now shone with moisture. She subconsciously covered her chest, keeping her wary gaze on the two Royal Guards to make sure they didn't attack her.

Red tinged Mímir's cheeks and he coughed. "I apologize about the water," he said quickly, raising his hands toward her. His tone was hesitant. "Do you mind if I draw the water out from your clothes?"

She nodded and he flicked his wrist. Almost instantaneously, all the moisture clinging to her body, dress, and hair, was removed until it was collected in a floating ball in front of him. He carefully molded the water until it was a cylinder, and then slid it into a bucket that was beside him.

"Please, have a seat." He motioned to the bed.

This whole thing was just bizarre. He wasn't being rude and throwing her around like she was a prisoner, so what exactly was his motive? She was still alive, so that must've meant *something*.

Kolfinna hesitated before climbing to her feet. She

stepped toward the bed but thought twice about it and crossed her arms. "I'm fine right here," she said.

He nodded. "That's fine. Whatever you're comfortable with."

He annoyed her with how polite he was acting; there was no doubt in her mind he was a duplicitous snake.

"What do you want from me?" She leaned against the wall and fit her fingernails into the grooves of the bumpy and grainy wallpaper. Her mana nudged against the wall and relief pooled in her chest at the pull of the stones beneath the pretty wallpaper. "I highly doubt you're being this nice just out of the kindness of your heart. There must be something the Royal Guards want from me if you're keeping me alive."

"You're right," a familiar, calm voice called from the doorway.

Fenris stood at the threshold of the room, his expression cool and his silver eyes dancing mysteriously. Mímir and Magni bowed their heads in respect as the leader of the Royal Guards pushed himself deeper into the room. Kolfinna pressed her back flush against the wall, ready for the wall to swallow her if she needed a quick escape. She couldn't defeat him, and she doubted she could run, but she had to try if it came down to it.

He had defeated her, but unlike Blár, she didn't feel a great fear when he was standing in the room. Her body didn't tremble at the thought of his fiery magic, and there wasn't a great despair in her chest like it was with Blár. Maybe it was because Fenris had shown mercy and hadn't brutally injured her? Or maybe it was because Fenris wasn't as cruel as Blár.

"We will do you a favor, while you do the same for us." Fenris stopped a few feet away from her. His face was blank, and she sensed no hostility from him. "That's what it means to do business. It is my hope that you will also give us our due respect, but it is not necessary."

None of this was fair. A favor? It was more like coercion. How could she even retaliate against a man like him? Whatever it was they wanted from her, they would take.

"Why should I have to respect you?" Her voice trembled, even as she tried to strengthen it. "You're ... You're a monster. All of you!"

Fenris tilted his head and watched her curiously. "We won't hurt you."

"Liar!" She pressed harder against the wall, her temple burning where he had struck her.

"Kolfinna—" He spoke softer now, as if she were a cornered animal he didn't want to frighten any further.

"All of you are just glorified soldiers of the king! Mere little dogs licking his feet," she hissed vehemently. Even she could hear the desperation in her voice. They would never understand her pain, her reality. "You're the monsters, not me!"

It didn't even make sense what she was saying, but maybe she truly was a cornered animal. And she was baring her fangs at them, threatening to bite even though she knew they had the upper hand.

"What—" Magni's face purpled and he took a step

forward as if to attack her, but Mímir placed a hand on his chest and held him back.

Fenris's expression didn't change, and Kolfinna tensed for the blow that was to come, but it never did. He remained peacefully calm, so much so that he reminded her of steady candlelight, so unlike the tumultuous fire he possessed.

"None of us here wish you harm," Fenris said with the same lulling calmness.

She shot a wild glance at Magni, who was practically fuming beside Mímir. "Really?" she said with a laugh. "I find that hard to believe!"

Fenris's silver eyes flicked to Magni. "He will not hurt you so long as you cooperate."

Cooperation? What exactly did they want from her?

She clung to the wall for support, as if it could protect her from this man. From these Royal Guards.

When she didn't say anything, he continued, "We have a proposition for you, Kolfinna the fae." He was the epitome of tranquil and unbothered as he spoke, as if he hadn't fought her that morning. "This proposition is from the king himself and from the Royal Guards. Two years ago, the military discovered a castle ruin thought to be older than the Great Purge."

Her body stiffened in response at the mention of the Great Purge, which occurred after the Last Fae War, where the humans overthrew the fae oppressors and took back Rosain, and which ultimately ended in the decimation of the fae civilization. Only a small percentage of her people survived.

Apparently, the fae were monstrous creatures that came from the Mistlands beyond the Forest of Great Divide, where only magic beasts and creatures that feasted on the flesh of humans thrived. That side of the world was uninhabitable. The fae left those lands and conquered the human world, only to be defeated and relentlessly hunted to near extinction.

If the ruins were truly that old, then it must've had some interesting and powerful fae artifacts that hadn't been used, or seen, in centuries.

Ancient fae artifacts were rare and powerful enough to be known as national treasures; all of them holding great primeval powers. How they were made was a mystery, but they belonged to the old fae civilization. Most had been destroyed during the Great Purge, either by the fae wanting to hide the power from human hands or by humans who didn't know any better.

"Naturally, this is all classified information. We wouldn't want other countries to swoop in and try to take what's ours," Fenris continued. "For two years, we've been trying to search the ruins and extract the artifacts. However, every time we send men into the ruins, they never come back. For two years, we've been losing men. A year ago, we teamed up with the military, but they too have failed. It doesn't matter which ranks we send forward —yellows or purples—they do not survive."

Kolfinna didn't like the sound of all of this. An

ancient ruin that killed everyone who entered it? It sounded spooky. Maybe this was a reason why fae artifacts were so hard to excavate—it was impossible for the average person to do it. And, by the sounds of it, still difficult for someone above average to do it.

But *why* was it difficult? Were there fae folk protecting the ruins? Ancient fae magic resisting the invasion? Or people who didn't want humans to see the inside of the ruins?

Whatever it was, she didn't want any part of it.

"The military and the Royal Guards hate each other," she mused. The king had his Royal Guards, led by Fenris, while the military had its commander-in-chief, Commander Steffen Bernsten. On paper, the king was in charge of everything, but in reality, he held no power over the military—and definitely no power over Commander Steffen Bernsten, who was rumored to look down on the king. As a result, both factions always tried to outdo the other and gain more power. "For the king to ask for the military's help, it must've hurt his pride."

Fenris blinked in surprise. "The military and the Royal Guards are both on the same side."

Mímir and Magni shared a glance. Clearly, it wasn't as simple as that.

Kolfinna's muscles grew taut with tension, but she remained silent.

"It's true that we will be splitting the goods with the military," Fenris said after a long pause. "But whether the imperial family receives the goods or the military, it, overall, will strengthen our nation. Which is why we have agreed to work with them."

An uneasiness stirred in the air. She could already tell where this conversation was going, but she still asked. "So ..." She licked her suddenly dry lips. "Where do I fit in all of this?"

"We wish for you to aid us as well," he said.

"You want me to throw away my life for *your* nation and for *your* king?" Kolfinna's fingers twitched against the wall, the stones beneath the wallpaper grinding against each other with her mana. She couldn't escape, and they must've been crazy to think she would willingly throw her life away like that.

"I'll have to decline," she said quickly, even though she knew it was futile. They could make her do anything now that they had her.

Mímir fiddled with the cuff of his white glove. "This nation and its king is also *your* nation and *your* king."

"As far as the king and this nation are concerned, I'm no different than an animal." She shot him a glare but averted her eyes when she saw a look of pity flash over him. She mumbled, "I'm not dying for your stupid artifacts."

"If you refuse, then we have no reason to keep you alive," Magni spat. A crackle and sizzle sounded in the room as fire danced on the palms of his hands.

"Do *not* attack her." Fenris's voice didn't rise in the slightest, but the temperature in the room rose significantly and he gave Magni a dark look that would've made any man drop to his knees in fear.

Magni's cheeks blazed red, but he listened and his flames flickered to sparks before dissipating altogether. He folded his hands behind his back and stared at his shiny leather boots.

"We wish to cooperate with you," Fenris said, turning his hard gaze away from Magni. "Please allow me to finish my proposition before you make your decision."

Kolfinna tried to keep some fire in her voice, even as fear ran through her veins. "Why me? I'm sure you can find a willing dog to do your dirty work."

"The ruins have many writings all over them, which we believe is the lost magic, rune magic," he said. "It is said that only powerful fae are able to read it. We think that by deciphering the runes, we'll be able to navigate the ruins and excavate the artifacts."

"You think I'll be able to read these runes?"

Her body went still. They needed a fae to read those runes, but she had never known anyone who knew how to read, write, or use that old magic. There was no way she was going to be able to read it right off the bat.

"You will be the deciding factor in our success or failure." He said it like it was supposed to make her feel important, but she only felt dread at those words.

It was a lot of pressure to put on her shoulders. Was she just a scapegoat everyone could use if the mission failed? Dump all the blame on her and save the disgrace the Royal Guards and military would otherwise face with failure?

But at least they didn't want to kill her. That was a start. As long as she was useful, they would keep her alive.

It should've comforted her that she wouldn't die today, but she couldn't shake her unease in that room. Even as these three men stood in the lilac room with mostly amicable words, she still felt like a cornered, trapped beast, being poked and prodded for a reaction.

"I'm ... I'm flattered." She swallowed; this was what they wanted to hear. She couldn't refuse them—she was a prisoner. But they wanted to keep up this ruse that she was going along with their plan out of her free will.

"Then—" Fenris started.

"Why pretend like you want my cooperation when you can just force me?" The words came out quickly, and she snapped her mouth shut.

"We want your cooperation because we need you. You're the most powerful fae that we know of," he said slowly.

She wasn't powerful, but there wasn't much competition when it came to the fae, since there were so few of them. A year ago, she would've agreed with him. But she had faced against Blár and had realized how weak she actually was.

Fenris's voice was soft, and she believed him as he spoke, "We don't want someone who's only there by force because you'll have the upper hand in those ruins. So we want a mutually beneficial relationship."

She laced her hands together to keep them from shaking. "Why should I help you? What's stopping me from agreeing and then escaping? After all, there are only three people in this entire country who can stop me." She raised her trembling fingers and tallied off, "Blár Vilulf, Hilda Helgadottir, and you, Captain Asulf." Kolfinna clenched her fingers into a fist. "I hardly see how a black rank like you would want to babysit me forever and keep me on a leash. And what's stopping me from leaving after *you* leave?"

She was bluffing. There were definitely more than three people who were stronger than her. But she had the upper hand because *they needed her.*

"You've raised some good points," Fenris said with a nod, as if expecting those questions. "You can leave whenever you want, really, but I wouldn't advise that. You don't want to become my enemy because that's exactly what you'll become. I don't enjoy being embarrassed, especially when King Leiknir gave me this mission personally. If you do try to leave, it won't be Blár Vilulf coming after you like last time. It'll be me. And as a word of caution, unlike Blár, I don't toy with my targets and I don't let them live just because I'm bored."

Even though he said that, the thought of Fenris coming after her didn't invoke the same effect as the thought of Blár coming after her—whenever she thought of that cruel monster, her palms grew sweaty and her stomach churned. Her shin would throb painfully at the memory of his ice semi-freezing the muscles and snapping her bones like a twig. His ice-blue eyes still haunted her even a year later.

Fenris must've misunderstood her fear of Blár for his threat because he continued, "I won't come after you if you cooperate with us. It's not all doom and gloom. We have incentives to make it so you *want* to fulfill this mission. If you're able to successfully finish this mission, we'll pardon you for your crimes. You'll no longer have to be on the run."

"You'll pardon which of my crimes?" Her voice was low.

He raised an eyebrow in puzzlement. "The crime you're well known for: murdering Lord Estur."

Lord Estur. She hated thinking about her old boss. An image flashed in her mind: Lord Estur holding a severed head in his hand. Slippery blood splattering the floor. A hollow laugh escaping from his lips.

She banished the thought and whispered, "And the crime of being a fae?"

"That's not a crime—"

"Oh, but it *is*." Kolfinna dug her nails into her bicep and crossed over her chest tightly, sternly. "You think I'm *solely* on the run because of my crimes? I'm mostly on the run because I'm a fae. I can be killed at any point for simply *existing*. How will you ensure that I can stop running when this country is filled with people who wish to kill me simply for existing?"

"You're strong enough to stop them," he said.

"I pride myself in being a relatively strong fae, something that isn't normal considering us fae aren't allowed to practice our magic freely for fear of being caught, but even

I can't face off multiple attackers. Especially if those attackers are a part of the Hunter's Association. You do realize a good portion of the Hunter's Association, a recreational club dedicated to killing me and my kind, comprises of the military and the Royal Guards? They masquerade as justice seekers hunting evil fae, but we all know that isn't the case. They kill any and all fae because they believe *all* fae are evil. What's stopping them from hunting me down? I might be a strong fae, but even I can't defeat everyone."

The conversation probably wasn't going the way he had planned, judging by the coolness of his gaze. "There's the fae protection act—"

Her piercing laugh broke the grimness of the conversation and made all the men in the room straighten. She tilted her head against the wall to feel the sturdy comfort of the stones against her body. The fae protection act was a joke. The fae could use it to go to a government facility and tell them they felt threatened and in danger, but there wasn't a single recorded case of it actually being enforced. No fae would outright tell anyone they were a fae, and no government facility would ever help a fae.

The hatred Rosain had for the fae ran deeper than any law could fix.

"Oh *please*." She gnashed her teeth together. "That law was passed in order to abolish the Hunter's Association from the military and force black rank Hilda Helgadottir to resign from her position as the leader so she could be better used by the military instead of being used for petty things like hunting poor, weak fae. That act doesn't protect my people from being killed by the Hunter's Association, or any group of fae hating people. Have you ever seen it used to protect a fae? And even when people kill fae, the dead never get justice *even though* that law exists."

Fenris watched her for a long while. "I cannot speak for the rest of your fae brethren, but since you're an asset for Rosain, we will do everything we can to protect you. If anyone tries to hurt you, you are free to use self-defense to protect yourself. And if it ever goes to court, that law will protect you. I can guarantee that," he said. "But in general, you won't have to worry about that because you'll be under my protection."

She waved her hand. "Just because you're a black rank doesn't mean you can protect me all day. And what about after we finish this mission? What happens to me then? Or will you continue to babysit me?"

"After this mission is over, there's no need for me to protect you because you'll become like any other citizen. I'm not sure if I'm making myself clear, but you're free after this mission. That means you will not be chased down by the military or the Royal Guards. The Hunter's Association is another matter. If they harass you, you can always make a claim with the courts."

The courts would do nothing to help her. The fae didn't bother to go to the courts if they were being chased by the Hunter's Association because once the hunters were onto them, it was usually too late.

Kolfinna held her breath. "And if I refuse?"

"You will be imprisoned and likely put to death for the murder of Lord Estur."

There wasn't much to consider. It was either die or go on a highly risky mission and potentially die there, but at least with the latter, there was a sliver of a chance of survival. Her shoulders sagged and she stared at the ground. She wasn't wearing shoes, so her bare toes splayed from under the hem of her dress on the gleaming wood floor. There was a jagged scar above her big toe where Blár's ice shards had impaled her right foot before freezing her leg up to her knee.

"I'll do it," she said so quietly that she was surprised they even heard her.

"Excellent." Fenris clapped his hands together. He didn't look too shocked by her answer because, after all, what other choice did she have? She wouldn't just keel over and die. If death was that easy, she wouldn't have been on the run for so long.

After the mission was over, she would go back to her life. She would be free from the authorities, but she would still be living in hiding. Except this time, she didn't have Katla to keep her company. Even if the military and the Royal Guards left her alone, she would still be running from everyone. Keeping herself hidden. Using different names.

Maybe this time she could be Lagertha or Aina. Or another pretty name that disguised her true nature.

"—we'll review the notes next week and—" Fenris was saying.

"Wait," Kolfinna said, an idea already formulating in her mind. Her heart pounded brazenly as the thought became more tangible. "I want to add a condition to the mission."

If they needed her like he had said, then she could make demands too. She didn't have to go along with whatever they said. If they needed her—*truly* needed her—then she had choices.

Fenris's silver eyes shifted to slits as he regarded her carefully. Mistrusting her. "Go on."

"If I go ... You'll make me a Royal Guard." The words spilled out quickly, like she was scared to hear them aloud and wanted them out of her mouth as soon as possible.

That seemed to be the last thing Fenris expected because his red eyebrows furrowed together and he appeared lost for words. Mímir blinked as if he heard wrong, while Magni's mouth was slightly ajar. For a moment, no one said anything.

Finally, Magni laughed harshly. "You've got to be kidding. *You*, a Royal Guard? Never in a million years."

If Kolfinna became a Royal Guard, she would be protected by Fenris and the law. Royal Guards were in prestigious authoritative positions of power. It wouldn't be easy for the Hunter's Association to target her, since they would have to go through Fenris first if they wanted to take his guard. She would be protected under him. It was the perfect, and most haunting, situation for her.

It made her nauseous to think about what it also meant. She would be under constant watch from Fenris and all the other people in positions of power. She might even be forced to come into contact with Blár. She would also be open to criticism from the Hunter's Association, the military, the Royal Guards, and the public. They would never truly accept her and would try to find faults in everything she did. There was also the chance they would treat her terribly.

But perhaps this was what she needed in order to truly be free.

Fenris's gaze was level and his tone was even more level. "Why do you want to become a Royal Guard? Surely, it's not to serve and protect."

"I need ... I want to be able to use my powers freely." Her voice thickened as she spoke. Her tongue felt like an anchor—she didn't like revealing her feelings, especially not to a human who would never truly understand. "I don't want to hide anymore."

"Being a Royal Guard will put you in the public's eye," he said slowly. "You'll be criticized heavily. Everyone will know you're a fae."

She could already imagine everyone staring at her in disgust, like they had during her fight with Fenris in the streets. They had avoided her like the plague.

She nodded. "I know."

"People won't be happy if you become a Royal Guard. It's incredibly difficult to become one and even more so to rise in the ranks. If I allow you to become a Royal Guard without any prior schooling or letters of recommendation, people will think I'm favoring you and that we're using you for power. The military will definitely be against it." He rubbed his chin thoughtfully. But she could see he was mulling it over, *considering* it. "Especially since you killed someone. The nobility, in particular, will not forgive you easily."

"Are you ... Are you considering this, Captain?" Magni's voice was barely controlled. His hands shook and he unclenched his fists before clenching them again, as if fighting the urge to lash out.

Mímir shifted on his feet and fidgeted with the cuff of his sleeve. "I think it's always a good idea to consider options ... Whether or not we follow through is another thing ..."

"As much as I would love to have you as a guard, I can't—" Fenris started.

"You can." Kolfinna met Fenris's eyes calmly, despite her body trembling from within and her toes curling against the floor. "You're Fenris Asulf. You're the captain. You can appoint anyone as a Royal Guard if you wanted to. Besides, it's not like I'm getting in for free. I still have to make it out of the ruins with the rest of the team, don't I? That's not going to be an easy feat. And besides, didn't you say that I would make or break this mission?"

He was quiet for a long time after that. He stared at her, and stared some more, and stared even more—until she felt like he was trying to make her crawl out of her own skin. Magni slowly simmered on the spot while Mímir was pulling a loose thread from his red cape.

"I've made a decision," Fenris said, his voice crackling like thunder in the quiet room. "If you show great strength, resilience, and mental fortitude—I will personally appoint you as a Royal Guard. But that's only *if* you're worthy. I'll put the responsibility on Mímir's shoulders since he'll be in charge of this mission."

Mímir straightened at the mention of his name.

"But if you're unable to show those traits and successfully clear the mission, I won't make you one. I'll also compile everyone else's opinion in case Mímir is biased. Does that sound fair?"

If she accepted, she was one step closer to becoming a Royal Guard. One step closer to freedom.

She felt lightheaded and her stomach churned as if to spill the contents all over the floor, but she swallowed that fear and kept her gaze level.

"Yes," she said, feeling like she was sealing a deal with a demon.

4

Kolfinna wasn't allowed to leave the lilac
room, except for bathroom breaks, but even then, a Royal
Guard always escorted her and checked in on her every
few seconds to make sure she wasn't trying to escape. She
was essentially a prisoner—her meals were brought to her
and she was under constant monitoring from the guards.

The week passed by mind-numbingly slow. Other
than a wooden chair, a bed, and a heavy chest brimming
with dresses meant for someone three times smaller than
Kolfinna, there was nothing in the room. Nothing to
entertain herself with and nobody she wanted talk to—
because she definitely wasn't keen on the idea of talking to
a Royal Guard.

Kolfinna braided her hair distractedly while balancing
a handheld, beveled mirror between her thighs; she had
found it buried in the bottom of the chest of clothes. Her
thick, frizzy hair stuck out in different directions from

tossing and turning in bed, and she silently cursed herself for not finding it sooner. She hadn't realized how untamed and wild her hair had become. The last thing she wanted was to show these Royal Guards an image of the generic fairytale fae—wild hair, wild eyes, and a wild smile. The only thing she was missing was bramble, twigs, and leaves sticking into her unkept hair.

Suppressing a chuckle at the idea of walking around like their tree-hugging, children snatching nightmare, she wrangled her hair into a tight braid and tied it with a pink ribbon one of the Royal Guards had given her earlier that week.

Her pink eyes matched the ribbon, and she had to pause to stare at herself. Kolfinna rarely saw her natural eye color since she always drank the weedy-tea when the effects of it ran out. But now that she didn't have to hide it anymore, she marveled without restraint. A long time ago, she had hated the pink color for being so conspicuous, but looking at her eyes now, with their vibrant, undeniably fae color, she found them beautiful.

A knock interrupted her thoughts and before she could ready herself, the door swung open and a young woman with honey-brown eyes poked her head through the doorway. Soft, blond curls framed her pretty face and she smiled tentatively. "You're being summoned."

The hair on the back of Kolfinna's neck rose and she jumped to her feet. The mirror clattered to the floor, but she barely registered it. Were they finally going to the ruins?

"Are you going to pick that up?" The woman pointed to the mirror. "I think it's broken."

But instead of looking at the mirror, Kolfinna stared at the woman's white silk gloves trimmed with lace. It was strange to see it with the Royal Guard uniform, since it seemed feminine in contrast to the masculine, militaristic uniform. Kolfinna blinked back and scooped the mirror off the floor. A thin crack spread like a spiderweb on the corner of it.

"Aw, yeah, it looks broken." The woman stepped into the room, her heeled boots clicking on the shining oak floors. "Sorry about that. I shouldn't have come so unexpectedly."

"No, it's not your fault." Kolfinna placed the mirror on her bed and hid her trembling hands behind her back. She peered into the empty hallway from the open door, her heart racing at the thought of leaving. "It's not mine, anyway."

"Huh. Yeah, that's true." She jerked a thumb at the door. "Let's go. We're going to be having a meeting to discuss the Eventyrslot ruins."

Was that what they were calling it now? The *fairy-tale castle*?

Upon seeing her expression, the woman suppressed a chuckle and said, "Yeah, it sounds lame, I know. The king chose the name."

"Right." So the king was strange, she settled with.

Kolfinna straightened her blue dress and ran a hand over the skirt. It didn't fit right, but it was the only dress she found she could squeeze into; it was meant for someone shorter and tinier, someone like the woman in front of her. On Kolfinna, it looked indecent. The skirt hung just over her shins, exposing her ankles, and the material stretched thinly over her shoulders, breasts, and stomach. She wanted to cover her body with how it accentuated all the features she wanted to hide—her wide hips, heavy breasts, and her belly. *Especially* her belly. She wasn't thin like the woman in front of her or like the rest of the lean and athletic Royal Guards. It was just another thing that made her stand out.

The woman placed a hand on her hip and tilted her head to examine the dress. For a moment, Kolfinna thought she would laugh at the fit and how it made her look frumpy, but she surprised her by saying, "Hm, maybe a blue ribbon would match better than the pink? I can find you one after the meeting if you'd like." She leaned forward to inspect the dress closely and when her gaze flew up to Kolfinna's face, they widened. "Oh, wow! It's just like they said! You have pink eyes!"

Her tone ... didn't sound mocking. Surprisingly.

Kolfinna threaded her hands together so tightly the knuckles became a bloodless white. This was the first time a human had seen her natural eye color, and she didn't know how to feel about that. She almost felt naked.

"It's a beautiful color," the woman said when she noticed Kolfinna's hesitation. She grinned widely, showing off her sparkling, albeit slightly crooked, teeth. "I had no idea the fae had different eye colors."

"All fae have colorful and vivid eyes," Kolfinna found herself saying. She really should've stopped and not told the woman any fae facts that could be used against her, but the woman's seemingly genuine reaction kept her going. "It ranges between gold, pink, purple, blue, and green ..." She cleared her throat and glanced at the woman to make sure she was still interested. "The colors are typically brighter than a human's."

"Can you see better?"

"I don't know." Kolfinna lifted her shoulders, the tension in her chest slowly unknotting itself. "I see what I see, and I don't know if it's better or worse for you humans."

"That's interesting." The woman bobbed her head and gestured toward the door. "But how about we talk and walk at the same time? We're running a bit late."

Kolfinna followed behind the woman as they entered the hallway. Her stomach twisted nervously as she looked from the woman to her surroundings. Tall sets of doors with gold handles mirrored each other on either side of the long and wide hallway. She couldn't shake the feeling that she was walking to her doom; everyone would jump on her like vultures and tear her apart.

"My name's Eyfura, by the way," the woman said.

"I'm Kolfinna."

"I know." Eyfura laughed, and it was pleasant to the ears. "Everyone here knows who you are."

Silence engulfed the space between them. Eyfura's glossy black boots clacked with every step as opposed to

Kolfinna's soft shuffles. The slippers she wore barely fit either; the dress was too tight, but the slippers too big. She could imagine herself tripping and falling and making a fool of herself in the meeting. Maybe the guards did that on purpose—to make her feel even more uncomfortable.

"No need to be so nervous," Eyfura said. "Everyone's here for work."

"I'm not nervous," she lied.

"All right." They stopped at a towering door and Eyfura twisted the gilded, lion-head knob before Kolfinna could mentally prepare herself.

She half expected a dungeon or a room full of guards sharpening their fancy swords and exchanging snobby tales about their wealth and status, but there was nothing of that sort. There were guards, yes, but the hum of their conversation seemed to follow mundane topics—like which jam from the side table was better, blueberry or strawberry? And there was no sharpening of sinister blades; they instead picked at the array of crusty bread, jams, and cookies sitting on porcelain plates. The guards either sat on the velvet couches arranged around a glass tea table, or stood beside the table of snacks. If they weren't wearing their uniforms, they would've looked like ordinary people.

But they weren't ordinary people—not in the slightest.

Kolfinna remained rooted in place; her body refused to move forward past the threshold and into the throng of guards. Her right leg weighed her down and she glanced at the end of the hallway; a thick, tight-knit, and rich-colored rug spread down the hallway in an unending line. She imagined herself running along it, but she knew they would catch her before she could make it to the bend of the hall.

"You okay?" A light hand rested on her shoulder.

Kolfinna gave a small nod and Eyfura waved her forward. Kolfinna stepped into the room, careful not to trip over her right leg with her oversized slippers. The door clicked shut behind them with finality, and Kolfinna forced herself not to turn back and run. She calmed the torrent of nausea building in her stomach and searched the crowd for familiar faces. She recognized Mímir, Magni, and Fenris.

A young man around her age bounded toward her immediately; he held two steaming, white porcelain cups delicately by the handles with his forefingers.

"Eyfura!" The young man stopped in his tracks and held out the cup. "I was thinking you'd never show up." His full head of dark honey-blond hair brushed along his shoulders messily. Green eyes sparkled with excitement and he held the other cup for Kolfinna. "Apparently there's going to be a fae here. Did you hear about it? I've never seen one."

Kolfinna gingerly took the cup from his hand while Eyfura shifted on her feet, shooting Kolfinna a knowing look. "Well," Eyfura started. "Guess—"

"Have you ever met one?" he asked Kolfinna, brows

raised as he glanced around the room. "I heard she's pretty powerful too."

"Err, yes, I've met a few," Kolfinna trailed.

Had he not noticed?

His head whipped in her direction, his eyes wide. "You've met a *few*? Wow, really? How? Are the Royal Guards really invested in catching fae?" He stuck his hand out to her. "I'm Nollar, by the way."

He didn't wear a Royal Guard uniform like the rest of everyone. Instead, his attire consisted of a dark blue military style uniform with charcoal buttons and dark boots. Nollar and Kolfinna were the only ones dressed differently in the sea of white uniforms and red capes.

She slipped her hand into his and he shook it gently. "You're pretty young," he noted, tilting his head to the side. "That's crazy that you're a Royal Guard while being, like, young. Don't you usually have to be eighteen to join? I mean, unless you're *really* good?"

Eyfura chuckled. "Don't bombard her with a million questions."

"I'm actually not a Royal Guard. I'm eighteen, by the way," Kolfinna said. "My name is Kolfinna. I'm the fae you're talking about."

His mouth hung ajar for five seconds, and Kolfinna's chest weighed heavily with those words—she had never openly said she was a fae to anyone.

He leaned in closer and stared into her eyes, just like Eyfura had done, and gasped. "Gosh, your *eyes*!"

"Err ... yes, they're pink. I know."

"I didn't even notice," he started. "My vision isn't that great up close ... But wow, I can't believe I didn't notice something so obvious. So you're really a fae?"

Kolfinna didn't sense hostility, only curiosity, so she nodded.

"Is it true you can shoot at stones from your hands?"

"No?" She raised an eyebrow.

"Or that you can control someone's brain?"

"Uh, no."

"Do you have wings?"

The question made all the pores on her back prickle like rose thorns. The two scars on her back stabbed into her flesh like phantom limbs; every fae child had their wings sawed off to stave suspicion. She had never felt the weight of her wings before they were ripped away from her.

Kolfinna found herself smiling tightly, the lie leaving her lips naturally. "Of course not."

"Is it true you're immortal?"

Kolfinna shook her head. Katla had told her that at one time, the fae were immortal, but that wasn't the case anymore. Not since the fae king from two thousand years ago traded their immortality to save the world. Or so the stories went.

"What about that you can grow plants really tall?"

"I can do that."

He breathed out quickly and didn't take his eyes off her. "So you could raise up a forest if you wanted to?"

"I don't see why not, but it would take a lot of time

and mana to do it."

"That's crazy." Nollar held up his hand and bluish-white lightning glinted at his fingertips in static waves. His jade eyes illuminated with the sparks. "I'm an elemental, so my power is pretty basic. I heard the fae can do a lot more than just one type of magic."

Eyfura rested a hand on his shoulder. "By the way, Kolfinna, Nollar is my younger brother. You both are around the same age."

"I'm two years younger." He held out two fingers. "I'll be graduating from the academy at the end of this summer and hopefully will join the Royal Guard after that."

"Are you going to be joining us on this ... expedition?" Kolfinna said, for lack of a better word.

"No, although I'd love to. Interns aren't allowed to go on *real* missions. Anyway"—Nollar's gaze shifted to someone across the room—"I'm going to talk to Mímir for a bit. There's this one thing he was showing me last week with his power that I wanted to check out." He gave a small wave. "So, bye for now."

He went over to Mímir, who was sitting on one of the couches flipping through a stack of papers.

Kolfinna turned to Eyfura. "Why is he here if he's a student?"

"He's interning with us this week and since this meeting isn't entirely confidential, he's allowed to be here. You'll see students interning here from time to time, since it's the Royal Guards' headquarters."

After a moment of silence, Eyfura continued with a

smile, "I hope you can get along with him. He might not look like it, but he's the top student in his class this year. Captain Asulf has high hopes for him."

Before Kolfinna could reply to that, Mímir clapped his hands loudly, drawing everyone's attention. "Everyone, please quiet down and take a seat," he said.

Eyfura nudged Kolfinna toward one of the couches. The hot cup of tea Nollar had given her stung her hand and when she brought it to her lips, it nearly scalded her tongue. She placed it on the glass tea table beside a plate brimming with butter biscuits meant to accompany the tea and a side of plump strawberries. If the circumstances were different, she could've scarfed down the whole plate of fruits and pastries, but her stomach was coiled so tightly she was sure she'd vomit with a single bite.

"Everyone, have a seat." Fenris's hair gleamed like fresh blood in the dim lighting. He folded his gloved hands together on his lap and waited for everyone to situate themselves on the couches. Silence hung in the air. "Before we begin, I'd like to properly introduce everyone to Kolfinna. She'll be joining us on this mission."

The room turned its attention to Kolfinna. Their expressions ranged from suspicion, curiosity, and disdain. Her skin crawled with all the stares; people didn't normally know she was a fae, and here she was in a room full of people who knew exactly what she was. Her stomach knotted together tighter and tighter. She fought the urge to shrink into the seat and disappear within its folds.

"Question." One of the Royal Guards raised a hand. "How can you expect us to fight alongside a murderer, Captain?"

Like a dam breaking from a flood, everyone started talking at once.

"A murderer?" a white-blond-haired man on the couch said. Kolfinna vaguely recognized him as the ice elemental she had faced on the day of her capture.

A mousy brunette with a mole beneath her eye leaned in toward him, eyes wide as she murmured, "Oh, I heard about that."

"*And* she's a fae."

"I heard one whole unit had to be sent out to subjugate her."

"My friend said fae eat the hearts of their victims."

"Didn't she murder a noble?"

Kolfinna's face grew hot under the weight of their sharp stares; it was as if they were peeling back the layers of her skin to see what was underneath.

A murderer. A fae. The two were almost interchangeable to these people.

I'm not a murderer, she wanted to say, but her tongue was too heavy and her throat had constricted at the thought of Lord Estur. And it would've been a lie if she said that anyway, because she *had* killed him, even if it was justified. Even if she didn't *feel* like a murderer—like a monstrous person for doing such a horrible thing to someone. Any time she thought of Lord Estur, she thought of Katla's hair woven between his fingers, her face crumpled into an expression of fear, and her headless body a few feet away. And each and every time, she didn't regret her actions.

Fenris's voice cracked like a heavy whip. "That's enough."

Everyone hushed until there was silence.

"We're here to discuss the mission," he said. "If you have a problem with Kolfinna being here, or if you're uncomfortable working alongside her, I'll take you off the list of participants."

The Royal Guards exchanged glances with one another. Kolfinna digested that tidbit of information: everyone was here voluntarily, which surprised her. If she had a choice, she wouldn't want to explore ruins that no one had survived. But there must've been some sort of prestige attached to successfully completing the mission. Maybe they thought they'd be able to get a firsthand look at the ancient artifacts? Or maybe the king would reward them greatly?

Nollar broke the awkward silence by jumping to his feet and pointing at the heavily embroidered, silver-threaded curtains. "Do you mind if I pull the curtains back? It's so dark in here. I'm sure some sunlight will help."

"Do as you like, Nollar," Fenris said.

Nollar unfurled the curtains, letting the sun's golden rays stream into the room. He cracked open the window a few inches to let the breeze kick in. Kolfinna briefly wondered what it would be like to raise her vines from the ground below and shoot off into the distance towards the chirping birds, the bright sky, and the soft breeze. How long would it take for the Royal Guards to catch her? If the room were empty, she might've dived out the window.

"Kolfinna is a valuable asset to this mission." Fenris's voice brought her back to reality. "She's a powerful fae, and what's more, she'll be able to read the runes written within the ruins. We hope these runes will help us navigate the ruins and their history. We truly believe she'll be the key to helping this mission," he said smoothly. "These ruins were investigated by a team of our most knowledgeable historians and they've concluded they're from before the Great Purge and the Last Fae War. These ruins are fae ruins where fae predominantly visited, *not* humans. This also means that there are possibly many things in there that are unbeknownst to us humans. Having a fae on our side is extremely beneficial for this mission. I don't want to hear any more opposition about her being here."

Kolfinna waited, but no one broke the uncomfortable silence. Mímir flipped through his notes, the rustling of paper the only sound in the room.

"Mímir will give you the rest of the information," Fenris said.

The white-blond Royal Guard raised his hand. "I have a question, Captain."

"What is it, Torsten?"

"You say that nobody has been able to get into these fae ruins, right?" He licked his lips and glanced at the others. "What if … what if it's because Ragnarök is there? What if that's their stronghold?"

Silence entrenched the room before everyone started talking all at once in hushed tones.

"Ragnarök? Those fae-loving freaks?"

"But they're not that strong, are they?"

"I haven't heard about them in years, not since *that* incident."

Kolfinna didn't understand what they were talking about. Ragnarök? It was her first time hearing the word. Kolfinna drew closer to Eyfura and dropped her voice so only she could hear her. "What's, um, Ragnarök?"

Eyfura smoothed the creases on her pants, her gaze darting from the guards to Kolfinna. "Ragnarök is, uh, a small group of people who want to change the world to, um, how it used to be back when the fae ruled."

Kolfinna must've looked confused because Eyfura continued, "I told you, it's a small group, so it's no wonder you haven't heard about them. They've been around ever since the fall of the last fae queen, Queen Aesileif. They're nothing you really have to worry about. The last big thing they did was six years ago—"

"Everyone, please quiet down." Fenris raised a hand to lull the voices to silence. Soon, everyone quieted until only the chirrups of birds outside the window sounded in the room. "We don't believe Ragnarök is a part of this. But if they are, they're simply humans and fae—nothing we can't face ourselves. You all have nothing to fear. Anyhow, let's stay on track." He nodded toward Mímir.

Mímir cleared his throat and scanned his papers. "I'll be taking the lead for this mission. As most of you know, and some of you who don't know"—he glanced up at Kolfinna, as if addressing her—"I love history and I'm very grateful to Captain Asulf for allowing me to take charge of this mission. I'm excited to see what the ruins have to offer. All the history that's in those walls ... It's likely been untouched for centuries." He licked his finger and flicked to another page. "Anyway, let's talk about the ruins themselves. They're located within a mountain. The mountain is cored out, and within it is a very large, expansive building with many sub buildings attached to it. We discovered it two years ago when military personnel stumbled upon it. We've sent air elemental soldiers to fly above it and see if they could enter, but there's a barrier covering the top of it like a dome. And what's more. There's a thick white fog that covers it. The soldiers were unable to draw near it due to those reasons. However, they were able to see some spiked domes and towers. From what they saw, the ruin grounds are extremely large.

"We've sent teams and teams of people out there, but once they enter through the doors of the castle ruins, they never return. We had historians scour all sorts of ancient books, writings, and notes ... And we uncovered that this castle was in fact discovered two hundred years ago, but the same thing happened: anyone who enters never returns. There are likely a great number of riches inside, according to historians."

"Wait, wait." Magni raised his white-gloved hand.

Rich brown locks fell over his brooding eyes, which he pushed back distractedly. "This was discovered two hundred years ago and we're just now finding out about it?"

"Correct." Mímir bobbed his head. "Two hundred years ago, the military did everything it could to try to excavate it but to no avail. They eventually gave up and it was lost since then. It was rediscovered two years ago. You have to keep in mind that two hundred years ago, this was all confidential information, so it's not like the public knew about it ... Which is why you've never heard of it."

"How long until they gave up?" This time it was Eyfura who asked the question. "I find it hard to believe the military would give up that easily."

"You're correct." Mímir hesitated. "They tried for twenty years before they quit."

A shiver ran down Kolfinna's spine. The military couldn't excavate it for *twenty* years? They must've sent out their best men, and they still couldn't do it?

"Excuse me?" All the color drained from the brunette with the mole below her eye. "This is a suicide mission then! What makes you think we'll be any more successful than everyone else who tried and failed?"

"Things are different than they were two hundred years ago," Mímir said. "Plus, the military didn't have a fae on their side."

"That's still pretty risky."

Cicadas buzzed from the window, mingling with the distant hum of city life. Kolfinna stared down at her hands, where flecks of dirt filled the space beneath her nails, and where thin scabs lined her fingers and palms from last week's fight. The descriptions of the ruins sounded ominous, but what she didn't understand was the Royal Guards' reaction—they had a *choice* on whether or not to participate.

Mímir brought his notes closer to his face. "We also —" He squinted. "We also have a black rank assisting us, so we're hopeful we'll be successful."

Kolfinna stiffened. A black rank?

The Royal Guards only had one black rank, and that was Fenris. The other two black ranks belonged to the military. Was Fenris joining them on this mission?

Magni must've been thinking the same thing because he tilted his head to the side. "Captain, are you coming with us?"

"No," Mímir said quickly. "Captain Asulf can't leave his post here in the capital for an extended period."

All was quiet as everyone turned to Fenris.

Kolfinna's heart raced. If Fenris wasn't coming—

Fenris reached forward for his teacup, calmly stared into the reflection, and took a sip. His voice was clear and low. "If any of you are unsure if you want to take this mission, you're free to go. Unlike your other missions and duties, this is purely voluntary. I won't force you to go somewhere you don't want to go." He placed the teacup back on the table, where it clinked against the glass surface. "I wasn't going to say anything since it doesn't matter too much, but the military got back to me with a list of their soldiers who will be joining us on this mission. And, like Mímir said, a black rank will be joining us."

Kolfinna's voice sharpened when she spoke. "Who?"

Fenris's silver eyes gleamed cruelly as he met her gaze. "Blár Vilulf."

"*No.*" Kolfinna sprang to her feet as the memory of his wintry clutches whispered against her right leg. "You didn't tell me—"

"I received the list this morning, so it's not like I'm hiding anything from any of you." Fenris turned to the rest of the room. "I know some of you have bad experiences with him, so I want you to put your differences aside and behave."

Kolfinna sank into the couch, her voice barely a whisper as she fought to steady her erratic breathing. "I can't work with him."

Fenris held her gaze unflinchingly, and she became increasingly aware of everyone's gazes from her peripheral vision. Eyfura watched her empathetically, Nollar wore a curious expression, Magni looked irritated, and Mímir had paused from nervously sifting through his notes to stare at her.

"You'll have to." Fenris folded his hands together. The inflection of his voice suggested there was no room for argument.

Kolfinna swallowed the bile rising up her throat. "You never told me any of this."

"It changes nothing."

"It changes *everything.*" Kolfinna cupped her knees

with trembling hands and focused in on Fenris, trying to plead with him with large eyes, but he seemed unaffected by her plight. Not a single red hair on his head was out of place, while she felt like she was coming undone from the seams. "I can't work with him." Hearing his name alone sent razors down her spine. There was no way she could work with him and be in close proximity to such a wicked monster.

"Are you scared of Blár Vilulf?" It was Magni who asked, his dark brown brows raised in question. He said it as if he couldn't believe it. As if she was childish to fear him. To treat him like the boogeyman.

But there was no way she was going to admit she had recurring nightmares of Blár trying to kill her almost every night, or that her body wasn't one hundred percent healed because of him. She had a niggling suspicion that if they met again, he would finish where he left off. That he would freeze the blood in her veins and carve her flesh with his ice.

Fenris watched her carefully. "He won't hurt you."

"Also," Mímir jumped in, "Blár Vilulf isn't a member of the Hunter's Association, if that makes you feel any better. Apparently, he doesn't like doing extra work outside of the military."

It was as reassuring as hearing she wouldn't fall to her death while walking on a tightrope between two mountains.

Mímir handed the papers to the person on his left. "Please take one and pass this to the person beside you."

Slowly, the papers were passed around the room. When Kolfinna got one, a sketch of an elaborate castle with many attached buildings inside a mountain sprawled over the paper. The separate buildings, or wings of the castle, were attached by suspended bridges.

"This is a drawing of the ruins. As you can see here"— he held up the sketch and pointed to the base of the mountain separate from the castle—"the first entrance is actually just a stone archway that leads to stairs attached to the mountain. Eventually, you reach an entrance that takes you inside the mountain. But here's the thing, the inside of the mountain is cored, so you're not going into a rocky, cavernous area. The mountain seems to serve as a *shield* for the castle ruins to keep them hidden. We've been able to get inside the mountain, to the bridge that leads to the castle, but everyone who has passed through the entrance doors of the ruins has never returned."

An ominous chill reverberated through her bones and she cast a quick glance at the room to see if everyone else felt the same; surprisingly, the Royal Guards shared her unease. Eyfura chewed on her lower lip as she inspected the paper, Nollar frowned deeply, and the others exchanged uncomfortable looks.

Kolfinna turned the paper over to find a scrawl of lines, symbols, and squares jumbled together in black ink. She studied the squiggles, trying to figure out what it was. Did it represent something?

"On the back of the sheet, you'll see the runes that are written on the front doors," Mímir said and the flaps of paper crinkling filled the air soon after. "We're hopeful that Kolfinna will be able to read them."

A jolt of panic stiffened Kolfinna's spine as everyone turned to her expectantly. These were runes? They looked like chicken scrawls! She licked her lips and glanced at the scribbles once more. The more she stared, the more it didn't make sense.

"Well?" Fenris asked. "Can you read them?"

She stared at the runes harder, her hands turning clammy. If she couldn't read them, didn't that make her pretty useless in the mission? Would they kill her if they realized she couldn't tell what they were?

Fenris noticed her hesitation and said, "I'm sure they'll look different in person. Try to decipher them in your free time."

Her face caught on fire and she nodded.

"You'll all be leaving next week." Fenris rose to his feet. "Prepare what you can during that time. If anyone wants to pull out of this mission, let me know as soon as possible. That's all."

Kolfinna continued to stare at the letters, but the more she stared, the more they didn't make sense. Her stomach dropped and a numbing frost spread through her fingers, chest, and then her whole body until she buzzed with the biting cold. If she couldn't figure this out, what did that mean for her?

5

IN THE MIDDLE OF THE NIGHT, KOLFINNA hesitantly sat up on her bed in the lilac room, the blanket falling around her hips. She needed to run as far away as possible. No one had told her that Blár Vilulf would be on the mission with her. She would rather take her chances with Fenris chasing her to the ends of the world than be in Blár's company. That wasn't the only thing that bothered her—she realized at the meeting she had made a big mistake. She couldn't be surrounded by those Royal Guards. If she became one of them, she'd have to endure their stares for the rest of her life. Not to mention that— just like that one guard had said—this Eventyrslot mission sounded suicidal.

There was always someone guarding her, so it wasn't like she could waltz out the door and book it, so she turned her attention to the wall. It was made of stone, and she could bend stone.

She pressed a finger to the wall and closed her eyes. Her mana spread across the expanse of the wall, but she narrowed it down to a hole the size of her finger. She could shift the wall to make a giant hole for herself to walk through, but that would mean the pieces of the wall she shifted would be moved somewhere else, which usually meant it was pushed off the very ends of the wall. In a building like this, that meant the foundation would be ruined and it would stick out into the hallway or the outside of the building. That was the biggest way to alert everyone that she was up to something. Her only option was to pull a section of the wall out and place it into her room.

Her mana twirled around the deep inner workings of the stone and she carefully pulled a cylindrical piece out until it fell on her bed. Her heart thumped loudly in her ears and she waited for a noise—someone to yell at her about what she was doing—but nothing happened. She peeped through the hole. Bookshelves lined one side of the wall and there was a love seat in the middle of the room, a short tea table across from it. Moonlight filtered through a giant window on one side of the room. Mímir sat there, a stack of papers laid in front of him on the table as he flicked through them and a sharp dagger balanced on his lap. A single candle flickered beside him.

She lurched back, her breath caught in her throat. He didn't seem to notice her, but that didn't mean he wouldn't. She fumbled with the cylindrical stone and slid it back into the hole and adjusted it so the wallpaper lined correctly. She pressed her palm on it and fused it together so it wouldn't look so clearly cut out, but if anyone looked close enough, they'd be able to see the circular cutout in the wallpaper.

On the opposite side of her room, she did the same thing with that wall, placed a finger on it and pulled a piece of it out so she could look through it. That room was different and appeared to be a storage room: there were stacks of boxes piled up in one corner, and a few lopsided and mismatched tables and chairs in the other. There was a smaller window at the far end of the room, which spilled speckled rays of moonlight onto the gleaming wooden floors. A smile stretched her face. Speckled light meant a tree was obscuring the window, and she could use the tree to guide her down.

It was perfect—almost *too* perfect.

Hesitation stalled her from moving another step. What if ... what if this was a set-up? But then again, the Royal Guards didn't have a reason to set her up. It was too elaborate of a story to set her up for anything. If they didn't need her, they could've just sentenced her to death immediately.

A movement in the room caught her attention and she held her breath as a guard she didn't recognize entered the room and rummaged through a box. He grabbed a handful of red capes, folded them under his arm, and left.

Kolfinna couldn't use that room to escape; if more Royal Guards came to get random items, she would be caught in no time.

She padded to the other wall of her four-walled room, the one opposite the door. She hadn't wanted to use this wall to escape since there was a possibility guards were watching this side from outside—maybe waiting for her to pull a stunt like this. But this seemed to be the only chance she had now.

Kolfinna touched the wall with fingers dripping with mana. She pulled out a piece of the wall the size of her head. She held the heavy stone and poked her head through the hole. The wind blew against her gently, tousling the unkempt hairs that had pulled away from her braid. Trees and winding roads intertwined below her. No guards waited below and farther away she spotted a tall iron wrought gateway.

Sweat formed between her brows and her heart rate tripled. If she was caught, swarms of Royal Guards could capture her, and there would be no telling what would happen to her afterward. Since she was in the Royal Guard headquarters in the capital, there were bound to be strong Royal Guards here, stronger than her. And the military was nearby; what if a platoon of military soldiers went after her as well?

"You've made up your mind," she whispered, placing the stone on the floor. She laid her hands on the cool stone wall and closed her eyes. Surely, staying was far more dangerous. She *couldn't* stay.

She willed the wall to move, but her heart faltered.

Blár's cold eyes came to mind. The freezing, cruel

touch of his magic brushed her leg and she shuddered. No. This was the right decision.

The piece of stone pulled apart like soft bread; she piled it beside her feet as she pulled apart more pieces of the wall. She could've easily shoved a giant hole through the wall and made the stone fall to the ground below, or fall into her room, but that would attract too much attention. She was in the heart of the Royal Guards; it would take seconds for them to surround her.

When there was a gaping cavity large enough that she could comfortably pass through, she willed a giant branch of the tree below her to grow and stretch until it was under her feet. Kolfinna immediately hoisted herself on the branch and controlled the tree to pull herself down. She went slowly and made sure to avoid windows.

A gentle, warm breeze kissed her skin and the shadows of the starless night blanketed her descent. When her feet landed on the ground, she waved her hand and forced the tree's branch to weave through its existing branches. Whenever her mana manipulated trees and plants to grow larger, taller, or wider, they would remain that way even after she was done using them. This created a problem when covertly trying to escape without leaving behind hints, but she figured it didn't matter since they would find out she was gone by the morning.

Kolfinna slunk toward the gateway, always staying behind trees and looking over her shoulder to make sure she wasn't being followed or watched. There were likely Royal Guards stationed all around the building.

Just as she inched closer to the gate, voices stopped her in her tracks. She dropped to her knees and pressed her back against a tree. The voices grew louder.

"I'm telling you, it's dangerous."

"I'll be fine!"

Kolfinna's eyebrows furrowed; she knew those voices. Poking her head out slowly, she recognized the petite Eyfura next to Nollar, who towered over her. Even in the night, his hair shone like pale gold.

They walked near her on the cobbled walkway and Kolfinna hugged the tree so tightly she was sure the ridges of the tree bark were imprinted onto her back.

"It'll be big for my career," Eyfura said. "The reward is too big to turn away and I might even be able to rise up in rank. You know how important this is for me."

"It's not as important as your life!" Nollar's voice boomed.

"Shush!" Eyfura said before whispering, "I won't die."

Nollar scoffed and Kolfinna could imagine him rolling his eyes, despite not being able to see him. "They say nobody has made it out alive from there! Seriously, you *can't* do this. I don't care how much the reward money is. It's not worth it."

"Nollar, stop yelling." Eyfura's voice grew stern. "Please."

"But—"

"Nollar, I'm going to do this."

"It's not worth it!"

Kolfinna stole a glance at the siblings; they were a

dozen feet away from her, and Nollar clenched his fists tightly while Eyfura squared off in front of him.

"Is this ... is this so you can pay off my school tuition?" Nollar's voice shook. "I'll drop out if you go on this mission, Eyfura. I swear."

Kolfinna couldn't see Eyfura's expression, but she could hear the tremor of anger in her voice as she said, "You won't do such a thing. You know exactly how important school is. It wasn't easy to get you to where you're at, and I won't let you just up and quit. Everyone has put all their hopes on you. You know that."

"I know." He shook his head, and the moonlight bounced off his golden hair. "But it's not worth you dying for."

"I won't die." She placed her hands on Nollar's shoulders. "This is important to me, Nollar. Please, you have to understand."

"I don't want to understand." He shook her hands off. "This is suicide."

"Come on, don't be like that! I'll make it back, I promise."

"If you—"

"Nollar." Her tone sharpened. "I appreciate your words and how worried you are about me, but you can't force me to change my mind. It's not right to threaten me to get what you want. I understand you're worried, I really do, but you have to respect my decision."

Nollar was silent for a long while, seeming to mull over what she was saying. Kolfinna felt like she was intruding on something she shouldn't have seen or heard, but she couldn't move even if she wanted to. She was somehow reminded of Katla.

"*We'll be fine here*," Katla had said to her when they started working in Lord Estur's mansion. Her smile had lit up the room and there had been a positive, hopeful twinkle in her voice. "*No one will know a thing, and the pay is great! We can't keep living like beggars, Kolfinna. We've got to aim higher than cleaning tiny homes. This is just our first step. Trust me.*"

Kolfinna's throat closed up as she remembered her older sister. Her enthusiasm. Her hopefulness. She was the only person who had understood Kolfinna. The only one who made her feel at home.

"Fine," Nollar said, the words coming out warbled. He sniffed and blew out deeply. "*Fine.* Just make it back, okay? I'll be waiting."

"Thank you." Eyfura reached forward and pulled him into a tight embrace. The moonlight illuminated his watery eyes and he quickly blinked, returning the hug. "I will."

"You better stick to that black rank."

"I'll try ... but I'm strong too, you know?" Eyfura laughed and pulled away to look at him with bright eyes, and an even brighter smile. "This is just the first step, Nollar! Things can only go up from here. And besides, things are going to be different this time around! We'll have a real fae there! Kolfinna will be able to understand the castle and figure things out. And coupled with Blár

Vilulf, we'll be unstoppable. We'll be successful this time around. I just know it!"

Kolfinna sank deeper against the tree and listened to their receding footsteps, their voices fading as they joked with one another. She blinked back the tears pricking the corner of her eyes and pressed the heel of her hands against her eyes. It had been a long time since anyone had pinned their hopes on her. But more than that, she missed having someone by her side. Someone who understood her. Someone who loved her.

She would never receive that here. They would never accept her.

But that didn't mean that Eyfura didn't have that with Nollar; or that the other Royal Guards didn't have that with other people in their lives.

She rose to her feet and headed back to the building she had come from. That inkling of hope Katla had nestled in her rekindled. Maybe it was time to stop running. Maybe it was time to take her first step.

THE AFTERNOON'S BREATH WAS HOT, HUMID, and sticky in the dusty attic of the Royal Guard headquarters. Kolfinna wanted to stick her head out the window and breathe, but she doubted that would help with the heat. Even with the windows open, the attic was unbearably hot. Her dress stuck to her sweaty body like a glove.

She rarely ever liked the cold since last year—since Blár—but she wished for a soft breeze at least.

Eyfura, who was guarding her for the day, was down to her knees in a pile of old, threadbare clothes. The makeshift storage room seemed to serve as an area to dump pretty much *anything*; it was apparently less used than the other storage rooms, which were more organized, according to Eyfura. A thick coating of dust covered all the boxes and piles of junk all around the room, indicating that nobody really used these things.

Kolfinna found it hard to meet Eyfura's gaze without remembering the events of last night and how she wasn't supposed to witness her moment with Nollar. Eyfura didn't mention that her brother was nervous about her leaving for the mission, or that this was an important mission for her, or that she had high hopes for Kolfinna.

Magni guarded the door and watched her with half-lidded emerald eyes, as if expecting her to leap into action and escape, or attack them—or whatever evil he thought she would do. His brown hair was slicked back neatly, a single curl hanging over his forehead. His white and silver uniform contrasted beautifully against his tanned skin, and for a moment, Kolfinna marveled at how handsome he could've been if he wasn't always scowling or huffing in anger. When he caught her staring, his eyes narrowed further.

Kolfinna looked away and dragged a finger over one of the chests. "I'm guessing people don't usually come here." She inspected the gray dust between her fingers.

"Gosh." Eyfura laughed in embarrassment as she pushed a dusty box away from her and inspected another one. Her cheeks were rosy in the heat. "You must think we're filthy slobs, but we're not usually *this* bad. I swear."

"It's fine," Kolfinna trailed, glancing at the stacks of chairs, boots, clothes, and other random things jammed into the crooks and crannies between brimming dressers and chests. "I used to be a cleaning maid, so I've seen all sorts of messes."

Kolfinna stopped when she noticed a flat wooden badge poking out from between two wooden chests, where the bottom half of it was wedged between them. Kolfinna tugged it free and spread her fingers over the unpolished wood. It was similar to the badges the Royal Guards wore, but it was much cruder. Unlike the gold lion badge that glistened in the light and was said to be made of real gold, this one was clearly handmade and had chipped yellow paint all over it. The lion's mane was roughly carved out and it was missing a tail.

"What's this?" Kolfinna flipped it over to find a name etched on the back.

"Hm?" Eyfura emerged from a pile of capes and loose tunics. Her lips broke into a smile when she spotted the badge. "Aw, you found someone's Hope badge! I wonder what it's doing up here. People usually treasure those."

"What is it?" The badly carved lion didn't look like something a Royal Guard—who were known to be snobby, smug, and noble—would treasure. Did it hold sentimental value?

"When someone is trying to become a Royal Guard, a friend or family member will make them a Hope badge and give it to them at their initiation ceremony," Eyfura explained. "It basically shows that your friends and family believed in you the whole time. Nollar and my aunt made me one. What about you, Magni?"

Magni rolled his eyes. "I don't care for stupid things like that."

"Aw, does that mean no one made you one?"

He shot her a dark scowl. "Of course I received one. I received *many*."

Eyfura exchanged a glance with Kolfinna and rolled her eyes, while Kolfinna bit the bottom of her lip to keep from grinning.

"Did you make any for anyone, Magni?" Eyfura cranked open the lids of a scratched-up box and peeked inside of it. "Magni is a brilliant artist. I've seen him make elaborate sketches in the dirt with just a stick—"

"No, I haven't," Magni bit out as he gave Eyfura a hard look, like she was telling a secret of his.

Eyfura's expression was hidden as she dug into another box, but she seemed to get his message because she said, "Well, uh, maybe it's really old? Does it have a name on it?"

"Maybe the person who owned it died," Kolfinna said, running her fingers over the wood. "Or maybe they lost it. It says Erik on the back."

"Usually, you put the person's name on the back, so

that's not unusual but ... Erik? Hm, I don't recall a Royal Guard with that name. What about you, Magni?"

Magni shook his head. "None that I know of."

"Well, it could be that Erik lost it, or died ... Or who knows." Eyfura lifted her shoulders and placed a hand on her hip. "Everything here is pretty old, so who knows how far back some of these things are."

Kolfinna placed the badge on top of one of the wooden chests and shifted her attention to the clothes in Eyfura's arms. "Did you find them?"

"Oh, yes!" She thrust the clothes into Kolfinna's arms. "I knew we had some training clothes up here! These should fit. We usually give them to trainees when they do an internship with us. Nollar did it here at headquarters last summer and this summer and it was a lot of fun! I wasn't able to do it when I was in school because I went to a smaller school back home ... Anyway, these are from last summer. They should be clean."

It was a simple black tunic with silver buttons and pants to match. She turned it in her hands. The material was soft and stretchy and reeked of lavishness; there was no way she'd find this fine of a material in the street markets. It wasn't silk, but she could tell the quality just by touching it. The Royal Guards were extravagant, even for trainees. She brought it close to her face and quickly pulled it away, her nose wrinkling. It also reeked of sweat.

Eyfura's smile faded into a frown and she stepped forward and sniffed. "Oh my gosh." She pinched her nose. "I'm so sorry, I didn't realize those ... well, *stink*. Gosh, the interns are supposed to clean all the uniforms before returning them." She held her hand out to the clothes. "I can take those and have them cleaned."

Out of all the Royal Guards Kolfinna had been acquainted with these past two weeks, Eyfura was definitely the nicest one. That should've comforted Kolfinna, but she still felt uneasy. She must've had an ulterior motive. Why would someone be friendly to her, a fae and a murderer? Her brother Nollar was the same: contagiously friendly. It was unnerving. She would rather deal with people she could easily read, like Magni.

Eyfura gathered an armful of clothes. "I'll take these to the laundry and have them cleaned. Magni, do you mind escorting Kolfinna to her room while I do this?"

His frown deepened. "That's why I'm here, aren't I?"

"So ... that's a yes?"

"No," he said sullenly, dabbing his sweaty forehead with a pure white handkerchief.

"Would you rather take this laundry then?" She held up the clothes with raised eyebrows.

He sighed. "No."

"Then I'll leave Kolfinna to you."

He didn't protest as Eyfura skipped out of the room, leaving Kolfinna alone with him. He stopped glowering at her and instead watched the hallway, where Eyfura's figure was slowly receding. When she was gone, he turned back to Kolfinna.

"I don't get why she trusts you so easily," Magni said with a scoff.

Kolfinna wasn't prepared for the fire in his eyes and the way his lips curled back in disgust. She stepped back subconsciously, her back bumping into a thin coat rack with red capes draped over it. She stilled it with her hands while Magni watched.

"And I don't get why you hate me so much," Kolfinna said, trying to keep her tone level.

"You're a fae *and* a murderer."

"You know nothing about me." Kolfinna's own eyes narrowed at him. "And that man—" The words caught in her throat and she couldn't spit them out. Couldn't tell him that Lord Estur had killed Katla. How it was either Kolfinna's life or his, and she had chosen her life. What was the point of telling him? By the way he was glaring at her with hate-tinted eyes, he would never believe her or care. Kolfinna being a fae was probably enough reason for him to hate her.

"That man," Magni continued harshly, "was a distinguished member of society."

"He was also a murderer," Kolfinna spat.

He ignored that, pushing himself off the wall by the door. He towered over her as he stepped closer, and she inadvertently stepped back. The gold Royal Guard badge shone on his chest from the flickering torchlights. "It disgusts me how Captain Asulf is fine with keeping you here so we can succeed in this mission. It pisses me off how low we've fallen, to trust a murderer. To trust a *fae*."

Magni spat out the word like it was poison to his tongue. It was inevitable that she came up against a reaction like this, but she hadn't thought it would be now. Right here.

Kolfinna's hands flexed, and she briefly glanced at the exit. Would it be considered self-defense if he attacked her? Her body tensed and she readied her mana for his first blow. If he came charging at her, she decided she would manipulate the stone walls and crush him with them before running out the door. He wouldn't die from that, but it would be enough to slow him down.

But he didn't attack. He continued watching her with narrowed, green eyes. "I don't trust you. I know you'll betray us at some point. You'll either kill us or make a run for it. You fae are all the same: manipulative, deceitful liars."

Kolfinna stilled. She recognized his language, the words he used. "Are you a hunter?"

Something flashed in his eyes—surprise, or maybe pride? "I am," he said. "I've only met two of your kind, but you're all the same."

A fly buzzed in front of them, momentarily distracting Magni as he swatted it away from his face. Kolfinna forgot to breathe and hid her shaking hands behind her back.

It didn't matter that he was a hunter. That he filled his free time with hunting her people. That he either found pleasure in killing her kind, or that he thought it was necessary to eradicate her kind. It didn't matter which hunter he was because he couldn't hurt her. Fenris had said he would personally protect her so long as she was on the mission. No matter how much Magni hated her, he wouldn't compromise his position in the Royal Guard ... Or would he?

She would beat him if she had to. Ever since losing to Blár, her insecurities had gotten the better of her, and she didn't know what to believe anymore. Was she strong, or weak, or average? Could she take down a Royal Guard? She had defeated the ice elemental guard back in the city when Fenris attacked her. That must've meant she could hold her own against Magni.

Before Blár defeated her last year, she had been confident in her abilities. After all, she had been better than Katla when it came to magic. When Katla had shown her how to use her magic to make a sapling grow when she was six, Kolfinna had been able to make it grow tall and wrap around her fingers at her will. Even Katla hadn't been able to do that, despite being older and practicing with their parents. Even their parents couldn't do that, according to Katla. So Kolfinna had always believed she was stronger and *better*.

She had defeated so many people in Lord Estur's house. She had killed him, and he was a purple rank.

But Blár Vilulf was stronger and *much* better, and that loss a year ago had humbled her. It now served as a direct line to how she felt about her magic abilities. Even now, standing in a dusty, steaming attic with sweat pouring down her chest, it taught her that she wasn't invincible. That there were people stronger than her. That she could likely never defeat Blár.

But it also reminded her that Blár was a black rank—there was no one stronger than him in the empire, only possibly two people, and even then, there was a chance he was stronger. She might not have been able to fight Blár, but Magni was *not* Blár.

"Are you *trying* to pick a fight?" Kolfinna kept her voice low and hard.

"Only if you're looking for one."

"I'm not," she said, "but you seem bent on picking on me."

"I'm only warning you, fae scum." Magni stepped closer, and his shadow loomed over her threateningly. "If you interfere in any way, I *will* kill you."

Kolfinna leapt away; she didn't like how close he was getting to her—how he was trying to intimidate her.

"Threatening me won't get you anywhere," Kolfinna ground out. "And don't be so confident. I won't hesitate to attack you if you attack me. Remember, yellow and purple ranks came to fight me, but I defeated them. It took a black rank to finally defeat me. What are *you*? A yellow? Purple?"

Magni's brow rose, and then he laughed. It sent shivers down her spine, and all the hairs on her arm rose as he spoke next. "Are you forgetting that same black rank that defeated you is going to be on the mission with us? If I can't defeat you, which I highly doubt, don't you think *he* will? I heard he's been itching to hunt something. Maybe this time he won't play with his toy and leave it after it stops moving. Maybe this time he'll actually finish the job."

Kolfinna sucked in sharply and stumbled back as if he had slapped her, her hand catching on a small box filled with worn, muddied, black boots and sending them crashing to the floor. A plume of dust rose between them as she found her footing.

"You're lying," she breathed, unable to hide the tremor in her voice. The dust sifted through the air, and her nose tickled with it. "Blár isn't a hunter."

"And how do you know that? Not every hunter *wants* people to know they're a hunter."

Kolfinna rounded a box of white uniforms, some of them sporting red stains across the front. There were two chests of clothes between them now.

"He's not a hunter," she said louder, as if increasing her volume would make it true. If Blár was a hunter, he'd definitely attack and kill her, because unlike Magni, he had no reason to hold back. And he was a black rank; nobody would miss her if she disappeared.

"Who knows," he murmured.

"He's not a hunter. You're bluffing." He was just trying to scare her, she told herself, growing stronger in her conviction. Blár couldn't be a hunter, because Mímir had said he didn't like doing things outside the military, right? "And besides, he can't hurt me, and neither can you. Fen—*Captain* Asulf said he'd protect me." She stared at him hard, hoping her pink eyes unnerved him enough to leave her alone. To believe her when she said she wasn't his enemy. "I plan on becoming a proper Royal Guard and you're not going to stop me. I don't care if you believe me or not, but I'm going to try my hardest to make this mission successful. You can't hurt me, or else Captain Asulf will deal with you personally."

Magni's lips curved and he braced his arms on a dusty bookshelf. "I believe that you want to join the Royal Guard, but you're not telling the whole story. You just want to join so you can ruin this country from the inside. So you can ensnare the men, kill them, and do whatever you want and get away with it. You want the power to freely do what you want."

Her nostrils flared and her hands twitched at those words. How dare he! The hunters were the ones killing her kind indiscriminately! And now he wanted to say that *she* was the one trying to do the same to humans?

"And what's wrong with freely doing what you want?" Kolfinna quelled the rage inside her that made her want to hurl chunks of the stone wall at him. She fought the urge to hate him for who he was—a hunter. It would've been so much easier to be the creature he believed her to be. To be truly evil and uncaring for living things just because she didn't understand them. It would've been easy to choose hate, but she was tired of hate. "You know nothing about me or my people. You think we want to run an evil scheme to take over the country? We just want to live freely and without fear! What's so wrong with that? Why can you do it, but we can't?"

Magni hesitated, as if not expecting that answer, but

then his face morphed into a scowl again. "I use my power for good, and your kind don't know what that means."

"Do you now?" Her bitter laugh tinkered through the thick, humid air. "You use your power for good when you're killing fae children, women, and men? When you're causing an entire group of people to hide for their lives because they're terrified that you'll kill them next? I was four years old when the hunters tried to kill me after killing my parents! What sin did I commit? What murder or evil did I commit? You know nothing about my people and our struggles. You know nothing about our magic or how much evil you commit as a hunter! Yes, we want to live freely, but what's so wrong with that?"

Something flickered in his eyes—hesitation, or perhaps guilt?—but it disappeared quickly and he whirled around until his back was to her. "Stop talking, fae scum. I don't have time to be arguing with you. Follow me." He headed to the door but then paused, glancing over his shoulder at her. She couldn't read his expression. "The instant you stop being useful, you're dead. Consider this a warning."

"I'll be useful," she spat. "And when I'm a Royal Guard, you'll have no choice but to accept me."

He shot her a glare but didn't respond.

6

———

THE STARLESS NIGHT SKY ENGULFED THE
makeshift camp in a blanket of darkness. Kolfinna and
the Royal Guards had started the trek to the Eventyrslot
ruins that morning. The majority of their travel was
through thick forests and unpaved paths, which made
sense since the ruins were in an uninhabited part of the
countryside. Kolfinna was thankful they didn't have to
travel through the city; she didn't want to face civilians
who would see her as a fae riding with the guards. There
was sure to be retaliation and nasty slurs thrown at her
face, and likely things tossed in her direction—she wasn't
ready for that phase just yet. The forest, however, helped
keep her calm and grounded, the peaceful shush of the
trees a reprieve from city eyes. But she still couldn't calm
herself completely. The closer they drew to the ruins, the
tighter Kolfinna's nerves pulled until her chest felt like it
would burst open. And maybe it would. If looks could

kill, she would've died a hundred times over that day alone.

Kolfinna rubbed her arms in slow circles; they had stopped in the middle of the woods and made camp when the sun waned. The eleven Royal Guards did their own thing—some attempted to make tents, others ate salted, dried meat and cheese from their sacks, others socialized with each other, and some tended to their horses. Kolfinna, on the other hand, sat in front of a flickering fire in the center of their camp. The fire licked and ate the logs, roaring quietly. She stared harder into it, her mind traveling to the far depths of her memories. She thought of Katla's smiling face as she taught Kolfinna how to use magic. She thought of Blár's ice magic as he froze the forest during their battle. She thought of Nollar's tears as he hugged Eyfura. The jumble of thoughts blurred through her mind, none of them sticking for too long before the next one began like a seamless dream. Her mind was a large, tangled ball of yarn; it didn't matter which thread she pulled, it refused to unknot itself.

Kolfinna's hand inadvertently traveled to her stiffening leg. The muscles around her shin and ankle throbbed from the jostling of the horseback ride. It wasn't just her leg that throbbed, but her hips, waist, and thighs from balancing upright on the horse and gripping so tight that the muscles screamed. It had been her first time riding a horse, and she had thought of Katla the whole time. She ached to tell Katla that she had fulfilled one of her sister's dreams. Katla had loved horses but had never even touched one. She had always wanted to ride one and would often tell Kolfinna that one day, she'd have a horse and she'd ride it around town. As if that was a grand dream to have. But it was to Katla.

There was also the matter of the runes that bothered Kolfinna. If she couldn't read them, did that make her useless to the party? What would the Royal Guard do to her if it came to that?

"Do you mind if I sit with you?" Eyfura stood a few feet away, her uniform bursting white against the vault of black sky. She pushed a strand of curly hair behind her ear. A flash of purple glittered on her earlobe.

"I don't mind," Kolfinna said as Eyfura thrust her cape away from her bottom and plopped beside her on the wooden log. Faceted, purple earrings clung to her ears and glittered against the red, blazing campfire.

"I thought earrings weren't allowed?" Kolfinna asked.

"Hm?" Eyfura touched her ears and smiled. "Oh, this. Well, technically, they're not allowed, but Captain Asulf doesn't mind. He said we can modify the uniforms to our liking so long as we do our job and don't stand out *too* much. So these earrings and these gloves"—she wriggled her fingers in the silk and lace trimmed gloves—"are fine. And so are my hair ribbon and this necklace." She tugged at the silver chain around her neck and held it up against the firelight. A sparkling gold butterfly hung on it. "Pretty, huh? It was one of my first purchases after becoming a Royal Guard. Just a little treat for myself."

Kolfinna stared at the butterfly longingly, wondering

what it would look like around her neck, warming against her skin. She had never owned any piece of jewelry. She and Katla had been simple maids. Their salary was never enough for extravagance and would've been wasted on such an unnecessary, vain thing. Not to mention that jewelry would make them stand out. Despite all of that, she couldn't help but imagine wearing pretty earrings and glittering necklaces.

Eyfura touched her arm, jolting her from her reverie. "Are you all right?" Her voice was as low as the soft crackling of the campfire. Her eyebrows puckered together in concern and a hint of worry laced her words.

"I am, sorry, I was just lost in thought." Kolfinna scraped her thumb into the rough ridges of the log she sat on, while her fingertips skimmed the bark slowly.

She didn't need jewelry, she told herself. It was unnecessary. She had lived without it, and she could continue living without it.

"When you're a Royal Guard, you can buy necklaces too."

"What? No, I wasn't thinking that." Her face heated up instantly, and she was sure it wasn't because of the fire. Kolfinna quickly pushed a strand of inky hair out of her face. "I was just wondering why Fenris—uh, *Captain Asulf*—allows that."

Eyfura didn't look convinced but shrugged. "He's young, so I think he doesn't really care for those kinds of things. Plus, he's the first Royal Guard captain who's not a noble. So I think he *really* doesn't care. Maybe he thinks it's a stupid rule to be strict about."

"Fenris isn't a noble?" Kolfinna tilted her head at that new tidbit of information. All Royal Guards seemed so … *royal* with their stiff, lavish uniforms, upright attitude, and immense influence and power. How was it that the captain *wasn't* a noble?

"No, he's not. He was raised in an orphanage on the south side of town." Eyfura smirked at Kolfinna's aghast expression. "Yup, the slums."

"But he doesn't seem …" Kolfinna waved her hands as she struggled to come up with a word to describe the slums. Her people usually hid in the slums. People didn't look twice at a beggar on the street; didn't look for too long to see that their eyes weren't exactly brown when the weedy tea started to fade. The people in the slums all wore the same expression as the fae did—survival toughened them. "I don't know the word for it … rough? And most people don't really get out of the slums."

"That's all true," Eyfura said. "But Captain Asulf is a genius with fire magic and has been since he was a child, so he was quickly taken out and put into a military academy. He ended up becoming a Royal Guard, and the rest is history." Eyfura stretched her legs out in front of her, her shiny black boots pushing against the bramble and twigs mulching the forest floor. "You know, I didn't really know what I wanted to be when I was in the academy. I felt like becoming a Royal Guard would be too hard, so the military was probably a better fit for me. But then I saw

Captain Asulf and I just knew I had to become one. I mean, if he could do it, why couldn't I? And well, it did help that he was just *so* handsome in that uniform."

Kolfinna continued pressing her fingers into the bark. Becoming a Royal Guard was apparently harder than joining the military, since the Royal Guards had a standard, and the military took just about anyone. "Why would you change your future for a man you didn't know?"

"I just saw how regal he looked and wanted to emulate the same thing. I felt like ... I'd get lost in a sea of military men and women, but a Royal Guard ... That's something extraordinary!" Eyfura nearly bounced in her seat, as if unable to contain her giddiness. "There are so many military people everywhere. A Royal Guard just seems more special. Like they do more for the people, not just go on military excursions and kill people because the commander-in-chief says so."

"But you'll kill whoever Fenris tells you to kill?"

Eyfura's smile faded. "No," she said, her tone sobering up. "I've never killed anyone."

The fire hissed as Mímir fed another log into it. Kolfinna stared at it for a moment longer, a gnawing feeling weighing on her heart like an impossibly heavy anchor into the tumultuous Northern shores. Eyfura came here to distract her from her thoughts, and Kolfinna had snapped at her. It wasn't fair, especially since Kolfinna was the murderer among the two.

"Eyfura ..." Kolfinna's fingers curled into the fallen

tree she sat on, the fissures of the bark digging into her skin uncomfortably. "I'm sorry, that was uncalled for."

"It's fine," Eyfura said airily, waving her hand.

"Do ..." Kolfinna tried to think of something to spark another conversation, something that Eyfura would want to talk about. "Do many girls like Captain Asulf? I always heard rumors about how handsome he is."

"Oh, yes!" The awkwardness peeled away and Eyfura giggled, leaning forward and pressing a hand on Kolfinna's forearm. "Practically all the girls in my academy gushed over him. We would travel to royal parades not to catch sight of the king or princes, but to see him! He's so dreamy!"

Dreamy? Those silver eyes were capable of skinning a man alive. And that fire of his could burn a human to charred bits.

Eyfura nudged her shoulder. "You can't tell me he's not handsome!"

"He's ... okay. Too old for me." It was true that Fenris was handsome, with his fiery hair and those stormy gray eyes, framed with blood-red lashes. His jaw, figure, facial structure all made him a beautiful catch. But she wasn't going to admit that to Eyfura. Or anyone.

"Too old? He's only twenty-nine!"

"That's old." Kolfinna laughed. "I'm only eighteen, remember?"

"Oh, right." Eyfura's lips formed a pout but then lifted into a smirk. "Well, I'm only twenty, so I'm not that far away from him."

"That's still nine years."

"Gosh, I know!" Eyfura sighed loudly, all the breath and enthusiasm leaving her as she slunk into her seat. "But it doesn't matter, because he's married."

Kolfinna's eyebrows shot up and she did a double take to see if Eyfura was telling the truth; she had never heard that the infamous Captain Asulf of the Royal Guard was a married man. "Really?"

"Yes, he got married like … hm, seven years ago?"

"Oh, I never heard about it."

"Yeah, I guess he's pretty private with his personal life. Apparently, he has kids too? I don't know, I'm not that high up in the ranks to know all these things. But I will say, if I didn't have morals, I'd be one of those girls pining after him! But I do, and I would *never* chase after a married man." Her gaze dragged over to the other Royal Guards who mulled around doing their own thing. "Any of these guys catch your eye?"

Kolfinna was already shaking her head. "No, not a chance."

"Really, none?"

"None." Kolfinna shot a glance at Magni, who was now tearing apart a hunk of bread and sitting with the white-blond-haired man she recognized from the meeting —Torsten? Then at Mímir, who was slowly but surely setting up one of the tents by himself, the firelight illuminating his mussed hair. And then at the rest of the group —half of whom had glared at her the entire ride here.

None were pleasant. "Not my type, and they're too old for me."

"Everyone's in their twenties or thir—"

"And I'm eighteen," Kolfinna retorted. "And besides, I'm sure most of them don't like me."

"Hm." Eyfura rubbed her chin thoughtfully. "Maybe I should set you up with my brother then?"

At the thought of Nollar's pale gold hair, sparkling green eyes, and cheerful grin, Kolfinna's face instantly bloomed with color. He was only two years younger, but that somehow felt too young. Or maybe it was just the thought of a romantic interest that scared her. "I'm not interested in romance," she quickly said. "Besides, I'm a fae! Who would willingly be with me while knowing that?"

The glowing firelight illuminated Eyfura's empathetic, almost pitying expression. "I'm sure there are people out there—"

"I'm not interested in romance." Kolfinna averted her gaze. A chill settled in her bones and she subconsciously reached for her right shin, her fingers curling over her knee. "Besides being a fae, I also have this terrible limp. I'm not exactly the ideal type for most people."

"That's not true! You're ideal to the people who matter!" Eyfura wrapped an arm around Kolfinna and kept it in place even as Kolfinna flinched at her touch. "You'll find someone who loves you for who you are—fae, limp, bad attitude and all!" Eyfura waggled her brows at the last part and rushed in with a laugh. "The last part is a joke."

Despite the joke, Kolfinna's expression soured. "I don't have a bad attitude."

"I'm joking with you." Her jovial expression softened. "But I'm serious when I say there's someone out there, Kolfinna. You should value yourself more."

She didn't say anything and continued looking into the fire. She did value herself. Why else was she always running and protecting herself? She couldn't trust anyone. Not a man or woman. Not a lover or a friend.

Her hands clenched into fists subconsciously. But wasn't that the whole reason why she wanted to become a Royal Guard? So she could finally find peace and be safe? Wouldn't safety mean she could try to find someone to love? Maybe there was someone out there who could love her. Maybe she could also gush over people like Eyfura.

No, a small voice in the back of her mind said. There was no one like that out there.

Besides, being a Royal Guard didn't mean that the people around her wouldn't backstab her.

"Are you nervous?" Eyfura tried dusting off a smudge of dirt on her white gloves distractedly. "Blár Vilulf will be there. I know you have history with him."

Kolfinna shivered as a breeze wafted through the camp, the trees rustling and the fire sputtering before tendrils of fire spread like outstretched hands toward the blackened sky. The cold bit her right leg and she reached for her shin, massaging her sore muscles. "He made my leg like this," she whispered. "I don't think I'll ever be ready to face him."

Eyfura's face grew white. "He what?"

"He attacked me and"—Kolfinna's voice grew thick—"he almost killed me. He could've killed me, actually, but he let me go for whatever reason. My leg broke in multiple places and it healed wrong, so I'm stuck with this."

She was reminded of Magni's description of Blár playing with her like a toy, and once that toy broke and stopped moving, he grew bored of it and left it there. She reached her hands out toward the fire to warm the numbing ice spreading over her body.

She shuddered as she remembered his tundra-like blue eyes. The evil curve of his lips. The way he peered down at her like she was filth.

"I'm so sorry," Eyfura whispered. "It must be terrible to have to see him and work with him."

"I'm nervous, but Fenris said he won't hurt me." Kolfinna didn't completely believe those words. Blár was the same power rank as Fenris, so what reason did he have to follow Fenris's order not to harm her? Besides, Blár wasn't a Royal Guard, so Fenris had no control over him. "He'll behave because I'm on his side this time. He has to."

"We'll protect you," Eyfura said. "I'll make sure he doesn't hurt you. You have all the Royal Guards here to protect you if he does anything to you. We might not look like it, and to be brutally honest, some probably don't like you, but we would never let the military mess with us like that. You're our responsibility."

That eased a bit of the tension cording her neck, but she couldn't help but ask, "Do you ... do you, by any chance, know if he's a hunter?"

The wind howled in the distance as Eyfura paused to think. "I don't think so. Mímir said he wasn't." Upon seeing Kolfinna's expression, Eyfura continued, "I really don't think he is. And besides, even if he were a hunter, would that change anything? He still can't hurt you."

Kolfinna's fingernails dug into the bark; that was true, even if Blár Vilulf was or wasn't a hunter, did that change that he was dangerous? Or that he wouldn't hurt her?

"By the way"—Eyfura grinned at her—"what can you do with your magic abilities? I think you mentioned they're nature-based?"

"Yes." She raised her hand above the grass below their feet. Her mana sizzled on her skin and the grass grew until it reached her hand. "I can do this. Among other things."

Eyfura's eyes were two wide saucers. "Gosh, that's awesome. I've never had a green thumb. All my plants always die."

"Fae are usually good gardeners." Kolfinna chuckled. "Before my sister and I chose to be cleaning maids, we thought about being gardeners and selling our vegetables, but that would be too suspicious. Plus, vegetables grown with magic don't taste that great."

"You'd be great in areas that have droughts. Imagine all the peoples' livelihoods you can help! That could be an awesome business venture. 'Kolfinna's Growing Aid' or something like that!" Eyfura leaned back on her log and grinned into the night sky. "You'd become stinking rich."

"And you? What's your power?"

"I'm an Enhancer." Eyfura held up her fist. "So I'm basically just strong."

"I heard learning to become an Enhancer is hard."

"Yeah, I guess so. Elementals have it easier, I think. Their magic comes easy to them since it's more natural, but Enhancers have to 'wake up' their magic since it's dormant." Eyfura sighed loudly, her gaze becoming distant as she peered up at the black sky. "It was so freakin' hard for me to awaken my abilities. I used to be so jealous of Nollar. My parents were so proud when they found out about his magic and they pinned all their hopes and dreams on him. They already were pretty proud that he was a Lightning Elemental, but they hoped he'd become big.

"On the other hand, nobody thought much about me, because I'm just a girl, and I didn't have any Elemental powers. But I didn't want to just become nothing. I wanted to prove myself too." The night cast shadows over her face, and her eyes grew sad. "To ... I don't know, win their love? Their attention? Or to prove *something*. I don't really know. I worked my ass off to awaken my Enhancer abilities. People say that everyone not blessed with Elemental powers have dormant Enhancer abilities, but as I tried over and over again to punch into a concrete wall and try to make a crack into it, my knuckles bleeding and my body breaking, I thought it was a lie. I thought there was no way I could ever awaken it. It took me years before I showed a *hint* of Enhancer abilities. The vast majority of the population never awaken their abilities because it's so dang hard. But I'm glad I never gave up."

Eyfura suddenly laughed, rubbing the nape of her neck and glancing at Kolfinna sheepishly. "I don't know why I'm telling you all this, but yeah, it's pretty hard. I guess I just get heated when I think about it … But you know, I'm pretty sure that's one of the reasons people don't like your kind … The fae, I mean. Magic comes so easily to your people. Or so I heard."

Kolfinna shifted in her seat. It was awkward and strange to think about—that she somehow had an advantage over a human. "It … it does come easily to us. I've never had to struggle to use my magic, if I'm being honest. Yes, there are a few things that are harder to do and harder to learn, but I never had to awaken my powers. What are you able to do with your abilities?"

"I can break boulders and buildings," Eyfura said. "And I can lift really heavy things. It's pretty nifty, to be honest. I'll show you my cool side when we actually fight whatever's in the ruins." She said the last part with a wink.

Kolfinna couldn't help the smile that lifted her lips. "That'll be cool to see."

"Oh, you never know!" Eyfura spread her hands out, her eyes wide with excitement. "What if there are evil spirits and bandits in there? Or ancient monsters our world has never seen?"

"I wonder ... But I don't think I'm excited to see that kind of stuff. What if they're stronger than us? Or I don't know, I'd rather face things I'm familiar with. That I *know* I can beat."

"Oh, come on. We'd be the first people in centuries to see some of the stuff in there! I think that's pretty exciting! But I'm pretty confident we could kick some monster butt if it came down to it, even if we didn't recognize them." Eyfura picked up a twig and twirled it around in her hand before pointing it at Kolfinna. "What do you think is in there that's strong enough to make it so no one makes it out of there? There has to be a reason nobody has made it out yet."

Kolfinna pondered for a moment. Magic beasts existed, so maybe there was a powerful magic beast stuck inside the ruins that no one could kill? Or maybe the ruins were empty because the first excavation team had taken all the goods and made a run for it? It was all a mystery.

"I'm not sure," she finally answered. "But I hope it's nothing too dangerous. I'd like to clear the ruins as easily as possible and then"—*become a Royal Guard and not have to run anymore*—"relax."

"I agree! The king is promising a hefty reward." Eyfura tossed the twig into the fire. "I'm excited to spend the money when we get back. Hey, maybe I'll show you all the good shops in the capital? We can go shopping together! That'll be so much fun!"

Kolfinna picked at the dirt beneath her fingernails. It was a pretty image: She and Eyfura waltzing through the capital streets with silk and fur clothes draped over their arms, smiling, laughing, having a jovial time. But it was too much like a dream.

"Yeah, sure." Kolfinna smiled hesitantly.

"That's a promise!" She held her pinky out and wrapped it around Kolfinna's without warning. Her grin was infectious. "When we're done here, we'll have lots of fun. I'll introduce you to all my friends, so you better not make a run for it, all right?"

"Yeah," Kolfinna murmured, "sure."

"Eyfura!" Mímir called out from half a dozen feet away. He stood with his hands on his hips and his tent was now a puddle by his feet. "Do you mind helping me with this? I've been trying to erect this thing, but it just won't work."

Eyfura giggled as she got to her feet. "You really do suck at those tents. Remember the last mission you needed my help too?"

"Ugh, don't remind me."

Eyfura went to the tent and examined it for a bit before waving to the other Royal Guards to help her. Magni grumbled and got to his feet. Kolfinna watched as Eyfura helped build the tent, laughing and poking at the other guards when they didn't pull their weight.

Kolfinna turned her attention back to the fire, where it continued to expand and wane with the wind. In a few days, she would see Blár Vilulf again.

❄

"WE'RE HERE!" MÍMIR CALLED OUT THREE DAYS later in the afternoon when they reached a makeshift military camp with two red tents and four gray tents erected in the forest clearing. Soldiers in gray military uniforms mulled around the clearing, and a few gave them pointed looks as they drew closer to the camp.

A chill settled in Kolfinna's bones; a chill that rattled her teeth and was cold in every sense: literally, figuratively, and metaphorically. Her injured leg ached terribly and she couldn't stop shivering. It was the kind of cold that tore at her skin and pricked her eyes. It was powerful and terrifying and horrendously ugly.

It meant that Blár Vilulf was nearby.

Kolfinna drew her cloak tighter around her body, her teeth chattering and her knees knocking together. Her cloak was meant for autumn's coolness, but it felt like a mesh sheet with how little it stood against the biting cold. Maybe it was the power of a black rank, but the last time she had met him, there had been a similarly unbearable wintry chill. A year ago, when she should've been sweltering under the summer heat, the weather had morphed into winter in the few minutes he came to find her.

She wasn't the only one who noticed the weather change; the entire party of Royal Guards shifted on their feet uncomfortably.

"It's supposed to be summer," Magni muttered with a string of curses to her left, while Torsten, the white-blond ice elemental, laughed beside him and said, "Well, you know what this means ..."

Their conversation drifted to silence as they stared ahead at the military camp, their once carefree mood shifting to a more serious note. It wasn't only them; Kolfinna could see the hardness in the Royal Guards' faces as they regarded the camp with narrowed eyes, as if looking down on something distasteful.

"You okay?" Eyfura came to stand beside her. A breeze tousled her hair and sent stray blond curls across her eyes. "I can tell by this chill that it's you-know-who exerting his power."

Kolfinna quickly gazed at the dozens of soldiers in the clearing, their faces blurring together as she tried to find *him*. Her breath caught in her throat when she couldn't find him, despite knowing he was close. "Is this normal for him?" Kolfinna asked, her voice carrying with the wind. "This cold, I mean."

"I think he makes everything cold around him on purpose. I don't know if it's to make himself more powerful or to make everyone more uncomfortable. You don't see Captain Asulf doing that." Eyfura sniffed, rubbing her reddening nose with her sleeve. "I heard he's hard to work with, so I'm not exactly excited to be working with him, but I'm sure it'll be easier having him on our side."

Kolfinna didn't share that sentiment. Sure, everyone was probably happy to have Blár there so he could save them, but that was only *if* he was willing to do that. And in Kolfinna's case, there was more of a chance of dying at his hands than being saved by them. What if he felt inclined to let her die since he hadn't been able to kill her the first time around?

No matter what, she needed to make sure she stayed far away from him. At least with Magni, she stood a chance against him. She wasn't sure if she could beat Magni, per se, but she had more of a chance of a fair fight with Magni than she did with Blár. An unsurmountable monster like Blár shouldn't have existed in the first place.

"Everyone, line up." Mímir clapped his hands to draw everyone's attention, though it felt unnecessary since nobody had moved since arriving. They stood rock-still, observing the soldiers warily, and the soldiers seemed to do the same from their position in the camp.

There were a dozen Royal Guards, Kolfinna included, and what appeared to be four dozen military soldiers. The last attempt at the ruins had tried to overcome them with numbers, and that had failed. Now, only twenty-four would enter. Twelve from the military side, and twelve from the Royal Guard's side. All the extra men would be staking outside the ruins and would wait for their return. *If* they returned.

Mímir cleared his throat and carefully looked at the Royal Guards. "We'll be entering the ruins tomorrow morning. Just relax for a bit and do what you want today because this is going to be our only real break for a while. Also, the red tents are ours. Women go in one, men in the other. If you have any questions, you can direct them to me. Remember, I'll be in charge of this entire mission, so if you have any quarrels with the military or anything, please bring it up with me first before taking matters into your own hands. The mission takes priority over everything."

Nobody said anything, so he waved them off. "All right, go relax. Introduce yourselves to the military and vice versa. And I hope I don't have to reiterate this: the military is not your enemy. We're all allies in this."

Despite saying that, none of the Royal Guards dispersed to the military side and instead remained in their own group on one side of the camp while Mímir went off to the military side.

One of the Royal Guards, a pretty brunette with a mole beneath her eye who Kolfinna vaguely recognized from the meeting, placed a hand on her hip and gazed at the soldiers with a scowl. "Do you think any of them will even be useful? Besides the black rank, of course. I mean, the military has like zero standards."

Torsten laughed and ran a hand through his wavy hair. "They're probably a bunch of sissies who've never been in *real* combat."

"They even smell like magic beast shit." The brunette chuckled behind her silk gloves.

"Bunch of lowlifes," Magni agreed with a sneer.

By the looks of the soldiers, they weren't thrilled for the Royal Guards to be there either. Instead of searching the shifting crowd of soldiers who went in and out of tents, Kolfinna turned her attention to the forest engulfing them all in a tight embrace. It was easier to feel the pull of life thrumming in each tree, each blade of grass, and each flower stem than it was to search for those haunting, cruel eyes. The trees swayed with the breeze, carrying a whiff of wild jasmine, and the sunlight dappled through the cluster of leaves and branches.

"I don't see him." Eyfura cut through Kolfinna's thoughts. "So you're in the clear."

"For now." Kolfinna stared harder into the trees and tried to pick out the various smells amalgamating into the clearing—moss, jasmine, and the sickly sweet smell of rotting wild fruits.

"Um, by the way"—Kolfinna finally looked over at the soldiers, and then at the Royal Guards—"why do the Royal Guards not like the military and vice versa? All I know is that the military is under the commander-in-chief while the Royal Guard is under the king. Is there anything that happened to create a divide?"

"Hm." Eyfura shrugged, casting a glance at the soldiers. "I don't really know, to be honest. I think it's just the type of work we do that they don't like and vice versa. I'm not so snobby to think I'm better than them just because I'm a Royal Guard, but I will say that being a Royal Guard is grander than the military, and we generally get paid more than the average soldier. I think that might have something to do with it."

Even as a normal citizen, Kolfinna understood the Royal Guards to be lavish in everything they did. From what she heard, the Royal Guard only booked the most expensive inns. They ate the most expensive food. And there was a slew of nobles in the Royal Guard. It didn't help that even their uniforms were fancy.

"What does the Royal Guard do?" Kolfinna asked. "Don't you guys just patrol the cities and capture criminals?"

"Yes, but we do more than that. We uphold the law, which is a pretty broad task, so there's a lot that goes into it. The military patrols the borders, deals with any foreign threats, handles any war, and they hunt down magic beasts that encroach on human territory. I mean, sometimes we also take down magic beasts if there's an immediate threat, but that's not our job."

"Are you nervous?" a voice came from behind Kolfinna.

Kolfinna jumped at the intrusion of their conversation and spun on her heels, mana working through her feet into the soil.

"*Mímir*"—her lips pressed together at his familiar face —"don't scare me like that," she hissed; vines were already slithering around her feet. Heat scorched her cheeks while Eyfura doubled over with laughter.

Mímir raised his hands as he eyed the vines close to his feet. "Sorry, didn't mean to sneak up on you."

Kolfinna cleared her throat and she sent the vines back into the earth. "Um, it's okay," she said, and then shot Eyfura a glare. "Come on, it's not *that* funny."

Eyfura laughed harder and pointed at the ground. "But you—you almost tied him up with that! What were you going to do, thrash him around like a doll?"

A hesitant grin spread across Mímir's face, easing the tension in his shoulders. "Were you really going to do that, Kolfinna?" he teased.

"No, I wasn't going to do that." Kolfinna's face radiated with heat.

"I didn't think you hated him *that* much," Eyfura joked between fits of laughter.

"That's not it." Kolfinna tucked her hands behind her back and cleared her throat again. "Anyway, did you need something?"

Mímir tapped the earth with the steel toes of his boots, as if waiting for the vines to spring out. "No, I'm just checking up on everyone. I mean, this is a very important and dangerous mission, so I'm just making sure everyone is on the same page and that there's no nervousness or something I should know about. How are you both holding up?"

Eyfura and Kolfinna exchanged glances. Other than worrying about a particular black rank popping up at any second, Kolfinna was relatively fine. Not great. Definitely nervous. But otherwise fine.

Eyfura gave a thumbs-up. "I'm peachy. And you? This is your first time leading a mission, so you must be nervous."

His eyebrows pulled together as if he hadn't expected her to ask him a question, and he rubbed the nape of his neck. "I'm actually doing really well. I'm excited, actually. I had begged Captain Asulf to put me on this case because it's something I truly wanted to do. I'm eternally grateful he allowed me to lead this mission. I've always loved history, so this is right up my alley. I mean, I'm sure it'll be difficult, but I'm hopeful that all will go well, and I really hope we get to see some neat stuff. I also want to prove my worth. So I'm really excited and hopeful that all will go well."

"I'm sure you'll do great!" Eyfura grinned. "There's no one better than you to do this."

Mímir looked over at the soldiers milling around the campgrounds. "Yeah ... except the military's not so happy that a Royal Guard is leading the mission, but I'm sure it'll go well."

"You'll do great!" Eyfura repeated. "And who cares what they think? They're just mad that one of their own isn't in charge."

"This mission is really important to me." He sounded lost in thought, his expression different—darker—before it changed again. "And you, Kolfinna? How are you doing?"

"I'm all right." Kolfinna kicked the fallen branches and intertwined bramble with her toe.

"This is your first ever mission, so I'm sure you're nervous."

"A bit ..." Kolfinna wasn't sure what she was more nervous about: the ruins themselves or confronting Blár Vilulf.

"Let me know if you need anything," he said. "I'm going to make the rounds and see how everyone's doing."

"All right, see you around." Eyfura waved as he went

to the next Royal Guard. Her voice dropped low and she turned her head toward Kolfinna. "He's doing surprisingly well in a leadership position."

"Why are you surprised?"

"He's too nice," Eyfura said with a sigh, and Kolfinna was reminded of the first time she met Mímir and how she had been annoyed at how polite he had been. Thinking back on it, he had treated her with respect despite her being a fae. Eyfura continued, "And too soft when making rules, so I figured this would be hard for him."

"But isn't he a lieutenant captain? Why would this be hard for him?"

"He got the position a few days before Captain Asulf brought you in, so it's not like he's been in that position for long." Eyfura lifted her shoulders. "There are ten lieutenant captains in the Royal Guard, and each of those lieutenants have their own unit of men. Our previous lieutenant captain retired, so Mímir was appointed as the new lieutenant. However, not many were happy with that decision. So he really has to prove himself for this mission to solidify his position."

"Ah, I see." Kolfinna wasn't the only one who had a lot riding on this mission, she supposed.

Eyfura's cheerful expression quickly soured. "Ugh, don't look now, but there's a girl headed our way. There are few people I dislike, but I *really* dislike her."

Kolfinna followed her gaze just as Eyfura swatted her shoulder. "I told you not to look—"

A short soldier with bobbed brown hair and matching

eyes walked toward them with a sly grin curving her plump lips. She couldn't have been more than a few years older than Kolfinna.

"Who is she?" Kolfinna whispered.

"Truda. An air elemental user. We went to school together. She's an absolute *delight*."

"Eyfura!" Truda's voice was shrill and grating. She stopped in front of them and rested a hand on her hip. The light gray military uniform clung to her athletic body snugly and she too had donned glittering earrings. "I see you're doing well. I was surprised to see that Mímir was leading the mission and not you. I thought you wanted to be in charge and rise up? That didn't work out, did it?"

Eyfura's smile was steely and her voice flat. "You're so full of charms so early in the mission."

"I just came to say hi." Truda laughed and tilted her head to the side, taking in Kolfinna's black trainee uniform that clearly wasn't meant for a Royal Guard. Understanding dawned in her eyes and she covered her mouth in mock shock. "Oh my, is this who I think it is? The infamous fae!"

Kolfinna rolled her eyes. "Did my pink eyes give it away?"

Truda's eyes narrowed a fraction of an inch as her sharp gaze cut to Kolfinna's face. She ignored the quip and instead turned to Eyfura. "Who would've thought the Royal Guards would stoop so low! I had heard the rumors, but I didn't think it was true. You let a murderer in your ranks."

Eyfura gasped. "What are you saying? Take that back."

"I don't think I will," she said in a singsong voice.

"If you've got something to say to me, say it to my face." Kolfinna took a step toward her.

"Oh, I've got nothing to say to you, *murderer*," Truda said, still smiling sweetly. She had her attention set on Eyfura. "I'll be the representative for the military. So if there's anything you need from us, please let me know."

"I'm an important member of this mission." Kolfinna made her voice chilly yet calm. "It would be wise if you got along with me."

"Excuse me?" Truda looked Kolfinna up and down, then turned her nose away. "Eyfura, tell your murdering little guard to learn some manners. And am I mistaken, or was that a threat?"

"She's not under me," Eyfura snapped. "And secondly, watch your mouth, Truda. You'll be getting in a lot of trouble from our side if you don't learn to respect us."

Mana sang at the tips of Kolfinna's fingers and she felt the life vibrating beneath her feet. But she had come here to become a full-fledged Royal Guard. She couldn't get in fights like this. She breathed out deeply, her mana ebbing from her fingers and nestling back into her chest.

Even as Truda sneered and turned away, an unbearable chill blew through the camp. Kolfinna froze, her body stiffening. The ice breath continued to breeze between the three of them. Even Eyfura and Truda straightened.

Blár was nearby.

Kolfinna rigidly glanced over her shoulder but didn't

find him anywhere. Not within the throng of gray uniforms, or within the sea of red capes. Her chest tightened at not finding the origin of such power. It probably would've been less scary if she could *see* him, instead of constantly feeling his presence and wondering when he would show up.

Truda's lips thinned into a firm line and she cocked her head in the opposite direction the Royal Guards had come from. A serious look passed over her face, and Kolfinna wasn't sure if it was fear she sensed in Truda or unease. "I have to go now," Truda said. "If either of you needs me, you know where to find me."

With that, she spun on her heels and joined the other soldiers, her gray uniform blending with the rest. Eyfura rubbed her arms slowly and shook her head in disbelief. "What an insufferable"—she paused and glanced at Kolfinna with a knowing look—"you know exactly what word I'm looking for."

"Yeah, I do."

"She's a ... brat, to put it nicely."

Even through the goose bumps, Kolfinna nodded grimly. "I agree."

7

Kolfinna couldn't sleep a wink that night. Sleep was the furthest thing from her mind. She kept thinking of various ways she would die on this mission, by the Royal Guards, the military, and Blár Vilulf. Or various ways that everything would go wrong—that she wouldn't be able to read the runes, and that they would all perish in the mysterious ruins. It also didn't help that she was sleeping with the female Royal Guards in the tent. Every time any of them moved—whether it was to stretch or change sleeping positions—mana pulsed beneath Kolfinna's fingers and she would lurch into a fighting position, only to find no threat nearby. Eyfura was kind to her, but she didn't trust the rest of them.

At the crack of dawn, Kolfinna swiftly and sound-lessly dressed in her black trainee uniform. Eyfura slept beside her in a lavender sleep sack, her chin tucked into the fitted blanket. Kolfinna was careful not to stir her as she stepped over her and the rest of the women in the women's tent.

Surprisingly, no one was awake yet. She had expected the high and mighty Royal Guards and the disciplined military to wake up and train the instant the sun rose. But no, everyone was snoring.

Today, they would be embarking to the ruins.

Birds chirped sweet songs, bugs buzzed near her ears, and the leaves rustled with every stir of the wind. Kolfinna breathed in the smell of moss, grass, wood oils, and pines. Magic danced under her skin as she stepped over the charred remains of last night's bonfire. The forest swayed and birds flew above her.

Kolfinna walked at the edge of the campgrounds, running her fingers over the bark of the trees. Tiny clusters of white wild mushrooms climbed the tree in front of her, and she felt the tiny surges of life force in each individual mushroom, dwarfed by the strong and old life of the tree they clung to.

The trees danced around her as a chilly wind thrust pine needles onto the forest floor. Fallen twigs snapped beneath her boots and she pushed her way through the dense bushes until she found a fallen tree to sit on. She was a bit away from the camp, but close enough that no one would assume she was running away.

Kolfinna sat on the tree and pulled the crumpled piece of paper Mímir had given during the meeting. The scribbled letters—the runes—looked back at her harshly. She stared at them, hard. If she wasn't able to read these, she would be useless. Then, being free to use her magic would only be a dream.

She glared at the paper until her head throbbed. It didn't matter how long it took, she *needed* to figure out what it said. She rubbed her eyes with the palms of her hands. Why couldn't she read it? Katla had never taught her anything about runes, and she doubted that her parents, of whom she had blurry memories of, had taught Katla anything about them.

The more she stared, the more the letters jumbled together and taunted her. It was impossible.

"What are you doing here?"

A chill ran down her spine and all the hairs on her arms rose stiffly. A familiar coldness swept across her body and held her hostage. She slowly craned her neck. Blár Vilulf's eyes were a tundra of snow and ice and frosty blue skies. There was a wicked gleam in his eyes: the gleam of a wolf that found its prey. Memories of last year stabbed at her leg and her stomach twisted painfully.

Her heart dropped.

Not him. Anyone but him.

Blár's lips twisted into a grin, and that hunter gleam intensified. White and gray fur lined the collar of his military uniform, matching his heavy fur-lined cloak. The silver buttons reflected the browns and greens of the trees surrounding them. "You trying to run away, fae?" His words held a taunting lilt.

Every fiber in her being screamed at her to make a run for it. To dash away and never come back. But she held herself still and watched him coolly. There was too much riding on this mission: her freedom, her safety, her life.

Running wasn't an option.

"What do you want?" She bottled the fear deep inside her, but her voice came out small like a frightened child's.

Blár tilted his head to the side. He was lean and towering, every bit the monster of her dreams. He had grown broader, bigger, and stronger from the last time she had seen him. He also lost some of his boyish looks, though there was a hint of youthful mischief in his features.

It was hard to believe that this monstrous man was only two years older than her.

"The Royal Guards are reaaally losing it if they think having you on their side is an advantage." A cool breeze froze her bones. His lips pulled back to reveal glistening white teeth; his smile was chilling. "What are you trying to accomplish by being out here, fae? And how's your leg doing?"

Kolfinna's heart thundered loudly in her ears. The more she stared at him—the mussed black hair, the mocking smile, the crisp uniform—the more her stomach churned. She was positive she was a few shades paler. She wanted to vomit. She wanted to run away. She wanted him to disappear. Forever.

The wind brushed her shoulders and carried the scent of wildflowers, as if reminding her she was in the folds of the forest, where her magic was the strongest. She would be fine, she told herself. She could use the forest to run away if it came to it.

Kolfinna squared her shoulders as she came to her feet and tried to appear as calm as still water. "I'm here because they need me."

"They need you?" His eyes narrowed. "Are you serious?"

"I am." Her hands trembled, so she clenched them tightly. "If I succeed in this mission, I'll be free and I'll be able to become a Royal Guard. You can't hurt me."

"You're a fae. Since when did your kind grovel at the feet of the Royal Guards?"

"Fae folk can be just like you, or anyone else. We should be able to join the military or live our lives." Kolfinna's voice wavered. "Why is it so hard to imagine us being normal?"

"Because you're not." He leaned against the tree, his broad back flattening the mushrooms she had been admiring a few minutes ago. "You're not normal. You never will be. What kind of fantasy are you living in? You're a monster."

Kolfinna shivered as another cold waft filled the forest clearing. "I don't want to hear that from you."

"I'll ask again." His eyes glowed and birds flew away violently. The temperature continued to drop. "Why are you here?"

Another chill rattled her core. "I'm here because Fenris said I have to be here. You're here because you're part of the military. We're both following orders."

"Fair enough." His laughter grated against her ears. "But I'm not buying it. You must have some sort of ulterior motive. What did they offer you for you to join them? Money? Freedom? Or was it just to pardon your crimes?"

"I'm sorry, but I wasn't under the impression that we were close." Kolfinna took a step back, and then another. "Why should I tell you any of that? We're not friends."

"We'll be working together—"

"Unfortunately," she cut in.

His eyebrows rose for a split second—as if surprised she had stood up to him—but then his smile grew wide and more sinister. "Yes, unfortunately. And, unfortunately, we'll be seeing a lot more of each other. So, fae, you better not compromise the mission. I don't trust you."

"I don't trust you either." Kolfinna's fingernails bit into the palms of her hands hard enough to draw blood. "And *you* better make sure *you* don't compromise the mission. I plan to do a dang good job." Kolfinna stepped away from him, the creeping vegetation crunching beneath her feet. "Leave me alone and we won't have anything to worry about."

Kolfinna spun on her heels and focused on where she had come from; she wanted to run to the camp so bad, but she quelled that urge. She couldn't let him know that she was terrified of him, or that he had that kind of power over her. She breathed in the leaves, the grass, and the sweet flowers to calm her raging heart.

She could do this. She had to bear with him and fulfill her mission. Her right leg dragged behind her with each step, feeling stiffer and heavier than it did a few minutes ago.

Ice shot from the ground beneath her feet and she only had a second to react. She lunged to the side and raised a bed of vines to break her fall before rolling around to face Blár. Her leg throbbed from the sudden movement and she gritted her teeth together to keep from crying. He was still leaning against the tree, this time with his arms crossed over his chest, watching her impassively.

"What was that for?" Kolfinna snapped. She balled her fists together and winced as a sharp pain stabbed her palms. Tiny crescents marks indented the flesh of her palms, blood beading where her nails had dug into. Her chest rose and fell erratically, and trembles overtook her body. She couldn't stop the shivering or keep her teeth from chattering. Even though the ice hadn't gotten to her, her body remembered the pain he had dealt her.

"Nothing." He pushed himself off the tree. "I was just testing you."

"Testing me?" She pointed at the ice shard that had solidified where she had been standing. From experience, she knew the tip was as sharp as a knife. "You almost skewered me!"

"I told you, I don't trust you."

"You've made that clear already." Her voice shook. "I'm on your side, Blár Vilulf. What do I have to do to make you understand that?"

"Leave this mission."

"No." Kolfinna glared at him, even as every instinct told her to run. There was nothing he gained from her leaving this mission. There was also nothing he gained if she stayed. And yet she could read the mischief in his eyes clear as day: he was toying with her. "I'm staying, whether you like it or not."

"Oh. I definitely don't like it," he said. "But it's not like I *dislike* it."

"What is *that* supposed to mean?"

"Oh. Nothing." He smiled, and that smile scared her more than if he had frowned. "I'm just excited to resume what I didn't finish last year. Our little cat-and-mouse game was fun, wasn't it?"

She shivered. "Why are you provoking me?"

"Because I'm bored. And it sounds like fun."

Her blood ran cold. Blár was a hundred times—no, *thousands* of times—worse than Magni, Truda, and everyone else she was dealing with who hated the fae. Because at least with them, she had the power to fight them back if they tried to mess with her. What was she supposed to do if Blár tried to fight her? She'd die. That's what.

There was not a bone in his body that was kind. And even if, by some miracle, there was, it wouldn't be directed at her.

"Leave me alone." Kolfinna stumbled away from him. She didn't even try to hide the fear as she spun on her heels and ran. Her right leg throbbed painfully with her uneven gait as she ran harder. The trees swayed out of her way, their branches missing her face.

Thankfully, he didn't follow her.

❄

THERE WAS A CLEAR DIVIDE BETWEEN THE military and the Royal Guards. Even when they were ready to discuss the mission plans, the Royal Guards chose to sit on one side of the clearing while the soldiers sat opposite. Both sides stared at each other in distaste. Although Kolfinna sat on the Royal Guards' side, she didn't feel like she belonged. She was the anomaly. The Royal Guards didn't consider her a Royal Guard, nor did the military. She was just Kolfinna the fae.

Mímir raked a hand through his dark hair and glanced over his papers. He had called everyone for a meeting, but he hadn't uttered a single word yet. He simply scanned the papers, his expression impassive. There was an air of authority around him that wasn't usually there. He seemed more like the lieutenant captain of the Royal Guard than he had earlier.

Blár sat on a boulder, slightly elevated from everyone else. Even his appearance wasn't normal. All the military wore drab gray uniforms, and from what Kolfinna had heard, they weren't allowed to alter them in any way. But Blár was clearly the exception. There was a thick, gray and white pelt around his neck, seamlessly sewn to his uniform. It appeared to be the pelt of a wolf, or some sort of fierce animal. And even the color of the gray uniform was darker, seemingly a mix between gray and navy blue.

"We'll be heading out to the entrance of the temple," Mímir's voice boomed. He raised his eyes from his notes.

"It has come to my attention that some of you have been questioning why Kolfinna, the fae, is here."

Everyone turned to Kolfinna, and their gazes crawled under her skin.

"She'll be helping us with the rune magic since she can read it. If you have any further questions, please feel free to talk to me privately." The papers in his hand rustled and he cleared his throat. "I'll give a little debrief for the military, who wasn't present during our meeting about the ruins ..."

Mímir began reading off information they had discussed about the Eventyrslot ruins in their Royal Guard meeting. Kolfinna fidgeted with her hair, which she had bound into a tight braid. Her gaze dragged across the faces in the clearing, but she paused when she landed on Blár. His knee was propped up and he had his elbow sitting on it while his chin rested against his closed fist. Boredom flitted over his face and, as if sensing her, he turned his head in her direction. Kolfinna averted her gaze, her heart racing in fear.

8

THEY WERE ON THE MOVE PRETTY QUICKLY later that morning. At the stone archway at the base of the mountain, the extra military men made camp and took the horses. Their job was to wait for everyone else's return from the ruins. Or to report back when the party *didn't* make it back. Kolfinna hoped it didn't come to that.

Kolfinna marveled at the stone archway and then at the sky-scraping mountain looming above them. This was the first step toward the ruins, and she could already feel the sway of nature around her, almost enveloping the mountain. Something powerful definitely resided in the mountain, she surmised.

After the archway, there was a winding path up the mountain made of spotty, crude stones meant to serve as a staircase. The first five minutes passed in a breeze, but the next five minutes after that, Kolfinna was wheezing and barely keeping up with the rest of everyone. Her right leg certainty didn't help her case and she could've sworn someone muttered "gimp" at her when she first showed signs of struggle. But the wind howled loudly, so she had no way to know for sure if she had misheard, or not.

"Climbing all these steps is tiring," Eyfura said from beside Kolfinna. Although Eyfura said that, she hadn't broken a sweat and was breathing normally.

Kolfinna peered ahead at the mountainous uphill battle. The other Royal Guards easily led the party. "It's a bit … much, I think," she breathed, her thighs burning with every step. "I'm not used to exercising."

"Oh, you'll get used to it."

"I hope so." Kolfinna's boots crunched beneath clusters of pebbles and crackled cobbled steps.

The higher they climbed the mountain, the more jarring it became to look down. There were rusty iron railings along the side of the stairs, but some parts were broken and sometimes the path became too narrow. One wrong misstep and she could fall to her death.

"It's definitely not easy going up." Eyfura wiped her forehead with her sleeve and squinted below them. "We're pretty high up."

Kolfinna had no idea how Eyfura was able to talk, because all Kolfinna could do was gulp in air and try not to pass out. Talking was out of the question, so she only nodded and forced her foot in front of the other. And then the other. Her focus remained on walking. Another step. And another.

"Gosh, I could really use some iced water," Eyfura

said. "Do you think I should ask Mímir for some water? Like cold water. Wait, no, I don't think he can make the water cold. That's more of an ice elemental thing. Maybe I should ask Torsten to make my water canister cold—"

"Don't complain just to complain," the brunette Royal Guard with the mole beneath her eye said with a short laugh. "*Especially* since you're an Enhancer."

"Me being an Enhancer has nothing to do with being thirsty!" Eyfura swatted the Royal Guard's shoulder. "Gosh, Thyra, if you're jealous, just say so."

"Jealous?" Thyra snorted, wiping the sweat beading her forehead with a handkerchief. "Hell yeah, I'm jealous! These steps are no joke, but it must be a walk in the park since you're an Enhancer."

"Hey, I'm not even using my mana for something like this, so I'm on the same level as you guys right now—"

"*Something like this*? So you agree that this isn't something you even need to use your mana for?" Thyra laughed and Eyfura hid a sheepish grin behind her gloved hand. "So this *is* a walk in the park for you, huh?"

"Well, I didn't mean it to sound like that—"

While they joked trivially, Kolfinna felt like a fish flapping on shore, the water a distance away, but her body slowly giving out. She was the only one truly struggling to even breathe or take another step. Eyfura and Thyra, for all their jests at each other, were still faring a hundred times better than she was. Was it because she was unused to exercise? Or maybe because everyone else had training? Or was it her weight that made her lousy at this?

Kolfinna couldn't help but glance over at where the military lagged behind, taking the rear. If the military hadn't been there, Kolfinna would drift back until nobody could see her struggling. She probably looked like a mess too—with her trainee uniform drenched, her braided hair frizzing with all the sweat, and her face likely a shade of beet red. Meanwhile, everyone conversed, laughed, and joked like they were on their way to the park, as Thyra had said.

It made her uncomfortable to be around all the joy and conversation—it was too foreign to her, and it was something she couldn't be a part of. But since she was smack dab in the middle of the line—the military behind her and the royal guards in front of her—she had to keep trudging forward and not fall into the military ranks. She was grateful Eyfura kept her company, even though it was obvious that Eyfura was the favorite among the Royal Guards. The whole group seemed to want her attention from time to time.

Half an hour passed before they finally reached another large stone archway, but unlike the first one, this one was attached to the mountain and led to an opening *into* the mountain. Beyond it, there was a straight, stone bridge, and what appeared to be the castle ruins.

At this point, everyone was breathing roughly and the wind had stopped howling so loudly when they stood beneath the archway. A shadow fell over the party as they remained there, all of them gaping at the bridge ahead. Kolfinna kept her hands on her knees and swallowed mouthfuls of air. It took all her strength not to collapse in a puddle of her own sweat and quivering muscles.

Kolfinna stumbled forward and peered up at what everyone else was looking at. Her jaw nearly dropped to the ground as the castle ruins came into view at the end of the bridge. The mountain perfectly surrounded the castle like a cloak; there was no ceiling to the mountain, and nothing covered the sky as light poured down onto the magnificent castle. To call it a castle wasn't an accurate description; it was more like a conglomeration of multiple castles jammed together and connected by suspended bridges.

The sound of birds cawing and flapping their wings overhead finally snapped her out of her reverie and she was reminded that the time to read the runes was now. Soon, everyone would find out she didn't know how to read them, but a part of her prayed she'd be able to do something with the runes. Maybe not read them exactly, but understand them to some degree? Or maybe the runes didn't matter in the grand scheme of the ruins?

Goose bumps ran across her arms and the back of her neck as the military swarmed behind the Royal Guards, finally catching up. She stared straight ahead, hoping she didn't look as nervous as she felt. What if they all died because of her inability to read the runes? She doubted Blár would let her live if he found out she was useless to them.

"Do you guys see the sky?" Mímir pointed up at the clear blue sky spotted with soft white clouds. "There seems to be some sort of ... I don't even know what to call it, to be honest. Magic? But anyway, there seems to be something covering the mountain to make it appear as though there's a mountaintop, when in reality there isn't one, as you all can see with the sky. Anytime we sent out someone to investigate and try to get in through the top, like an air elemental user, they're not *able* to cross over for some reason. The winds grow too strong, they can't get close, their magic stops working, etc."

Torsten raked a hand through his hair and followed Mímir's gaze at the sky. "Um, what do you mean by their magic stopped working? How's that even possible?"

"I don't think they meant it literally," Mímir said. "Maybe more like, the sky wasn't cooperating and allowing them to fly? I don't know."

Blár squinted against the blaring sun when he came to stand on the stone bridge. He glanced at the rest of the party when they remained rooted in place. "We didn't come here to sightsee," he said. "Let's get this over with."

Kolfinna's previous fatigue washed away as she began crossing over the bridge, her nerves pulling tighter as they drew closer to the castle doors. Even the bridge they walked along was suspended between the mountain wall to the castle.

"It's ... bigger than I thought," Eyfura whispered.

Kolfinna's jelly legs nearly gave out and she tripped forward, her hand launching out to grasp the stone railing with swirling designs carved into it. She steadied herself and caught a glimpse of the deep, pitch-black ravine below the bridge. Her heart squeezed tightly and the color drained from her face. Falling would be lethal.

"You okay?" Eyfura placed a hand on her shoulder.

"Um, yeah." Kolfinna's face bloomed with color and she ignored the snickers from the soldiers behind her. Even though she wanted to move on like nothing had happened, she wasn't used to such rigorous exercise. And she seemed to be the only one still affected by the climb.

How many people had traversed this bridge all those thousands of years ago? Her ancestors had likely crossed this very bridge. The thought made her shiver. This bridge was built when fae were powerful and abundant. When their civilization was thriving. And now? It was being raided by humans with the assistance of a fae.

"Do you sense anything from it?" Eyfura asked as they reached the end of the bridge.

"Yes." Kolfinna couldn't keep her eyes away from the ruins and how impossibly tall they were. A powerful presence drenched the place, but she couldn't pinpoint what it was. Usually, she could feel the life force of trees when she walked in a forest, and the presence was always powerful and heavy, similar to this place, but the difference was that she knew she was sensing the trees when she did that. Here? She had no idea what it was. Was there a lot of nature inside that was exhibiting such a powerful force? Or was it a powerful monster? Or was this the power of runes? She really had no idea.

"This place is abundant with ... power?" Kolfinna settled with as she eyed the wide, twenty or thirty-step long staircase leading up to the entrance doors. "I don't know how to explain it, but it feels powerful."

The birds stopped tweeting, the chirr of crickets disappeared, and even the wind ceased breathing when they approached the entrance of the castle ruins. Life seemed to stop moving as the ivory castle walls loomed in front of them. A heavy tension filled the air as everyone looked at one another.

"Everyone, remember to be on your guard. We have no idea what's in there." Mímir's voice echoed and his back straightened as he glanced around himself with an uneasy expression. "There, um, might be magic beasts we've never encountered, or powerful bandits—"

Mímir continued talking, his voice bouncing around the walls of the mountain in softer tones over and over, but Kolfinna could barely pay attention to what he was saying as she peered up at the tall walls and towers of the ruins. It didn't look like a ruin with crumbling foundations or broken pieces. In fact, it shouldn't have even been called a "ruin" since it didn't look ruined at all. Just abandoned.

Moss, creeping vegetation, and vines wrapped around the domes on the tips of the towers and over the walls like splayed fingers. Something about the ruins made the hairs on her body stand stiff.

Mímir led them up the stairs and Kolfinna tentatively followed close behind; she didn't know what it was, but she couldn't keep her eyes off the set of double doors leading to the ruins. They stood tall and proud, embellished with gold and with carvings of trees over each door, the branches stretching out to the corners of the frame. Ancient writing was sprawled across the doors in a mixture of gold and silver. Kolfinna's breath caught in her throat as the words lulled her forward like a lost tune that sounded impossibly familiar.

"That's the writing we told you about. The runes, I mean." Mímir came to stand beside her. "It was on the paper I—hey, are you okay?"

"Huh?" Kolfinna brought a hand to her face and touched her damp cheeks. She hadn't even realized she was crying. She rubbed her eyes vigorously, heat creeping up her face as she felt the various eyes on her. "It's just so beautiful," Kolfinna murmured without thinking.

She knew almost instantly these were runes. They pulled at something dormant within her and her chest ached as she stared at them. She had never seen runes, had never interacted with them, or even knew much about them. All she knew was what everyone else knew: runes were a lost fae magic. But they were so much more now that she stood in front them.

The meaning formed in her mind without a second thought. As if she had always known what it said.

"*We send our greetings to our fellow fae.*" Kolfinna's voice echoed and the others fell silent.

"What?" Mímir asked.

"That's what it says." Kolfinna yanked out the piece of paper from her pocket and held it up against the runes on the door. The designs on the crumpled paper were similar but different. It was like a child trying to draw an intricate painting of a tree; the essence was there, a tree, but it was nowhere near as fleshed out or correct. "This is incorrect. You guys incorrectly transcribed it."

Relief washed over her so powerfully she sank to her knees and could finally breathe without feeling like she was inhaling nails. The tightness in her chest fell away and she didn't know if she should jump with joy or cry. She was useful to the party and would *live*.

"Kolfinna!" Mímir kneeled beside her, concern making his forehead pucker. "What's wrong? Did something—Did the runes attack you? Or ... um ...?"

"I just—" A blush stained her cheeks as she pulled herself to her feet. "My legs are still sore. Sorry."

"Oh." He tilted his head as if he didn't believe her completely, but then turned to the door. Everyone remained silent as they stared at him. "It's wonderful news that you can read it. I knew you had it in you."

Mímir clapped his hands together. "All right, everyone. We'll be heading inside now. If you have anything to say, say it now." When no one said anything, he motioned to the door. "Let's go. And everyone, remember to stay on guard. We have no idea what's beyond these doors."

Mímir and Magni pushed open the doors of the ruins, and they creaked open slowly, before everyone filed inside. Beyond the door, Kolfinna couldn't believe her eyes. The ceilings were tall, and a majestic power filled the air. She still couldn't pinpoint what was powerful about it, but all her senses screamed that this was a place of great magic.

Kolfinna stepped forward, almost in a trance as she took in the ruined insides. Light spilled from giant windows and holes in the walls. Moss covered the walls and dusty, threadbare rugs half-covered the floors, the marbled floor peeking from torn sections of the rugs. Debris, pebbles, and cracked tiles ran all throughout the entry room. Beyond the foyer, a giant lobby that must've been a quarter of a mile, lay out in front of them with arched doorways leading to different areas of the castle along the walls. At the end of the lobby, a staircase led deeper into the castle. Halfway up the staircase, it split into two, one going to the right and the other going to the left.

"It's so old," Truda murmured as they walked deeper into the castle.

After the last person entered, the doors slammed shut with finality. Kolfinna jumped and whirled around.

"W-What the—" One of the soldiers stared at the door, dumbstruck.

"Hey!" Another soldier pounded on the door and wrestled with the doorknob. "It won't open!"

"Who locked it shut?" Magni demanded, and Kolfinna didn't miss the way his glare fixed on her, even though she had been one of the first to enter.

Thyra paled as the soldiers tried yanking the door open. "This is creepy as hell."

An uneasiness ate away at Kolfinna's stomach and she threw a glance at the lobby. Was it the castle that closed the door? Or was someone messing with them?

A murmur of unrest filtered the air and Mímir raised his hands. "Calm down," he said. Kolfinna had to hand it to him. He didn't look the least bit worried. "We knew there were magical properties in this ruin. If it was that easy to leave, there would be some survivors at least. But there aren't any. We expected this. Please calm down."

All the noise died down until the only sound reverberating in the lobby was shuffling feet as they stepped deeper into the building. Cracks formed along the walls and pillars in some areas, but everything still held its form. Kolfinna walked toward one of the pillars and brushed her fingers over the cool stone. How many fae walked through this hall? How many centuries old was this place?

"What is *that*?" Torsten's voice boomed like thunder.

Kolfinna followed his gaze to where an enormous gray statue sat at the center of the lobby. A stone beast stretched across its monstrous four legs on the floor, mouth open in a half-roar position. Even from their distance across the room, she could see a set of jagged teeth overflowing from its mouth. A tail curled around its spiky body and skeletal wings spanned across its back.

Kolfinna reeled back, her body tensing as if she should run, but her legs were leaden. The sudden deep fear she felt when seeing it didn't seem to affect anyone else.

"It's just a statue." Truda snickered from beside her. "You can't piss your pants *just* yet."

Some of the soldiers chuckled, and Kolfinna's cheeks seared with heat.

"Let's go forward," Mímir said.

Kolfinna strode forward and shot the statue an uneasy look. It appeared far too realistic for her liking, as if it would take a step forward any second. She turned her attention away. Truda's comments couldn't dull the unexpected excitement bubbling in the pit of her stomach. When she had first heard of the mission, she hadn't wanted to be a part of it. But now that she was here, surrounded by the beautiful history of her people, she wanted to explore every crook and cranny of this place. Her people had once walked through these halls. What kinds of things would she find?

The farther they walked into the lobby, the more curious she became about her surroundings. The lobby was rather symmetrical, with three doorways on each side of the walls, adjacent to the staircase. Although a part of her wanted to rush forward and inspect everything, another bigger part of her wanted to soak in the moment and take it slow. She doubted she'd be able to visit this place again after they finished excavating it this time around.

A part of her was sad at the thought of that; of humans looting this place with her help, but she banished that thought. She didn't allow herself to wallow in guilt; she needed this for her survival. Her ancestors would understand.

A cold breeze gusted over her shoulders and she whipped her head to the side, where there was an undeniable coldness. Blár walked with the other soldiers, his expression stony. His cold gaze swept around the room warily, and there was an air of hostility around him. Kolfinna quickly looked away before he noticed her staring; the last thing she wanted was his attention.

They neared one of the first doorways. Mímir held his hand up and poked his head inside. When he deemed it safe, he beckoned everyone forward. One wall of the room was completely made of glass windows, allowing light to abundantly flow into the spacious room. At least thirty rusty swords hung on the walls, and even more littered the floor by the wall.

Kolfinna drifted toward the windows while the others inspected the contents of the room. From the window, she could see the flying buttresses and the walkways beneath them just outside. There were rusted latches on the bottoms of the windows and she could probably heave the windows open and walk underneath the buttresses if she wanted to.

Kolfinna turned to leave but froze midway and returned to inspect the window. A splash of brown and black splotches painted the walkway in giant streaks. Blood?

"Kolfinna, look at this," Eyfura called to her. "What does this say?"

"Hm?" She spun around.

Eyfura held up a broken, circular shield with an inscription etched in the center of it. "It says something here. Can you read it?"

Kolfinna pulled away from the window and came to inspect the rusted shield with chipped edges. The bottom half of the shield was missing and its strap had snapped.

Kolfinna eased it out of Eyfura's grasp and brushed her fingers over the lumpy, dented shield, and then to the inscription, which was written in runes. She knew the words immediately. "*The serpent army will devour—*" Kolfinna raised her eyes. "The rest of it is gone."

"The serpent army?" Eyfura rubbed her chin. "That sounds spooky."

"The serpent army," Mímir murmured, coming to stand beside them. "I wonder who that army is. And what are these weapons for? This doesn't appear to be an armory."

"There are snake symbols on the swords," Truda called out. She picked up a half-broken sword and held it up, pointing to the flat of the rusted blade where a snake engraving slithered along it. "See?"

"I don't remember reading about serpents in fae history," Mímir mumbled to himself, "but then again, it's not like we know much about fae history. Most is unknown and what little we do know is spotty at best."

Truda didn't seem to hear him, because she asked, "Does the serpent mean anything?"

"I'm not sure. In our literature—" Mímir frowned when she tossed the sword aside. "The serpent almost always symbolizes a two-faced evil person, but that might be different for other civilizations like the fae. There's just so much we don't know."

"You got any insight, fae?" Magni asked.

Kolfinna narrowed her eyes. "I have a name, you know. It's not just 'fae' this and 'fae' that."

"Do you have any insight or not?" Truda asked, tapping her foot on the floor and glancing around the room distastefully. "If not, let's move forward. We don't have all day to be dawdling in a dingy room with rusty swords."

"I don't know," Kolfinna said. "I can't think of anything with serpents."

"Let's move to the next room," Mímir said.

The neighboring room was empty save for a statue of a woman wearing a draping dress at the center of it. The woman had her eyes closed and held long chains that dangled down to her feet. But what caught Kolfinna's attention were the delicate, gossamer, butterfly-like wings clinging to her back.

As if instinctively, the long scars on Kolfinna's back tickled and she swallowed down the sadness and anger suddenly broiling within her. She could've been just like this woman—free and able to have her beautiful wings. And yet, she had never been able to see them, much less use them. This world wouldn't have allowed it.

"What the ...?" Torsten murmured. "Who is she supposed to be?"

"She looks a bit ... strange to me." Thyra reached forward and tentatively poked the statue's arm.

"It's just a statue," a soldier in his mid-thirties said, gulping and looking around himself. "Can we just move on?"

"Does this place scare you, Eyjarr?" Truda asked with a smirk as she dragged her hand over the moss-ridden wall. "I think the stories of the soldiers never making it out of here are just lies. They probably just looted the place and made a run for it so they could keep the riches."

Kolfinna crossed the room until she was face to face with the statue. The rune on her hand read *War*. Kolfinna studied the woman, trying to remember if Katla or her parents had ever mentioned a woman with chains, or serpents, from the other room. But she came up with nothing. Was this woman a historical figure? A myth? A symbolism for something? There was so much Kolfinna didn't know about her own history. Guilt, shame, and sadness washed over her. All of that had been ripped away from her because the humans waged war on her people centuries ago and wiped their history clean.

"She looks a bit ... creepy," Eyfura said with a nervous laugh.

"Maybe she'll attack us," Torsten joked.

"Oh come on." Magni gnashed a broken piece of tile beneath his boot. "Don't joke like that. With how freaky this place is, I wouldn't be surprised if she started moving and jumped on us."

"Maybe she'll move and"—Truda jumped in front of Eyjarr, the soldier she had teased earlier—"eat you up like in the stories!"

Eyjarr flinched and she burst into laughter. "Oh, screw off," he muttered.

"Is she supposed to be a fae?" a soldier asked.

"The fae don't have wings like that."

Click. Clack.

"And how do you know that?"

"Well, look at her." Magni motioned to Kolfinna. "She doesn't have wings."

"Maybe she can grow them."

Click. Clack.

Kolfinna tuned the conversations out and looked around herself. Where was that clicking noise coming from? No one was doing anything that warranted that noise. The Royal Guards and military were either swarming the statue or looking at the walls, which had crude drawings of flying birds etched into them with faded black paint.

Click. Clack.

She drew herself closer to the window and scrubbed the dust coating it so she could see better. As she had suspected, it was identical to the previous room: a walkway underneath the flying buttresses. It was all probably connected; maybe it acted as an escape route if people were trapped in the rooms? Or maybe the walkway wrapped around other parts of the castle as well?

Click. Clack.

Kolfinna squinted through the window. Was it her imagination or was there a shadow warping across the walkway? Just as she was thinking that, she followed the shadow to where a figure lumbered forward.

A humanoid creature that was twice her size trudged along the walkway. Its cream-colored bald head looked like moldy cheese, with dents and craters and splotches of green. Milky blind eyes flitted over the ceiling of the buttresses and then to the floor, its head bobbing right and left. A rag hung over its emaciated body, and it held a rusted sword, its mouth gaping open to reveal rows of razor-sharp teeth. Its skin was a withered gray, and there were rotting pieces of flesh on its legs and arms.

What the—

It craned its neck in her direction and Kolfinna's heart froze as its blind eyes met hers.

This can't be real—

It opened its mouth and shrieked, the glass vibrating from the earsplitting noise. Kolfinna stumbled backward as it launched at the window. Glass shattered and sprayed the room, and she brought her hands over squinting eyes just as the monster tackled her to the floor.

Spit splattered her face and sharp glass cut into her back. The creature pinned her down with its weight. Its mouth opened wide and it screamed again, this time louder. Kolfinna's ears rang as it continued screaming.

Kolfinna couldn't breathe, couldn't think. The room disappeared and all she could see was the creature screaming at her face. She had no idea where everyone else was. She couldn't even think to ask for help.

The creature pressed its sword to her throat and her hands automatically wedged into the space between the sword and her neck. The corroded edge of the blade bit into the palms of her hands, but she didn't even register the pain. Her mind was blank.

In a split second, ice splintered forward and shoved the monster off her. The monster shrieked as it hit the wall, which dented and cracked on impact. Debris fell on their heads with the force of the attack. The monster lurched to its feet, screeching as it ran toward Eyfura, who was closest to it. Ice shot from the floor and gripped its feet, halting its movement and making it fall. It bellowed incoherently and clawed at the floor before the ice spread across its whole body and encapsulated it.

Everyone watched in stunned horror. The creature's mouth was frozen open in the ice, its claws stretched forward as if to grab the nearest person. Kolfinna pushed herself into a sitting position, her breaths ragged and heavy. *What just happened?* She ripped her gaze from the monster to Blár.

"What is that?" Blár asked, stooping low to inspect the frozen creature on the floor. He raised an eyebrow and glanced at the party. "Why are you all acting like we haven't been trained to hunt down monsters?"

"Magic beasts don't look like that!" Thyra sputtered, pointing at it with a trembling finger. "What the hell is that?!"

Another Royal Guard cursed loudly. "Man, this isn't right. Things like that aren't supposed to exist."

"I've never seen anything move like that," Thyra said, eyeing the creature uneasily. "Is this normal for you soldiers?"

Truda snorted. "You ivory-towered pricks wouldn't know how to fight a monster if it bit you in the ass"—

she motioned toward Kolfinna—"or came close enough to."

"She's not a Royal Guard. She doesn't speak for all of us," Torsten snapped as he picked out a shard of glass from his forearm. "And it's not like we saw you running into action."

"You don't have to be deep in monster shit to know that *that*"—Magni pointed at the frozen creature—"is not normal."

"E-Everyone, calm down," Mímir said, raising his hands, but even he was trembling and wide-eyed.

Kolfinna's hands burned from holding back the blade, blood dripping from the cuts. Her gaze drifted to the sword; the monster had dropped it when it was struck by the ice. If the blade wasn't rusted, her hands would've been cut off. If Blár hadn't frozen the creature, would she have been able to stop it?

"Are you all right?" Eyfura kneeled beside her. A rivulet of blood ran down her cheek, which she promptly rubbed away with the back of her white glove. "Those cuts look bad ..." She searched inside her pack and took out bandages and a salve. "Here, let's put this on it."

"I'm ... all right," Kolfinna said carefully.

"What is that thing?" Eyfura looked over her shoulder at the Royal Guards and soldiers huddled around the monster.

"I ..." Kolfinna swallowed the bile rising in her throat. "I don't know."

"No one said anything about *that*!" one of the soldiers

said as he prodded the ice encased monster. "What have we gotten ourselves into?"

"Come on, we knew exactly what we were signing up for," Magni scoffed. "Don't go around acting like a wuss now."

"You royal ass-kissers are the ones shitting your pants over—" a soldier started.

"What did you say?"

"You heard me—"

"Calm down!" Mímir shouted. "Look, everyone! I understand that this is a lot to take in, but we have to remain calm. That ... that thing is, well, out of a children's story—I understand that, but we can't dwell on that too much. The fact remains that we've been trained to handle these kinds of situations, and we're strong. Blár was able to kill it rather easily. We all can take it down as well. Everyone here is a yellow rank and above. We can survive these things. It might look strange, but just think of it like any other magic beast."

Once Kolfinna's hands were bandaged, she unsteadily rose up to her feet. Her legs still quivered and her heart pounded so loudly she was surprised no one heard the *thud thud thud* of it beating like a drum.

"Let's move forward," Mímir said.

Everyone filed out of the room, but most of the group walked with rigid shoulders and sharp eyes as they scoped their surroundings. Kolfinna shot the monster one last look. That ice likely wouldn't melt, unless someone with Fenris's fire abilities came along, or if enough time passed.

No one joked, laughed, or made crude comments anymore. There was only an uneasy silence. Kolfinna tried to relax, but her heart was nearly jumping out of her chest. She focused her mana on her fingertips, so it would be easy to launch an attack if another thing came at her. She could feel nature around her, but it wasn't as strong, since she was in a building. She would have to rely on the stones for quick attacks.

The next room was similar to the previous ones, but instead of weapons with cryptic rune writing or a statue, this one had stacks and stacks of spears. They were falling apart and most of the spearheads were rusted and dull.

"Were they preparing for war?" Eyfura's voice seemed to carry to the far ends of the room.

"I don't know," Mímir said. "But I'm sure ... I'm sure there must be some reason why they're here."

Kolfinna shifted on her feet and found herself staring at the windows. There were things she hadn't noticed before that she was suddenly aware of. There were dried brown spots on some of the pillars, as if blood had splattered. And what she had thought were signs of wear and tear, were possible signs of a fight. Uneasiness grew in the pit of her stomach. There were probably more of those monsters out here, and people had likely died fighting them.

The next room was as strange as the others, but this one had a small statue of a ship in the center of it. Old, broken swords hung on the walls. Everyone entered the room warily, some with their hands on the hilts of their weapons, and others with their hands raised for an attack. Kolfinna kept her back close to the wall as she inched close to the window and then peeked around the edge. Thankfully, there wasn't a creature waiting for her like last time.

"This place is full of junk," Truda said. "I doubt we'll find anything valuable here."

"We should—" Mímir started.

A gong interrupted him, reverberating against the castle walls.

Before the sound ended, the room shook and spun, and everyone lurched forward as the floor disappeared beneath their feet. Kolfinna stifled a scream as everything washed away into a whirl of black. Her stomach churned and her body felt like it was being ripped apart. A splitting headache threatened to knock her unconscious.

And then, everything became quiet for a second before she crashed to the floor. Her back slammed into hardwood flooring and a shock of icy water splashed over her body. Kolfinna's body swayed one way and then another, and she finally managed to peel her eyes open. The world still spun and her stomach twisted with the urge to vomit. A fishy, briny smell pervaded the air, followed by the stench of rotting meat.

The room came into view again. But this time, it wasn't a room. Kolfinna looked around herself violently, her heart sinking. What was going on?

9

THE OTHER ROYAL GUARDS AND SOLDIERS ALSO lay on the floor, groaning and moaning and showing the same shock she felt. Thunder crackled in the dark bluish sky and a blustering gust of wind slapped cold rain water against Kolfinna's skin. She tried to stand, but she was thrown aside as everything rocked from side to side. Lightning dragged squiggle lines over the darkening sky. Ripped sails barely hanging on their masts quivered like streams of ribbons. Kolfinna tried to right herself again but fell on her knees, water sloshing on the deck and soaking her in frozen salty water.

She was … on a ship? Where was the castle?

"What's happening? Where are we?" someone screamed above the wailing of the wind and rain.

Water slapped down on Kolfinna, hard. She struggled to her feet and steadied one hand on the foremast for support, and that's when she noticed them. Dozens of half-dead monsters with rotting hands pulled their skeletal bodies over the railings of the ship. Water slopped over their bodies. Skin and rotting flesh hung to their bodies, and white bones poked through their ragged clothes. Patches of hair clung to their skulls. They held sharp swords and screamed a battle cry when they jumped onto the deck.

One of the half-dead monsters ran to Kolfinna. She raised her hands to force the stones in her vicinity to do her bidding, but nothing happened. She tried to feel deep inside herself for her mana, for a life force, for *anything*. But she felt empty, as if her magic had been cored out of her being. And in that minuscule second, the monster lunged at her.

Kolfinna ducked and stumbled backward, tripping on her own feet and planting on the floor. Salt water entered her mouth and she sputtered, her eyes tearing. A wave crashed against the ship and sent a flood of water to wash over her. She coughed, water clogging her throat, as she tried to pull herself back to her feet.

More and more monsters boarded the ship. Screams filled the air, mingling with the clapping thunder and pelting rain. Royal Guards were falling to the floor, crying and screaming as the monsters plunged their swords into their chests or lopped their heads off. All the blood drained from Kolfinna's face.

What in the world was happening?

These weren't magic beasts. Magic beasts were simply

animals with magic. This? This was straight out of a nightmare.

Another skeletal creature pounced at her, sword swinging at her head. She rolled over and away from the creature before grabbing the foremast and pulling herself upright. Her hands trembled and wet tendrils of her hair stuck to the sides of her face. *Breathe, breathe.* Her heart raced as the skeletal creatures zoomed in on her. Three surrounded her in an instant. Their mouths creaked open in sinister smiles.

The closest one swung its sword at her, and she jumped away, but another one was in front of her in a second. It gripped her shoulder tightly, its pointy skeletal bones piercing her flesh. Pain bit into her shoulder as the monster raised its sword to slice her head off. Kolfinna pulled her fist and punched the skeletal creature in the face —once, twice, and three times. Half its skull broke beneath her fist and it stumbled back, stunned. In that split second, Kolfinna tackled it to the floor and yanked the sword out of its hand. She had never touched a sword before, much less used one, but she didn't need to be taught a lesson on how to chop something up. She swung at its head. Bones and flesh crunched beneath the corroded steel. Her breathing was heavy and she braced herself for the other two creatures closing in on her. The smell of rotting fish and flesh intensified when they drew closer.

The first one jumped at her and struck her abdomen with its sword. Kolfinna swerved to the right, but the tip of the sword nicked her stomach. The ship tipped to the side and she flung with the motion. She threw her hands in front of her to lessen the fall, but she still slammed into the slippery flooring painfully. Salt water splashed over her face and stung her cuts. She glanced over her shoulder to find the monsters had also fallen and were rising up. She pushed herself to her feet just as the monster swung at her, aiming for her neck. She reeled back with the sway of the ship and instead of the sword burrowing into her neck, the blade slashed her arm. She bit back a scream and swung her sword wildly while she steadied herself once again.

Kolfinna stabbed her blade into the fleshy part of the monster's chest, but it did nothing to the creature, who only tilted its head and instead brought its sword down on her. She lurched back just in time, but the monster's blade slammed into her shoulder. Pain exploded in her shoulder and she chewed her inner cheek to keep from screaming. Great. She was injured and she lost her sword—it was still stuck in the creature.

Her breathing hitched, and her heart raced faster. Blood ran down her arm freely and her legs shook as she tried to stumble away from them. She blinked rapidly against the rain. The two creatures stepped closer to her, their skeletal mouths curved into grins. One of their eyeballs dangled out of its socket by a cord, while the other one was missing a jaw. This was it, she would die, wouldn't she? Against these ghastly beings.

Just then, Blár came out of nowhere and kicked one of

the skeletal creatures. It flew into its partner and they fell to the floor before Blár smashed their skulls with his booted feet, brain matter and bits of skull smearing the floorboards.

"What the hell is going on, fae?" he shouted above the storm. Thunder boomed above them and another wave of brackish water splashed over the deck.

"I-I don't know!" Kolfinna cried.

More monsters boarded the ship, their eyes glowing as they screamed for blood. Kolfinna's heart sank as a realization dawned on her: no one was using their magic. Thyra was tackled by three skeletal creatures, screaming as the monsters bit into her flesh and stabbed her repeatedly with their swords. Kolfinna's stomach twisted and she covered her mouth with her hands. Thyra was dead.

Kolfinna turned just in time to see another Royal Guard thrown off board. And then another. One of the military men tripped over the body of his ally and was stabbed to death by two creatures.

Kolfinna couldn't contain the contents of her stomach and retched on the watery floor.

"Calm down!" Blár grabbed her shoulder and shook her. She bit back a scream, tears forming in her eyes and pain shooting through her injured shoulder and arm. Blár released her, scanning their surroundings. "Get a grip! There's no way I'm dying here."

Another monster ran to them, but Blár ducked, tackled it to the floor, and pummeled it with his fist. Its skull cracked into multiple pieces, chunks of flesh painting the wet floor before being washed away. Kolfinna's watched in muted horror. Blár was strong even without his powers.

"Why is magic not working?" Blár shouted at her, shaking pieces of the monster's skull off his knuckles.

"I don't know!"

A skeletal creature catapulted on her and she slammed onto the floor with a scream. The monster's teeth tore into her injured arm and she screamed louder as her forearm throbbed painfully. She writhed beneath the monster, its rancid odor making her eyes water. Even when she punched it with her free hand repeatedly, it wouldn't release her. Finally, Blár ripped the creature off her and kicked it. It skidded into another monster, where it twitched but didn't get back up.

"Get up!" Blár grabbed her uninjured shoulder and pulled her to her feet. "There has to be something we can do!"

This was it. They would die in this hellhole. These demonic creatures would kill them all.

"Hey! Calm down! Why are you freaking out?!"

"How can I not freak out?" Kolfinna shouted over the sound of one of the half-hanging sails cracking with the wind as it snapped back and forth.

"Calm yourself and *think*!"

There was no way she could think straight. They were being attacked by grisly half-dead *monsters*. What was there to even think about? More and more of those beings were boarding the ship and they were already outnumbered. No matter how much Blár and the rest of the group killed off the creatures, more kept replacing the dead ones. It wouldn't be long before everyone died.

"Do you sense anything? Any mana?" Blár scooped up a fallen sword and wedged it into the face of one of the beings. He yanked it out and stomped on the skeletal face, crushing it effortlessly. "*Shit*. These things just aren't dying."

Kolfinna realized with a start that the beings she thought were dead, were in fact *still alive*. Having their skulls smashed only seemed to stun them for a few minutes before their bodies convulsed and they pulled themselves up. Even headless, *they weren't dying.*

"I don't sense anything! I can't use magic at all." The ship swerved and she flew forward, tripping over a body. Blood stained her hands and she glanced at the body. That was a mistake. It was one of the soldiers. He had given her a dirty look at the start of the mission, but she could hardly think of that as she looked at his boyish face. His eyes were glassy, and there was a gash in his neck, revealing the shiny white bone underneath the flesh and blood.

"Watch it," Blár shouted above the howling wind and the sound of clashing blades. He barreled another creature out of her way. "Pull yourself together. Now, do you sense anything or not?!"

"No! I don't!" She was on her hands and knees, a crash of water dousing her and knocking her to her side.

"Try harder! There has to be *something*!"

"I don't—" The words were stuck in her throat when

she realized there was *something* she felt. She had been trying with no avail to reach her own mana this entire time, but she hadn't noticed that there was something faint pulsing in the background. She swiveled her head right, left, and right again. Where was it coming from?

"What are you looking for?" Blár tried to follow her gaze, but another creature was already on them. It jumped and latched itself on him, wrapping its rotting legs around his torso and gnashing its teeth into his arm. Blár gritted his teeth together and punched the creature with the pommel of the blade before its skull caved in.

Kolfinna could barely see in the distance due to the lashing rain and the swarm of bodies struggling onboard. She curtained her eyes with her hands and searched quickly until she found something. At the opposite side of the ship where the main mast was, she sensed mana thrumming on the wood.

"There!" She pointed at the mast. "I sense magic there! Rune magic!"

"Don't just stand there—go!"

Kolfinna didn't need to be told twice, but it was daunting. A sea of creatures fought with the military and the Royal Guards; she would need to weave her way through it to make it to the mast. But even then, she didn't know what she would find there.

When she took too long, confused by the constantly moving bodies and flying swords, Blár grabbed her hand and yanked her forward, *hard*. She yelped in pain and surprise; her arm felt like it was going to be ripped out of its socket. She didn't have time to protest because another being was on them, swinging its sword at Blár's head. Blár let go of her hand and lopped the creature's head off in one smooth motion.

"Keep going!" he shouted, thunder snapping above them, followed by a flash of lightning. "I'll protect you."

Those were the last words she expected from Blár, but she had to trust his word.

Kolfinna bobbed her head in agreement and ran forward, stooping low when a monster came toward her. Blár slammed his blade into the monster and kicked it, sending it reeling back. Kolfinna lurched forward. Water violently spat on her face, obscuring her vision. The cold bit into her bones, but she trudged forward. Men and women screamed all around her, and she made sure not to look at their faces. She didn't want to see the terror coloring their faces, or see their grisly deaths.

A sudden, sharp pain shot through her back and she was launched forward, her forehead cracking against the slick floor. Her vision momentarily darkened before she came to. Her arms shook and she cried in pain as she tried pushing herself up, but her injured arm gave out underneath her. Sweat and tears and salt water stung her eyes. Her back throbbed and a sticky warmth trickled down her back. Had she been slashed? She craned her neck to see behind her and found a bloodied sword on the floor; had one of the creatures thrown it at her? Wasn't Blár supposed to protect her?

That villain. Kolfinna shouldn't have trusted him.

But Blár wasn't behind her. He was instead on the floor, four different monsters clinging to him. One was biting his leg and the other was on his arm. He struggled against them and kicked them, swinging his sword. Kolfinna didn't have time to worry about him as she pulled herself to her feet. She needed to go to the mast. *Now.*

But her feet had plans of their own. She rammed into the skeletal creature clinging to Blár's arm. They both fell together in a heap of tangled arms and legs. Kolfinna hooked her fingers into the monster's eye sockets and yanked its skull as hard as she could. She grunted as it clawed her chest and dug its sharp talon-like fingers into her flesh. The skull finally gave out and snapped off the neck. She chucked it with all her might at the water.

Blár was back on his feet. Kolfinna pushed herself up and didn't look back at him as she headed to the mast once more. She held no warmth for him, but she acknowledged that he was necessary. He was strong, and she needed to use that strength. With the way he was fighting even without his magic, she saw clearly that any hope of them surviving lay with him, as much as she hated to admit it.

Kolfinna flung herself to the mast, her hands flying over the wet wood. She felt for the threads of magic, her eyes darting over it before she found it. Inscribed in glowing gold letters, runes were etched into the wood; there were two holes below the inscription. *Magic will not enter this area. The draugrs will keep multiplying to no end.*

Find the rubies and place them here. Draugrs? That must've meant the undead demons.

"R-Rubies!" Kolfinna shouted, another wave crashing over the side of the ship and drenching her. Wet tendrils of hair stuck to the side of her face. "We need to find rubies and put them here! Then it'll stop!"

"Rubies?" Even through the rain, Blár looked at her like she was crazy. "Where are we going to find rubies?"

"I don't know! We have to look, though!" Kolfinna scanned their surroundings quickly. Where would rubies be in a place like this? In the water? No, that seemed highly unlikely. They would die if they flung themselves overboard. Then where? The floorboards? In the dim lighting and with the water sloshing everywhere, that also seemed unlikely.

Kolfinna spotted Mímir on the floor, trying to push off two skeletal creatures. She ran and kicked the first creature off him. He managed to shove the second one off him, and Blár sliced its head off with his sword. Mímir then jumped to his feet.

"Kolfinna! You're alive!" Blood dripped down his temple and one of his eyes was swollen shut, the budding bruise matching the ocean surrounding them. "Magic isn't working!"

"I know." Kolfinna's eyes darted around the ship. Rubies, rubies! Where would rubies be here? Another strike of lightning flashed above them, coloring the ship in white before darkening again. "I found rune magic on the mast of the ship! It says that we have to find rubies in order to leave!"

"Rubies?"

"Yes, rubies."

He looked confused but nodded nonetheless. "Let everyone know! The faster we find them, the faster we can get out!"

Kolfinna omitted the part that she wasn't exactly sure if finding rubies would necessarily get them out of the ship because the runes hadn't exactly stated that. For all she knew, they could still be killed after finding the rubies.

"Everyone!" But Kolfinna's voice was lost in the raucous wind. "We need to find rubies if we want to get out—"

She was thrown to the side by one of the draugrs. She rolled on the floor like a rag doll, slamming into rotting legs. Another wave crashed against the ship and sloshed over the floorboards. Water obscured her vision and she gasped for air, trying to sit up when something kicked her face. Her head cracked onto the floor. The seconds ticked by and she inhaled sharply, saltiness biting her lips.

Everything hurt. Her back, her arm, and her shoulder in particular. Not to mention her muscles were screaming in agony, her body was littered with budding bruises, and she was freezing cold. Was this how she was going to die? Alone, cold, and powerless?

But she was always fighting to survive, so Kolfinna pulled herself to her feet. She couldn't focus on that right now. Rubies. She needed to find those blasted rubies. In the sea of demons, it seemed unlikely that there would even be anything as precious as rubies onboard, but they had to be here. So where? Where were they?

One of the creatures closed in on her, its eyes fixated on her. It screeched and lunged at her. Kolfinna scrambled away. Rubies! Where were the rubies?

All she saw was a sea of green, glowing, hateful eyes.

Except one.

In the distance by the helm, one of the draugrs had glowing red eyes.

That was it. The one with rubies. Kolfinna didn't think twice and pushed through the crowd of skeletal hands, feet, and swords; if she took the time to fend off against every half-dead monster, she'd be stuck on the ship forever. All she needed to do was get to that one creature and rip those red eyes from its skull. Her thighs still felt sore from this morning's trek and like they would split open. Her wounds dripped with blood and her vision darkened from blood loss. But if she passed out here, that would be the end of them all.

By some miracle, she managed to get to the draugr. It turned its crystalized eyes to her and raised its sword. She pushed herself off her feet to the side and slammed her fist against its jaw. It felt like punching a wall. She bit back a yelp and kicked its midsection. Her shin screamed. But she didn't stop there; she shoved her body against the monster and slammed it to the floor. Her fists came raining down on its face. It clawed at her, its sharp fingers slicing into her back.

Kolfinna dug her fingers into its eye sockets and ripped the red crystals out. She tightened her hold over the rubies, protecting them. She just needed to put those into the mast now, and then they'd be free from this hellhole. She started toward the mast, pushing away from the skeletal being.

"Cursed fae!"

A crushing pain in her back sent her dropping forward, her chin slamming against the floorboards. Stars danced in her vision, but she was brought back to reality when someone's boot ground into her back, specifically the wound on her back. She screamed and tried to jerk away, and one of the rubies slipped from her fingers and clattered to the floor. Water picked it up and threw it a foot away from her.

"What did you get us into?" a familiar voice angrily shouted, trampling her back with the heel of his boot.

"Stop!" She craned her neck to find Magni glowering at her. Blood streaked down from a cut on his forehead, and his clothes were drenched. "Get off me!"

"What did you get us into?" He kicked her again, his voice rising in panic, almost as loud as the screaming monsters. "I warned you not to try anything! If we're going to die anyway, I'd rather kill you myself!"

"Get off me!" Her gaze darted to the ruby she had dropped. The waves were pushing it farther away. She crawled toward it, but Magni's foot pinned her down again.

"This is all your fault! You did this on purpose!"

"Magni!" It was Blár, suddenly back to her side amidst all the chaos, the throng of bodies, and the wailing storm. "You miserable little snob!" Blár shoved Magni and sent him hurling forward. Magni blinked back and spun to face him, surprise written all over his face.

"What was that for?!" Magni shouted and thrust a finger in Kolfinna's direction. "She's the reason we're in this mess!"

Kolfinna scrambled toward the ruby, her back stinging from the salt and her shoulder stiff with pain as she snatched it off the floor. The palms of her hands throbbed when she grasped the rubies tighter. The bandages Eyfura had tied over them were long gone. She couldn't care less about Magni right now, or the fact that this was the second—or third? —time Blár had saved her.

"We really don't have time for this, you hagfish," Blár snarled.

"You—"

Kolfinna ignored Magni and said, "I got the rubies! Take me to the mast!"

Blár's lips twisted and even with all the chaos surrounding them and the darkened skies enveloping them, she could see the flash of annoyance in his icy gaze. He probably didn't like being ordered around, she realized, but he surprised her by giving a small nod.

Kolfinna ran straight for the mast once more. This time, with Blár fighting off the creatures beside her, it was easier. She kicked and shoved as many as she could, but dodging them was faster. Unfortunately, the thicket of monsters was only increasing.

She almost ran headfirst into the mast. She scanned the wooden mast for the inscription and quickly shoved one of the rubies into the holes. It slid in perfectly. The rain pelted down on her hard and she almost dropped the second ruby before lodging it into place beside its companion.

Thunder slammed onto the ship and it rocked violently from side to side. Kolfinna wrapped her arms around the mast and buried her face into it as the ship rocked faster and faster until everything blurred. It felt like she was plucked off the ship and flung across the sea. The wind swallowed her scream.

Finally, she hit the floor, gasping. Her eyes adjusted and she inhaled sharply, feeling as though her chest would crack open. She blinked against the blinding light, so different than the stormy dark sky. And that's when she realized she was in that room again, the room with the ship statue—where all of it began.

10

All the tension left Kolfinna's body and she was like a puddle on the floor. And then the pain hit. Her arm, shoulder, back, and the palms of her hands screamed in agony. She chewed the inside of her cheek to keep from crying. Her entire body quivered and her teeth chattered against the biting cold. Her bones were weak, her flesh was half frozen, and she was minutes away from curling into a ball and sobbing once the shock wore off.

But she wasn't the only one in pain and at least she wasn't dead. About a dozen of their party was sprawled on the floor, groaning and shivering and bleeding. They had started with two dozen men, and now that number was cut in half.

"W-What was that?" someone cried.

Mímir's hands shook as he wiped the blood from his face. "I don't know. I-I never read anything about—well, whatever *that* was."

"I've never heard of such a thing." Truda's teeth clicked together and she tried snapping, but her fingers were too stiff to make a *snap*. "W-Who knows how to do fire magic? We could really use it right about now."

Kolfinna realized with a start that their magic was back. The familiar thrum of her mana nuzzled deep inside her and she sighed in relief. At least that hadn't been taken away for good. But one thing was clear—this castle was dangerous. For all of them. What good were they if they couldn't use their magic?

She quickly scanned the party, looking for Eyfura, but didn't find her familiar face. Kolfinna's heart sank and she recalled the screaming from the ship, the bodies being torn to pieces, and the creatures attacking mercilessly. The back of her eyes stung; had Eyfura died like that? She bottled the feeling deep inside and tamped it down for a later date, when she was ready to face her emotions.

"We need to treat everyone's injuries," Mímir said, eyeing the crowd. He frowned and pointed to each member, seemingly counting to himself. Before redoing the count again. And again. Kolfinna followed his gaze; there were only fourteen that survived.

Mímir cleared his throat and tried to smile encouragingly, but it came out forced. "All those who are able to, please help each other with the wounds."

Kolfinna scanned the crowd once more, trying to see who had made it. Unsurprisingly, Blár was one of the surviving people. And another among the surviving people was Magni, who was shrugging off his soaked cape.

His dark hair was matted against his slick forehead. Kolfinna's blood suddenly boiled. *That weasel.*

Earlier, in the capital, she had been scared to face him and the other Royal Guards, but her confidence was slowly renewing itself. She was on the same level as them. Definitely not at the same level as Blár, but she was just as worthy, just as strong, to be standing with everyone here.

And if she wanted to fight—she could.

She was in front of him in a split second. Mana pulsed beneath her fingers and she shoved him as hard as she could. He stumbled back. She raised her hands and the stones beneath his feet rumbled. In seconds, they snapped off the floor and slammed into his chest. The force of the stones hurtled him backward and she manipulated the stones to attack him until he was pinned to the wall by a mountain of stones. For extra measure, she forced the wall to wrap him in a tight embrace, both of his hands and feet pinned to it. Swords that had been hanging on the wall clattered to the floor in a heap, some of them breaking with the impact.

"What were you thinking?" Kolfinna snarled, her back throbbing with the memory of the way he stepped on her as if squashing a bug.

"Kolfinna!" Mímir shouted, but she had her focus on Magni, who was trying to rip the stones off him.

Fire sputtered at Magni's fingers, so she enclosed his fists with stone. Her eyes blazed. "You miserable little snob!" she snapped, tightening her grip on him. "You almost killed me!"

From her peripheral vision, Blár raised an eyebrow. *Miserable little snob.* That had been his insult back when Magni stomped on her back. Normally, she would've shied away from anything to do with Blár, but she was too blinded to care for any of that. She shook with rage as the scene replayed in her mind. He had tried to kill her and, in the process, almost killed them all.

Mímir grabbed her injured shoulder and pulled at her painfully. "Kolfinna! Stop this!"

"Get off me!" She shook his hand off and pointed at Magni. "That guy tried to kill me! I was trying to save all of us and he attacked me!"

"Kolfinna, let him go." Mímir's jaw tightened. "We can talk about this peacefully—"

"Screw that!" She wanted to rip Magni to pieces. *How dare he?*

"Kolfinna!"

"We're all in this mess because of her!" Magni shouted and tried wriggling his shoulder. "She didn't tell us anything about this! Now let me go, fae scum!"

"Let him go!" Truda stepped in front of Magni, as if she was the protective barrier he needed. "He's just as scared as the rest of us! Besides, what he's saying is true. You didn't tell us any of this would happen! Isn't that your job?"

Kolfinna clenched and unclenched her fists. "My job? Are you freaking serious right now? How was I supposed to know we'd be thrust onto a *freaking ship* in the middle of a storm?!"

"You're a fae!" Truda said with a twisted expression. "You should know this place better than us. Your kind lived here! And besides, you're fine and well right now, aren't you? Think about the people who lost their lives! Let him go!"

Kolfinna's mouth hung open and she almost couldn't speak with how much anger was boiling her veins. "You cannot be serious right now. So I should ignore the fact that he tried to kill me? And are we just going to gloss over that I helped save us all? That he was about to doom us all?! None of that matters because we're fine now? Are you serious?"

She turned to Mímir and the rest of everyone. She expected some sort of rebuttal, or for them to realize how ridiculous Truda sounded, but almost everyone had the same hostile gleam in their eyes. It then hit her. They needed someone to blame. And she was the perfect target.

Kolfinna felt like someone punched her in the gut. "This isn't my fault," she whispered as the gazes in the room turned sharp—hostile. She looked for a familiar face, for someone to believe her, but all she saw was a sea of hatred. Kolfinna's voice lowered, her tone losing its steam. "Don't trivialize what Magni did to me just because he didn't succeed. He tried to *kill* me."

For a moment, no one said anything and Kolfinna feared they would all turn on her. Her body trembled and she wasn't sure if it was from the cold water drenching her bones or from the current situation. She cast a quick glance at the doorway; she could make it if she ran. Maybe.

Finally, Mímir stepped forward. "Kolfinna is right. This isn't her fault. Also, no one could've imagined that this would happen."

"We all need to stick together." Truda placed one hand on her hip while she motioned to Magni with her other hand. "Let him go."

"Stick together?" Kolfinna laughed hollowly and her eyes stung. "You seem awfully bent on making me look like the bad guy here."

"You *are* the bad guy," Magni hissed from the wall. "You're a murderer."

"We're a team, so let him go." Truda glowered at Kolfinna and crossed her arms over her chest. Kolfinna had the urge to knock her back along with Magni. "Besides, isn't the whole reason you're here so you can read the runes and warn us about something like this? Why didn't you? Why didn't you read the room or find clues or something?! If you had warned us, we wouldn't have—"

"Truda, shut up." Blár's voice cracked like a whip.

Truda blinked in surprise and opened her mouth to protest, but no words came out. Blár was now shirtless, sitting on the floor with a roll of bandages in one hand and an open jar of salve balanced on his thigh. He was in the middle of wrapping his arm, a wad of bloody rags beside him. His ice-cold eyes narrowed at Truda.

"Stop with your accusations. You sound like a dung

beetle." He wrapped the bindings tightly around his bulging forearm. Water glistened against his rippling chest. "She saved all our asses by reading that rune shit and putting those rubies where they needed to be."

"D-Dung beetle?" Truda sputtered, opening and closing her mouth, cheeks ablaze. "What does that even—"

"I don't think it's right that Magni tried to kill her and you're brushing it under the rug just because she didn't die." Blár's face twisted in pain when he tightened the bandage around his bicep; blood seeped into the bindings and colored them a deep, rich red. He continued wrapping the bandages until there was enough padding to hide the flowing blood. He raised his sharp blue eyes to pin Truda with a withering stare. "Stop making excuses for your own pathetic uselessness. I've told you several times that the next time you talk shit, I'll freeze your half-wit mind."

Truda flinched as the temperature of the room dropped. Despite the sudden coldness, Kolfinna's chest tightened with unexpected warmth. He was the last person she expected to stand up for her.

Magni writhed against the wall, trying to free himself again; he reminded Kolfinna of a butterfly pinned to a wall by its wings. "Why are you siding with the fae?" Magni spat. The rage brewing on his face made it seem like it was personal, even though it shouldn't have been. "She's not on our side."

"Oh, I almost forgot about the talking pond scum."

Blár rolled his eyes and finished binding his arm. He then took a rag and blotting another nasty cut on his stomach. "I'm not siding with anyone. You guys are acting like headless chickens who've never gone on a mission. You think we all like each other? *Hell no*. But we work together because that's our job. Or have you forgotten that?"

Kolfinna couldn't believe the words coming out of his mouth. Wasn't *he* the one who threatened her before the mission? But she ignored the quip fighting to loosen her lips; he had saved her several times on the ship before he even realized her usefulness, so she let him off the hook for that. But just for this moment. She allowed the warmth in her chest to spread and tingle over her whole body.

"Huh? Why are you all looking like that?" Blár scoffed as everyone goggled at him like he'd grown three heads. "Your faces look like there's shit leaking from them."

"S-She didn't save us fast enough. She must've delayed it," Magni sputtered, his face turning a shade of blue as he struggled to breathe against the rocks. Kolfinna loosened the stones a tad bit and was relieved when some color returned to his face; she didn't *actually* want to kill him.

"No, she didn't. I was watching her and I was by her side for most of it." Blár slowly unrolled another set of bandages and Kolfinna fought the urge to stare at his body —at his sculpted chest, the lean cut of his abdomen, his biceps. "Stop pointing fingers and focus on your own wounds. You might not like her because she's a fae, but we need her on our side if we want any chance to survive. We wouldn't have survived without her. Do any of us know how to read that rune stuff? What would we have done in that situation? We would've all died."

"It's like you said"—Kolfinna turned to Truda, who had remained like a rock since Blár snapped at her—"if we want to survive, we have to stick together." She then turned to Magni. "And *you*. You're absolutely despicable. You've shown that your hatred is more important than the mission!"

Kolfinna wanted to squeeze him harder and thrash him on the floor a few times, but that would only make everyone more hostile toward her, so she released him, but not before giving him a little push on the back with a stone so that he face-planted onto the hard floor.

"Hey, I agree with Kolfinna and Blár," a familiar voice said.

Kolfinna quickly scoured the party until her gaze landed on Eyfura, and a tension she hadn't realized that had been building up inside her loosened tremendously. *She was alive*. Kolfinna could've sunk to the floor with the relief she felt.

Kolfinna could see why she hadn't been able to recognize Eyfura from a quick glance. Eyfura's usually gold-blond hair was mostly doused with dried blood, and the cuts and bruises on her face dampened her typical cheerful disposition.

"We really shouldn't be fighting," Eyfura said, clutching her side. Her silk gloves were ripped and barely hanging onto her dainty hands. "It's really dangerous, so we can't be fighting like this. Our powers didn't work back then, but the rune magic did. I don't think we'll be able to survive without each other."

"We knew this would be a tough mission," Mímir said with a nod. "Let's not split up. We need to work together." He laughed uncomfortably. "How about we bandage ourselves up first and then fight later, huh?" It was a sad excuse at lightening the mood, but it calmed the room a little.

"I'm not done." Kolfinna's fists were clenched so tightly that her fingers dug crescent-shaped marks into her already bleeding palms. "We're supposed to be a team. I don't want to have to worry about someone backstabbing me while I'm just trying to do the mission. We're all here for a reason."

"Kolfinna is right." Eyfura came to stand beside Kolfinna and rested a hand on her shoulder. "We have to trust her and we can't fight her or blame her just because something goes awry."

"All right." Mímir clapped his hands together, a tight smile on his face. "We all agree that it wasn't right for Magni to try to kill Kolfinna and that Kolfinna is an integral part of this operation. Now that we have that settled, let's bandage ourselves up. It'll be best to stake out here in this room tonight and try again tomorrow when we're better rested. We'll take turns guarding. Is that clear?"

A deep silence permeated throughout the room while everyone shifted on their feet to bandage themselves up. Pieces of the wall Kolfinna had manipulated crumbled and fell onto the cracked tiles.

Torsten suddenly burst into tears, breaking the silence. "I didn't think"—he hastily rubbed the tears on his cheeks, his shoulders racking forward with sobs—"I didn't think Thyra would die like that!"

Kolfinna remembered the petite brunette and how she had teased Eyfura when they climbed the mountain. She had been so full of life. And then she thought of how Thyra had been brutally attacked by three of the skeletal beings, and how they had killed her mercilessly and gnawed on her limbs.

Torsten continued crying, but his cries grew a bit softer when Mímir placed a hand on his shoulder, his own face twisted with pain. Kolfinna stared at her shiny boots that were a tad too big. It always made her feel awkward when someone cried in front of her. She didn't know what to do. Was she supposed to comfort him? Let him cry alone? Or leave him to it? It was too intimate.

"I'm so sorry," Eyfura said, her shoulders drooping and her eyes shining with unshed tears. "I know you both were really close. That must've been terrible to witness."

"We'll avenge her. We'll avenge them all," Blár said with a frown. He had finished bandaging himself up and was shrugging his uniform back on. "There must be somebody or something pulling the strings to these ruins. We'll find them and gut them alive."

Guilt grew in the pit of Kolfinna's stomach and if she hadn't vomited all the contents of her stomach already, she was sure she would've retched right then and there. Although Magni was wrong in thinking she purposefully delayed the whole situation, it was true that if she had been faster, if she had figured things out sooner—maybe there would be more survivors. Maybe Thyra wouldn't have died.

Everyone worked quickly and methodologically after that, as if they were used to the aftermath of a battle: disinfect, bandage, move on to the next injured person, repeat. The women huddled together when there was a private wound, to prevent the men from seeing anything, but it didn't matter, because everyone was in their own little world. The silence was grim and haunting.

"Thyra was such a sweet girl," Eyfura murmured. "I … I just can't believe it."

"Brynhild was like a sister to me," one of the female soldiers said through half-sobs as she tied a bandage around Truda's ankle. "We went to school together and she was supposed to marry this autumn—"

"I'm so sorry, Embla," Eyfura said, her voice growing thick.

The guilt grew heavier and heavier on Kolfinna with each passing moment as everyone spoke about their friends and coworkers they lost. Some of the people they knew for years. Others were young in their careers and new to it all.

Kolfinna gritted her teeth together and peeled back the shredded sleeve of her injured arm. She flinched at the slight movement and sucked in her cheek. Thick blood crusted her stiff arm. Every movement felt like her flesh would slide off the bone. Teeth marks formed half crescents all over her arm. She squeezed her eyes shut. The more she looked, the more her stomach turned. Cuts, some jagged and some clean, peppered her broken skin. Her shoulder hurt the most and was by far the deepest of her wounds. Every time she moved her arm, it burned and throbbed relentlessly. She hadn't realized it earlier because of all the adrenaline, but now that the rush was gone, all she felt was the constant throbbing.

Eyfura kneeled in front of Kolfinna, a roll of clean, new bandages in one hand and a small jar of green salve in the other. She smiled faintly, revealing two dimples on her cheeks. "Kolfinna, let me help bind your wounds."

"Oh, uh, are you sure? There are people who are worse off—"

Eyfura waved her hand. "Don't be shy. Your shoulder doesn't look too good. Let me help."

Kolfinna opened her mouth to protest, to tell her she was fine and could manage by herself, but Eyfura cocked a brow, giving her a look that told her she wasn't taking no for an answer. It reminded Kolfinna of Katla and how she always insisted on bandaging up the scrapes on her knees whenever they played as children. Kolfinna bit her bottom lip and nodded. "I would appreciate it, thank you."

Eyfura hummed softly as she went to work. She cut the sleeve of Kolfinna's uniform and threw it to the floor, where it plopped in a sad, wet, bloody heap. Kolfinna tried ignoring the needle in Eyfura's hand as she brought it to her shoulder and started sewing the wound with lightning speed after dabbing it clean with a rag.

"My mother and father work in the medical unit in the military, so I've been in and out of government hospitals since I was a child," Eyfura explained. "Blood and gore don't really bother me."

Kolfinna flinched as the needle dug deeper into her skin. "You must be pretty knowledgeable in medicine then." Medicine wasn't an easy field to get into, whether as a nurse, doctor, or simply a helper. At least not on the military level. Small villages were always looking for medical help, but they usually only had superstitious healers who would use herbal treatments that weren't as effective as the knowledge a medical practitioner had. "Why didn't you become a nurse or a physician?"

"Surprisingly, the money is not *that* great," Eyfura said with a laugh. "At least when you're a woman. And, to be frank, it didn't align with my interests. I wanted to be out in the field and use my abilities. I don't think I can handle it mentally, either. It was too much for me most days. Seeing people I cared for pass away, or just seeing others in pain ... It took a huge mental toll on me, and I just helped out occasionally! I can't imagine doing it every day." The needle went in and out of Kolfinna's skin. "My parents didn't really have many expectations for me, so it didn't matter what I did. I think I mentioned it to you already, but they put all their hopes and dreams on Nollar."

"How do they feel about you being a Royal Guard?" Kolfinna traced a crack on the tile she sat on and she tried to focus on Eyfura's words rather than Eyfura closing her wound.

"That I'm taking up a spot that could've—and *should've*—belonged to a well-deserving man." She cut the thread with her teeth and tied the ends before applying the salve thickly. "There's a limited number of people who can become a Royal Guard and they think it would've been better if a man who has to provide for his family took that spot instead of me. I'm essentially taking somebody else's job!"

Kolfinna blinked. "But that's ridiculous. You deserve to be a Royal Guard just as much as anyone else does."

"I think so too, but ..." She shrugged and rolled the bandage around Kolfinna's shoulder. "But they've got their minds set. Nothing's going to change how they feel."

"I wonder how they'll feel when they find out a fae—a woman at that—is trying to be a Royal Guard."

"Oh, they'll pass out." Eyfura laughed and applied salve to the bite marks on Kolfinna's forearm. "They'll never believe it. And they'll hate you for it."

"That's a shame that people don't think you deserve to be where you're at."

"I suppose, but I don't let it get me down. At the end of the day, I'm a Royal Guard and I'm proud of myself." Eyfura paused at the wound on Kolfinna's back. "Can you take your shirt off? I need to work on this."

Kolfinna's gaze darted to the other soldiers and Royal Guards mulling around. A few were done with their treatment, while others were in the middle of it.

As if sensing her discomfort, Eyfura offered, "How about we do it outside the room?"

"But what if ..." The question hung in the air. Kolfinna didn't want to finish it. *What if we're attacked by another monster?*

"It'll only take me a moment." Eyfura pointed to the corner of the room. "Or we can do it there."

Kolfinna weighed her options. "All right. Let's do it there."

When they reached the corner, Kolfinna constructed a thin stone barrier between herself and the rest of everyone. It was the little privacy she could have.

Eyfura blew out air as she inspected the little hideout the stones created. "That's a useful trick."

Kolfinna carefully undid the buttons on her dripping uniform and slowly eased it off her body. It stuck to her like a second skin and she gritted her teeth together to keep from crying as her injured shoulder throbbed, the new stitches threatening to burst open with every move-ment. Finally, with Eyfura's help, she managed to remove it. She threw it to the floor, where a wet puddle was already forming.

"You have a lot of glass in your back," Eyfura murmured.

Kolfinna grimaced when Eyfura picked and prodded her exposed back. "It must've happened when I was attacked by ..." She was at a loss for words about what to call the first creature she had encountered.

"Yeah, I figured."

Like Eyfura promised, it didn't take her long to clean the wound, pick away the pieces of glass, stitch the cut, and bandage her. The bandages wrapped over her chest and back, acting like a shirt of its own.

"That was scary out there," Eyfura said, wrapping the roll around Kolfinna's chest. "I'm almost done, by the way."

"It *was* scary." Kolfinna shuddered to think about the two very different monsters they had met. The worst part of it all was being helpless and unable to use their magic.

"I've never seen such ... monsters." Eyfura patted Kolfinna's uninjured shoulder. "All done."

"Thank you." Kolfinna's gaze drifted to Eyfura's own wounds. She wasn't as badly hurt as the others, but her right thigh was bandaged heavily and her left arm was padded in bandages as well.

"Of course!" Eyfura peeked over the stone wall at the rest of everyone and sighed. "Everyone's shaken up. It's kinda embarrassing, but what Blár said is true. We're acting like we've never been on a mission before." She pushed back a strand of hair and chewed on her lower lip, lost in thought for a second. She smiled, but it didn't reach her eyes. "I think it's because we've never seen such things. Like, magic beasts are a different breed to handle. They're not like *that*. They're more like pesky birds that shoot out fire from their wings. Or a giant horse that flies and spits acid. Something normal—definitely not like a nightmare. I don't know how Blár is able to just ... I don't know, jump into action and not think twice about it? It's hard. I guess it's because he's a black rank. But it motivates me to do better. I mean, we have to."

Yes, they needed to do better. When the first monster struck Kolfinna, she had been frozen in fear and confusion. If she had been alone, she likely would've been seriously injured before remembering to fight back. Blár had been the one to attack and kill it. If he hadn't been there ... she didn't want to think about how wrong everything could've gone. A wave of uneasiness made her stomach knot together. What if there were more powerful, more sinister, and more bizarre things waiting for them?

"Hi, ladies." Mímir's voice invaded her thoughts. He stood a few feet away from them, turning his head slightly so as not to catch sight of Kolfinna. "I'm the only water elemental left and instead of having a fire elemental dry the clothes, I thought it would be easier and quicker for me to just draw the water out."

"Mímir! Yes, thank you. I've been feeling wet and soggy since we got back!" Eyfura said. "Please, go ahead."

Mímir waved his hand and the water pulled away from Eyfura's clothing. He splashed it against the wall, where it left a streak. Eyfura held up Kolfinna's shirt. Mímir wordlessly did the same to the shirt and the rest of Kolfinna's outfit.

"Great! You're the best," Eyfura said, beaming.

"Thank you," Kolfinna said. She definitely felt better without the squelching, blood-soaked wetness of the clothes.

"Mímir, what's our next plan of action?" Eyfura asked while Kolfinna hurriedly donned her uniform shirt. It still smelled strongly of briny ocean water and blood, but at least it was dry. "Like tomorrow morning, I mean."

"You know that big staircase in the lobby? We'll be moving up." Mímir ran a hand through his hair and he peered over the party. "One thing I'm certain about is that this castle *must* have a powerful artifact or two, if not multiple. We need to find them and get out of here as soon as possible."

"All right, sounds like a plan."

"You both should go to sleep. You look exhausted." His smile was thin and weary. "I'm thinking we should stand guard two at a time, and maybe in two-hour intervals. I'll take the first watch with Magni, and when it's your turn, I'll wake you both. Unless you want to guard with someone else—"

"That's fine," Kolfinna said, glancing at Eyfura, who bobbed her head in return. She would rather stand guard with Eyfura than any of the other Royal Guards or soldiers. "If Eyfura is okay with me, then I don't mind."

Mímir nodded. "Perfect."

Kolfinna unfurled her pack and pulled out the thinning, scratchy blanket. She wrapped herself in a cocoon and curled into a ball on the floor, her eyelids suddenly heavy. She caught sight of Torsten, who was leaning against the wall covering his face, his shoulders quaking with silent sobs. Her chest tightened painfully at the lives lost. She needed to do better. She needed to be better. If she had any hopes of becoming a proper Royal Guard, she had to protect everyone.

Her eyes fluttered shut, but not before the flickering faces of the dead soldiers and Royal Guards flitted through her mind. She seared their faces into her memory. She couldn't let any more die, because this place was dangerous, and maybe she was the only one who could protect them all.

11

Kolfinna was startled awake by a stifled scream. She jerked upright in her makeshift bed of blankets and noticed the other soldiers and Royal Guards do the same. They pushed their blankets off and looked ready to jump into action, hair mussed and drool still smeared on their faces. Kolfinna shifted her attention to the door, where a Royal Guard stood at the entrance, his legs bowed together at his knees. He craned his neck to look at them, his skin pale and his lips quivering as he pointed in the distance.

"I-It's a monster," he said under his breath.

Mímir ran to the threshold, squinting at where he was pointing, while everyone else lurched to their feet, bundling blankets under their arms and quickly stuffing them in their packs. Kolfinna jammed her blanket in her pack while jogging to where Mímir stood. She slung the pack over her shoulder and she peeked over the doorway.

By the large staircase at the end of the lobby was the same type of creature that had attacked her yesterday. The hairs on her arm stood up as she remembered it tackling her to the floor. The milky-eyed monster's head kept shifting in different directions, a sword dragging behind it as it descended the stairs. *Clank, clank.* The rusted sword scratched the floor with each step.

"Let me take care of it." Kolfinna turned to Mímir.

Mímir hesitated and studied her carefully. "If ... if you think you can handle it, then go ahead."

Kolfinna pushed forward, leaving the room. She didn't think too much about the way he paused and what that meant—he didn't trust her abilities. She probably wouldn't trust her abilities either, with how she had handled the monster the first time it attacked her. But she drowned away all background noise, her intrusive thoughts, and poured her focus onto the creature. Mana pulsed beneath her fingers; she breathed deeply, feeling it circulate her body. She didn't have to worry—she could use magic. She repeated it to herself as her mana vibrated beneath her flesh.

The creature's head bobbed in her direction and it tilted its head. A ghastly smile curved its mouth. It was still three dozen feet away from her, but it ran toward her, its arms flailing behind it. The sword bumped against the floor with every stride. It was unnerving seeing its quick, uneven gait, but she kept reminding herself that she was strong enough to face it.

Before it could get close to her, she forced the stone

floor to open up beneath its feet. The monster fell, and Kolfinna manipulated the stones in the floor to fall back in place and crush the monster. It screeched loudly, its white eyes shifting around the room. It could only move its head at that point. Kolfinna squeezed her fingers together, shoving the stones to squash the monster. It screamed louder, the bones and skin and flesh crunching beneath the weight of the stones. Finally, its head fell forward limply.

She expected to feel powerful, fulfilled, and happy at crushing it so easily. But instead, she remembered the ship incident and how powerless she was against those skeletal creatures. How so many soldiers and Royal Guards—who were *trained* to fight—had died mercilessly. She had seen what a fight like that would have looked like without her powers. What if it happened again?

"Good job," Mímir said.

The corner of her mouth rose, but it quickly fell when she caught sight of everyone's patchy appearance. Some wore slings, others had padded legs. They were all in bad condition, so this was nothing to be proud of. It was a normal takedown of a magic beast. She couldn't celebrate until they found an artifact and got as far away from this place as possible.

"All right, everyone, I think it's best we keep moving. I know we can sleep a bit more, but it's already morning and I don't know about you guys, but I'm ready to get this mission done with. Just one artifact." Mímir raised his finger to solidify his point. "Just one good artifact and we've accomplished our mission and can head out."

Mímir gestured to everyone to follow him as he led them toward the staircase. A few paused to examine the corpse of the monster Kolfinna had defeated, and a few cast her quick glances. Whether it was awe or uneasiness, she couldn't tell. Or maybe it was a mixture of both. She was sure none of these people had ever witnessed fae magic, which wasn't as simple as their magic.

They passed the statue of the monster with its mouth open, as if ready to eat them next. Kolfinna tried to keep away from it. Even though it was just a statue, it was unsettling to look at.

The staircase was partially covered in what probably once was a fancy, rich, velvety carpet, but was now so worn down it was discolored to brown and was missing chunks, revealing the marble stone underneath. As they went farther up the stairs, a swirling embossed design on the wall below the half-rotted wooden hand railing caught her attention. At first, it appeared to be a pretty design for beautification, but upon closer inspection, it depicted a tale. A woman with a crown sat upon a throne holding a chain attached to the necks of the people below her. An army of half-fish people was beneath her image, swords in their hands, seeming to oppose her. Kolfinna scanned the walls, but chunks of it were broken and crumbly. Was this a piece of Kolfinna's history? What did it even mean? A queen and half-fish people? Was the queen supposed to be Queen Aesileif?

The last fae queen, said to be the oppressor of all humans? Or was this supposed to represent another queen?

She wanted to stop and stare, to breathe in the knowledge of the past, but the party was already moving forward, so she couldn't study it for too long.

Kolfinna tried to imagine what the castle was like all those centuries ago, before the descent of her people. Hundreds of fae filled the castle floor in her mind, a few scholars running with scrolls bunched together in their hands. Maybe families were walking inside, holding their children's hands and telling them about fae abilities. Everyone would be laughing and freely talking amongst each other, proud of their shared powers.

But it was all a fantasy. This castle was in ruins. It was a reminder of what the humans did to the fae.

"*Help*," a feminine voice called from behind her.

Kolfinna whipped around, only to almost run headlong into Blár and Truda, who halted in their steps and both narrowed their eyes in unison, as if looking for a fight. Kolfinna studied Truda for a split second. It couldn't have been her, could it?

Truda's brows pulled together angrily. "What?"

"Nothing." Kolfinna continued climbing the steps, her heart rate picking up. She had no idea Blár was directly behind her. Was he trying to keep a closer eye on her? Or was she overthinking it? His words at the forest clearing sent chills down her spine. He wanted to toy with her and resume their "cat-and-mouse" game. Just because he had helped her during the ship ordeal didn't mean they were magically buddy-buddy.

"Hey, you doing okay?" Eyfura popped up beside her. Her cheery disposition was a stark contrast to Truda's—or, honestly, everyone else's. "How's your shoulder feeling? That was a really nasty cut."

The tension and adrenaline had assuaged the sharp stabbing pain, but it was a constant dull throbbing that wouldn't go away that easily, and all the distractions couldn't hide her discomfort. Kolfinna kept imagining herself unraveling at the seams, her blood and flesh slipping off her frame. It was a gruesome imagery, but the culmination of wounds made her feel that way.

Kolfinna shrugged but winced when her shoulder stung. "It's all right," she settled with. Blár was still behind her and could probably hear every word. "And you? How are your wounds?"

"Oh, I'm doing all right." Eyfura placed a hand on her cheek. "Anytime I feel down, I just think of Captain Asulf's face, and all my negative feelings disappear!"

Kolfinna raised an eyebrow. "I thought you wouldn't pine after a married man?"

"Ugh, don't remind me!" Eyfura sighed. "If I can get cheered up by thinking of his handsome, regal face, then I will! Come on, tell me you didn't once think he was incredibly gorgeous? The red hair, the silver eyes, that pretty physique—ugh, I swoon every time!"

"I'm not interested."

"So you say." Eyfura giggled, leaning closer as if

sharing a secret. "But, you know, *all* the single Royal Guard ladies have a little crush on him. Sadly, I'm not the president of the unofficial fan club, but I was *this* close"— she pinched her fingers together—"to becoming vice president."

Kolfinna couldn't help the wry smile forming on her face. She couldn't imagine all the uptight Royal Guard women swooning over the captain in such a way, or having a fan club. Before she joined this mission, she was under the impression that all Royal Guards had a stick up their asses. "I had no idea there was such a thing."

"Oh, there is! After this mission, we could totally go to one of the meetings together!"

"Um, no, thanks."

"What, he's not your type?" Eyfura elbowed her in the abdomen softly. "You into the tall, dark, and handsome kind?"

The only tall, dark, and handsome guy who came to mind was Blár Vilulf. But he just happened to be rude, sinister, and villainous. "Hell no," Kolfinna said sharply, all too aware that Blár was behind them.

Eyfura's laughter tinkered over the group, but despite her bubbliness, Kolfinna noticed the tension stretching the skin around her eyes. And then it hit Kolfinna what Eyfura was doing: lightening the mood. Before talking to Kolfinna, she had been huddled between soldiers, chatting airily and giggling about something.

"Can you two get serious for once?" Truda snapped

from behind and rolled her eyes. "My ears will bleed listening to your stupid ramblings."

Eyfura's gaze darted between Kolfinna, Truda, and Blár. She winked at Truda. "Oh, Truda," she said in a singsong voice. "Don't get jealous because we've got a hunk for a captain. I'm sorry your commanding officer is an old guy in his forties."

"I literally do not care," Truda huffed.

Eyfura's voice dropped to a whisper, "Don't think I don't notice you staring at Blár. He's your type, isn't he?"

Truda's cheeks instantly fired up. "I do *not* like him. I used to before he opened his mouth and I realized how much of an asshole he is."

Kolfinna stifled a laugh; at least there was one thing they could agree on.

Eyfura didn't have time to reply because their party came to a screeching halt. They were at the fork, where the staircase split into two directions. Both staircases ended with the same thing: darkness. Even if she squinted, she couldn't imagine what was beyond them. There was only one way to find out.

Mímir paused for a moment, contemplating, and then motioned to the right. They all followed behind him, but just as they started climbing up the stairway, Kolfinna sensed a surge of magic behind her. She spun around to find two demonic dog-like creatures dashing down the opposite staircase, froth flicking from their open mouths. Razor claws tore the carpet beneath their feet as they ran. Now she understood what had contributed to the torn carpet on the stairs. Black, leathered skin covered their entire body, but what was the most terrifying was their wrinkled, squished faces with protruding teeth.

Shards of ice slammed into the dog-monsters' faces and pinned them to the floor. The ice spears stuck out of the corpses. Blue blood and pieces of flesh splattered the staircase and the walls. Kolfinna flinched at the impact, her breath caught in her throat. Blár was unfazed, his expression schooled to boredom as he brushed off flecks of ice from his fingers.

Eyfura whistled before whispering, "He's annoying, I'll admit. But damn."

Blár, who had been inspecting his work, glanced over at her sharply and scowled.

"You think he heard me?" she whispered again.

"Come on, everyone. Let's keep moving!" Mímir called. "Blár, I'll leave the rearguard to you."

Blár frowned, looking none too pleased with that, but he didn't say anything.

They continued up the stairs into a spacious, empty hallway. Tall arched double doors stood at the end of it. The off-white floor tiles were cracked and smeared with dirt and dried, brown blood. There was a dent on one side of the wall. A fight had ensued at some point, but who knew how long ago that fight was? Hundreds of years? Or maybe within the past two years?

"U-Um, I-I can't go back—" Torsten pointed to the staircase they had come from. His hand trembled and he swallowed, his Adam's apple bobbing up and down his throat.

Mímir tilted his head. "Excuse me?"

"I dropped my handkerchief on the top step, so I thought I'd grab it … But I can't." Sweat beaded his forehead and he placed his hand over the air. As if there was some sort of glass, his hand splayed against … *nothing*. He pressed harder, but his hand didn't budge. It was like there was a wall in place.

Kolfinna strode to where he was and tentatively tried to pass her hand back to the staircase, but her fingers met with an invisible wall. And then, golden runes floated along the invisible wall. She stared at it for a second. *Barrier*, it read.

"We can't go back," she whispered.

Torsten looked at her; he had been one of the people who, when traveling with her, had shot her dirty looks along with Magni. But this time, he appeared serious. As if realizing he needed her. "This is getting a little …" He paused. "Unnerving."

It looked like the castle ruins wanted them to go forward. The arched double doors seemed to beg their attention. Kolfinna chewed on her lower lip, something stirring within her. The ruins wanted them dead. At least that's what it seemed like. But during the ship ordeal, the runes had helped them escape. Why? What was the purpose of it all? What was the castle hiding or protecting?

The double doors didn't have anything special on

them; Kolfinna couldn't trace any mana from them. But when she reached out and placed her hand against them, she could feel the faintest whiff of it. She closed her eyes, willing all her senses forward. Mana from humans and other fae were relatively easy to sense when one reached a high enough proficiency with their own mana, but rune magic was trickier for Kolfinna to figure out. She needed to put all her focus into it, or else she couldn't sense it— like the barrier that had formed after they left the staircase.

"Kolfinna?" It was Mímir. She could imagine him staring at her with that worried crease between his brows. But she didn't look at him and kept her attention on the door.

After a few seconds, she found it, eyes snapping open. "Mana," she said. "There's rune magic behind the door."

"Is it ... another monster?" Eyjarr, the middle-aged soldier with peppered hair, said. His eyes were wide saucers. "Is it another ordeal? Like on the ship?"

"Not the ship ..." Embla, one of the other soldiers, whispered.

Sweat dampened Kolfinna's hands, nearly soaking through the new bandages on her palms. She didn't have any answers for them. The party watched her expectantly, even Magni and Truda. They all seemed to hold their breaths for what she was going to say.

She didn't like them by any means—except for maybe Eyfura and Mímir, the only two people who had been welcoming and kind to her—but she couldn't have them all die unprepared, especially when she could help.

Blár watched her with an uninterested and unbothered expression. There was a budding blue bruise on his cheek, making his contemptuous blue eyes more intense. She bristled under his scrutiny and turned to avoid his gaze. Even though he saved her life twice, she was uneasy around him. He was being cooperative, but there was no kindness in him. He would toss her aside if she proved to be useless.

"Rune magic," Kolfinna repeated, finding strength in her voice, "exists beyond this door." She spoke loud enough for all of them to hear. "There are powers beyond this door that, most likely, we've never seen before. The castle isn't letting us leave." She gestured toward the staircase they had come from. "It wants us to move forward. And if that's what it wants, there must be something waiting for us."

Her throat closed up and she grasped for words, her gaze flitting over the blur of faces. They didn't trust her, did they? She could feel it in the stirring air as they stared.

Kolfinna fidgeted with her sleeve, her voice dropping. "Runes ... Only I can read them here, and from what I've gathered, it's imperative that we ... that we follow what they say. They have clues to help get us out of situations, I think."

If she wanted to become a proper Royal Guard, she needed to protect everyone here. Even if they disliked her. Even if they thought she was nothing more than a fae monster.

Kolfinna pressed her hand against the door once

more. Rune magic was still such a mystery to her. She could sense it enough to know that it was there, but not enough to have any idea what was beyond the door. "At the ship, the runes told me to find rubies and place them where they indicated. The rubies were one of the monsters' eyes. It's almost as if that ordeal was a *test*. I think the castle is testing us. Testing *me*." Her stomach churned with the weight of their stares. Anxiety twisted and knotted in her throat. She didn't like all the eyes on her. "You need to listen to me beyond this door. I'll try my best to figure out if there's something I can do. But you *cannot*"—she turned sharply to Magni, who straightened —"hurt me or compromise me."

"Why do you think it's testing you in particular?" Truda crossed her arms over her chest. "It could be testing all of us. It's not just specific to you."

"I'm the only fae here." Kolfinna pointedly stared at Truda, the thorn in her side. "I'm the only one who can read, interpret, and follow the runes. What would you all have done without me? Would you have figured that out by yourselves? Also, this used to be a castle for fae. It was designed for my people. So it seems the temple is speaking to me, a fae, directly. *Not* to humans."

Truda screwed her mouth shut.

When there didn't seem to be any more opposition, Kolfinna breathed out deeply and pushed the door open.

12

There was nothing extraordinary about the room except the green, white, and black checkered floor. It was what was in the center of the room that captured everyone's attention—a large, *living* monster. Folds and folds of fat rolled off its grotesque, white, and greasy humanoid body; it was bigger than all of them combined. Its head was tiny and perched on top of its round blob of a body. Six spikes protruded from its fleshy body, extending at least five feet. The ghastliest feature was its face: completely bone white, with large owl-like eyes that were too big for its head, and a mouth that took over half its face, pointy teeth sticking out from it at different angles—as if there were too many teeth jammed into its mouth. It was staring at them, and it was *smiling*.

Kolfinna and the rest of the party held their breaths, frozen and suspended as the creature stared at them, because although the monster was gruesome, another alarming fact hit everyone at the same time: their powers didn't work.

"What is—" Torsten started.

A split second was all it took for the creature to lurch forward and swipe Torsten's head with its claw. Bone crunched, blood splattered, and flesh fell into ribbons at his feet before his body fell to the floor. Something warm splashed on Kolfinna's face. Blood pooled on the floor around everyone's feet.

The creature held Torsten's decapitated head in one claw. It tossed it in the air and chomped down on it loudly. It slurped and chewed until there wasn't a trace left. Another claw wrapped Torsten's arm and it dragged his corpse to where it was originally sitting. It plopped down on its seat in the center of the room, a dangling arm hanging out of its mouth. A smear of blood stained the tiled floor. The monster ate, not taking its eyes off them. It all happened in a split second.

Someone screamed. Kolfinna's knees gave out.

"H-Help us!" Embla grabbed the doorknob, but it was too late.

The creature snapped forward and did the same with her. Her body hit the floor and she was dragged away in the same manner. The monster smiled as it ate their flesh. It picked at the bones and munched, bones snapping and flesh slopping down its mouth.

More people screamed and backed into the doorway. They tried opening the door, but it was locked in place.

"It won't open—"

Despite its monstrous size, it was too quick on his feet. So quick that when he charged past Kolfinna and grabbed the man, her hair blew to the side and stuck to her blood-covered face. The spikes on its body were inches away from slicing her head off.

Kolfinna covered her mouth with trembling hands. The stench of death, decay, and blood made her stomach drop. Blood spotted the floor. Eyfura's face was gray. Blár's back was pressed against the wall. Magni and Truda were frozen by the blood smears on the floor, as if they had tried reaching down to help before it was too late. Everyone else hugged the door as if it would save them, watching in muted silence as the monster ate their friends.

Kolfinna couldn't utter a word at the scene. The creature had finished its meal and watched them in silence, its grin now bathed in blood. Shaky breaths filled the air; fear struck everyone into silence.

The creature continued staring, but after a few minutes, nothing happened. It felt like hours before Kolfinna noticed glowing words on one of the walls. She zeroed in on it. The runes shimmered gold. *Speak, and the Jötnar will silence you forever.* Her eyes widened at the name of the creature—Jötnar. A troll.

But trolls didn't exist, and they weren't supposed to look like *that*.

Nothing made sense anymore, so she clambered to her feet unsteadily. The three who died had spoken, hadn't they? Was that why the monster was just sitting there, waiting for them to make a mistake and utter a word?

Kolfinna tamped down the fear in her heart and tried to focus on the room.

As she was thinking that, she spotted a door at the end of the hall-like room. That must've been the escape. On another wall, the runes swirled and curved in such a way that should've made it hard to decipher, and yet the meaning came to her mind instantly.

Green will burn your feet, and black will fill the Jötnar's belly. Green and black? It must've meant the floors, since two of those colors filled the tiles. There were five rows of white tiles, which they were all currently standing on. Beyond that was a mishmash of greens, whites, and blacks—in no particular pattern whatsoever. Around the Jötnar were mostly black tiles.

Kolfinna raised her finger and pressed it to her lips, trying to indicate to everyone to be quiet, but no one was looking at her. They were too focused on the imminent threat the Jötnar posed to even look her way. How would she lead them all forward when she couldn't speak?

She had to try something. She couldn't let any more people die.

Kolfinna cleared her mind and filled it with the calmness of the trees stirring in the wind gently, to the stillness of water puddled on the ground after rain, to the coolness of the forest's canopied shade on a hot day—she tried to emulate the strength of her powers. The strength of nature itself. She had to focus on what she could do: get everyone to the doorway. The rest she would figure out when it happened.

Kolfinna clapped her hands. Almost everyone flinched, turning to her as if she were crazy. She placed a finger on her lips. *Silence*, she mouthed.

She pointed to the white tiles. They were safe, she presumed, since they were standing on them. *Safe*, she mouthed. A few confused looks stared back at her. *Safe*, she mouthed again, giving a thumbs-up. Understanding dawned on some of their faces. She pointed to a black tile and shook her head. *Death*, she mouthed, dragging a hand over her neck to gesticulate her point.

There were a few among the crowd who didn't seem afraid. Blár was one of them. Despite the terrifying situation, he was calm and composed, his face seemingly carved from stone. But despite his calmness, there was a hard set to his mouth. Eyfura was trembling, but she was somewhat composed too. As was Mímir.

Maybe they weren't as broken as she thought. They were militarized. She could still read the fear on their faces, but one by one, they rose to their feet, survival and a hardness taking over their sweaty, pale faces. The switch was amazing. They were ready to move forward.

Kolfinna's heart was in her throat, sweat dribbling down the sides of her face. The Jötnar watched with owlish eyes. What if it attacked them anyway? Kolfinna shook the thought out of her head. No, she had to move forward. She willed her lead-laden legs forward and waved everyone to follow her.

The black tiles were scattered beyond the rows of white ones, but Kolfinna jumped to a white one that was about two feet away. She swayed on her feet and sharply turned to the Jötnar. It watched her but didn't move. She jumped to the next closest white tile. Once again, the Jötnar didn't move.

Behind her, Mímir jumped on the white tile, but his foot slipped a bit and his toe touched the green tile right beside him. He quickly pulled his foot back and inhaled sharply, his face contracting in pain. Kolfinna winced. She should've mentioned the green tile was also dangerous.

Truda shot her a dark look, and Kolfinna averted her gaze. Everyone was already on the move, finding their own paths to the doorway at the end of the room. Some were already ahead of her, and others followed behind her. Kolfinna had to focus on the task at hand. Getting to the other side was more important than thinking too much about what others would think. Or how they were faring.

Each tile was about one square foot, so if a white tile was two tiles away, it was a small jump. But if it was three tiles away, it was a bit harder to jump and make sure she didn't tip over and face-plant onto the black or green tiles. And they were everywhere: black and green outnumbered the white.

After a shaky breath, she jumped to the next white one. She held her breath, finding the nearest white. She scanned the tiles and made a viable path in her mind first, since backtracking was hard when there were other people following.

Sweat formed on her brow, a stress headache building in the back of her head as she focused on every jump. Her right leg felt like an anchor every time she moved. She was halfway through her path before she was a dozen feet away from the Jötnar. The next closest was four tiles away, bringing her even closer to the monster. She hesitated. Four tiles away was a big jump. Her headache intensified and she rubbed her sweaty palms on her thighs. The white tile was on an island of black tiles. Failing the jump meant death.

A loud clapping broke her from her concentration. Eyfura was ahead of her by at least half a dozen feet. Eyfura shook her head and pointed to the tiles behind Kolfinna and mouthed, *turn back*. Kolfinna's brows came together; behind her, Truda was occupying the step she had been on.

It would probably be easier to turn back and find a different path instead, but going back meant making a mess of everyone else's paths. Kolfinna mulled it over and shifted her attention back to the tile. She had to jump. It was doable, and it was easier for everyone else this way.

I can do it, she nodded to Eyfura.

No. Eyfura grimaced and she glanced from Kolfinna to the Jötnar.

I can do it, she mouthed again, giving her what she hoped was a reassuring smile.

She readied herself mentally and looked up at the Jötnar. Its eyes were directed at her, its smile grim. She released a shuddering breath and turned back to the tile.

And then, she jumped.

For a split second, she thought she would trip, but she

landed in the center of it. Her feet slid toward the corners and she flailed her arms to balance herself. But she made it. She let out a shaky breath of relief.

Eyfura's hand flew to her chest in relief and her shoulders relaxed. Eyfura looked like she aged ten years in two seconds. She gave her a thumbs-up and moved on. Kolfinna did the same and went forward. It didn't take long for everyone to reach the end of the room by the exit.

There was only one problem: the door was locked.

Truda yanked at the heavy iron handles, but they didn't budge. She turned to Kolfinna sharply, as if to tell her she had lied to them.

They had done what the room had asked, so why—

Kolfinna's heart sank when she noticed the runes above the double doors. *Take the spikes off the Jötnar and place them in order into the appropriate holes.* She hadn't noticed it before, but there were three holes flanking both sides of the door, and now that she looked at the Jötnar more closely, it had exactly six spikes in its body.

Of course it wouldn't be that easy.

But what did it mean by *appropriate* holes? What would happen if she made a mistake?

Kolfinna twisted around until she faced the Jötnar, which still had its predatory gaze on them all. She could feel the weight of everyone's stares; they wanted her to save them all, but she could also tell they didn't trust her.

She would take the spikes off and put them in the holes—alone.

Since they couldn't speak to each other, it was pointless to hope for anyone's help. They also didn't know about which designated hole the spikes went into—granted, neither did she, but she could figure that out.

Before anyone could grab her and try to ask her why the door wouldn't open, she hopped to a white tile. A few of the party members clapped to draw her attention, notably Mímir. His forehead was creased and he clapped incessantly. *What are you doing?* He seemed to say. But Kolfinna pressed forward, jumping to another white tile. The clapping grew louder, as did the sound of boots slapping the hard floor behind her.

She twisted around to find Blár two tiles behind her. His blue eyes were too ... *loud*. His emotions shone harshly in them: the animosity, the mistrust, the murderous nature of his ways. Kolfinna froze, absorbing the coldness that exuded from him. Even without his powers, he had the ability to shrink the room and all its occupants; and even without his icy magic, everything about him was so *cold*.

Kolfinna's breath faltered, as did her step. Why was he following her, and why did he look like that? So angry and mistrusting? She was trying to save them all. Couldn't he have a little faith in her?

She shooed him away, but he remained. Did he not understand? No, that was impossible. But why? Why did he want to follow her? Kolfinna pointed back to the party. *Go,* she mouthed. But he stayed rooted in position.

A million questions swarmed her, but the only logical one was that he was wary of what she was doing. Did he think she was going to leave them all behind? Sabotage them somehow?

Whatever the case, she leaped forward, toward the Jötnar. As she jumped closer to it, the clapping dwindled into silence. When she was three tiles away from it, the smell of it hit her. It was an acrid, rancid, decaying smell. It hit her like a mace, smashing into her until it was hard to breathe. Up close, the Jötnar was even more hideous. Its skin was shiny and slick with an oiliness. Bits of flesh clung to the gaps between its pointy teeth and there was another ribbon of flesh that had fallen from its mouth and was lying on one of the spikes. Blood coated its teeth and dribbled out of its mouth.

Her stomach churned at the thought that these pieces of flesh had been her companions.

Kolfinna reached for the nearest spike with trembling hands. The Jötnar peered at her as she wrapped her fingers around the warm, black metal. Its mouth opened and it hissed, flecks of blood spattering across her cheeks. She gasped and released the spike, taking an involuntary step back. But Blár's hand was on her lower back in an instant, stopping her. She realized with a start that she almost stepped onto a black tile. And the Jötnar noticed too because its smile widened.

Blár saved her, *again*. Heat rose to her cheeks in embarrassment, but she pushed that thought away as she focused on the spike. It was plain, long, and had a pointed end. Nothing about it was extraordinary. She grabbed it once more, her fingers curling over it. It yanked out easily, as if she were pulling a knife out of a slab of butter. The Jötnar screamed and her entire body flinched, waiting for the attack to come.

It never did.

The Jötnar watched her as she held the spike in her quivering hands. It was heavier than she thought it would be. She twisted it in her hands and noticed the number *two* etched in runes on the side of it. That must've meant something.

For a second, she thought she had to take it back to the doorway and retrieve each spike, one by one. But a better idea sprang to mind when she looked at Blár.

She held out the spike to him. He tilted his head to the side in confusion but took the spike anyway. Unlike Kolfinna's arms, which had bent at the weight of it, he hardly budged at all. Kolfinna moved a tile over and grabbed the second spike off the Jötnar's body. It pulled away with ease, and another scream emitted from it.

A ribbon of flesh slid off the spike and slapped the floor. Kolfinna's stomach dropped and she swallowed the bile rising up her throat. The Jötnar's claw grazed Kolfinna's arm as it shot out and snatched the piece of meat. Kolfinna held her breath, watching as it devoured it hungrily. Sweat rolled off her and dampened her hands to the point that she almost dropped the spike.

Kolfinna turned to Blár, who took it expressionlessly. Slowly, they rounded the Jötnar and Kolfinna removed the spikes, handing them to Blár. The weight didn't seem to bother him, but by the sixth spike, he broke out into a sweat. Kolfinna reached for one of his, but he shook his head and headed toward the rest of the party. Her heart tightened with unexpected warmth. Why didn't he let her carry any? It couldn't be chivalry; there must've been an ulterior motive. There had to be because Blár Vilulf was anything but chivalrous.

They made it back to the door wordlessly. Blár held the spikes, and she went to the holes. There had to be a reason each spike had a number on it. As she thought, inside each hole was a number. Relief pooled in her chest. This made sense!

She took one of the spikes from Blár's hand and aligned it with its appropriate number. She slid it into the hole and it clicked in place. Kolfinna smiled. This wasn't so hard. She moved to take another spike, but Mímir already grabbed one, seemingly keen to help.

Kolfinna opened her mouth to say something, to tell him to *stop*, but the Jötnar's gluttonous, oily profile in her peripheral silenced her. She clapped her hands loudly to get his attention and snatched the spike from him when she drew near.

Mímir seemed to understand because he backed away as she went to work. When she slid the last spike into its hole, a hissing click sounded at the doorway. Kolfinna scrambled toward the handles and placed her shaking hands on them. *Please*. She begged. *Please open.* She didn't want to stay a second longer with that monster.

Her prayers came true as the door creaked open.

"Thank go—" one of the soldiers, Eyjarr, accidentally whispered.

Kolfinna's eyes widened and the Jötnar screamed, lurching forward. Without thinking, Kolfinna shoved him through the doorway and sprang inside herself. Everyone spilled out of the room while the Jötnar screamed, its claw slamming the floor where Eyjarr had been.

"Close the door! Close the door!" Kolfinna screamed, crawling further away from the room.

The Jötnar screamed again from the open doorway, but it didn't pass through, its beady eyes narrowed in fury. Mímir slammed the door shut behind him loudly.

For a moment, it was hard to do anything but stare at the door, as if the Jötnar would come crashing through it. Kolfinna's body shook with adrenaline and she ran a shaky hand over her face.

That was close.

All at once, everyone released a breath of air.

Kolfinna took notice of the room they had entered. Torn paintings hung on the walls, various broken statues littered the carpeted floors, which were splattered with who-knows-what, and moss covered the pillars in the rooms. There was nothing out of the ordinary compared to the previous rooms. Light spilled from an open doorway to another room that, from the outside looking in, was more spacious and must've had many windows with how brightly lit it was.

"That was intense," Eyfura breathed. "Gosh."

Eyjarr stumbled back against a broken statue of a man,

and it crashed to the floor, where it splintered and white chunks of it sprayed the grimy floor. Eyjarr's body racked back and forth and Kolfinna realized he was crying. He was a robust man and although he had appeared easily spooked these past two days, Kolfinna hadn't expected him to openly bawl. A sturdy, manly man like him?

"Oh, Eyjarr, it's all right." Eyfura stepped over the sharp edges of the statue pieces and patted Eyjarr's shoulder in a comforting manner, but she looked just as shaken as he did. "I'm sorry."

He cried harder and the discomfort was palpable. Magni stiffened and pursed his lips together. There was a haunted look on everyone's faces. Kolfinna couldn't fault them for being shaken; she felt the same. First it was the draugrs and now the Jötnar. What more was out there for them? But she didn't allow herself to think too much about it. It must've been worse for everyone else; they watched their friends and colleagues die in that room in a gruesome way.

"Pull yourself together," Magni snapped at Eyjarr, who was still sobbing silently.

"Excuse me?" Eyfura's mouth hung open. "Don't say that to him! We've just been through something highly traumatic—"

"And you don't see the rest of us crying!" Magni's nostrils flared and his eyes grew flinty. "He needs to toughen up. Stop your crying and let's move on. You knew this would happen."

"No, we didn't!" Eyjarr bunched his hands into fists.

Tears glistened on his cheeks. "This isn't what we signed up for! What was that over there? It *ate* them! What the hell are we supposed to do against something like that?!"

Magni cringed. "Don't yell at me about that. I don't know how you military folk are trained, but we Royal Guards are trained to be on our toes at all times. So yes, toughen up. You don't like it? Well, you're free to leave where we came from."

"Stop." Mímir placed a hand on Magni's shoulder. "Eyfura is right—"

"Screw you!" Eyjarr shoved Magni and he stumbled against the wall, where an indecipherable decaying painting broke and crumbled to the floor upon impact. A plume of dust rose around him. "Unlike you, I've got kids to look after! I can't die here! And if I could go back, I gladly would!"

"You—" Magni hauled Eyjarr close to him by the collar of his uniform, fire glinting on Magni's free hand.

"Stop, both of you!" Eyfura grabbed Magni's bicep and pulled his fiery hand. "Magni, *stop*! We're supposed to be a team! Fighting amongst ourselves isn't going to solve anything!"

Eyjarr slapped Magni's hand away, breaking his hold on him. "You're lucky she's holding you back, or I'd pummel your face."

"Eyjarr!" Truda's mouth hung open in surprise. "Stop—"

A muscle on Magni's jaw twitched, but Kolfinna noticed he didn't shove Eyfura away from him like she expected him to. "You act like you're the only one who has something to lose. Maybe you should've thought twice before having kids and being in the military. It'll be nobody's fault but your own if you end up dying and making them orphans. Don't have kids if you can't keep yourself alive."

Eyjarr stomped his foot and the uncovered sections of the floor cracked, forming an imprint of his foot. *He's an Enhancer*, Kolfinna realized with a start.

"What did you say?!"

"That's enough!" Truda moved in front of Eyjarr, creating a barrier between the two men. She looked at both of them incredulously. "I understand we're all riled up and shaken at what just happened, but come on! We've been trained better than this!"

"If you both don't stop arguing, I'm going to throw both your asses back in that room." Mímir jabbed a thumb back toward the Jötnar's room. "I don't need men like you making the rest of everyone uneasy. Do I make myself clear?"

Tension roiled in the room, thickening with every passing minute. Finally, Mímir spoke again. "Let's move."

Out of everyone to lead, why did Fenris pick Mímir? Because as much as Kolfinna liked Mímir, there was something about him that felt ... lacking? If Fenris were here, Kolfinna could imagine everyone whipping up into shape and relying on him. He had the kind of personality that made these kinds of situations bearable and doable. Mímir wasn't bringing anyone together, and the anxiety was rising.

Kolfinna cast those thoughts away. She was in no position to question his authority or how the Royal Guards ran things. Maybe this was normal. And even if it wasn't, it wasn't like she knew much about leadership positions.

Kolfinna noticed Eyfura's hand was still on Magni's bicep. Eyfura leaned in closer, her tone low. "I understand you're upset seeing Torsten die like that ... You were close to him and he deserved better than that, I understand how painful that must've been, but we need to stick together. You can't lash out like that—"

"I'm fine," he bit back, shaking her hand away.

"Magni—"

Kolfinna averted her gaze from them and instead found herself watching Blár, who was hanging in the back of the party. Why had he joined her in removing the spikes? Did he not trust her? Was he going to get in her way? What was he trying at? He had helped her, somehow, but there wasn't an ounce of trust in his hateful gaze. Was he going to get in her way later on? Was he going to resume the "cat and mouse" game?

Everyone filed into the next room, but Kolfinna hung back and tapped Blár's shoulder. He was about to step through the threshold, but he stopped, glancing down at her. A draft sent shivers down her body.

Wintry blue eyes narrowed at her. "What?"

"Why—" Her voice caught in her throat as a sudden rush of mana surrounded the room. As if in slow motion, she looked at Blár and then at everyone else, who were already in the next room, mere steps away from them. No one seemed to notice until it was too late.

A gong boomed through the air.

The floor shook, and then she slipped as the walls disappeared. Kolfinna couldn't breathe. Her body felt like it was being pulled at every angle. Her head felt like it would burst, like there was too much information for her to process and it would squeeze out from every orifice in her body. She opened her mouth to scream, but nothing came out. Only blackness filled her vision. She clawed her neck for air, she fought to scream, flail, do something—but she was suspended in black space, unable to move.

Finally, her body slammed into something and the breath was finally knocked into her. She gasped, coughing and clutching her chest before a searing light blinded her. She squinted, blinked, and then gasped again. The sun shone down on her, and a warm wave blew against her, sending sand against her skin.

Kolfinna's blood ran cold.

There was sand, and more sand, and rocks, and boulders, but mostly just sand. Kolfinna found it hard to breathe, her body suddenly trembling. It had happened again. They were somewhere else. And it wasn't in their world because there were *two* suns in the sky.

And unlike last time when the whole party was with her, the only one beside her was Blár, who appeared just as stunned as she was. He pushed himself to his knees and turned his head left and right, his mouth slightly ajar, but he quickly screwed it shut and rose to his feet, his face growing stony.

"Damn it," he muttered, looking down at his hands.

Once again, Kolfinna didn't feel the pull of her mana.

Kolfinna wanted to throw up. Not only was she in a different world, but she was also with the last person she ever wanted to be with.

13

WHEN KOLFINNA WAS WITH THE PARTY, SHE could pretend Blár wasn't her constant nightmare. Honestly, she hadn't felt the numbing fear of being around him when she was with the Royal Guards and the soldiers. But now that they were alone, it came crashing back to her. Every fiber of her being screamed at her to run away. Her right leg felt stiffer, heavier, and cold despite the scorching heat.

Blár dusted his pants distractedly with a hand, the muscles on his jaw clenching. In the harsh sunlight, it was easier to see all the imperfections blotting his usually handsome, albeit intimidating, appearance: the purple bruise on his cheek, the dirt and grime coating his skin, the dried blood and sweat greasing his hair and smudging his neck. Not to mention his now worn-out uniform, which had tears and blood splatters all over it. It was hard to imagine that all these changes happened within two days. Kolfinna didn't want to think about how terrible she looked. Her wavy hair had transformed into a ratted nest, dirt and blood clung beneath her nails, and she stank of rotted fish and sweat—thanks to the ship incident. Her own uniform was torn in odd places here and there, the torn sections accompanied by a blooming of dried, stained blood. Not to mention she was missing a sleeve from when Eyfura cut it off.

"Where are we?" Blár shielded his eyes to peer at the sky. "Why are there two suns?"

Why did the castle ruins do such a thing? It was indeed a magical place, because how else would they be thrown in such a situation? How was it possible to teleport someone to another ... world? Dimension? Kolfinna couldn't help but shake at the thought of it. If other worlds existed, what did that mean for her world? Was this world even real? It definitely felt real. But how was any of this possible?

A roar resounded in the distance, booming across the landscape and causing sand to quiver in the air. Powerful mana radiated and blasted like a shockwave. Kolfinna fell to her knees, her body tensing. Even Blár flinched in surprise.

She had been so dazed by the bright suns and the sand that she had forgotten monsters existed. Who was to say there weren't monsters here in this area? Kolfinna clambered to her feet, but there was nothing around them but sand and rocks.

"We don't know when monsters will come," she said quickly. "We have to—"

Her mind went blank. What did they have to do?

"We have to ...? What?" Blár raised a dark eyebrow.

That was right. They needed to find the runes that would set them free.

"Rune magic," she finished, scanning their surroundings. "I need to find the rune magic."

Every turn she took, she was met with mounds of golden sand. From her peripheral, she became more and more aware that Blár was blatantly staring at her. She avoided his gaze and put more attention on sensing her surroundings, but she could barely pay attention to the dull sand, the sharp rocks, and soft blue sky. His scrutiny was blazing, even hotter than the two desert suns above her. She stared harder in the distance, where mountains of sand etched the horizon.

When there was nothing more to look at, she finally braved a glance back at him. His face was a blank canvas, betraying no emotion, but there was a spark in his eyes she didn't like.

Her lips pursed together. "What?"

"You wanted to tell me something before we were"— he struggled to find the word, waving his hand—"*warped* here."

"I did," she said, remembering how she had wanted to ask him why he had helped her. Why he was pretending to be chivalrous. What his ulterior motives were. But without everyone's presence, she felt she couldn't ask him out loud. "It doesn't really matter anymore."

"What is it?"

"I said it doesn't matter."

"On the contrary, I believe it does matter."

Kolfinna clenched her fists together. "Why do you say that?"

"Because it has to do with me. So I have a right to know, don't I?" Blár inched closer and glowered at her, as if he wanted her to vanish on the spot. "So, what is it? What was so important that you wanted to pull me aside and tell me?"

What did he mean he had the *right* to know? Was he one of those people who had to know anything and everything concerning them? Kolfinna couldn't hide the irritation on her face.

"Stop with this childishness," she said, walking past him. "We have other things to worry about."

"You're really annoying, you know that?"

"*I'm* annoying? You're the one who keeps badgering me!" She placed a hand on her hip. "I've done nothing but keep quiet and follow orders. You're the one who's—" Her words faltered on her lips. What exactly had he done? Other than following orders, scowling, and showing off how strong he was, he hadn't done anything atrocious.

"We really don't have time to argue right now," she finally declared, spinning on her heels so he wouldn't see the embarrassment flushing her cheeks. "Anything can attack us at any moment."

"What was it that you wanted to tell me?" His expression hardened. "I don't think you would want to talk to me unless it was something important."

Kolfinna waved her hand dismissively. "How many times do I have to tell you that it doesn't matter? Are you *that* curious?"

"Yes, I'm *that* curious." Blár took a step closer to her, his tall figure casting a shadow over her. "Why would you want to talk to me? I see the way you're around me. You *fear* me. You cower when I'm around you. And you dislike me. I can see all of that. So, it really piques my interest when you decide to pull me aside and have a private conversation with me."

She felt her cheeks blossom with color. "I don't fear you." She avoided the coldness in his eyes and focused on her boots, which had dried blood smeared over the toe cap. "And I definitely don't cower."

"Oh, please. You're always shivering whenever I get too close." Blár laughed, but there wasn't a hint of laughter in his eyes. He pointed to her leg and a malicious intent glimmered in his expression. "I'm not faulting you. I get it. I skewered you."

Kolfinna's hands bunched together and she had the urge to smack him across the face. Maybe she should've done it, since he couldn't use his powers anyway, but he had proven himself to be strong even without his powers —strong enough to overpower her.

"You're a monster," she hissed. "All you have is your power. And now that it's gone, you're useless."

Even without his icy powers, the temperature dropped as his face darkened. A muscle on his jaw clenched. "The pot calling the kettle black." He chuckled shortly. "You've only ever relied on your powers. I've been watching you. Without your powers, you can't do shit. You don't know how to fight and you're clumsy on your feet. You think you can best me in a fight? I'm twice your size, and I can fight without my magic."

"You think everything is a fight," she snapped. "I said you were useless, not that I can beat you."

"Then what does that make you? Someone *even more* useless?"

A roar in the distance interrupted their conversation. Kolfinna shuddered and almost fell to her knees. The mana was so immense that her ears rang. Her gaze followed the horizon, where the puffy white clouds had separated from the boom of the roar, but there was no monster there. Goose bumps rose on her arms and the back of her neck; whatever was out there, it was terrifyingly strong. And close.

"I really don't have time to argue with you." Kolfinna cast her attention on her surroundings, trying to pinpoint the runes. "I don't intend to die by whatever is making that noise. Oh, and in case you forgot, you're at *my* mercy."

"What?"

It probably wasn't a good idea to provoke him: he was a monster in his own right. But the undiluted anger and hatred from the past year overcame her better judgment.

She wanted him to feel a sliver of the fear she had when she faced him. And now the tables were turned.

"You can't do anything without your magic," Kolfinna murmured, relishing in how his eyes narrowed. She had struck a nerve. "I can read the runes. If I decide to let you die, then you die."

Blár grabbed the collar of her uniform and yanked her close until she was inches away from him. The smell of vanilla, spice, and sweat assaulted her nose. She was on her tiptoes, and his grip was like iron. "Do not provoke me, fae," he said through clenched teeth.

Blár released her and she stumbled a few feet back, her arms flailing as she regained her balance. It was infuriating how much stronger he was than her. What could she do to reach his level?

"Asshole," she muttered, dusting her clothes with trembling hands.

Kolfinna shifted her attention back to finding the runes. For a few seconds, she stood still, scanning the sands, before she felt the tiny pull of mana. She followed that pull of mana to a rock in the distance. There was nothing extraordinary about it, but she felt that there was something powerful on it. Runes, most likely.

Without waiting for Blár, she jogged to the location. She could hear him following behind her, and a part of her couldn't help but smirk. He needed her. He knew that, and she knew that. It must've infuriated him to rely on her. She didn't peg him as the kind of person to rely on anyone but himself.

When she reached the rock—upon closer inspection it was more of a boulder, since it was half her size—sure enough, shimmering runes were inscribed into it. It said in simple words, *Slay the dreki; magic does not work.*

The dreki? Was that what was making all that noise? Her blood ran cold and she reread the sentence. How were they supposed to slay it without their powers?

"What does it say?" Blár asked.

Kolfinna ignored him and brushed a hand over the runes. There had to be something else written there. Some clue to help them kill the dreki, because there was no way she could fight without her powers. They didn't even have weapons.

"Well?" His tone grew more annoyed and he kicked a rock the size of a small animal to the side as if it weighed nothing. It plopped into the sand. "What does it say?"

"Wouldn't you like to know."

"Stop." He slammed a fist against the boulder, his body positioned in her direction. "Weren't you the one saying we should work together?"

"No." Kolfinna stared at the silver clasp of his cloak, and then at the dried blood on the collar of his uniform shirt, and lastly at the column of his neck. And then she met his icy blue eyes. "You rejected the idea of me working with you. You said you didn't trust me. And that you wanted me to leave the mission."

His lips thinned down. "I've saved your ass plenty of times."

"That doesn't negate what you said. You told me you

wanted to continue our little cat-and-mouse game, and that you wanted me out of the mission. You said it clearly before we left. You threatened me and then tried to attack me with your ice."

Blár hesitated and for a moment, she feared he would tell her he didn't remember, or that it never happened. She wouldn't have expected anything less from him. But he muttered, "I was wrong."

Kolfinna blinked. Had she heard right? "You ... were wrong?"

"Yes. Now what does it say?"

"No." She couldn't help the grin that twitched at the ends of her lips. "You said you were wrong. You should apologize as well."

"You're being as stubborn as this ugly-ass rock." He slapped the rock to emphasize his point. "Now just tell me. What does it say?"

"That doesn't sound like an apology."

"I still haven't heard a thank you."

"Excuse me?"

"I saved you multiple times throughout the two days." A sheen of sweat dampened his forehead. "If you want me to apologize, you have to say thank you first."

"No."

"Then you won't get an apology."

"And *you* won't know what *this* says." Kolfinna pointed to the rock with the runes before pushing past him.

It was foolish to exclude him—she wouldn't be able to

accomplish her goal without him, and vice versa. But she wanted to feel … *something*. To hear him apologize. To have him acknowledge her. To acknowledge all the pain, fear, and anger she had felt the past year because of him. To have some sort of *power* over him.

After trudging forth for a moment, she paused. How was she going to defeat the dreki? What even was it? They didn't have any weapons on them, and they couldn't use their magic. Dread built in the pit of her stomach. If it was as powerful as the last creature they faced, they would die.

"What is it this time?"

"Nothing," she said quietly. The stubborn part of her didn't want to cave in and tell him, but the logical side wanted to do exactly that. Two heads were better than one. And they needed to work together to get out of there.

"It doesn't look like nothing."

Her right leg dragged behind her, reminding her what he had done to her. "It's nothing," she said, louder this time.

"What the hell is your problem?" Blár yanked her uninjured shoulder and violently twirled her around until she was facing him. His brows were pulled together in an angry V, and there was a winter storm brewing in his icy eyes. Rage rolled off his body and her courage quickly withered at the sight of him. He was absolutely *livid*.

"W-What?" Kolfinna slapped his hand away. She couldn't hide the tremor in her voice. "There's nothing wrong with me—"

"Yes, there is! We're supposed to work together! Now tell me what's going on."

"N-No—"

He glared at her. "Tell. Me."

She opened her mouth to say something—she wasn't even sure what she was going to say—but an earsplitting roar broke her thoughts. She cupped her hands over her ears, her body instinctively curling within itself as the enormous mana blasted through the air. She turned toward the sound, and she truly forgot to breathe. Because on the horizon, she saw it.

The dreki was at least fifty times their size; it was larger than a few houses combined. Glossy black and blue scales covered the entirety of its body, and it seemed to draw the suns away from it. Large skeletal wings kept it upright, each flap sending a gust of wind to blow away sand hills. Even from the distance, its teeth were visible and bared, as if ready to chomp. It cried again, and everything shook.

It was the same creature they had seen in the lobby of the ruins; except this time, it wasn't simply a statue.

Kolfinna went white with terror. Her legs felt like lead, and she turned to Blár, who was just as stunned as she was. Without thinking, she found herself grasping his hand.

"R-Run," she croaked.

It was the first time Kolfinna had seen Blár so wide-eyed. The weight of the situation dawned on her. They needed to get far away from it because there was no way they could defeat it at their current level.

"Run!" she screamed.

Kolfinna released his hand, spun, and shot in the opposite direction of the dreki. Her heart felt like it would burst out of her chest, and not from exertion. Adrenaline and fear pumped through her veins. How were they supposed to beat *that*? It was impossible without their powers. And even if they had their powers, she had never seen something that monstrously large or with that much mana.

The dreki roared and picked up speed, rushing toward them. Kolfinna's feet sank into the sand with every stride she took. Her calves burned with exertion. Blár was already ahead of her; his speed picked up and his strides grew wider. Kolfinna struggled to maintain her speed, her right leg dragging behind her painfully, the stiff muscles resisting. She was no match against him or the dreki.

"Come on! Haven't you ever run before?" Blár shouted over his shoulder.

"I can't run like you, remember?!" Her scream was ripped away with another roar from the dreki, and whatever else she wanted to add dissipated on her lips. She gasped large mouthfuls of air. She couldn't waste her energy on talking.

Blár slowed down and captured her hand in his, wrenching her forward. Her feet sank into the sandy ground. She had no idea where they were headed. All there was in front of them was sand and more sand. But farther ahead—too far ahead—was a rocky area with what looked like a small, cavernous opening. Blár seemed to notice too, because he shifted toward it.

The dreki breathed and fire stung her back. Kolfinna glanced behind her shoulder. That was a mistake because its ruby eyes zeroed in on her. It was twenty meters away, its wings flapping and a swirl of sand dusting off its feet and claws.

"F-Faster!" she screamed, trying to run with all her speed. Her arm felt like it would rip from its socket as Blár yanked her forward. It must've been killing him to keep a slower pace because of her, and yet he did. If he ran too fast and dragged her, there was the chance of her falling. If she fell, the dreki would catch her. They both seemed to know that fact.

Kolfinna felt the wind from the dreki inhaling behind them. The cave was closer. It roared again, the sand trembling with the shockwaves. Kolfinna stared at the cave—it was close. Just a bit more.

A loud inhale sounded behind them and fire shot from its mouth. Just as the fire was about to hit them, Blár wrapped Kolfinna in his arms and dove into the rocks. They crashed into the opening of the cave, and fire blasted against the entrance. Kolfinna crawled deeper into the opening, but it was shallow. She pressed her back against the wall of it, and Blár threw himself after her.

Fire continued blowing into the opening, but it was a few feet away from them. The dreki cried and landed in front of the opening, slamming its wings against the cave. Kolfinna squeezed herself against the wall.

Leave, she prayed. *Please!*

It shrieked so piercingly that debris and pebbles fell onto their heads with the reverberations. Then, after a moment of ramming its wings against the cave and jumping on it, it sprang up into the sky. Kolfinna's hands were pressed against her mouth the entire time, as if breathing would make it return. It felt like ages before either of them moved.

"W-What was *that*?" Blár breathed.

"The ... the dreki ..."

"The what?"

"The dreki." She hugged her elbows to herself as the adrenaline ebbed away.

"You know what that thing was?" He pointed to the mouth of the cave, his eyes narrowing. "Did the runes say something about it?"

Her voice was small. "Yes."

"That would've been very freakin' helpful to know."

"The only thing the runes said was that we have to defeat it, and that magic doesn't work." Kolfinna shrugged as if it wasn't a big deal, but flinched as pain rocked her injured shoulder. She bit her bottom lip to keep from crying out loud. "We already figured out the latter. Whether you knew or not wouldn't have prepared you."

"You were fighting with me the whole time," he accused. "We could've, I don't know, run away sooner if you had told me!"

"*You* were fighting with me too!" Kolfinna jabbed a finger at his chest. The darkness of the cave obscured half his face, but she could still see the anger carving his features. "I was going to tell you anyway, if only you apologized first! Why is that so hard for you? To admit you were wrong and to apologize?!"

"I already admitted I was wrong!"

"But you didn't apologize!"

"Who the hell cares for that?"

"I do!" She threw her hands up but cursed loudly when her injured shoulder throbbed painfully, the stitches likely coming undone. She doubled over and tears formed in her eyes from pain. Her voice lowered. "I freaking do!"

"You should put your personal feelings aside and focus on the mission! You should've told me about that-that-*that thing*!"

"I didn't know anything about it either!"

Blár pushed himself off the wall and winced. He fumbled with the clasp of his cloak and quickly undid it, letting it fall in a heap around his feet. He pressed a hand on the wall and tried looking over his shoulder at his back. Kolfinna sucked in sharply as she realized the back of Blár's uniform was burnt in some places, revealing red, peeling skin. The cloak had protected him to some degree, but it wasn't enough. Was that when he grabbed her and threw himself, along with her, into the cave?

Her chest swelled and her throat closed up. Now she looked like a brat withholding information and throwing a tantrum.

"Are you okay?" she asked tentatively.

"I'm fine," he bit out. "More importantly, anything else I should know?"

She flicked a pebble away from her. "No."

Why did he protect her? He should've just let her get burned a little. She didn't want to feel gratitude. It was easier to hate him. Was this the third time he had saved her? She didn't want to keep track anymore.

They stayed that way for hours, staring at the opening of the cave and watching the suns dip into the horizon until an orange glow lit the dunes. Then it darkened completely.

"We should probably head out," Blár said. "It looks like it left for good. It probably sleeps at this time."

"No." Kolfinna rolled a jagged pebble in her hand before tossing it into the opening. "Who knows if it's just waiting out there for us? And besides, we're both injured and tired. Let's sleep and eat for a bit."

"Sleep?" His eyebrows skyrocketed. "And eat?"

"Yes."

"Eat what?" He spread his hand out to the small cave, which was only big enough for them so long as they were huddled. It was completely empty, the ground cool but dusted with grainy sand.

"We have food ..." she trailed, realizing with a start that her pack was missing. Did she drop it before they were transported here? Blár also didn't have his pack.

"We have no food." Blár raked a hand through his inky strands and cursed loudly.

"Let's at least sleep."

"Sleep? Here?" He laughed harshly. "You're just asking for something to come and kill us. We have no idea what's out there! We can't just sleep. We need to move, find shelter and food, and find a way to kill that thing."

"We have shelter." Her face was growing redder by the second. He was treating her like a child. "We need to rest, or else we'll burn out! Maybe you don't know because you're a black rank, but normal people have to sleep and recuperate! And besides, I doubt we can see anything out there with how dark it is."

"Then *you* can sleep. I'll wait it out."

"Gladly." She turned away from him and lay on the ground, positioning herself so her back was to him.

"You can't seriously be going to sleep."

"I am."

"We need to move!"

"No."

He cursed again and then again. His words drowned away as she thought about Eyfura and the rest of the party. Where were they? Had they also been teleported here? Or were they still in the ruins? Wherever they were, how were they going to fare in the ruins without her? A jumble of thoughts streamed through her mind until she slowly drifted away to slumber.

14

"*Help them. Please.*"

The desperate, feminine voice startled Kolfinna awake. She jerked upright and then hissed in pain as her shoulder ached. She tried to grasp onto the ends of the dream, but it receded in the back of her mind.

Morning light spilled into the cave. How long had she slept? Beside her, Blár sat with his head propped against one of the cavernous walls, his eyes sealed shut. His chest rose and fell rhythmically. When he slept, he appeared younger and less harsh than his usual self. But even in sleep, his brows were twined together into a soft scowl.

So much for keeping watch. Hadn't he thrown a fit about not sleeping since anything could attack them?

Kolfinna winced when she stretched her arms and legs. Her injured arm and shoulder were stiff, the padding seeped with blood. She felt a dry, crusty feeling on her back when she moved. Most likely her wound had opened during their run. She wasn't as refreshed as she would've liked, but that could've just been the stress talking.

Blár didn't move in the slightest, even when she drew closer so she could take a better look at his face. He was extraordinarily handsome, which was more apparent now that he wasn't glaring, shouting crude things, or trying to kill her. His lashes were long and black against his pale skin, and his hair was silken and glossy. She wanted to run her fingers through it, but she didn't dare. He was a beautiful monster, after all.

Before she could think anything stupid and unlike her, she tapped his face lightly. When he didn't stir, she slapped him a little harder. He flinched and his icy eyes fluttered open in confusion.

"Wake up," she said, her voice still gruff from sleep.

"Did you"—he rubbed his cheek—"Did you slap me?"

"No."

He narrowed his eyes, but Kolfinna was already talking before he could ask anything else. "I thought you said we shouldn't sleep."

Blár frowned. "I said that, but I never said I *wasn't* tired." He stifled a yawn before stretching his arms. He grimaced and keeled over his knees, his teeth gritting together. Like her, his wounds probably ached. He breathed out deeply and slowly straightened, his jaw tightening in pain. "You were out cold. Drooling and all."

Her eyes widened. Drooling? "You're lying."

"No, I'm not."

Blár watched her with a raised eyebrow as a blush stained her cheeks and neck. How embarrassing! And she had been sure to position herself so he couldn't look at her.

As if reading her thoughts, Blár spoke, "You rolled over and grabbed my arm."

"No—"

"You were hugging me."

Kolfinna thought her eyes would pop out of their sockets. Her whole body erupted in waves of fire and she shook her head. "That's impossible!"

"Unfortunately, no." He was calm—*too calm*. As if it didn't bother him.

"You ... you're joking."

"I'm not." This time, he smirked.

Kolfinna couldn't mask her horror and audibly gasped. She was *hugging* Blár Vilulf in her sleep? The mere thought was bizarre and preposterous. She hated the man! Her own body had betrayed her. Now that she thought about it, as a child, she always woke up clinging to Katla when they used to sleep in the same bed together.

"Let's get a move on." He sighed. "I highly doubt yesterday was our only run-in with that *thing*."

Right. She needed to focus on the matter at hand: the dreki. Kolfinna pushed all her embarrassments to the side and straightened at once. The dreki was a creature they knew nothing about. Even the magic beasts were nothing like this.

"Have you ever seen anything like that?" she asked as

she poked her head out of the cave. She squinted in the early morning light but didn't see anything except sand and rocks, the same as yesterday. Not even insects buzzed around. It was dreadfully silent, save for the howl of the wind. "Or any of the monsters we've encountered?"

"No." He joined her and scanned the horizon. "The magic beasts I've encountered aren't as big or as powerful. Magic beasts are just animals that have mana. *But* I've heard of stories about beasts that look like that. Depends on where you go. It's regional, I think. Those dogs we saw, for instance—that wasn't too strange. The closer you get to the Great Divide, however, the weirder the magic beasts get. But those walking dead looking corpses from that ship? No way in hell have I ever seen or heard anything like that."

The two suns greeted Kolfinna when she stepped out of the cave. A gust of wind blew sand into her eyes and she blinked away the grittiness. Blár's cloak lashed against her thighs with the wind. He shifted the corner of it so it didn't strike her, and she momentarily felt her cheeks warm at the small gesture.

"We'll die by starvation and thirst, or from that monster." Kolfinna's stomach growled loudly as they trekked in a random direction.

"Don't talk like that." Blár's tone was harsh. "You're not dying out here. And neither am I."

"Are you trying to console me?" Kolfinna fought the wry smile twitching her lips. If someone had told her a year ago that Blár Vilulf would attempt to comfort her in any way, she would've lost her mind. But then again, maybe she was losing her mind because she couldn't help but think he wasn't *that* bad of a person.

"No way." He ran a hand through his tousled hair. "I'm the last person you should go to for consolation."

Kolfinna's throat dried up and they continued for a few minutes. The sun relentlessly beat down on them. "We need water," she said quietly. "Food is important, but water is more important."

"I know."

"Maybe we should find a source of water first."

"We don't even know if there's any water out there."

"We can't just give up."

"I didn't say that."

They walked in silence for a while, their boots sinking into the sand. Kolfinna's thighs, calves, and butt burned with exertion from trudging through the sand. She had never pushed her body to the limit, but it sure felt like she was reaching a limit. Not to mention her body was littered with bruises and wounds. To make matters worse, the beating rays of the suns seemed bent on peeling her skin away.

Kolfinna leaned down and rubbed her aching right leg. All that running made the soles of her foot, her ankle, and her calf throb like it was half-broken again.

"Are you okay?"

"Hm?" She raised her head to look up at him.

"Your leg ..." Blár stared at her and an unreadable look flitted over his face.

"What about it?"

"It's ... I really did that, huh?"

She rolled her eyes. "Screw you."

"I didn't mean that in a smug way—"

"Screw you, nonetheless." Kolfinna waved to her leg. "Thanks to you, my leg is messed up permanently. I don't care which way you meant it. Thanks to you, I can't run like you, or walk fast, or be on my feet for too long without being in excruciating pain—"

"You're full of sunshine early in the morning."

"Screw you."

"You also get a lot of nightmares." Blár didn't look at her.

Ice ran through her veins and she couldn't look him straight in the eye. Did she have a nightmare about him last night? Did he know that he killed her in her dreams?

"What's that?" Blár shielded his eyes from the sun and squinted in the distance.

From far away, it appeared to be a boulder nestled in a spread of other boulders. But then it twitched. And Kolfinna realized, in horror, that it was the exact thing they were running from. Blár's eyes widened and they both exchanged glances; they needed to run, again.

Neither waited another second before spinning around and running in the opposite direction. They ran, but Kolfinna wondered if it was useless. They had to fight it at some point, didn't they? Without her powers, she was unable to do anything. She had kept her powers hidden for *years*, but she had known that if she was thrown into any dire situation, she'd be able to fight her way through it. But here, all she could do was run.

She was so utterly powerless.

She refused to die in a place like this, but what else could they do against the dreki? Maybe if they had weapons, they could stand a chance. But as they were, what could they do? And what *should* they do?

They ran for what felt like forever, and it wasn't until they couldn't see the dreki in the distance that they finally slowed down to a trot. Both breathed heavily, but Kolfinna was noticeably more out of breath than he was.

"D-Don't you have—" Kolfinna wheezed, hands on her knees as she gasped for breath. Sweat dribbled down her neck and pooled around her chest and back. "A weapon?"

Blár raked a hand through his sweat-dampened hair. "Why would I need a weapon? It'll only be more weight to carry."

"Why?" She narrowed her eyes accusingly at him, as if it was his fault they were weaponless. "Maybe because you're a soldier? Don't the military carry weapons?"

Blár wiped the sweat pouring down his forehead with his sleeve. "I can say the same to you. You Royal Guards always have swords on you. Where's yours?" He waved at her hips, where there was no sword whatsoever. There was a hardness in his tone. The kind of hardness that made her flinch. "Also, in case you forgot, I don't need an ornamental weapon. Because that's all it'll ever be on me —ornamental."

"In case you didn't realize, I'm not a Royal Guard!"

"I *know* you're not a Royal Guard, but you're *with* them, so they should've given you one."

"I'm hoping to become one, but I'm not one of them." She waved to her dark uniform, which was so different from the white uniform the Royal Guards wore. "In case you didn't notice, I'm not dressed like a Royal Guard."

"Huh, I didn't notice," he said sarcastically. "And I guess they didn't bother giving you a training sword either?"

"A training sword?"

"All Royal Guard trainees have one. Where's yours?"

"I ... I didn't receive one," Kolfinna whispered so quietly that she was sure he didn't hear her. Why had she not received a sword? All the Royal Guards had swords, but she hadn't given it much thought.

"What?"

Kolfinna straightened. "I forgot it."

"How—" He pinched the bridge of his nose and sighed. "You know what, it doesn't change anything. Let's just keep moving."

"Keep moving where exactly?" She waved at the hills of sand.

"I don't know. Somewhere." Blár jabbed a thumb in the direction they had come from. "Anywhere away from that monster."

"What can we even do without our powers?" she whispered.

"We can do *something*."

"But what? What exactly can we do? How are we going to kill that thing?" She swallowed the lump that was forming in her throat. She saw the desperation of their situation more clearly in the light of day. There was a high probability they would die. How could they survive against that thing? "Oh, man," she whispered. "We're going to die."

Kolfinna's throat constricted and her chest tightened, as if a giant rope was wrapping around her lungs and squeezing the life out of them. An unbearable weight crushed her shoulders. There was no way they could survive against the dreki.

She would die.

She breathed in deeply, her vision darkening as the realization hit her.

Tears sprang in her eyes. She didn't want to die. She really, *really* didn't want to die.

Her whole life had been about survival. She never had a moment's rest. It was always go, go, go—survive no matter what. Deep down, she always had confidence that she could make it out of any situation because unlike Katla, she wasn't scared to use her magic if she had to.

"Get a hold of yourself." Blár grabbed her by the shoulders and shook her. The pain from her injured shoulder brought her back to reality. "Breathe."

She inhaled shakily before exhaling. For a few minutes, she simply breathed.

Kolfinna squeezed her eyes shut. She didn't like

showing her emotions so wildly like this, but she wasn't sure how to mask her fear of death.

"We'll get through this." Blár released her gingerly. There was a softness in his gaze—a look she didn't like. As if he was obligated to take care of her. As if he saw her as human.

It didn't suit him—this softness. She preferred him crass and crude.

Kolfinna didn't have time to wallow in self-doubt and self-pity. There had to be a way to solve this. If the first two ordeals—the ship and then with the Jötnar— had solutions, then this too must've had a solution. Each of those scenarios had rules and a way to get out. There must've been a catch. Maybe there was something beyond this sandy wasteland? What if there was somewhere they could find weapons? There had to be something.

Or maybe they should try fighting the dreki? Maybe it wasn't as strong as it looked? Or maybe it had a weakness?

"We have two options," she finally settled with. "We can either run away and try to find something to fight the dreki with, or we can try fighting it right now with what we have."

Blár stared at her for a few seconds. "That's it? That's all you came up with?"

Her cheeks flared. "Do you have something better in mind?"

"Fight with what we have?" Blár laughed, ignoring her question. "What do we have, exactly?" He rummaged in his pockets and pulled out crumpled notes and a few paper wrappers. He tossed them to the ground. "Great. Freakin' great."

Kolfinna eyed the things he threw and bent down to pick them up. The note was the sketch of the castle they had been given at the start of the mission. The wrappers, on the other hand, piqued her interest. There was a white, grainy powder on them. Sugar?

"Candy?" she asked.

Blár looked at her like she had lost her mind. "Why are you going through my trash?"

"I was wondering what a black rank would carry around." She tossed the wrappers to the ground. "But was I right?"

He gave her a look that said she was stupid. "Yes."

"I didn't think you would like sweets."

"Okay, what is wrong with you? Why are you talking about this? It's so ... irrelevant? I don't understand."

Maybe she really was losing her mind. Kolfinna held up two fingers. "Which choice do you vote for? Run and find weapons, or fight it head-on?"

He kicked at the ground, a spray of sand and pebbles arcing the air. "Those can't be the only two options."

"I opt for the first one, for at least a day or two. And the reason I say that is because we can't run and search forever. We don't even know what's out there. So, if we don't find anything initially, we'll have to rule out the possibility that there's even anything out here that can aid us."

Blár ran a hand over his face but nodded. "It'll also

give us time to scout for an area to fight it. Because by the looks of it, it'll come find us sooner or later. We'll have an advantage if we choose a good location. But before that, we really need to get water first."

"I think so too."

"I still think there's maybe something more we can do."

"I'm not hearing any suggestions. Just complaints." Kolfinna undid her braid and cringed at how matted her hair had become. She wove her fingers through it distractedly.

Blár glared at her. "Don't you have fae powers? Can't you sense runes or something? I don't know. Maybe there's something out here we can use. Maybe we can escape this place without fighting the dreki."

"I don't think so. I can't really sense much out here. And if there is something, it's not within my range ... And whenever I sense mana, it's the dreki."

"I guess all we can do is just walk now."

Kolfinna turned to look over the vast expanse of golden sand. The wind blew her tangled hair over her face. "I'm sure we'll find something useful."

She truly hoped so.

15

———

THEY WALKED AND WALKED BUT CAME ACROSS nothing but sand and more sand. The horizon stretched with the same scenery. It was as if nothing else existed but that. And they found nothing useful at all. Nothing they could use as weapons, and nowhere they could potentially have a battle with the dreki.

Blár lay on the ground by a cluster of jagged boulders and stones. The harshness of the suns had faded into the night, and more surprising than the sandy environment—where the sand was like hot coals and the suns scorched their skin off—was that it was freezing now that the suns had set. Their breaths puffed in front of them and Kolfinna was grateful she hadn't thrown her cloak aside. How had she not noticed the cold last night? Was she so exhausted that it didn't register to her?

Kolfinna sat cross-legged on one of the smoother rocks and tipped her head back to gaze at the starry sky.

Three moons hung in the black sky, casting soft, shimmery moonbeams across the sand.

"I'm thirsty and hungry."

Kolfinna glanced down at Blár. All the running, the fighting, and arguing seemed to have worn him down. His lips were twisted into his signature scowl, but on the ground with his hair messily kissing the sand, he looked more boyish.

"I'm starving," he repeated with a sigh. "Screw this place."

Kolfinna licked her dry lips. "We just have to move forward and hopefully we'll find something ..."

"I'm gonna skin that bird and eat it," he growled.

"Bird?" She raised her brows. "You mean the dreki?"

"Yeah, that bastard."

"It looked more like a lizard than a bird."

"Doesn't change anything." Blár pulled his cloak tighter around himself like a blanket. "Why is it so cold?"

"I thought you liked the cold."

"No." Blár rolled his eyes as if she had said something stupid. "I mean, I don't dislike the cold, but just because my powers are ice doesn't mean I love the cold. Or that I'm immune to it." He closed his eyes, the moonlight glistening on his black hair. "Man, if only I could use my powers. I'd skewer that bird so quick."

"We wouldn't be in this state if that were the case." She dragged a finger over the grooves and fissures of the rock she sat on. She reached for a thread of mana in the stones, something to help her manipulate it, but she felt nothing. The emptiness within her widened. She missed feeling the pull of life in the stones, in the surrounding nature—she had taken that feeling for granted. When she hid her magic, she had at least still been able to feel the life force of nature around her. Now she was just an abyss of nothing, her connection to everything severed. "Your ice powers ... aren't they weak in hot weather?"

"No." He shrugged, though the movement was awkward since he was lying down. "My ice is stronger than typical ice. It doesn't melt like regular ice. It's fortified with my mana, after all. So, the weather doesn't necessarily make it weaker ... But if I'm being honest, I'm stronger in cold climates. It's easier to make more ice. However, I wouldn't say I'm weaker in hot weather. I guess ... I don't know. Even if I do get weaker, it's such a minuscule amount that I don't notice."

"I ... see." It was unsettling how abnormal he was. Moments like this made her realize just how powerful and rare he was in the world. "I only ask because I heard that fire elemental users have a harder time in extremely cold climates, and that ice elemental users have a harder time in extremely hot climates."

"Well, I don't notice a difference." He turned his head toward her. The moon bathed his face in silvery light. "And you? Does your magic suffer in extreme weather?"

She couldn't help but scowl. "Why would I tell you?"

"You think I'll use it against you?" Blár rolled his eyes and crossed his arms behind his head. "I don't need to do that shit. And you know that too."

He was right, he didn't *need* an advantage over her to beat her, but she didn't like the way he said it. Regardless, she answered, "In ... in winter, it's harder to use my magic. A lot of plants and nature are already dead or hibernating, so I can't draw on them that well. Or in places like this ..." She waved at the hills and hills of sand. "I can't really do much since there's no nature. But I guess I could just use the rocks."

"You wouldn't do well in my hometown, then." Blár kept his gaze on the moons. "Or maybe you would. I don't know."

"I read somewhere that you lived in a mountainous area."

His sharp blue eyes shifted to her. "You've read about me?"

She was grateful for the night's canopy that hid the heat from her cheeks. "Y-You were an enemy, so I had to research," she quickly said. "I'm not, like, looking into you for fun. You should know that."

There was a lot of literature about the three black ranks in the country, though most of it was gossip, irrelevant, or unverified. Most of it was about the missions they went on, their power levels, and their current positions in the government or military. People were curious about the powerful people in the nation. From what she read, none of the three black ranks indulged the crowds or the curious folks trying to milk information. All three had one thing in common: they kept to themselves. Blár was no exception. There was limited information on him.

The corner of his lip twitched. "I grew up far north. All that's up there is ice, snow, and mountains."

"I wouldn't do well in that weather." She tried to imagine a younger Blár climbing up mountains, bright-eyed and bundled in sheep's skin. It was a different image than the current Blár. "But I guess I'd do well with the mountains, since there are rocks and stones there."

Silence engulfed them for a while, wrapping them tightly until the only noise was the soft waves of the wind against the sand. It was so quiet that Kolfinna thought he fell asleep, but when she glanced at him from the corner of her eye, he was awake and staring at the sky.

"You know, I hate you," she whispered.

His gaze flicked to her. "I don't like you either."

"Yes, but I *hate* you." Her nails dug into her elbows. She wanted to look away from him, but she couldn't. She stared at the dark bruise on his cheek the size of a fist, at his long lashes, at the rippling muscles tight across his uniform. "Every time I see your face, every time I limp with this leg, I'm reminded of my greatest loss. You almost killed me, and I hate you for that. And do you know what really bothers me? It's that you *didn't* kill me. And I just can't wrap my head around it. Why did you let me go?"

The wind ruffled his hair and sent a gust of sand to dust him. He appeared unbothered and turned back to stare at the stars.

"You could've killed me. You could've chased me. You could've put in more effort." Her skin broke underneath her nails, blood clinging to them. "Why didn't you? Was it because you were bored? Or you couldn't be bothered to? Or that you pitied me? Why?"

Blár pressed his lips together. "None of those."

"Then *why*?"

"I was pissed off." He breathed out deeply as he pulled himself into a sitting position. Sand fell off his shoulders and hair with the movement. "My orders were to kill you. But that little shit Sijur was getting on my nerves. If I had killed you, he would've gotten the credit. I wanted to piss him off. So, I disobeyed and let you go."

Kolfinna finally had the answer to the question that had been plaguing her the past year but instead of feeling satisfied, a numbing feeling spread through her chest at the memory of the attack. The temperature in the sweltering summer heat had plummeted, and everyone in the streets of the town had been confused. Kolfinna had made a mistake earlier that morning when she didn't brew a strong enough "weedy" tea to completely cover her pink eyes. She thought no one had noticed, but when she heard rumors of Blár Vilulf being in town that evening, she realized her cover was up. She had to run. And so she had run to the forest, thinking it would protect her. She had thought she was the strongest in nature, and that no one could touch her there. But he had proved her wrong.

She had realized she was in over her head when the entire forest suddenly froze and was coated in a thick, hard, bluish-white ice. She had been so cold as she tripped and slipped, trying to get out of the wintry forest. She hadn't been able to draw from the plants surrounding her because they were too frozen and her mana couldn't break them free. She must've been stumbling in the forest for hours before he found her. It was like from a nightmare when he had walked toward her. The only sound had been the crunch of his footsteps. And then those eyes had come into view. So icy, so blue. So murderous.

She had thought she would die right then and there at the hands of a monster.

"Did you want me to kill you?" His voice broke through her memories and the cold air breezed over her shoulders.

"Of course not," she responded quickly and slid down the boulder to protect herself from the chilling wind. "Why would I want to die? I've spent my whole life trying to survive."

He dusted sand off his hair distractedly. "I wouldn't be surprised if you wanted to. It's not like you have anything going for you."

"What?"

"I mean, you don't have family or anything. That shit gets depressing."

She fell silent for a moment and stuck her hand into the sand. She raised it and watched the sand granules slip through her fingers. She hadn't done much reading about Blár, but what she had read hadn't listed any family. "You speak like you know how that feels," she said carefully.

"Is this the part of our journey where we unload all our burdens and become friends?" Blár snorted, laughed, and then grew quiet. He lay back down and stared up at the vault of black sky peppered with white stars. "This sucks."

"Nobody said anything about becoming friends." Kolfinna pulled her thin cloak tighter around herself until she felt like the fabric would tear. It did nothing against the freezing climate, but it covered her smile when she pulled it over half her face. "You tried to kill me, remember?"

"I was following orders."

"What about that stuff you said about the 'cat and mouse' game?"

He smiled, and his vibe seemed to lighten from that single smile. "Well, I *am* an asshole."

"Oh? So you knew this whole time?"

"Don't pretend like you're not one either." Blár suddenly became serious again. "We're not friends, and I don't think we'll ever be. But at least we can be ... I don't know, *civil* toward each other?" He spoke clumsily, as if the words didn't fit right in his mouth. And he fidgeted, like he knew it didn't suit him. "And yes, I did say some stuff I shouldn't have said. And ... I'm sorry."

Kolfinna blinked. The moons seemed to still in the sky as she looked at him, and even the wind seemed to stop howling. Did Blár Vilulf actually *apologize*? She hadn't expected or prepared for that.

"I didn't think—well, I don't know—I thought you were going to sabotage the mission," he continued. "Why would a fae want to help anyone? You guys, I mean, the fae, probably hate everyone? At least that's what I was thinking."

"We're not hateful creatures."

"I wouldn't blame you if you did hate everyone." Blár carefully placed his cloak on the sand and laid on it. He moved slowly, and Kolfinna wondered if his back stung when he lay on it. "Look at all the crap you've all been through. A lot of people kill fae. Most of them aren't even bad people."

"The people who're committing the murders or the fae?" She could hear the edge in her voice. A prickling, awkward sensation crept into her chest. She didn't want to hear him talking crap about her people, or to ruin her suddenly bright thoughts about him.

"The fae." His gaze was level. "I would probably hate everybody if I were a fae."

"Why ... why do you think like that?" She drew circles into the sand to distract herself from the growing hollow pit in her stomach. She didn't usually have conversations like this. In fact, nobody had ever empathized with her. It should've made her ecstatic to talk to someone, but she just felt angrier. How could he empathize with her and still treat her so viciously? "You accepted a mission to kill a fae. If you believe we're justified in hating humans, why would you accept that? And why would you still treat me badly?"

"A mission is a mission. I don't get to be choosy. And besides, my mission was to capture or kill someone who was wanted for murder. How was I supposed to know if you're guilty or innocent? I got my orders and the facts were there that you killed someone." He closed his eyes. "Honestly, even now, I'm not sure if you're innocent or not."

Kolfinna waved her hands over the series of circles she had traced into the ground until it was smooth once more.

"If I was ordered to—I don't know—kill a kid, then yeah, I'd refuse. But kill someone wanted for murder? It's not that hard of a choice. Just, okay, fine, I'll do it. I already don't cooperate much with the military and they've been on my ass multiple times for disobeying. Why should I disobey for something that isn't even that big of a deal?"

She let out a throaty sigh. "Fine. Whatever. Fair enough."

There was a tense silence for a moment before Kolfinna decided to lie down on the ground too, the fatigue getting to her. Just a moment's rest wouldn't hurt.

"What are you doing?"

Kolfinna created a mound of sand with one hand and unclasped her cloak with the other. She popped her head on the makeshift pillow and threw her cloak over her like a blanket. "Resting."

Blár scoffed. "What if it attacks us? There's no cave to hide in this time."

They had tried to find another cave during their search but to no avail. "I can't just *not* sleep."

"One of us has to stay on guard and then switch with the other."

"Then—"

"No, I sleep first." Blár spoke as if his word was final. "Last night you slept first and I stayed up."

"But—"

"Play fair."

Kolfinna opened her mouth to retaliate, but then sighed and propped herself up on her elbow. "Fine," she ground out.

"You better not let me die."

Kolfinna rolled her eyes and threw her cloak over herself again, but this time she leaned against one of the boulders instead of on the ground. At least this would give her some time to think. To reflect on her life. And to maybe think of a plan.

She stared up at the starry sky and watched the three moons in silence.

16

<hr>

"*Wake up*," a feminine voice said. "*Kolfinna, wake up!*"

Kolfinna's eyes sprang open into the bright sky and a hundred thoughts ran through her mind: *when did I fall asleep, where am I, who spoke to me?* But they all came to a halt at the creature in the morning sky, descending on them and blocking one of the suns.

The dreki's eyes glowed a blood lusting red—so red that it reminded her of murder and hatred. Its wings flapped in the air with enough force to send giant gusts to split the clouds in half and push them farther away into the corners of the sky. When it opened its mouth, she could see three rows of sharp teeth, drool and fire dripping from its scaly mouth.

It took Kolfinna a split second to spring to her feet. Just as her cloak fell to the ground in a puddle by her feet, she charged at Blár and kicked him in the hip. "Get up!"

Blár jerked upright but was too disoriented to make a move as he looked around himself in a confused daze, so Kolfinna jumped in front of the dreki and waved her hands, trying to catch its attention. Adrenaline pumped through her body and kicked her into high gear. She jogged away from Blár, flailing her hands all the while. She ignored the guilt knotting her stomach at her mistake—if she hadn't fallen asleep, they wouldn't be in this mess.

The dreki's roar sent waves over the sand dunes, disrupting their once still formation. The sunlight glistered off its glossy scales and Kolfinna had to squint to keep it from blinding her.

Blár lurched to his feet and all drowsiness washed away with a single glance at the sky. She half expected him to blame her, to ask her how it got so close and why she didn't warn him, but he surprised her by shouting, "Let's fight it!"

Kolfinna wanted to give him a look like he was crazy, but she was too busy diving out of the way as the dreki breathed fire at her. Heat stung the skin on her face, hands, and neck, but it wasn't as hot as Fenris's fire. The fire fanned out of its mouth, but surprisingly, its reach wasn't as wide as she thought. As long as they avoided the fire head-on, they would be fine.

The dreki's wings flapped furiously as it steadied its back legs on the ground. It roared again, sending another shockwave over the sandy hills. Now that it was even closer to them, it looked even more hideous. The distance had hidden the crackling, black skin around its mouth, which wasn't covered with scales. Its teeth were yellowed and caked with thick, white grime near its bluish gums. And its breath stank of death and decay as it breathed down on them heavily, inhaling as if to breathe another breath of fire.

It shot fire from its mouth again, and Kolfinna jumped out of the way once more. She rolled and managed to come to its side, as did Blár on its opposite side. The dreki slowly shifted toward Blár and screamed at him. Kolfinna took that moment to kick the dreki's back leg. The scales were hard as steel and she bit back a string of insults.

They needed a sword to fight because Kolfinna couldn't see how else they could hack away at it. The only parts that were fleshy and not covered with scales were around its mouth and its eyes.

Without thinking too much, Kolfinna dodged its skeletal wings and jumped onto its hind leg. It was too busy aiming fire at Blár to notice her climbing its massive body. Her fingers gripped into the grooves of its scales and she hoisted herself higher until she grazed one of its jutting spikes along its back. She grabbed it and climbed up until she was on top of it. The dreki finally seemed to notice her and tried shaking her off, but it was too focused on Blár, who was running in circles around it and garnering its attention.

"What are you doing?" Blár shouted, easily jumping away from the dreki's fire breath. He was out of breath and sweat ran down the sides of his temples. "This thing is surprisingly stupid."

Kolfinna made it to the neck and wrapped her arms around it as the dreki thrashed for a minute. "I'm gonna—" Her right foot slipped and she fell forward. Her hand shot out to grab the spikes along its back; her legs dangled in the air and a flash of panic washed over her. Her biceps cramped and she hauled herself back onto its back. "Distract it!" she shouted instead.

"That's what"—he lurched away and shouted a curse—"I'm doing!"

She tightened her thighs between the creature's neck and hugged it with her body to keep from falling. She tapped its eye and was surprised to find it was hard as glass, but fleshy at the same time. It reminded her of an egg, and she sure hoped it would be as easy to crack as an egg. Without wasting time, she balled her fist and smashed it into its eye. Her hand squelched inside its socket. Time slowed and the dreki screamed deafeningly loud—so loud that Kolfinna wondered if her eardrums had burst. She dug her hand deeper, her fingers warm with flesh. She didn't have time to do the other side, because the dreki thrashed its head from side to side, and she was thrown off like a rag doll.

The sand softened her fall and she rolled before falling face first into a mound of sand. Her injured shoulder slammed to the ground and a jolt of pain shot through her. Everything went black and she struggled to push herself to her elbows. The dreki let out another earsplitting screech. She flinched and turned to watch it roar and spray fire in its path.

Blár launched himself onto the dreki's back like she had done, but he was lither and quicker than she was. He easily climbed its back, despite the dreki whipping its head from side to side, and made his way to its neck. He hung there with one arm and did the same as she did, but instead of his fist, he jammed a stone into its eye. The dreki screamed louder, and Blár hopped off its neck, narrowly missing a slash of its claw to his face. He rolled on the ground and bolted toward her.

His eyes were bright with excitement, but when he opened his mouth, there wasn't a hint of excitement in it. "Run!"

"W-Why?"

"What the hell are we supposed to do now? We blinded it. That's good for now!" He scooped her arm and pulled her to her feet. "Now start running! We'll think of a plan later. Now that it's blind, we probably have an advantage—"

They both lurched in opposite directions as the dreki's fire breath blazed toward them. Kolfinna scrambled to her feet and started running without direction. Soon, Blár was beside her. Behind them, the dreki screamed and flapped its wings to become airborne. It teetered to the side in the sky, but then flew above them and zoomed into the distance unevenly. And like that, their third encounter was over.

They had stopped running to watch it retreat into the

horizon. Kolfinna breathed heavily and winced as her shoulder ached with every breath. Sure enough, the wound had opened and blood seeped through the thick padding Eyfura had bandaged her with.

"It escaped."

"Not much we can do." Blár didn't breathe nearly as roughly as she did. He ran a hand through his sweaty hair before rubbing his shoulder. "Damn. That thing's body is hard. I slammed into it, and I'm pretty sure I almost dislocated my shoulder."

She remembered the pain in her foot when she had kicked it and grimaced. "How are we going to be able to defeat it then?"

"I ... don't know."

"Even with weapons, it'll be hard if its body is that hard." The wind ripped through her hair. "Maybe if we had a spear, we could jam it into its eye sockets and somehow kill it that way?"

"Maybe ..."

"Or ..." She chewed her lower lip and sighed exasperatedly. "I don't know."

Kolfinna's nose twitched and she quickly looked down at her hand. Slick, reddish-yellow gunk dripped from her fingers and coated her wrist. Bits of red flesh clung to her fingernails and her stomach churned as she realized it was the dreki's eye fluids and possibly chunks of its eyeball. She didn't have the guts to wipe it on the front of her uniform, because the flesh *stank*. Her eyes watered and the acrid stench of it blocked her throat; she couldn't even vomit if she wanted to. It was too disgusting, and the feeling of its slimy eye juices running down her wrist made her stomach roll. She gagged and scrunched her nose.

"Here." Blár held out a handkerchief, his own nose crinkled. "Wipe that shit off."

Kolfinna snatched it and quickly engulfed her hand in the thick material, her skin crawling as the flesh clung to her. She kept wiping, her stomach twisting further as the white handkerchief morphed into a yellowish red. She was glad she hadn't eaten anything, because she was sure she would've vomited it all up right then and there.

"Thanks," she muttered and held it back to him. She kept it pinched between her fingers to keep from touching the stained, stinky material. The smell of raw, rotten meat made her gag when she flailed the material. "Here."

Blár stepped back and held his hands up as if she had asked him to murder someone. "Keep it."

"This is yours. You keep it." She waved the handkerchief again.

Blár's face shifted to a shade of green and he backed away up a sand dune, so he was even farther away from her. "No. You keep it."

"I *must* return your kindness."

"I'm not taking that."

"Take it!" Kolfinna laughed and tossed it in his direction. The wind seemed to be on her side because it carried it toward him, and he had to jump to the side to keep it from smacking his face. Kolfinna doubled over as he kicked the handkerchief away in horror.

"I'd rather eat sand than have that touch me." He shivered in disgust and ran a hand over his stubbled jaw. His sharp eyes found her as she continued laughing. "And why are you still laughing like a fiend?"

"Oh, gosh, you're too funny—" Tears pricked the corner of Kolfinna's eyes. Who would've thought that black rank Blár Vilulf could make a face like *that*? Like he had witnessed the greatest injustice in the world.

"Save your tears for *after* we find a source of water." He straightened his uniform and cast a suspicious look at her. "And don't touch me."

Kolfinna's laughter subsided and she was reminded for the umpteenth time that they were parched, and if the dreki or the hunger didn't get to them first, the lack of water would.

"Why would I want to touch you?" She rolled her eyes and wriggled her fingers at him. "My hands are clean."

"Let's say you dig your hands in horse shit. If you wipe it with a cloth, are you suddenly, *magically*, clean?"

"Well, no—"

"Exactly. So don't touch me or my things."

"I don't want to touch you."

They continued their journey once more, but this time it was steeped in silence. The suns started to dip closer to the horizon, and she surmised it would take an hour or less for them to set—and hopefully, they would be spared from their heat.

Kolfinna kept shooting glances at Blár and averting her gaze whenever he noticed. It was strange being around him. There was still a part of her that didn't like him, but there was another growing part of her that actually *liked* being around him. And that shocked her. Because he was *supposed* to be the epitome of evil and crude and terrible. And she wasn't *supposed* to enjoy being with him.

Kolfinna combed her hair with her fingers and detangled it slowly as she tried unraveling her thoughts. Blár was still her enemy, she told herself. And she wasn't laughing *with* him but *at* him. So it wasn't like she was enjoying herself with him. Right? And it was normal to admire how strong he was—they were fighting for their lives, so of course she was naturally drawn to his strength. So long as that admiration stayed as admiration, she was fine. And it was normal to find him attractive since there was no one else around her.

Blár's voice interrupted her thoughts. "Do you sense any runes or anything?"

"No."

"Maybe we can make our own weapons?" He peered ahead at the scattered boulders and stones on the sandy skyline. "I don't know."

Kolfinna rubbed her chin thoughtfully. They needed to come up with an answer, because they were both starving, and she doubted they could survive for long in their current environment. From the looks of it, there was no life besides their own and the dreki, which meant there were likely no food sources for them.

"How exactly do runes work?" Blár unhooked his heavy cloak and draped it over one arm before yanking at the collar of his uniform. Sweat formed on his brows. His chest and arms filled the uniform snugly, and Kolfinna wondered what it would feel like to run her hands over it and feel how hard it must've been.

Kolfinna's cheeks stained with color as she realized where her thoughts were running. What in the world was she thinking? He was the enemy! And she did *not* want to touch him. Ever.

"Well?" He glanced down at her, his attention anything but comforting. Thankfully, he didn't seem to realize her inner dilemma.

She cleared her throat. "I'm not exactly sure. It wasn't like I was taught about them. It's just ... I look at the runes and the meaning pops up in my head, as if it's like second nature. It's like ... You don't think about how you're moving your arm when you move it, right? Your muscles move it without you thinking. It's the same principle with the runes."

"That complicates things." Blár frowned. "I guess it's not that easy to decipher them, then. They have magical properties, I suppose?"

"What do they look like to you? From my understanding, humans can't read them."

"They just look like squiggles." He made swirls in the air with his finger. "Looks like a bunch of gibberish. But the weirdest thing is that I can't pick it up. Just looking at it, it doesn't make any sense. All languages have some sort of pattern and repetition in sentences. Like nouns or transition words. But I can't even try to comprehend runes. It's like they scramble my mind when I look at them."

"Are you familiar with other languages?"

"A few. In my village, we spoke two languages—the common tongue and then our native tongue. And when I joined the military, I was taught Skarl—that's the language of Skarlland. They're to the east of us. I was stationed near the border there, so it's useful to know the language if there's ever an attack or just for negotiation purposes or if there are merchants wanting to travel through. And then when I became a black rank, they wanted me in the southeast border, and I picked up—" He stopped abruptly, as if realizing he was going off on a tangent. Kolfinna wasn't sure if it was the two suns making his face red from heat or embarrassment. "Well, to make a long story short: yes. I think runes might be protected by magic or something, to keep humans from understanding them."

"You know, now that I think about it," Kolfinna mused, "there seems to be two types of runes. The ones with magic, and the ones without. The ones without magic, like the runes outside the castle, are like regular writing. But the ones with magic ... It's more complex and I can feel more mana in them than regular writing ... I think there's a lot that goes into runes. But I can't figure it out completely. I don't have anyone to teach me ... And, well, I don't know much about them in general. My sister never taught me about runes."

"Is it true that only powerful fae can read them?"

"Maybe? Runes are imbued with mana—no, actually,

they're magic in themselves. I would guess that a fae with lower powers wouldn't be able to decipher them ... But I really don't know."

"We really have no idea what we're dealing with."

"No, I guess not."

Sweat beaded her forehead and whenever she wiped it away, more formed just as quickly. Her mouth was drier than this desert and she would've given her arm to have a taste of water. Blár was probably thinking the same, but he didn't voice his concerns. Instead, he squinted into the horizon, as if a weapon would appear if he stared hard enough.

Kolfinna followed his gaze and blinked back in surprise when she saw a small structure in the distance. It couldn't be ... Was that a *house*?

She slowed in her steps and her mouth dropped open. It *was*.

A tiny house sat in the distance. They were too far to see any details on it, but a plume of smoke exited through a chimney.

Blár grabbed her forearm. "I'm not hallucinating, am I? Do you see a house?"

"I do."

For a stunned moment, they both stared at it.

"It could be dangerous. Like a trap ..." He licked his chapped lips. But they both knew a house meant someone was living there, someone who had food and water.

A shiver ran down her spine. "Whatever it is, it might be the answer to our plight."

17

As they neared the house, they realized it was entirely made of stone. Its windows were impenetrable black glass and the heavy wooden door had golden inscriptions on it. Streams of iridescent gold runes skirted around the walls of the house like a million spidery chains. The chimney puffed out silver and golden dust, with a few speckles that glowed. Mana spilled forth from the house, but it felt oddly different from the dreki or the castle ruins; it was powerful, and yet so hidden. How had she not felt any trace of it until that moment?

They stopped a foot away from the door, neither of them sure if they should proceed further. From afar, the smoke was an indication that someone was living inside, but now that they were here, with all the mana and magic surrounding the place, she wasn't so sure if she wanted to go inside. What would they meet? After the draugrs, the

Jötnar, and the dreki, Kolfinna wasn't so keen on surprises. For all they knew, there could be a humanoid monster behind that door.

"What do the runes on the walls say?" Blár asked slowly. His steps were cautious and calculated, as if something would pop up in front of them and they'd be forced into combat mode.

The way he carefully inspected the house and kept glancing around looked funny, but she knew she was doing the same. Kolfinna was drawn to the mana of the house—to the shining runes wrapping around it. She wanted to splay her fingers over them and absorb the life pulsing from them. She missed the familiar nestling of her mana in her chest, like the heartbeat of a hummingbird vibrating beneath her skin.

"Let me see," she murmured, drawing close to the door. The radiant runes were tightly packed together and so small she had to bring her face closer. Before she could start reading, the door yanked open. Kolfinna stumbled back and gasped; in front of her was a humanoid face.

No, a *human* face.

An older woman stood at the threshold with one hand leaning against the doorframe and another holding a ladle. Black and gray hair streamed down her shoulders, and a pair of vivid purple eyes peered back at her. And her ears —they were strangely *pointed*.

No, not a human, Kolfinna realized. *A fae.*

The woman's mouth dropped, and she looked

between them. "People? Here?" She swung the door wider. "What brings you here? Come in, come in! I haven't had people over in *years*!"

Kolfinna hesitated, then looked at Blár, who hadn't moved and wore a guarded look. "Um," she said. "I ... Who are you?"

"Revna," the woman replied airily. "And you?"

"Kolfinna."

The woman paused and watched her carefully, the gears in her head practically grinding together. Finally, she said softly with a tinge of sadness, "Kolfinna, hm? What a beautiful name. I knew a Kolfinna once. She was the sweetest, tiniest little thing. It's a shame she was sealed away during the war. She even had your eye color. What a beautiful color it is."

Kolfinna was at a loss for words. What did Revna mean by "sealed" away? She didn't have time to ask her, because Revna was already speaking again.

"And you?" Revna gave Blár a once-over with a deep frown. "What exactly are you?"

Blár scowled. "The hell does that mean?"

"What exactly are you?" She tilted her head, her blue-stone earrings catching in the light, and pointed a long nail in Kolfinna's direction. "She's normal. But you?" Revna rubbed her chin thoughtfully, her purple eyes flashing. "I've never seen someone like you. Your mana is strange."

Kolfinna couldn't follow the conversation, and by the looks of it, neither could Blár. There was nothing about

Blár that was inherently *different*, other than that he was a black rank. But it didn't seem like this woman, Revna, was prodding at that fact. It was like there was something deeper than that.

"Oh!" She snapped her fingers. "Are you a human?"

He raised an eyebrow. "Uh, yes."

"My, I would've never thought I'd see a human here." She leaned one hip against the doorframe and regarded Blár calmly with half-lidded, sharp purple eyes. If she was hoping to unnerve him, it didn't work because he narrowed his eyes in question. "You're not much to look at."

A muscle on Blár's jaw twitched.

"Who are you?" Kolfinna interrupted before Blár could react; she didn't want to pry him off Revna if he decided to go ballistic and attack her. "How can you survive here? And where exactly are we?"

"This is a dimension created for the Black Castle." She sounded as if it were obvious. The sauce coating the ladle dribbled down the handle and dripped down her wrist until smatters of red flecked on the stone floor. Revna brought her wrist to her lips and licked it off. "I haven't cleaned up at all. I didn't expect visitors." Her eyebrows puckered as she looked at Kolfinna closely. "Darling, where are your wings? And why are your ears so ... round?"

Kolfinna stiffened at the question, while Blár glanced between them with raised brows. "Wings?"

"My ears have always been like this ..." Kolfinna had

never heard of fae having sharp, pointed ears, so she was confused at the woman's appearance.

"And your wings?"

"My parents cut them off when I was born," Kolfinna said quickly, noting that she also didn't have wings. "And yours?"

Revna's mouth hung open in a wide O like it was the most bizarre thing she had heard. "Heavens, that's horrid! Why would they do such a thing? You didn't commit a crime, so I really don't understand."

"Everyone—" Kolfinna spared a glance at Blár, who watched her silently but with a hundred questions reflecting in his blue eyes—surely, he wouldn't tell anyone the fae secret? "Everyone cuts their wings off. It's ... normal."

"Very strange. Mine were cut off during the war." Revna cleared her throat. "Anyhow—"

"The Black Castle? Is that what this place is called?" Blár asked impatiently. "You know this place? And what did you mean by dimension?"

"This dimension was created solely for the Black Castle." Revna's gaze flicked from his head to his toes, a frown twisting her thin, dry lips. "Which is why I'm so shocked to see a human here. This place isn't for your kind."

Blár's mouth pursed into a firm line and irritation flashed over his face. He likely wasn't used to people talking to him like he wasn't a black rank.

"We've been stuck here for two days now," Kolfinna said. "We're very confused as to what's happening."

"Huh? Why's that? Aren't you training here?" Revna waved a hand and ushered them inside. "You must be famished and thirsty! Come inside and we can talk. I just finished making some beet soup!"

Kolfinna's stomach rumbled as if on cue and her mouth watered at the thought of finally filling her belly with something other than sandy air. They hadn't eaten or drunk water in two days and it was taking its toll on them; Blár was noticeably more irritable and snappier while she was weak to her bones. The thought of a home-cooked meal sounded better than the riches of the world. She took a step forward, but Blár grabbed her wrist, stopping her.

"We don't even know if we can trust her." His voice was sharp but low.

"This is our chance to find out information." She shot a glance at Revna, who had her back to them. "Besides, we need food and water, or we'll die. I know you're just as hungry as I am."

Blár mulled over that a moment before sighing and releasing her. "Fine."

"You know I can hear you both." Revna chuckled and waved them forward with one hand while her other hand pulled her cape hood over her head. "Come inside, please. I'm not a monster waiting to eat you up."

Kolfinna ventured inside eagerly. Mana spilled forth

from every inch of the house. Her footsteps slowed. The interior was cozier than she thought it would be. Rich and colorful tapestries hung on the walls, and intricate rugs and cushioned seats of every color covered the floors. A spicy, herby, and aromatic smell pervaded the room, welcoming them.

"Have a seat," Revna said, waving her toward a chair in front of a small four-legged table. The dining table had bowls of dried colorful fruit and an assortment of cheeses on it. Crusty baked bread sat in the center, beside it a cluttering array of nuts and jars of jam.

Kolfinna mutely sat down, her stomach growling louder by the second. It took all her willpower not to devour everything that sat on the table. The jams, nuts, bread—they must've tasted like heaven. She licked her lips and finally tore her gaze from the food and forced herself to stare at Revna.

"I didn't expect guests, so I just have a few things around. Help yourself to whatever you'd like." She scurried into the kitchen, leaving them alone in the dining area. "Give me a second while I finish the soup!" she called out from the other room.

Blár pulled back the chair beside Kolfinna and it screeched along the wooden floor before he gingerly sat down, his gaze locked on the jams and cheeses. "What's going on?" he muttered, grabbing a piece of dried fruit. "I've never seen some of these." He held up a dried green and yellow fruit. "None of this makes sense. Who is she and why is she here in the middle of nowhere in this … this world, whatever it is? What if she's a monster just like those undead soldiers— on the ship? Or the dreki?"

"I don't know, but she seems nice. We can probably find out something useful … Or maybe she can help us find a way to kill the dreki and get out of here." Even through her words, she couldn't stop ogling the food, her mind completely taken by the buttery smell of bread and the fruity scent of the jams and dried food.

Kolfinna plucked one of the dried fruits and inspected it carefully. It was clearly a raisin, but how did grapes grow here? And where did the cheese come from?

She bit it, while Blár hissed, "What are you doing? It could be poisoned."

It tasted sweet like a raisin. "Too late," she murmured, her stomach churning in hunger. She poured herself a glass of water and downed it in a second. She then popped one of the white cheeses into her mouth. It was creamy, rich, and salty. "It's good."

Blár eyed the nuts and his lips formed into a tense line. "We can't just trust her. Who is she and why is she here? How is any of this possible? And why is she so surprised by me?" The last part came out with a hint of irritation. "Last I checked, humans weren't rare."

Kolfinna chewed thoughtfully. It was strange, *very* strange. But things had stopped making sense ever since they stepped foot inside the castle ruins.

"What if she attacks us?" Blár's frown grew wider and

his blue eyes attacked her accusingly as she took another bite of cheese. "This is a trap. It has to be. In my village, there's a story of a girl who loses her way in the woods and a demon gives her a berry. She accepts and is whisked away to his world."

"How does the story end?"

He stared at her levelly. "She's eaten by a horde of demons."

"Why a girl? Why are all these horror stories centered around foolish girls?" Kolfinna scoffed and picked up another dried fruit. "If we get attacked, at least we'll have full stomachs."

Blár narrowed his eyes. "I, for one, do not plan to die here. I don't trust that woman and I don't plan on becoming another Gertrude."

"Who's Gertrude?"

"The stupid girl in the story."

"Oh. Well, I don't want to become Gertrude either, but we need food and information. She clearly knows about this place. Much more than we do." Kolfinna poured herself another glass of water and then began cutting into the bread with a butter knife. "It's weird. It's almost like—"

"Almost like what?" Revna called from the entrance of the kitchen. She balanced two steaming bowls in her hands. She placed the bowls in front of them and grabbed the back of one of the seats before yanking it and plopping down on it. Her hood slid down to her thin shoulders. "I see you're eating well, Kolfinna."

"Ah, yes." Kolfinna paused from smearing jam on the slice of bread she had just cut. "It's good."

"And you?" She turned her vivid purple eyes to Blár. "You, who refuses to say his name and who smells weird."

Blár looked taken aback. "I smell just as bad as she does." He jerked a thumb at Kolfinna. "Anyway, who are you?"

"I've already told you." She sighed, as if the question inconvenienced her. "Revna is my name."

"Why are we trapped here, Revna?" Blár pinned her with a stare that would've made Kolfinna wither on the spot. "Are you behind all of this?"

Revna looked at him like he was a bug who crawled in her path. "Heavens, boy, why would I be behind all of this?"

"That's what I'd like to know."

She sighed, as if she was speaking to a child. "No, I'm not behind all of this." She shifted her gaze to Kolfinna and helped herself to a piece of cheese. "I'm trapped here the same as you both."

Kolfinna stilled. "How long have you been trapped here? We got here a few days ago. Were you part of the previous party?"

"No," she said. "I didn't realize there were parties of people entering the place recently. I'm sure I would've met them by now if they made it this far."

"So how long have you been here?"

"I have no idea. It feels like forever." Revna smoothed the checkered tablecloth with her hand and scratched an old bubble of food that was stuck to it. "Centuries, perhaps. Time doesn't seem to move at all."

"If what you're saying is true, how are you alive if you've been here that long?" Blár crossed his arms over his chest and didn't seem convinced.

"Because it's only my soul that's here. My physical body is in the castle."

A chill settled in the room and Blár gave her a hard look. He turned sharply to exchange bewildered stares with Kolfinna.

Kolfinna lowered her bread onto the plate. "What do you mean your body is in the castle?"

"It's as I said, my body is in the castle. I'm just a soul right now." Revna didn't look like a soul. She looked like a flesh and blood person, like Blár and Kolfinna. Weren't souls supposed to be transparent or shift from opaque to invisible? If they hadn't been in a dimension with two suns and three moons, she would've thought Revna was either crazy or a liar. But all things considered, Kolfinna half-believed her.

"How is that possible?" Kolfinna asked. "If you're here in spirit form, how come we can see you and how can you be sitting here and talking to us like you are?"

"Because we're in this dimension and everyone who enters this dimension, whether a spirit or like you, will be corporeal."

"Are our bodies just lying in the castle right now? Are we spirits?" Blár asked.

"No. There are two ways you can enter a dimension like this: with your body or your soul. If you enter with your body, you'll die if you die here. If you enter with your spirit, you might be hurt, but you won't actually die if you die here. You both likely entered through the normal means with your bodies when the gong sounded, unless someone maliciously sent your souls here. But you would know it because it's excruciatingly painful and it's a very in-depth process with heavy rune magic to make that possible." She tilted her head and regarded them strangely. "How do you not know this? Aren't you here for training?"

"No." Kolfinna paused. "What do you mean about training?"

"Trainees come here to train and become full-fledged warriors. That's the whole purpose of the Black Castle," she said with a wave. "Why are you here then if you're not a trainee? Who let you into the castle?"

"No one let us in," Kolfinna said. "We just walked inside."

"How?"

"The castle ruins have been abandoned for centuries."

Revna's lips parted as shock flitted over her face. She opened her mouth and closed it, like a flapping fish gasping for air. "*Ruins*? What? When did that happen? How was it abandoned? This is the greatest training facility in Drivhus. How ... Why?"

Drivhus was the name of the country when the fae

ruled, before it was changed to Rosain when the humans overthrew the fae rulers. Kolfinna couldn't contain the curiosity and awe sputtering in the pit of her stomach. If Revna was truly as old as she claimed to be—if she truly was from before the Great Purge—she must've known so much about fae history. Revna was a piece of Kolfinna's lost heritage and she didn't even know it.

"There was a war between fae and humans," Kolfinna said when she found the words. "The humans won and freed themselves from the fae, and then soon after there was the Great Purge, where the majority of the fae were exterminated."

Revna went very still, the color slowly leeching from her skin. There was a pin drop silence as she absorbed those words. "What did you say? Exterminated?"

"For the most part." Bitterness seeped into Kolfinna's tone. "Only a few are left and we're all in hiding because we'll be killed if we're found out. That's why we cut our wings off and hide our eye colors."

"That's ridiculous! How has our society sunken so low? We ... we did so much for the humans! How can they just—" Tears glistened in her eyes and she sniffled, rubbing her nose and turning her head away from them. "Forgive me, this is ... this is a big shock for me."

Blár drummed his fingers on the tabletop but, thankfully, kept his silence. Kolfinna scratched the nape of her neck. She hated that she had been the one to deliver such news to Revna, but she also felt ... strange. Revna was from a time where fae were powerful and equal to humans. In the span of centuries, so much had changed. If Kolfinna was born in Revna's time, no one would've thought to kill Katla, or her parents, or any of them simply because they were fae.

Revna let out a shaky breath as she dabbed her damp, red eyes with a handkerchief. "I can't believe it," she said. "To think we … Forgive me, I'm just so shocked. Are there any of us left? Is there any safe haven?"

"If there were," Kolfinna said sadly, "I would already be there."

"And you?" She pointed a trembling finger at Blár, her eyes reduced to slits. "Where do you fit into all this?"

"What do you mean?" Blár didn't look guilty or ashamed—and why should he? He wasn't personally invested in the fae, their history, or their genocide. His gaze was level and clear, unafraid and comfortable. "Do you mean where do I fit in terms of the historical aspect? Look, lady, I'm only twenty. I haven't lived long enough to kill you all, so don't look at me like I'm a mass murderer."

Revna clucked her tongue. "I find it hard to sit with a human knowing what your people did to mine!"

"And I find it hard to sit with someone who claims to be over a thousand years old," Blár said with an eye roll.

Kolfinna kicked his shin, hard. He winced and shot her a dark look. "He didn't mean to sound so rude," she explained. "A-Anyway! I have so many questions—"

"Yes, me too." Blár eased into his seat. "What I want to know is what exactly did you do to land yourself here? You said you were trapped. If you actually were trapped for centuries, you must be here because you were punished. Especially since you say you've met other trainees before. Why would the people in charge of this castle, this training ground, as you said it, keep you stuck here unless it was a punishment?"

Revna bristled, likely not appreciating Blár's accusatory tone or the way he was staring at her like a wolf waiting to devour its prey. Maybe she didn't like being viewed as a tiny rabbit. Kolfinna had felt the weight of those predatory blue eyes; it was heavy and prickly.

Revna smoothed the material of her cloak with unshaking hands. "You're correct," she said. "I indeed am here for punishment, but it's not as black and white as you make it sound. I was wrongly put here and now ... now I'm just stuck."

Blár leaned forward like a wolf ready to pounce. Teeth bared and ready to sink in. "What did you do?"

"I was part of a faction that wanted to make a difference ... That wanted to create a better world for my people, for other fae," she said with a sigh, waving her hand. "There were others who disagreed, naturally, and they were powerful. This was a long time ago. My group of sisters and I were attacked one night and imprisoned here. Our bodies are in the castle, bringing life to it and helping train the new fae warriors, while our souls are stuck in these dimensions, unable to leave. We're repeatedly attacked and killed for training purposes, only to be brought back the next day, since only our souls dwell here."

"That ... sounds terrible," Kolfinna murmured.

"If that's true"—Blár cut in sharply, not a hint of empathy dredging his tone—"why did you let us in so eagerly? Why would you let us into your home if you thought we were trainees? Didn't you think we were here to kill you?"

Kolfinna wanted to tell him he was being too rude, but even she leaned in to hear the answer to that.

"You don't understand what it's like to be trapped here for so long." Revna folded her hands over the table, her eyes shining with unshed tears. "I've gone centuries without seeing anyone. I felt the presence of two people— you both—and I ... I craved that connection. It's been so many years since I last spoke to anyone."

"I'm so sorry," Kolfinna whispered. "That must be terrible. I can't even imagine the loneliness."

Blár studied her with a scowl but seemed satisfied enough with that answer.

"It is terrible," Revna sniffed. "Rune magic can't work without a source of mana. How else do you think this castle, even abandoned as it is now, is running still? There always needs to be a power source for any type of magic. We—my sisters and I—are that power source. We're running the Black Castle with our bodies and mana, without our consent, of course. Our magic is leeched and used to preserve the castle, this dimension, and *all* the dimensions in this castle."

"We were in a dimension before this one, and we didn't run into any of your 'sisters,'" Blár said.

"There are dozens of dimensions in the Black Castle and there are only ten of my sisters, myself included. It only makes sense that some of those dimensions don't have my sisters in them. But regardless of that, we still run this whole place. Whether we're in a specific dimension or not."

"Is there any way you can break free?" Kolfinna asked.

"No, unless someone else helps me." Revna smiled sadly at Kolfinna. "Unfortunately, I don't think you have a high proficiency in rune magic, do you?"

Kolfinna shook her head. "No ... I don't. Rune magic is a lost magic. No one really knows how to use it."

"That's a shame. It was a backbone of our society. Everything ran because of rune magic." Revna sighed, suddenly looking very bone-weary. "Such a shame indeed ... If you'd like, I can teach you."

"Let me guess?" Blár's voice was like steel against Revna's vulnerability. "You want Kolfinna to learn rune magic so she can free you?"

Revna matched his cold stare and she regarded him silently. Kolfinna felt the air stir uncomfortably as the two shared frigid looks with one another. Finally, Revna spoke, "Why, of course. I've been trapped here for centuries. I would like to be released from here. I don't think it's unreasonable. Kolfinna needs to learn how to use rune magic if she wishes to survive in the Black Castle. Not to mention that it's part of her heritage! She's a fae. Do you wish to rip that part away from her? The purpose of the Black Castle is to help sharpen your rune magic abilities. I'm surprised you both made it so far *without* using rune magic."

Kolfinna didn't miss the suspicious gleam in Blár's eyes, nor the way his mouth tightened in rage. She reached forward without thinking and placed her hand over his. His cold eyes shifted to hers and she gave him a pleading look. *Please*, she tried to say through her eyes.

She waited for him to lash out, to rip his hand away from hers, but he did no such thing. He only flattened his lips together, clearly not happy with the idea of it. Kolfinna clung to his silence, relieved. She doubted an opportunity like this would ever come her way again. What better way to learn the lost rune magic than to have someone well versed in it teach her?

Kolfinna withdrew her hand from his and bobbed her head. "That sounds fair. I would love to learn." She practically sat on the edge of her seat. All thoughts of the Black Castle and their trials were forgotten as she imagined herself wielding rune magic. The imagery was exhilarating; she wanted to touch back to her roots. To be a fae without fear. "Maybe even now."

"I love your enthusiasm, but I think we can try tomorrow. You're exhausted."

"Ah ..." Kolfinna sank back in her seat, her excitement deflating. "All right."

"Don't look so sad! You'll feel a lot better if you rest and then we try tomorrow. Rune magic will drain you, trust me. You'll need the rest."

Blár sat rigidly, as if the seat could never be comfortable enough for him. Thankfully, he didn't object, though he sure looked displeased. Kolfinna's gaze cut over to the window on the wall; golden inscriptions wove over the glass from the outside in hundreds of horizontal lines. She turned back to Revna and tried to keep the disappointment out of her voice.

"Um, I feel fine, so we can definitely start now, but if you think it's better to start tomorrow, that's fine too ..." Kolfinna folded her hands atop the table. "Oh, and I did have another question that was bothering me."

"What is it?"

She glanced at Blár. "We actually came with a party of people, but for some reason, only Blár and I were warped here. I don't know where the others went. But during our first trial, we were all warped to the same location—a ship. Why is it different now?"

Revna's gaze shifted between the two of them and she seemed to weigh her options carefully before picking a grape from the fruit bowl. "Were you two in a separate room than the rest of the party?"

Now that Revna mentioned it, Kolfinna had pulled Blár aside to ask him something while the rest of the party moved forward to another room. "Yes."

"There's your answer."

"Why did we get warped, though, and not everyone else?"

"It happens at a random time, but once a day, people are teleported into a dimension within the Black Castle. Each room is linked to a different dimension. If you happen to be in that room when the time for being warped happens, you'll get warped. Simple as that. Some rooms are immune to that, but you'll know which rooms they are because they'll be written on the walls."

"You seem to know an awful lot about this place," Blár said slowly.

"Yes," Revna said with an exasperated sigh. "I would know a lot, considering I've been trapped here for so long. But I also trained here when I was younger and taught here too."

"Really?" Kolfinna perked up; Revna had been a trainee and a teacher in the Black Castle when it was still thriving? There must've been so much she knew about the castle then. About what it was like before it became a shadow of itself.

"Yes, really." She smiled, but it didn't reach her eyes. "You—"

"Wait, I have a question," Blár said. "You mentioned that each room is linked to another dimension. Does that mean the rest of our party was warped to another dimension since they were in another room than us?"

Kolfinna's breath caught in her throat as she waited for the answer; she had hoped the rest of the party was in the Black Castle and hadn't been warped, since they couldn't survive without understanding the runes.

"I'm not sure," Revna said as she picked up the pitcher of water, her thin fingers wrapping around the glass handle. "It depends on the room they went into. If they entered a hallway or a room without runes, then they should still be in the castle. But you mentioned you've been here for a few days, yes? If they didn't get warped the same day you did, then perhaps the next day they did, or the day after that. Because if they're unaware of the rules, they'll have a hard time navigating the castle. My best bet? Yes, they're likely trapped in a dimension."

It felt like a sucker punch to the gut hearing those words. Kolfinna couldn't bear to think of what everyone else was enduring. Were they on that ship again? Or maybe they were in another dimension more harrowing than that? How could they survive? She thought of Eyfura, who swore to Nollar she would make it back alive. She thought of Mímir, who was trying so hard to prove himself. She thought of Magni, Truda, Eyjarr, and the others whose names she hadn't caught. She didn't know them very well, and some she disliked, but she wasn't so cold-hearted to wish for their deaths.

Blár seemed to be thinking the same thing because the color drained from his face, but it was Kolfinna who jumped to her feet. "I need to learn rune magic *now*! If they're trapped in a dimension, I need to save them!"

The guilt was so powerful that she nearly drowned in it as she thought about how Blár and her had wasted time trying to fight the dreki, how they had slept through the nights instead of moving, how they had joked along the way when they should've stayed focused—if they had gotten here faster, then Kolfinna could have saved everyone even quicker. Maybe there was still time. Maybe they were still alive.

She didn't want to think of anyone as dead.

"Kolfinna, I understand, but you need to rest," Revna started.

"No, you don't understand! They're just humans. They can't survive!" A selfish, niggling part of her mind whispered that if they all died, there was no way she could become a Royal Guard. But she pushed that thought away. She needed to save them, first and foremost.

"Why can't you teach her today?" Blár asked, his words dripping with acid.

"Because it'll put too much pressure on your already weary body," Revna answered calmly. "You need to be fresh when you start learning runes. It takes a toll on you."

"But—"

"Kolfinna, please. I know more than you do." Revna stared at her with a stern look. "Don't you trust me?"

Kolfinna fell back into her seat, her body screaming at her to do something. But she nodded slowly instead. "I trust you."

"Then believe me when I say that I have your best interest at heart. You need to rest. We can start training in the morning." She motioned to the dark windows, which showed miles and miles of sand stretched across a black skyline. "It's already night. Rest and once the suns rise again, we'll start training."

Kolfinna bunched her fists together onto her knees. She didn't have time to rest or dillydally, but she needed to cooperate with Revna; what if she refused to help Kolfinna if she didn't cooperate with her rules? Then rune magic would forever be a lost cause.

"We can talk more about this tomorrow. Now, it's my turn for the questions." Revna pointed at Blár. "Your name?"

Blár narrowed his eyes and made a face as if he was offended by being asked such a thing, but answered curtly anyway. "Blár Vilulf."

"Why are you two in this castle if not for training purposes?" Revna leaned in closer, her purple eyes flaring as she inspected them both. "Don't lie to me. I can tell if you lie."

"We're here as an order," Kolfinna answered honestly. "By the king."

"Why is the king interested in this place?"

"Treasure." Blár tapped the table with his forefinger. "Money? More power? Maybe to have us killed? Who knows what that greedy bastard wants?"

"And what's your relationship with each other? You're wearing different uniforms."

"We're in two different military units," Blár said.

"And your relationship?" She smiled, and Kolfinna could've sworn there was mischief in her eyes. "Are you two lovers?"

Kolfinna's face heated up in different shades of red. Lovers? Was that what they looked like to her? She had never thought of such a thing about Blár. He was handsome, and she was sure there was an odd attraction she felt toward him, but lovers? They were the farthest from that. He had once tried to kill her!

She opened her mouth to deny it, to tell her they would never be anything like that, but Blár surprised her by saying, "Something like that."

Kolfinna blinked and thought her face might explode from heat. *What?*

"How'd you meet?"

"That's a long story," Blár said.

"But you're a human and she's a fae?" Revna raised an eyebrow. "How did you fall in love?"

"Ever heard of star-crossed lovers?" Blár stared at the platter of cheeses and nuts. "Anyway, how do you have food here when there's nothing out there but sand?"

"Magic," Revna answered like it was a normal part of life. "It's rather easy for me. I can still conjure things."

"How?"

"Rune magic," she said. "It only works in these kinds of dimensions, though."

"What are these dimensions? Different worlds?"

"No, they're constructed with magic. All this food in front of you isn't real. It'll still taste real, fill your bellies like real food, and make you defecate like it's real food— but it's made entirely with just magic. This"—she picked up an apple—"is not actually an apple. It's condensed magic that's formulated to taste like an apple and to give nutrients like an apple, but it's not an apple. These dimensions work the same way."

Kolfinna struggled to wrap her mind around that. The food in front of her wasn't real? It was hard to believe they were eating magic. But even as she was thinking that, her gaze drifted to Blár. Magic food was interesting, but why had Blár lied about them being lovers?

"I'm sure you both are very curious about everything, but I think we should take a break from all the questions." Revna leaned back in her chair as if done with questions. "Anyway, eat your supper and then rest a little. I'd also like to take a look at your wounds. I have some bandages and things I can—"

"We can bandage ourselves up," Blár interrupted. "Just tell us where the stuff is."

Kolfinna internally cringed. Blár didn't have to be such a jerk about the whole situation. They should've been grateful Revna was even helping them. How would they have survived without water and food? And although not absolutely necessary, shelter and having their wounds checked was a luxury. Maybe they could also get weapons from her? And more importantly: she needed Revna's information and to learn rune magic.

And yet here he was, blunt and brisk and rude.

Revna frowned. "I'll bring it out to the living room. You two also need a bath. I'll draw—"

"We don't need a bath," Blár snapped like she had said something ridiculous.

"No, you *certainly* need one." Revna's nose crinkled as she looked down at Blár, and then at Kolfinna. "Both of you."

Kolfinna would've loved to dip her toes in warm water and rid herself of all the grime and gunk clinging to her, but then she remembered how everyone else was likely dying. A bath didn't seem appropriate.

"Um, I don't need—" Kolfinna started.

"Nonsense! I'll prepare one immediately. Trust me, you need it. It'll make you feel much better." Revna rose from her chair and gestured to the food. "Please finish eating while I prepare the bath, all right? I'm not taking no for an answer!"

Kolfinna could only bob her head while Revna disappeared up a flight of stairs. When they were alone, Blár turned to Kolfinna and scoffed, "Really, you're just going to let her treat you like that?"

"Huh?" Kolfinna didn't appreciate the edge in his tone. "What are you talking about? She's treated us great —food, shelter, information. That's a lot."

"She doesn't let you voice what you want. You didn't want to take a bath, she ignored you. You didn't want to learn rune magic tomorrow, but she ignored you. All she says is 'trust me' and you *trust* her."

"I'm not as cynical as you. She's been kind to us, and yes, I *do* trust her." Kolfinna's face began warming up again, but this time it wasn't from embarrassment. "Anyway, what was that whole deal about us being *lovers*?"

"I needed to gauge her reaction. Notice how she said

she would know if we lied to her? Well, I lied, and she didn't realize it." Blár glanced around the house suspiciously, his muscles pulled taut. "I don't know. Something's up with this lady. I don't like her and I don't trust her."

Kolfinna picked up her silver spoon and tasted the beet soup, chunks of beef floating in the oily, rich broth. She ate a mouthful and closed her eyes as the meaty flavors rushed her palate. "You should eat. We need to replenish our strength." Kolfinna slurped the soup while Blár stared at the soup like it was poison. But she didn't miss the way he licked his lips, or couldn't rip his gaze from the cheeses. "And besides, what if she noticed you were lying but didn't want to say anything about it since it wasn't like you were lying about something serious?"

Blár gripped the edge of the table until his knuckles turned white. "How can you trust her so blindly? I would think someone like you would be more cautious than me."

"I'm not trusting her blindly." Kolfinna sipped her water and watched him over the rim. "You really need to drink water at least."

"You're practically throwing yourself at her feet."

"No, I'm not." She slammed the cup on the table, water sloshing over the rim. "I'm just not as cynical as you. She's offering us shelter, food, and information. She also offered to teach me rune magic. I don't think you understand how valuable that is to me. I don't know much about being a fae, and she can teach me! She can bridge that gap. And we need her if we want to get out of here." She gave him a long look. "You should try to be a bit more grateful."

"You're too soft." He rubbed his face like he was tired of the conversation. "Man, everyone's going to be dead by the time we get out of here."

"No, they won't. I'll make sure of it." Her tone hardened and she tightened her hold on the spoon. "If you don't eat, though, *you* will be dead before we even get out of here."

"I'm not eating this shit."

"Are you seriously scared?" Kolfinna pointed at his soup with her spoon. "A black rank like you, scared of eating *soup*? Losing your powers has really stripped you down, hasn't it?"

Blár's eyes narrowed. "Shut it."

"Oh, but it's true." She broke a piece of the soft and fluffy bread and took a bite of it. It melted in her mouth and she ignored the guilty thought that everyone in the party was likely starving and dying. "You're scared of food. You're scared of *her*." She pointed up the stairs where Revna had disappeared. "You're not so tough without your ice."

"I'm cautious, not scared. We know nothing about this place and it's not like we can trust her. What if she's the monster we're supposed to slay?"

"You're being ridiculous."

"Am I? Really?" He glared at her. "After all the weird

stuff we've been through the past week, I'd say I'm being reasonable."

Kolfinna drank water in response.

After what felt like forever, Blár finally took a piece of cheese and turned it over, inspected it, and took a bite. He chewed, swallowed, and took another bite. In seconds, he had a piece of cheese in his hand and a slice of bread in the other. He devoured it in seconds, scowling at her the whole time.

"It's good." He ate a spoonful of soup. "Damn it. I hope this doesn't anchor us here."

"Are you talking about the story of Gertrude?" Kolfinna shoveled spoonfuls of soup into her mouth; it sounded like a ridiculous story to teach children not to trust strangers. "You think demons will eat us?"

"I wouldn't be surprised."

Revna entered right then, her hood pulled down to reveal her midnight locks and pointed ears. She smiled warmly at Kolfinna. "The bath is ready."

"Oh, thank you," she said, rising.

"Would you both like to join?"

Kolfinna's mouth hung open and she glanced at Blár, who didn't look as alarmed, but who had gone still. "N-No!" she said. "We're not, um, at that stage."

"*Yet*," Blár added.

Kolfinna wanted to smack him across the back of the head, but she simply stood there while her face grew redder.

Revna chuckled and waved her forward. "I understand. Come this way."

Kolfinna quickly scurried after her, looking once over her shoulder at Blár, who sat eating his soup with the spoon in his mouth. Their eyes met, time slowing, but instead of the predatory glimmer of her nightmares, there was a hint of mischief in the harsh blue. He looked good when he smiled genuinely, she thought, and she felt her blush deepening.

18

―――――

The smell of lavender clung to Kolfinna's skin and as she pulled the blanket over her chin, a breezy, clean smell tickled her nose from the blanket. The bath helped ease the tension in her body, but it did nothing against the guilt expanding in the pit of her stomach. While everyone else was suffering—maybe even dead at this point—Kolfinna had eaten a full meal, bathed, and now was going to sleep in a cozy living room.

Kolfinna closed her eyes, willing those thoughts away, but she was all too aware of Blár's glare set on her. Silence spread thickly across the room, suffocating them like a plush blanket on a summer night. She gingerly opened one eye to find Blár silently fuming against the wall, the blanket draped over his legs.

Kolfinna turned on the couch so she wouldn't have to face him. Staring at him for too long made her stomach twist and tingle like she had a host of butterflies caged in her belly.

She still felt his eyes on the back of her head, as if drilling holes into her skull. She gritted her teeth together and squeezed her eyes shut. She tried to think about nature and trees and everything that helped calm her nerves, but she couldn't shake his stare.

"Okay, what?" Kolfinna jerked up into a sitting position and shot him a hard look, ignoring the way the moonlight danced silver streaks over his midnight hair. "Why are you pouting like a child?"

"Why are you cozying up to that freak?" he hissed between clenched teeth. "And I can't believe you actually took a bath."

Hearing him talk so harshly made her forget how brilliantly his blue eyes shone in the dark room.

Kolfinna raised an eyebrow. "She's been nothing but kind to us and even answered all of our questions. Why can't you be more appreciative and grateful? And I took a bath because I needed one. We can't do anything until tomorrow anyway."

"That's what she says—" He forcefully pointed to the staircase where Revna had gone up to. "She probably wants them to die. That's why she's not letting you learn."

"What? That doesn't even make sense!"

"She needs *you* to help her escape. You'd think she'd give you more bargaining power. But she's letting you think she has your best interests at heart, even though she never once asked you what you wanted, and that she knows better than you. She didn't even try to compromise. Look, I've been around people who are manipulative, and they prey on people like you—people who want to believe them."

"You don't know me." Kolfinna kept her tone low so as not to wake Revna with their arguing. She bunched her fists into the blanket and tried to keep her tone neutral. "She's not a bad person."

Blár laughed mirthlessly. "You just want to ignore everything and live in your la-la land where fae are accepted and normal."

Kolfinna resisted the urge to chuck the embroidered couch pillow at his face. She instead kept her hands busy by fluffing the pillow, her words coming out rigid. "I'm not living in a la-la land. I'm keeping an open mind."

"I say we find a weapon and make a run for it. Kill the dreki and get out of here."

"No," Kolfinna said a bit too sharply. She cleared her throat. "I need to learn rune magic. It'll help the others."

"You're being delusional if you think she's going to help you."

"Why can't you be nice for once? Why can't you just appreciate that we're not starving or freezing or dying anymore? We have a roof over our heads and we have full bellies. We can worry about our task *tomorrow*. For now, we should enjoy the blessings we've been given."

"Who says we'll be alive tomorrow?" he snorted. "How did you survive all these years being so trusting? I really don't get it."

"I don't trust—"

"The only reason you trust her is because she's not human." Blár's words were like salt on a gaping sore. "We've eaten in her home. Now we can't escape." The last part came out in a whisper, like an ominous breeze.

"Not that stupid tale again."

"Then walk out." He pointed to the door. "Walk. Out."

"I'm not going to play this game with you."

"I bet my entire life savings that she won't let us walk out of this house."

In order to prove him wrong, Kolfinna pushed her blanket off and rose to her feet. Revna wasn't a bad person. She fed them, sheltered them, and offered her assistance. And she had so much to offer: information, history, things about the fae nobody knew about anymore. Maybe she was the key to getting out of these ruins alive.

Kolfinna walked toward the front door. She didn't want to leave the house and go into the cold, sandy desert that was beyond the door, but if it was to prove a point to Blár, she'd climb mountains if she had to. Besides, all she had to do was step outside for a few minutes and come back inside. Revna would never know, and maybe Blár would shut up and let her sleep then.

Her heart picked up in pace and she placed her hand on the doorknob. What if Revna was exactly what Blár thought she was? A monster in disguise? What if she was feeding them to fatten them up for the dreki? What if she was a liar? What if everything Kolfinna hoped for was actually a mountain of lies and there was no connection to her past? That there wasn't a mysterious fae who knew all the answers?

Kolfinna twisted the doorknob and flung the door open. A chilly breeze blew against her body and she waited for her fantasy to crumble to dust like the sand sifting through the mounds. She waited. The cool touch of the night air shocked her skin and she shivered, turning her face away from the biting wind, but nothing came. Not the dreki and not Revna. She stepped outside and inhaled the scent of rocks and earth and sand. She waited again, but still, nothing happened.

The tension released from her shoulders and she released a deep breath. Her grip on the doorframe loosened and she spun around and headed inside to face Blár, whose lips twisted into a sheepish frown.

"See?" The door clicked shut behind her. "We can leave whenever we want."

"I still don't trust her."

"I think you're going to have to learn to trust people a bit more if you want us to make it out of here," she said with a wave as she tiptoed to the couch. She bundled the blanket over her body. "She's going to help us and hopefully I'll be able to get us out of here tomorrow."

"I *do* trust people, by the way, but I just don't trust her."

"Why not? Because she doesn't worship you?" Kolfinna scoffed; it was hard to believe the man in front of her was one of the most important men in the county. Revna didn't need to know that the man on her floor was a great portion of the country's military strength. "She doesn't know about your abilities or your status in the military, so she has no reason to bow down at every word you say."

Blár gave her a bewildered look. "Is that what you think of me? That I *like* when people treat me like an otherworldly being?"

"Then why else are you arrogant?"

"I'm not arrogant."

She snorted and settled herself into the couch. "That's a lie."

"I'm not a liar either."

"Maybe, but you're definitely arrogant."

The moonlight bathed half his face in a silvery cast while the shadows of the room obscured the other half. He blew out air. "I don't trust her because she just seems off. And maybe you're right—it bothers me how she talks to me like I'm irrelevant."

Kolfinna couldn't help the grin that stretched across her face. "Ah. So now you know what it feels like to be a fae."

"I'm going to sleep," Blár said gruffly. He threw his blanket over his body and positioned himself so his back was to her. "Good night, fae."

Kolfinna mimicked him so her back was facing him as well and curled up in a ball and closed her eyes. "Good night, human."

He made a noise that could've been a muffled laugh, but she was already drifting off to sleep.

EARLY THE NEXT MORNING, KOLFINNA STUFFED A handful of berries in her mouth, chewed, and chugged a glass full of water. Blár sat opposite her at the table, with his elbow propped on it and his head lolling onto his hand as he drifted forward before snapping awake, and then repeating the cycle.

"I'm awake," he said when he caught Kolfinna staring. But his eyes were glassy and glazed over, as if he wasn't actually seeing anything. He sliced a piece of bread from the serving platter at the center of the table and placed it on his plate, along with a chunk of yellowish-orange cheese.

"We slept about the same amount of hours." Kolfinna sipped her water slowly and raised an eyebrow as he stared blankly at his plate. "How are you still tired?"

"Shut up," he mumbled, rubbing his eyes. "Man, I feel like crap."

"You look like it too." Revna snickered from the end of the table.

"You shut up too." His lips curled back and he breathed out deeply. "It's too early for this."

Revna chuckled and stirred her cup of tea with a small silver teaspoon. "Are you always like this?"

"Like what? Sleepy?" Blár's body was rigid as he

stacked his cheese and bread together and took a bite. He chewed, watching Revna with barely concealed annoyance. "Yeah, it happens when I don't get enough sleep."

Kolfinna quickly cut into the loaf of bread centered on the table. The faster she finished eating, the faster they could get on with training and hopefully get out of this desert dimension. She didn't know how she had been able to sleep last night, considering all the negative thoughts plaguing her and the excitement coursing through her veins. She was going to learn a *lost magic*.

"So you're always sleepy?" Revna said, shifting her bright purple eyes to Blár. She folded her hands on top of each other and leaned forward, suddenly interested in him. "That's highly unusual. Do you have a lot of mana? People who have a higher amount of mana actually require a bit more sleep and energy than the average person because their body needs to replenish that mana."

Blár's forehead puckered. "Hm, is that what it is?"

"Can I—" Revna snatched Blár's hand before he could answer, but he recoiled abruptly, ripping it away from her grasp.

"Don't touch me," he snarled.

Her smile was thin and she held her hands up apologetically. "I'm just trying to see something about your mana." She motioned to his hand. "Can I?"

He stared at her for a few seconds, an uncomfortable silence stretching between them. If it were anyone else, they would've likely squirmed under Blár's icy glare, but

Revna simply stared back, unfazed. Finally, he gave a curt nod and held his hand out rigidly.

Revna's wrinkled hand shot forward and clutched onto Blár's. He made a sour face but didn't pull away this time, while she tightened her grip and concentrated, her forehead forming a deep wrinkle. After a second, she audibly gasped and dropped his hand like it burned.

"H-How?" Revna reeled back in her seat and stared at Blár with wide, unblinking eyes. "How is that possible?"

Blár looked just as confused as Kolfinna. "How is what possible?"

"How do you ... How much mana do you have?" Revna reached for his hand again, but he withdrew it before she could touch him.

"I told you not to touch me," he snapped. "And I don't know what you're getting at."

"Your mana ... I've never seen such a large amount of it. How is that even possible? I've met hundreds of extremely talented people in my life, but their mana pales in comparison—"

All of Kolfinna's confusion burst like a bubble and she slumped back in her seat, suddenly uninterested. Of course Blár had an insane amount of mana—all black ranks did.

Kolfinna had known it would only be a matter of time before his abilities were noticed, but she didn't think it would be this soon, especially since he wasn't able to use his powers. "He's a black rank," Kolfinna explained with a non-enthusiastic wave in his direction. "He's one of the three most powerful people in the country. It's not surprising that you're this surprised."

"A black ... rank? What does that mean?"

"It's a power ranking system," Kolfinna said. "It's supposed to gauge how strong your magical abilities are. The ranking goes from white, gray, yellow, purple, to black. White being the weakest and black being the strongest. To give you reference, my power level is probably ... a gray."

Blár snorted, and Kolfinna shot him a dark look—why did he make a face like he wanted to laugh? He placed his arm on the back of the empty chair beside him and said, "A gray, really? That's not being generous. You're closer to an upper yellow. Maybe even a purple rank."

Did he really think that? Or was *he* the one being generous? Kolfinna wasn't sure what power level she was at anymore—last year's defeat was still raw and had tanked her confidence.

"That's extraordinary," Revna whispered. "To think a human can be that powerful."

Blár's mouth pursed together and he took another bite of his food. "How can you feel my mana if I can't use my powers?" Blár asked. "I can't even feel it right now."

"Your mana isn't gone. You're just restricted from using it. It's simply dormant right now." Revna leaned closer to Blár and reached over as if to grab his hand, but plucked a cherry from the fruit platter beside his plate. Revna's hand flattened against the table and she smiled tentatively. "It's impressive that you have such a large store of mana. Were you always this way or did you train to get to that level?"

He shrugged, averting his gaze and letting the question hang in the air. Kolfinna watched him carefully, remembering his words last night. Was he uncomfortable talking about his powers? Kolfinna certainly felt uncomfortable and *slightly* jealous talking about Blár's capabilities. She could only wonder how he felt. A month ago, she would've said he was more than happy to have people fawn over his monstrous powers. But now, she could detect an inkling of discomfort by the way he nonchalantly picked at something under his nail. Like he didn't want to further the conversation. Maybe that blank expression wasn't arrogance? But a mask?

She couldn't say for sure, so she sipped her water and slammed the cup on the table, drawing their attention. "I'm ready to train," she said with renewed eagerness.

Revna clapped her hands together. "Wonderful! That's the spirit." She rose from her seat and motioned to the cushioned couch. "I would like to teach you in a larger room or more preferably, an open field, but I'm confined in this house and can't leave. Therefore, the living room will have to do."

"Oh, that's fine." Kolfinna pressed a hand into the back of the chair and she hoisted herself up, her gaze lingering on Blár and his unfinished breakfast. He still wasn't comfortable eating here, it seemed. As if sensing her unease, he picked up his piece of bread and brought it to his mouth, his eyebrows quirked in question. She pulled away from the table and headed to the couch. He didn't need her to babysit him.

"Did you enjoy your meal?" Revna lowered herself onto the couch. She moved the embroidered pillows aside to make room for Kolfinna and patted the couch. "Sit with me."

"It was good," she said, joining her.

"You should maybe try to eat a bit less, though," Revna said. "If you want to be a proper fae warrior, you need to lose a bit of weight." She pinched Kolfinna's arm and gave her a long look. "Fae are supposed to be lean and muscular, you know. I think you have too much human blood diluting your fae blood. It would explain why your ears are round."

The blood rushed to her face and she quickly glanced at Blár to see if he had heard, but he was staring out the kitchen window, seemingly lost in his own world. She straightened the front of her uniform. She wanted to snap at her like Blár had done—to tell Revna not to touch her so freely and to not comment on her body—but Revna was the only one who could teach her rune magic. So she instead tried smiling. "Um, shall we start?"

"Yes, let's get to the fun part, shall we?" Revna held her hands out to Kolfinna. "Let me feel your mana."

Kolfinna slipped her hands in Revna's.

"Your mana is strong. That's a good sign," Revna murmured. "It means you're ready to learn runes. Your mana is practically begging for it. That's a good thing. A really good thing."

Excitement bubbled in the pit of Kolfinna's stomach. "Really?"

"Yes, really." Revna dropped her hands. "It's not as impressive as your partner's, but it's good. It'll do."

Her happiness waned as those words struck a chord; being compared to Blár was like comparing a pebble with a boulder. Or maybe even a boulder and a mountain. She knew her capabilities were nowhere near his, and having such a prodigy so close to her sent a shard of jealousy through her heart.

"Rune magic is versatile," Revna said, bringing her back to the conversation. "It's a set of rules you impose with your magic onto the world, the space, or whatever item you're casting it in. Take—" Revna looked around herself and picked up a silver spoon on the tea table beside a half-finished cup of tea. She held the spoon up. "Take this spoon for example. I can imbue rune magic into this spoon. Like this." Her eyes shifted to gold and immediately, magic charged the air in a thick haze and singed the handle of the spoon with sparkling lettering. When Revna held the spoon out to Kolfinna, her eyes melded back into a deep purple. "What do the runes say?"

Kolfinna squinted at the writing on the handle. "*The breath of the sun will kiss this metal,*" she read with bunched brows. "What does that mean?"

"Here, take it."

Kolfinna almost dropped the spoon when Revna handed it to her from the unexpected warmth of the handle. "It's ... warm."

"It is." Revna smiled. "You can only use runes depending on your abilities and power level. That's a relatively easy and mild rune, but there are more complicated ones as well. Take, for example, Blár." She gestured to Blár, who was eating his meal slowly and watching them with glinting eyes. "You can't write runes on a living being that's meant to harm them, because their mana will naturally reject it. Remember, the soul is more powerful than any rune you can create. But you can do other things to him with rune magic that he won't reject. For example, healing his wounds."

"I don't like the way you're talking about me like I'm not here," he said, taking another bite of his bread.

"You're free to leave," Revna said. "Actually, I'd feel more comfortable if you weren't here."

"The feeling is mutual." Blár rolled a cherry between his thumb and forefinger, then twisted the stem. "But if I leave, then Kolfinna will be taken to the underworld with the rest of your demon lackeys. She's surprisingly gullible."

Revna's forehead creased and she tilted her head to the side in confusion, while a blush stained Kolfinna's cheeks. Not that story about Gertrude being eaten by demons.

"You're free to leave at any time," Revna said. "In fact, why don't you? You can explore the rest of the house and maybe have a seat in another room. Or maybe take a bath. Or"—she motioned to the pile of blankets in the corner of the room—"maybe you can take a nap?"

"Maybe you should," Kolfinna added. "You look like you're about to fall asleep anyway."

He bit into the cherry and pulled it away, picked at the seed, and let it drop on his plate with a *plink* before popping the rest of it in his mouth. He fixed her with a level gaze. "Maybe I will."

"Humans are not to be trusted," Revna said to Kolfinna under her breath, but by the way Blár was now glowering at Revna, Kolfinna surmised he had heard her. "I don't know what you see in him."

"He's—" She swallowed, unable to form the words.

The chair screeched behind him as he rose to his feet. His nostrils flared and he loosened the collar of his uniform. Kolfinna forgot to breathe as his deep blue eyes shifted to a tightened, icy glare. But this time, it wasn't aimed at her. He swept past them and went to his pile of blankets.

"Wake me up when you figure out how to get us out of here," he called out to Kolfinna, sinking into the floor and wrapping himself up. It was hard to take him seriously as he flopped over, baring his back to them. "Or when we decide to kill this hag."

Revna's eyes narrowed to slits.

"B-Blár!" Kolfinna winced, a tingling sensation spreading from her chest, neck, and finally across her face. She turned to Revna, who was glaring at him like a hawk eyeing its prey. "He didn't mean that! I'm so sorry. He's just rude sometimes."

"Don't apologize to her," he called from his position.

"Go to sleep!" Kolfinna hissed.

"Gladly."

Minutes ticked by and he remained silent, so Kolfinna took that as her cue to return to training. She held the spoon higher, examining the glimmering runes. "So," she said, "these runes don't ever disappear?"

"They'll eventually weaken with time since your mana won't last forever." Revna pointed to the runes. "You can also erase runes. Use your magic to overpower the rune and break it. You can only break it if your mana is more powerful than the rune magic. This is a simple rune and I only put a little bit of my power into it, so even you should be able to break it. Try it."

How was she supposed to overpower it? The more Kolfinna stared, the more her stomach stirred nervously. Revna's eyes darkened and she stopped moving, staring solely at the spoon in Kolfinna's hand, but nothing happened.

When it became obvious that Kolfinna didn't know what to do, Revna huffed and motioned to the spoon impatiently. "Look at the rune magic and imagine your mana circling around it, grasping it tightly, and then shattering it. Your mana must become a chain to squeeze and crumble the runes. Try it, *dear*."

Kolfinna's eyebrows came together and she stared intently at the spoon, willing the runes to disappear. The seconds blurred together and her fingers ached from clenching the handle too tightly. Finally, she shook her head. "It's not working."

"Use your imagination."

"But I can't even feel my mana."

"It's in there." The lines around Revna's mouth tightened. "Dig deep."

"But—"

"*Try.*"

Kolfinna chewed her lower lip and squeezed her eyes shut, the spoon singeing her fingers with its heat. She had never had a teacher other than Katla, and even then, because Kolfinna's magic had exceeded hers, Katla had only been able to show her the basics. Having someone breathing down her neck and watching her carefully made her skin prickle, as if a worm was crawling beneath her flesh.

She reached deep within herself for her mana but felt nothing. She tried again, reaching and reaching until she finally felt a tendril of it. She gripped that tendril and worked it toward her fingers like unrolling a ball of yarn. Slowly, it spread around her hand. It wasn't the usual rush of mana she felt, but it was something.

She thrust the inkling of her mana over the runes. Slowly, she twisted it around the runes and then squeezed it tightly as if she were knitting over the words with her mana. Tighter. And then tighter. Until finally, the runes crumbled and dissipated into gold dust. In an instant, the spoon went from hot to cold.

"I-I did it!" Kolfinna wanted to show Blár how cold the metal suddenly was, but he was fast asleep in his heap of blankets, so she turned to Revna instead. She held the spoon proudly. "Look, I did it!"

"That you did." Revna chuckled. "That wasn't so hard, was it?"

"Surprisingly, no."

"Sometimes, it's not possible to break it. Sometimes, the caster is too powerful, or the magic has been done with years upon years of rune magic that multiple people have enforced. In times like that, it's pointless trying to break the runes and you're better off overwriting them."

"How do you overwrite them?"

"Take that spoon and try to make it hot like I did," Revna said. "When making runes, you simply command your mana to spell out what you wish for it to spell out. So think about what you want it to do, and then it'll come naturally."

"Even if I don't know the specific runes?"

"Yes, rune magic is something that comes naturally to us. You'll be surprised at how your mana will understand what to do."

Kolfinna held the spoon tightly in her grip and imagined the spoon growing hot in her hand. She willed her mana onto the spoon and focused it on the handle. *Hot, I want it to be hot*, she thought. Mana buzzed in her fingertips and the handle glowed as runes were written on it. *Hot*, it read. Her hand warmed and she quickly dropped the spoon, sucking in a pained breath.

"Good," Revna said. "A bit simple, but good. It's

usually better to write an intricate rune in flowery words because it's harder to break, but that's good."

"Why is it harder to break?"

"Because there's more that you have to break down. More words mean more mana to break and it's harder to counteract something that's too flowery and specific. That's the key to making runes work, specificity. The more specific you are, the better the runes will work in your favor and the harder it will be for someone to find a loophole. If the runes are *too* abstract or vague, the runes won't work because it's unclear what you want it to do. Does that make sense?"

"Yes, kinda." Kolfinna thought for a moment. "The runes in the castle were pretty simple, though."

"Yes, they're supposed to be simple for the most part," she said. "Because they're there to help you learn. Now, back to the spoon." She pointed at it. "If you want to counteract that rune, what do you think you should put on it?"

"Cold?" Kolfinna asked.

Revna's cheeks lifted as she smiled. "Yes, that's correct. Simple, isn't it? Try it out."

Kolfinna did as she was asked. She thought of a tundra and winters, of the coldness of snow and the bone-chilling feeling of ice. Her mind traveled to Blár—to the very frigid and cruel nature of his magic. She harnessed that imagery and wished the spoon would emulate that feeling. Suddenly, the heat dissipated from the spoon until it became a normal temperature. She stared in amazement.

Cold like Blár's winter runes etched into the space below the *hot* rune.

"Perfect! Just like that," Revna said with forced enthusiasm. "People usually learn the basics faster than that, but ... well, I guess you should blame your human blood. Anyhow—let's move on."

Kolfinna's smile fell and she stared at the runes on the spoon; was it true that people learned faster than her? That didn't seem like the case with the fae she knew. Katla, her parents, and the others she had met over the years had never been able to match her abilities. Simply because they were scared to practice, but also because she seemed to learn faster. But was it different when it came to runes?

And this was the second time Revna had mentioned human blood "diluting" her abilities. As far as Kolfinna was concerned, she didn't think she had human blood.

"If you physically touch the runes, it'll be easier to break them." Revna pointed to the rune that said *hot*. "If you destroy this rune, then there's nothing negating the cold rune, so your spoon will then become cold."

"That makes sense," Kolfinna said. "But something's been bothering me for a while. How are we able to use rune magic if this place says we can't use any magic? Doesn't rune magic fall in that criterion?"

"Rune magic is magic, but it's more complex than that. It's an ability that all fae have. We can read runes and write runes and imbue those runes with our mana. It doesn't actually count as magic. It's a written language with mana imbued in it. Also, when you write runes that say no magic, how can that operate if your runes are magic in themselves? Your rune magic is the one doing all the rules you've set in place, so if you say no magic, rune magic doesn't count because then your own runes that set that rule wouldn't work. Does that make sense?"

"It does ... kinda." Kolfinna nodded, taking mental notes in case she needed it in the future. "It is a bit complex, I suppose. But if that's the case, why can't you get out of here?"

"The runes state that if I try to break them, my physical body will perish. The runes are very powerful, so there's nothing I can do to break out. I've tried, I really have, but there's no way out of it."

Kolfinna silently placed the spoon back on the tea table, her gaze locked on the heavy pile rug her feet sank into. It must've been horrible to be stuck here for centuries on end in complete isolation.

"Well, anyway, that's the basic gist of runes." Revna folded her hands on her lap and eased into the couch, her purple eyes drifting from the spoon, to Kolfinna, and then to the window overlooking the drab desert. "You can use it for anything, really. You can make your sword have the power of fire with every strike. You can make your dagger freeze what it touches. You can make the bathtub water warm when you sit inside it. You can make it so no bugs enter your home. The possibilities are endless. Our society was built with runes. Skilled rune users were in high demand. They would engineer all sorts of gadgets and weapons. Things from exploding balls to books that read by themselves to rugs that flew. Rune magic was everywhere. There weren't many people skilled in runes, but that didn't matter since there only needed to be a handful of skilled rune users to make sure society ran accordingly." She sighed. "I'm assuming that's not the case anymore since the fae are nearly extinct. Is that true?"

"I've never heard of what you're speaking about," Kolfinna whispered in awe. "What you're saying is out of a storybook."

"I assure you, it's not a storybook!"

"If our society was so advanced, how did it fall?"

"Blame the humans." The lines around her face were pulled taut. "I didn't realize our society had fallen, but if it's as you say ... then I suppose we lost the war."

Kolfinna's breath caught in her throat. Was Revna alive during the war between the humans and fae over Rosain—previously called Drivhus under fae rule?

"Were you ... a part of the war between the humans and fae?"

Revna's expression grew dark and her hand clutched the armrest so forcefully her fingers blanched. "That's a talk for another day, but all great empires fall at one point or another. Anyhow, let me show you a skilled move. Bring your leg up here. I'll show you how to heal."

Kolfinna stilled. Heal ... her leg? Had she heard right? That shouldn't have been possible. How could runes heal something when they were just a set of rules?

She gave Revna a strange look, trying to discern if she

was serious, but when Revna only raised an eyebrow, Kolfinna's body went slack. That couldn't be right. Could she actually heal her?

"You can ... heal my leg?" Even saying the words out loud felt like a hopeless dream. If her leg was healed, she wouldn't have to endure the stares. Or the frustration of not getting to one place fast enough like she used to. Or especially the pain. Would she really no longer have to feel her muscles resist and strain with every forward movement?

Revna nodded.

Kolfinna's lower lip trembled and she fought the urge to cry. She didn't want to grasp onto such a notion. It shouldn't have been possible. She didn't want to bring her hopes up. "Are you telling the truth?" she asked. "How can runes do that?"

"Runes can do many things," Revna said. "If it's to benefit you, your mana will not repel it. You weren't born with a crippled leg, were you? Because if that's the case, I can't 'heal' it because there's nothing to heal. That's your body's natural state. But if it's an injury that didn't heal properly, I can heal it. So, were you born like that?"

"No."

"I expected as much. Let me see your leg."

Kolfinna repositioned herself on the couch and brought her leg up to rest on Revna's lap. Her body bristled when Revna pulled the hem of her pants all the way up to her knee, exposing the jagged scars running up the length of her shin and ankle. Revna examined it for a minute and placed her cold and leathery hands on Kolfinna's bare skin.

"Using rune magic to heal is extremely difficult to do and you need years of practice to do it properly. I'm not saying I'm a master, per se, but I can do it," Revna said. "How did you damage your leg?"

"I shattered it." Kolfinna fought the urge to glance at Blár. "It didn't set correctly."

"So I'll have to force all the fragments to mend together the way they used to be," Revna murmured, as if speaking to herself. She tightened her hold on Kolfinna's leg and gave her a hard look. "This *will* hurt."

Revna's eyelids lowered and heat spread from her fingers onto Kolfinna's skin. Kolfinna lowered her head on the armrest and closed her eyes, anticipating the pain. All she felt was the thrum of mana bursting from Revna's hands, warming her leg. It wasn't bad at all. She had been hurt far more than just that. Injuring her leg had been an excruciating experience. Her ankle had snapped and her shin had shattered, making her leg useless. At the time, she had fallen to the ground, screaming and holding her thigh, too scared to look or touch anything beyond her knee. And then those cold eyes had fallen on her. That scene had replayed in her nightmares over and over again.

Kolfinna shifted in the seat, trying to get more comfortable, even though that task was nearly impossible whilst having her bare leg in a stranger's lap. She instead focused on the crackly ceiling with peeling white paint.

Uneven breaths stole from her chest as she waited in anticipation for the pain to come, but it didn't.

"I don't feel any—" she started.

And then it hit her, the feeling that her leg was being broken all over again. She gasped and gripped the armrest below her head to keep herself from spasming on the couch. Shards of glass seemed to shred through her calf muscles. She squeezed her eyes shut and gritted her teeth together to keep from screaming.

"Just a bit more," Revna said.

She held her position and focused on her breathing. In and out. In and out. Even when her muscles felt like they were tearing from her bone. In and out. In and out. Even as her bones tugged out of place. In and out.

She couldn't take it anymore.

But just as she thought that, the pain stopped altogether. In the absence of it, even breathing felt like a chore. She tried unclenching her jaw. Her body trembled and she pushed herself into a sitting position. A thin sheen of sweat dampened her skin.

"Try to walk now. It should feel much better." Revna leaned into the couch, her face pale and sweat beading her forehead. "I'm sure you were in constant pain just walking and standing."

Kolfinna quickly pulled down the hem of her pants until her leg was covered, then rose to her feet slowly, unsurely. She didn't feel any different, but when she took her first step, there was no shooting pain. No awkwardness that forced her to walk on the side of her foot.

Kolfinna took a few steps and then jumped. And then jumped again. It was like she had never been injured in the first place.

Shock stunned her to silence and she walked around the room. She turned to Blár to show him, but he remained in his mountain of blankets, his whole body hidden within it. A frown twisted her lips. He had been the one to do it to her, so why was she so excited to show him how her leg was now?

"Thank you." Tears formed in her eyes and her face crumpled. "You have no idea how much this means to me."

"I can imagine." Revna's eyes saddened. "Kolfinna, someone did that to you, didn't they?"

Kolfinna pressed her palms into her eyes. How could she tell her that Blár had been the one to cripple her? To cause her so much pain for months on end? He didn't even realize how much he had hurt her when he shattered her leg. How immobile he had made her.

"It doesn't matter," Kolfinna said with a strained smile. She stretched her leg forward and wriggled her toes before taking another step. She could walk without pain; it was the strangest feeling, but it felt so natural at the same time.

Revna's hands clenched the sides of the couch and she leaned forward. "What is the world like right now for our kind?"

"It's not easy."

"Will you tell me about it?"

Kolfinna eased onto the couch, her smile fading. "What do you want to know?"

"What's your life like? How did you grow up? Were your parents fae? Do you have any family or friends that are fae?"

A pang shot through her chest. She didn't like to dwell on her family, but Revna had done so much for her, and she was the first fae she had met in a long time. She didn't even know what to say, where to begin, so for several moments, she said nothing. She simply stared at her hands, mulling over the words she had never spoken. Finally, she started from the beginning.

"My parents were both fae," she said, the previously unsaid words tumbling out awkwardly. "I had a sister as well. There were only four of us. We lived in the countryside in a cottage but somehow the villagers found out we were fae. I don't remember all the details because I was only four. I do remember my house catching on fire. I remember my father protecting us ... And then I remember running. They killed my parents." She shivered at the blurry memory. "We ran as far as we could. We kept running and running, and moving farther and farther away from our village. Katla was only three years older than me, but she suddenly had to raise me. It must've been difficult for her, but she managed. We just lived like that, running from one place to another. For years.

"But Katla was a dreamer. She wanted more and she wanted to be normal. She wanted to find love, she wanted kids, she wanted freedom. She wanted so many things, but most of all, she wanted both of us to live carefree lives. She wanted to go to school, to make friends, to meet people. She just wanted something normal and stable. A job opened up at a noble's home and she took it. I didn't want to take the job. I felt like it was too … personal. We would be living there, and when you live with people, they notice details. They notice that the flowers sway in our direction. Or that the trees seem to shade us. Or that the garden is suddenly thriving. Things like that. I'm sure they did notice.

"Well, a little over a year ago, I wasn't feeling well. I was feverish for days." Her throat closed up and she clenched her fists tightly together to keep them from shaking, then sat on them to keep them still. "I was in the courtyard with Katla and she was saying something, but I couldn't hear it. I just felt hot and uncomfortable. And then … I … I lost control. It had never happened like that." A sob escaped her throat. "Vines and trees and stones were flying everywhere around me. Katla tried to stop me, but it was too late. Everyone saw. Lord Estur was in the military and he was pretty powerful and he saw too. I don't remember much after that, but Lord Estur tried to kill me. Katla protected me. She used her power … And she never used her power. She hated it, in fact. She didn't like being a fae … But she used it because he would kill me … and … and the next thing I knew …" She inhaled sharply, tears rolling down her face. "He was standing there with her … with her head." She wept into her hands, the memory burned into the back of her mind. "Everything was a blur after that. I killed him and I ran away. I was such a coward. I didn't even take her body with me. I didn't think of anything. I don't remember what happened after that."

Kolfinna tensed when Revna pulled her into an embrace; it had been years since she had felt the warmth of a hug, and her body struggled falling into it. "You did what you could, dear," Revna murmured, rubbing her back. Pain colored her tone. "I'm so sorry you went through that. It's okay to cry. You tried your best."

Kolfinna's body went slack and she cried on her shoulder, finally letting out everything she had held in for the past year. Katla's death, her inability to save her own sister, the guilt hanging over her head—it had haunted her more than Blár ever could.

When her tears dried, Revna patted her hand. "What you experienced was an awakening. When your powers grow into a mature state, they become more powerful and you're able to use rune magic. It happens during the teen years, usually, but only when you're skilled. Some people awaken later in life when their magic finally blossoms."

Kolfinna sniffed. "It came at the wrong time."

"It would've happened at some point or another," she said, shifting in her seat so she could look over her shoulder at Blár. "When did you meet him?"

A knob of guilt grew in her chest. Was it still necessary to keep lying to her? It felt too awkward to admit to the lie now, so Kolfinna said, "Um, soon after that, actually."

"I'm surprised you were able to fall in love with a

human considering ... everything, really," Revna said, frowning at the Blár's blanket heap. She clucked her tongue. "Humans have done so much wrong to you, Kolfinna. You've lived your whole life running and hiding ... and never trusting anyone. So how can you fall in love with one? I could *never* trust a human."

"I ... I know," Kolfinna stuttered, but there was something else, a knowledge that had been growing the past few days. "But he's different."

"Really?"

"Yeah ..."

"He just seems rude and mean," Revna said with a frown.

"He's got a great personality," Kolfinna said with an awkward smile. "And ... um, it helps that he's got a cute face."

"That's it?"

"And, and ..." She glanced at Blár; he wasn't as terrible as she had made him out to be in her mind. Yes, he had plagued her nightmares, and yes, he was rude and mean and occasionally crude, but she didn't have that animosity and fear burning in her chest at the mere thought of him anymore. But what about him could she even say was great? That his insults were actually kind of funny? That he saved her life multiple times and didn't ask her to repay it? Or that he was just too beautiful.

She grasped onto those feelings.

"He's ... He's beautiful and kind, and he treats me like

I'm ... I'm, uh, normal," she said. "And—" Heat crept up her cheeks. "He's got a great ass."

Kolfinna could've sworn she saw the heap of blankets move.

Revna blinked rapidly, clearly not expecting that answer, and then burst into a chuckle. "All right, all right. I get it. You both do make a good couple, though. You look nice together."

"Thanks ..." Kolfinna's face blazed with warmth and she cleared her throat, ready to move on from this topic. "Anyway, how can I help the rest of my party?"

"Ah, ah—" Revna tutted. "First, you'll have to free me, and then I'll help you."

"But there is a way to help them, right?" Kolfinna noticed from her peripheral that Blár had poked his head out of the blanket pile; his hair stuck out in every direction.

She *really* hoped he didn't hear what she had said about him.

"There is."

The rest of the party came to her mind and she jumped to her feet. She had done enough dillydallying; it was time to save them. Or at least, *almost*. "Well?" She walked a few steps, her body relaxing with the smooth movements of her walk. "How can I free you?"

Revna's smile sent shivers down Kolfinna's spine, but she ignored the sensation. "The runes that imprison me are outside the house," Revna said. "You saw some of them when entering through the front door, I assume?

There are hundreds of runes wrapped around the house like chains. With your abilities, I don't think you'll be able to break them all and thus free me, but you'll have to try."

"All right, I'll try."

"It'll take you months—"

It felt like a bucket of ice water was thrown over her head. "I don't have months to give you," she said slowly. "Everyone will be dead by then."

"Then I suppose you should work quickly." Revna shrugged as if it wasn't her problem—and it wasn't, but she could've at least *pretended* to care.

"All right," Kolfinna said, stretching her leg. "And thank you, by the way. For healing my leg."

"Certainly, dear." Revna pushed herself to her feet and bounded to her front door. She yanked it open and gestured to the doorway, where sand was already blowing into the house. "Now, I suggest you work fast if you want to save them all."

Kolfinna didn't appreciate being told what to do, but she headed to the door nonetheless. Revna had healed her —that was enough reason to help her. But she couldn't stop the anxiety from growing in her chest, tightening like a corkscrew. Eyfura, Mímir, Magni, and the rest of the party needed her.

But, she supposed, Revna needed her too. And a deal was a deal.

19

GOLDEN RUNES SPANNED ACROSS THE DOOR IN swirls and overlapping lines. *Revna cannot use rune magic to break out of the house. Revna can use rune magic to fight students, but she cannot escape the house. Revna cannot escape the house. Clause: Revna's body will die if she leaves the house. If the house is left by Revna, her real body will crumble to dust. Revna cannot leave no matter what. Clause: no clause can be made to make Revna leave the house. Revna will be trapped here until the end of time. Clause: no clause can be made to change the duration of her imprisonment unless it is to increase the time. Clause: no decrease of time can be made. Revna will not be able to ever leave.* Hundreds of similar lines were carved into the door, the walls, and even the windows. They all essentially said the same thing, except worded differently each time. They snaked around the house in tiny never-ending lines and glittered under the harsh two suns.

Kolfinna pressed her hand against the first rune she could. *Revna cannot escape the house.* Her brows pulled together as she wisped her mana around the words. She imagined a snake wrapping around the runes, pulling tighter and tighter. She concentrated, and the words crumbled. A grin spread across her face as the first rune was destroyed, but her smile disappeared when she glanced at the thousands upon thousands of runes that filled the walls. It would be a long, arduous task to break each one.

She set to work, first focusing on the door. She grasped another rune and forced her mana to crush it with the weight of her power, and then moved on to the next. And the next. And the next. Sweat dampened her brow, but she kept at it. She used as little mana as possible to conserve her energy, since she would probably be here for a while. She found that grabbing two different runes with both hands and breaking them simultaneously worked faster, so she resorted to that.

"You're working fast." Blár poked his head from the window; the blue of his eyes was bright in the sunlight.

Kolfinna shattered the rune beneath her finger, the light dying from it as it disintegrated into gold dust. "I see you're finally awake."

"Looks like it," he said, pushing the window higher above his head. He leaned his muscular forearms on the windowsill and watched her with a curious expression.

"What is it?" She moved to the next rune and watched

him from her peripheral vision. "Is there something on my face?"

"Your eyes glow gold when you do that." He pointed to her hand, which hovered over a rune. "It looks cool."

"Oh." She inadvertently tucked a strand of hair behind her ear. "I didn't know."

"How long until you're done? I don't know about you, but I want to get out of here as soon as possible."

"I don't know ..." She broke another rune. "I have to break all of these first."

"Isn't there any way you can do it quicker?"

"No, there isn't." The heat of the desert beat down on her and sweat dampened her uniform. She turned toward the expanse of sand surrounding them and curtained her eyes with her hands to peer at the sky and the position of the suns; she didn't need anyone to tell her that time was of the essence. She wished there were another way.

He stayed there and watched her, his head propped against the side of the window frame and an unreadable expression painting his striking face. She wasn't lying when she said he was a looker. The fear she had of him had masked that beauty, but now she could openly gawk at it. He was prodigal in his abilities *and* he was handsome. Life truly was unfair. She frowned and moved to the next rune.

When had her fear turned into civility? Or whatever she felt toward him. It wasn't admiration, and it definitely wasn't friendliness, but it was *close* to the latter. When did that happen? When they were on the ship and he saved her? Or when they traveled together to get to this house? Or had it happened when they were in the castle ruins?

She finished the runes on the door and moved to the left side of the house, which was also where Blár was situated at the window. He was now sitting on the windowsill, watching the desert sky with the two suns. An awkward silence stretched between them. They weren't buddy-buddy with each other and even if Kolfinna had wanted to say something, there was nothing to talk about.

Blár finally broke the silence. "Why do you want to become a Royal Guard?"

Kolfinna faltered at those words. What did it matter to him? But it was a conversation, and it was better than the silence. The wind howled above their heads, sending a gust of sand against her face. "So I can be safe," she answered truthfully, blinking away the grittiness that had gotten in her eyes. "I don't want to keep running anymore. If I'm under Fen"—she cleared her throat—"*Captain* Asulf, then I'll be protected. I want to live a somewhat normal life."

It's what Katla wanted, she thought, but didn't add.

Kolfinna's fingers brushed the next set of runes and she broke them beneath her fingers. "And you? Why did you join the military? I heard you joined when you were twelve?"

"No," he said. "I was actually thirteen."

Extraordinary people with extraordinary abilities sometimes didn't go through schooling and were placed straight into the military. Such was the case for Blár, who was the youngest person in Rosain's history to become a black rank at age fifteen. Prior to Blár, Fenris Asulf had been the youngest black rank.

"I didn't like my powers when I was a child," he said. "I mean, what's the use of ice when you live in a village where it's winter all year long? Back then, I wished I had fire powers. My siblings used to tease me about my abilities." He tipped his head back against the window frame to gaze at the cloudless sky, a wistful smile on his face. "The military noticed I was strong and asked my father if he would be willing to let me join them. My father asked me what I wanted, and I said yes. Not because I actually cared about being in the military, but money was tight and I figured I'd help out that way. They offered a pretty hefty sum, I'll tell you that. That's how I joined."

"Do you regret it?"

He turned to her sharply. "Why do you ask?"

Kolfinna shrugged. "You were just a kid."

He cracked his knuckles distractedly. "If I could go back, I'd never join. They're all parasitic tapeworms. They'll drain you dry and toss you aside like trash. I should've stayed home and enjoyed being a kid. Joining the military is a huge regret of mine."

"Why don't you just quit?"

"I can't. I'm too far in." He scoffed and tilted his head to look at her more levelly. "And besides, do you think they'll let me live if I leave? I'm a national threat if I'm not on their side. If I'm not leashed up and behaving. They use me, but they're also scared of me."

"Who is 'they'?"

"I can't say." He dusted flecks of sand off the front of his uniform. "The higher-ups, I guess. But I can't really say."

"Come on, we're in the middle of a weird dimension. I doubt anyone will find out if you say anything."

Blár gave her a long look, and his blue eyes flashed with *something*—a memory, maybe? "You're better off not knowing all the specifics. Trust me."

"But you're a black rank. How can anyone boss you around?" Kolfinna had a hard time wrapping around her mind that Blár wasn't the all-powerful person she had in mind. How could anyone defy him when he had such monstrous abilities? "You can defeat pretty much everyone in the country except for Fenris and Hilda Helgadottir."

His nose crinkled as if she had shoved a lemon in his mouth. "You don't think I can beat those two geezers? Hilda's an old hag and Fenris hasn't had a proper battle in years. I can easily wipe the floor with them."

She snorted back a laugh. Such a typical Blár response. "Okay, sure, but my point stands."

"Kolfinna, it's not always about power," he said. "I might be the most powerful in the country when it comes to my abilities, but I'm not powerful politically, and these assholes have too much on me for me to just up and quit. I can't leave right now anyway. I've got too much to do."

Kolfinna's hand grazed another rune and she squeezed

it with her mana; it instantly faded from the wall. "Is it true the military cages you up sometimes?"

He frowned. "No, why would they do that?"

"Because you're"—she broke the next chain of runes with both hands; she lifted a hand from the grainy texture of the wooden wall splattered with sand, and waved it at him—"uncooperative."

"The military wants to keep me on their side, so they would never do that." Blár gave her a look like she had asked a strange question, even though it was a common rumor among the gossipers. "I'm not a dog."

"So I'm guessing they don't drug you either?"

"Who comes up with this stuff?" He cocked an eyebrow, the corner of his mouth lifting in an amused smirk. "Do people really think I'm a drugged puppet? Or a caged dog?"

"From the gossips, people don't know anything about you. Other than that you're powerful, scary, and uncontrollable." She grabbed the next runes and shattered them easier than she had the others. Was it her imagination or was she getting better at this?

Her mind wandered to when Magni at the Royal Guard headquarters had told her Blár was a hunter. "Um ... one of the rumors also says you're a part of the Hunter's Association."

"I don't have time for that, and there are a million reasons why I wouldn't join them."

That sparked her attention almost more than the

unexpected relief that he wasn't a hunter. "Oh? Like what?"

"Well, for one, I don't have time for that. Those losers really spend their free time killing innocent people? That's not my thing. Secondly, I don't like that shitbag Hilda Helgadottir, so the thought of her ordering me around would piss me off. Thirdly, I don't agree with them morally. And so much more."

Kolfinna crouched below Blár's window where ribbons of runes spiraled beneath it. "You ... you don't hate fae?"

"No."

"Why?" Her hand hovered over a rune, but she couldn't focus enough to break it, and instead peered up at him.

"You're all just ... people." He shrugged. "People with weird power, sure. But just people."

"Many humans don't agree with you."

"I know. But I used to know a fae when I was younger, and it really just made me see that the fae are just ... people."

That was even stranger—why would a fae reveal themselves? Or did something happen for Blár to find out the person was a fae?

Blár must've seen the questions on her face because he said, "It's a long story. I'll tell you about it later."

"Ah, okay ..." Taking the hint that he didn't want to talk about it, she asked instead, "So ... um, what's your take on the Royal Guards? Do you think they'll use me and toss me?"

"Of course. That's what they all do," he said. "But you'll be in better hands than if you joined the military. Fenris isn't a bad guy. He's annoying, but he's not a bad guy. He'll take care of you. But you have to keep in mind you'll be under the king, and the king is like every fat political bastard. He's a greedy, miserable shit. So be careful not to get noticed by him."

"I think that's hard to do." Kolfinna's hand hovered over the golden inscriptions below the windowsill. The air buzzed with her mana as she made the runes disappear before she waved at her body with her free hand. "I mean, look at me."

Blár peered down at her with intensely blue eyes, his brows pulled together. "What do you mean? You can blend in even if you're chubby."

"W-What? What does that have to do with anything?" The shock sent her stumbling onto her bottom and she looked up at him with wide eyes. Her face tingled as the blood rushed to her ears. She didn't mean it *that* way! "I mean, like, look at me—I'm a fae!" she sputtered, pushing herself onto her knees, the hot sand grinding beneath her movements. "Obviously, I stick out like a sore thumb. And, I mean, my eyes, Blár—they're pink! There's no way he won't notice me."

His eyes widened with realization, and then his face slowly flushed red. "Oh. Oh, uh, well, it seems I misinterpreted." He cleared his throat, then rubbed the nape of his neck. "I thought you meant like you didn't fit in with the other Royal Guards because you're ..."

She covered her face with her hands, suddenly feeling like the double suns were starting to burn her. She didn't know what was more awkward: Blár commenting about her body or that he noticed she didn't belong. "Ugh, let's just drop this!"

Kolfinna straightened and moved to another part of the house, turning so he couldn't see her red face.

"I don't mean that you look bad. I mean it, you look great." Blár jumped off the windowsill and stepped toward her until he was inches away. He gently placed a hand on the crook of her arm. "Look, I didn't mean to, uh, comment on your body. I know that can be a sensitive topic ..."

"Blár, just drop it."

"You have a nice figure." He dropped his hand. Wind tousled his hair and the sun continued to redden his skin. "Kolfinna, I'm serious—"

"I get it, I get it!" A sudden burst of wind raged over them and made her clothes cling to her even more tightly. She pushed back her hair with one hand and pressed the other over a string of runes. "I'm not fit like the others. I get it. Let's just move on from that—"

"Hey, it's nothing to feel bad about—"

"It's everything to feel bad about." She overpowered a rune with her mana, watching as it perished. She didn't need another reason to feel out of place, but now she was even more self-conscious. "The training will help me slim down," she reasoned more to herself than Blár. "So it's not like I feel bad—"

"Stop, stop." He blew out air and leaned against the house. "Man, I feel like the biggest asshole right now. Look, I don't think you look bad. I shouldn't have said anything about your body or called you that. I'm sorry. Your body type is fine the way it is."

Between the glare of the suns and Blár's stammering, she needed more time to get over the embarrassment, but she nodded anyway. "Thanks, I guess."

"If it makes you feel any better, your body type is my type."

"You're not chubby. Or big." She raised an eyebrow and glanced at his muscular physique. Even with his thick uniform, she could make out the strong planes of his chest and the fullness of his biceps.

"That's not the type I meant," he said with a smirk.

Her mouth dropped open in mortification as the words hit her. He didn't mean that his body type was the same body type she had. Her face grew hotter and now she was the one stammering. "I didn't need to hear that, but thanks. A-Anyway, I have to get back to work."

Blár motioned for her to continue and perched himself back on the windowsill. He tipped his head back to stare at the sky while Kolfinna broke another jumble of runes, her face steaming from embarrassment. That was the weirdest conversation she'd ever had with him, but it didn't make her feel bad like she thought it would. And she couldn't shake the feeling that he was glancing at her from time to time. She didn't dare look.

IT WASN'T UNTIL THE SUN DIPPED INTO THE horizon that Revna opened one of the windows and waved to Kolfinna, careful not to stick any part of herself outside. "Why don't you both come inside and have some dinner? I'm sure you're starving."

"I want to keep working," Kolfinna murmured, stifling a yawn.

"Kolfinna, it'll be days before you finish," she said. "Come inside and rest. You've been at it for hours."

"I'm almost done."

Revna froze. "What?"

"I'm almost done," Kolfinna said, just as another rune vanished at her fingertips. She tried to pull more mana from within her, but it felt like touching raindrops instead of a full pond. "I have maybe a hundred left? Maybe less."

"Are you sure you got them all?"

"Not all, but most, yes." Most of the runes were gone and she could see the pale-yellow wood of the house.

"But …" Revna opened her mouth and closed it, like a gaping fish. "That shouldn't be possible at your current level. Are you sure you've never used rune magic?"

Kolfinna had nothing to base her progress on, so hearing that brought a smile to her face. Was she actually, maybe, *good* at this?

"Yes, this is my first time," Kolfinna answered, careful to hide the undercurrents of excitement in her voice, "but ... it's not hard, per se. It's just very tedious and it gets monotonous."

Revna snapped her fingers. "I didn't think about it before, but it's been centuries since anyone has fortified the runes. They've likely lost a significant amount of their power ... Let this be a lesson to you," she said, her voice quickening in giddiness. "Runes must always have a power source. You can write runes and leave them there and they'll stay up for decades because your mana is inside it, but once you're dead, it weakens. And as time goes on, it weakens more and more. Unless they're runes with souls and the dead mingled in, like with items ... they can't last forever. It doesn't make sense that a newcomer like you would be able to break centuries' worth of runes just because you're slightly gifted. Isn't this great news? And, I suppose, you must be one of *those* types."

"Those types?" Kolfinna lowered her hand from the wall.

"Yes, usually there are two types of rune users. Those that are good at breaking runes, and those that are good at making runes. The latter is favored in society more than the former. Seeing as how you could only write 'cold' on the spoon, I suppose your rune making abilities are abysmal. But that's good that you're able to break them."

Kolfinna's smile faltered; was she supposed to feel happy hearing that? "Um, yeah, thanks."

Blár, who had been lying on the ground with his arms

behind his head, stretched his arms out as he sat upright. Sand coated his cloak and hair. "Are we almost done?"

"We?" Kolfinna raised an eyebrow. "I don't recall you helping."

"I offered conversation." He jumped to his feet and dusted the sand off his pants. "How is your mana doing? You've been working for a few hours now, so I imagine you're drained."

She wanted to refute him and say her mana was perfectly fine and that she could finish breaking all the runes, but she could barely feel the mana inside her. "Unfortunately," she said, "I think I've exhausted a lot of my mana."

"You can work on it tomorrow," Revna said. "Come inside and eat. Come on."

Kolfinna hesitated even as her arms felt heavy and her eyes drooped. She *needed* to finish tonight. Eyfura and the rest of the party needed her help; she couldn't waste time here. But she was running on fumes. Maybe an hour or two would help rejuvenate her mana?

"Eat and rest, and you can start again," Revna insisted, as if reading her mind.

"All right ... But only for a bit."

20

⁓

After a two-hour break that helped Kolfinna replenish some mana, Kolfinna set to work on the rest of the runes. She felt like a stick in the mud as she tried to garner the willpower and strength to shatter the runes. Blár was sprawled on the ground again with his arms crossed beneath his head. Two swords sat beside him; swords that Revna had given them to defeat the dreki when the time came.

She tried concentrating on the rune at hand, but her mind drifted to Blár, and then to the swords, and then to the sky—as if the dreki would swoop down and gobble her up.

"What's wrong?" Blár asked, startling her from her reverie.

"I don't know." She betrayed a glance at the window, hoping Revna wasn't eavesdropping. She wrung her aching hands together—they were sore from opening and closing her fist to grasp the runes, which she later realized she didn't need to do and only needed to touch them with her mana to break them. The joints popped with every twist and her knuckles cracked when she distractedly pulled her fingers. "I think I might've gone overboard earlier, and now I'm just burned out. It's hard to focus."

Blár considered that for a moment. "Then let's just go. We have weapons. Someone else can save her dusty ass."

"What? And what about helping the others? Revna knows more about this place than we do."

"We'll find a way now that you know how to use runes—"

"No, it's better if we learn the proper way. And besides, I made a promise! How can I just abandon that?"

"Easy. You just walk away." He said it as if it was the easiest thing in the world. "Not everyone needs to be rescued, you know."

"That's not comforting coming from a military black rank," she huffed as the cool night air tickled her down to her bones. "Aren't you supposed to save people?"

"No, that's the Royal Guards' job. My job is to obliterate whatever they tell me to." He sat upright, the moonlight glinting off his hair. "But anyway, why can't you focus?"

"Maybe it's you." She waggled her finger at him. "You're distracting me."

He rolled his eyes. "I'm just making sure you don't get roasted by the dreki when the time comes. So keep working and ignore me. I know that may be difficult."

"Ha, ha." She concentrated her mana on a rune. *Revna, the liar, shall never break free.* Kolfinna brushed a finger over the *liar*. Why would it say such a thing?

"Is it difficult?"

"Hm?" She burst her mana over the rune.

"The runes," he said. "Is it hard breaking them?"

The rune shifted to dust in her hand and she spread her fingers to the next one. "Not really. Revna said these runes are weak since time has worn them out and the people who put them here have long died. I'm sure it'll be harder once we get out of here."

Blár rubbed off the sand stuck to his elbows. "That's a bummer. Do you think we'll have trouble with the rest of the castle?"

"I'm not sure ... Let's hope not." Her mind wandered to the others again and her chest tightened with the weight of their lives resting in her hands. "Do you ..." Her voice softened and she tried to hide the tremble in her words. "Do you think they're still alive?"

Blár rubbed a hand over his mouth, as if thinking of what to say. "I hope they are. I trust their abilities, but what if they're in a place where their magic doesn't work? This place"—he paused and he peered at the three moons— "doesn't care for our rules or our abilities. It favors the fae. So I don't know. I hope they are, but I really have no clue."

"If I ... if I were better at reading runes"—her voice cracked—"maybe there would be fewer deaths—"

"Don't talk like that." His voice snapped like the

crackle of a whip. "Once you start feeling guilty, there's no going back. You're the only one not trained to be here, do you understand?" His voice lowered. "The burden of everyone's safety is *not* yours to bear."

Kolfinna dug her feet into the sand to keep from looking at him as her throat constricted; she hadn't realized how much she needed to hear that.

"I've been meaning to ask you." He cleared his throat and averted his gaze, instead choosing to examine the star-speckled night sky. "Your ... um, leg ... Does it still bother you?"

Kolfinna wriggled her toes subconsciously, the movement causing no usual discomfort. The scars were still there—she had checked—but there was no pain. No awkward movement. No limping. "It's back to how it used to be," she said quietly, "but with scarring."

He grimaced and picked at the dried blood on the cuff of his sleeve. "You know, under normal circumstances, I wouldn't apologize, because I don't necessarily think I did anything wrong, but these aren't exactly *normal* circumstances." He rose to his feet and dusted off the sand on his pants. The moonlight bathed his face in silver. "And honestly, seeing you hobble around and just look outright in pain, made me uncomfortable. And yes, I was just doing my job and for all I knew, you were a crazy murderer fae and ... I kind of figured I'd let someone else catch you since I wasn't in the mood, but looking at it in hindsight, it was a pretty shitty thing to do. And ... Well, what I'm trying to say is—I'm sorry. I really shouldn't have done that to you."

The cold desert wind blew against her face and sent her hair fluttering over her face wildly. The cold contrasted with the budding warmth in the pit of her stomach. She had never thought he would apologize for injuring her. Though the apology sounded a bit awkward, he still owned up to his mistake. Sort of.

"Are you trying to apologize?" Kolfinna placed a hand on her hip and raised a brow. "Because that's a weird apology. Especially starting it off that you wouldn't normally apologize. So do you feel like you did something wrong or not? Because your words are a bit contradictory."

"You're making this way more awkward than it should be," he groaned and kicked the ground, which sent a flurry of sand to carry with the wind. "Yes, I'm sorry. I truly mean it."

"Then maybe you should reword it." She curled her fingers over the rough siding of the house, the runes buzzing beneath her fingers. "Like, 'hey, Kolfinna, I'm terribly sorry for crippling you. I'll make sure not to do it again.'"

"I apologized." Blár blew out air, his ice-blue eyes flashing in the moonlight. "Do you want me to be eternally at your mercy?"

The corner of Kolfinna's mouth lifted into a smirk. "*Eternally* at my mercy? Does that mean you plan on sticking to my side for that long?"

"Only if you want me to stay."

The wind seemed to stop blowing and the moons wilted in her peripheral until all Kolfinna saw was the intense frigid blue of Blár's eyes. She forgot to breathe and could only stare at him—at the serious expression on his face, at the blue bruise on his cheek, at his pale skin illuminating silver from the moonlight. He couldn't have meant that seriously, could he? Kolfinna ripped her gaze from his and turned to the golden iridescence of the runes. He was too powerful, too beautiful, and too monstrous to mean it seriously when it came to her.

She forced herself to smile and drilled the runes with her mana. "I'm surprised you know how to joke. You're always so serious looking." She laughed, and it came out hollow. A strange part of her wondered if she wanted him to be serious.

"Do you think I'm a soulless monster? Of course I know how to joke." Blár leaned a shoulder against the wall and watched her. "I'm just not great at it. Or funny, to be honest."

"So you're the kind that does self-depreciating humor?" Kolfinna broke another rune.

A rare smile lifted his lips, but the shadows of the night swallowed it up as he turned his head to the ground. "Well, *anyway*, I hope you can learn to, um, accept my apology. That doesn't mean you have to forgive me, but it was important for me to put it out there."

The pit of her stomach fluttered unnaturally and she quickly went back to the runes. Nothing he said was outright romantic or extraordinary, so why did it feel like she was being swept away?

"Thank you," she said, her words barely a whisper. "I appreciate it."

He didn't have time to say anything else, because the last rune crumbled beneath her mana and the door to the house flung open with gusto. Kolfinna nearly fell backward in surprise as Revna stood in the doorway, her trembling hands pressed together. Had she felt the last rune disappear?

"Is it done?" Revna's eyes were alight with hope. "Have you finished?"

Kolfinna gave the house a quick inspection and bobbed her head. "Yes, I got them all."

"Really? Truly? Can you check again?"

Kolfinna checked every crevice of the house before circling back to the doorway. "Yes, I got it all—"

Revna jumped through the doorway and flung her arms around Kolfinna, capturing her in a bear hug. "Oh, goodness! Thank you! Thank you so much, Kolfinna." She tightened her grip on her, her thin shoulders quivering as she swallowed a sob. "You have no idea how lonely, and tiring, and horrible it was to be stuck in there for so, so long. Thank you, thank you so much."

"Um, you're welcome—" Kolfinna started just as Blár said, "Don't act like she did it for free. Now tell us how to get our comrades out of here."

Revna pulled Kolfinna out of the embrace and held her at arm's length, a scowl twisting her face. "I really don't see what you see in him, darling," Revna said with a sniff. "And yes, I haven't forgotten my end of the deal."

"Now that you're free, will your soul return to your body?" Kolfinna asked with a head tilt.

Revna's shoulders dropped. "My body is still in a comatose state, so I'm going to try to see what I can do ... I fear I won't be able to do much, but at least if I leave here and go back to my body, I won't be stuck. I'm sure I'll be able to wake up somehow ..."

"If I run into your body," Kolfinna said, "I'll try to wake you."

"Thank you, dear." Revna gave her another tight embrace. "You've already done so much for me. I promise I'll make it up to you somehow."

Blár drummed his fingers against his sunburnt crossed arms. "Hate to break this touching moment, but we kind of have to go and kill the dreki and free our comrades. So, maybe you can just tell us already how to help everyone?"

"You're as pleasant as always, human." Revna sighed loudly and detached herself from Kolfinna. "I hope I don't see you on the other side. And as for the matter of your comrades—they're likely already dead, so don't bother."

Revna held her hand up in the sky and twirled her fingers above her head. Runes glared in the space above her, glinting harshly like the blinding light of the two suns. Kolfinna covered her eyes and when the light died down, Revna was nowhere to be seen.

Blár stared at the spot she had been standing; her footprints indented the sand. "Did—Did that hagfish just *ghost* us? After all the trouble you did for her?"

All the color blanched from Kolfinna's skin; what about Revna's end of the deal—did she really just betray her like that? And what runes did she write over her head to make her disappear from this dimension?

Blár cursed under his breath and kicked the wall of the house. "Damn it! We could've left this place much earlier if we'd known that shitbag wouldn't even help us!"

The strength left Kolfinna's legs and she sank to her knees, the cool sand cushioning her. She covered her face with her hands. Revna had betrayed her. Kolfinna had trusted her, and she had in turn *used* her! All that time she wasted trying to break the runes in the house was precious time she could've used to help everyone.

"Hey—are you crying?"

She felt Blár tentatively touch her shoulder, but she brushed his hand away. "She probably made a mistake," she heard herself say between bitter breaths. "W-Whatever the case, we should go. Let's find the dreki and get out of here."

"Kol—"

"Blár!" Kolfinna turned her face toward him and hated the way her eyes stung. "We don't have time for this. Let's go."

Blár studied her for a moment before nodding.

If Kolfinna saw her again, she had a lot of questions to ask.

21

Kolfinna's thighs burned as they trekked the sandy dunes of the desert. The dreki was nowhere to be found, even though they had been walking the whole night until dusk. The suns beat down on the back of her head and sweat poured down her face, drenching her uniform. Blár's own uniform was similarly soaked with sweat. He had discarded his cloak at some point and had unbuttoned the first three buttons of his uniform. Neither of them talked about Revna; their sole focus was on finding the dreki.

Kolfinna blotted her sweaty forehead with the sleeve of her uniform. "When we were running from that monster, it came upon us every chance it got, but now that we're actively looking for it, it's disappeared."

"What's our plan anyway?" Blár shifted his sword in his other hand, careful not to let the sharp edge drag across the sand like Kolfinna was doing. He eyed her sword, which sliced into the granular ground, with a frown. "Once you're a Royal Guard, you can't do that."

"Do what?"

"Actively drag it across the ground. Royal Guards are supposed to uphold an image." He rolled up one sleeve at a time, balancing the sword and revealing his sunburnt, red skin. Kolfinna couldn't stop staring at his forearms and the way his muscles bulged. "Well, I guess it doesn't matter," he continued, oblivious to her stare. Sweat dotted his forehead, and sand particles clung to the sunburnt skin on his cheeks and nose. "Anyway—are you going to change the runes or are we going to fight it with these?" He motioned to the sword. "I'm not much of a swordsman."

Despite his words, Kolfinna still dragged the sword behind her. She didn't want to admit it to him, but the sword was too heavy to carry upright for hours on end.

Slaying a monster with a sword shouldn't have been as daunting of a task as it seemed, but the thought of killing it with a weapon instead of using her magic made her uncomfortable. Attacking something with magic was quick and she didn't have to get so close to it, but with a sword, she would deal the finishing blow.

"I don't think I can create new runes. I'm only good at breaking them, not making them." Kolfinna's feet dragged into the thick sand with each step. "I guess we'll have to fight with these swords."

"You only had your first rune lesson two days ago.

How do you know if you're good or bad at creating them?"

The deafening silence stretched between them as Kolfinna pondered those words. She had listened to whatever Revna had told her, but it was true, she had only tried once to create runes. Maybe it would be different this time?

A sizzle of mana caught her attention and she froze as the sensation sent a jolt of warmth up her spine. She whipped her head up to the sky, but there was no familiar flapping of its wings or the pressure of the wind as the dreki flew. She waited with bated breath, gaze flickering over the clear skies, but there was no dreki. The wind howled and she remembered to breathe.

She craned her neck to where the mana sizzled and found a boulder with mana spilling forth from it. Kolfinna ran to the boulder, her sword clanking behind her as it bumped across pebbles. She heard Blár's footsteps disrupting the sand behind her.

Kolfinna stopped when she reached the boulder; golden runes danced over the rough ridges of the stone. *Slay the dreki; magic does not work.*

"This is where we started," she said.

Would she be able to break the runes here? Her fingers splayed against the runes and she quickly withdrew her hand from the scorching boulder. The rays of the two suns made the boulder unbearably hot, but she hesitantly placed her hands an inch away from the runes and she closed her eyes, feeling her own mana deep within herself.

She called it forth and imagined it like a rope lassoing around the runes and suffocating them.

The runes didn't break.

Sweat dotted her forehead as she focused her mana on the runes again. Breaking the runes at Revna's house was like butter melting in her hands, or like antiques withering to dust at her very touch. These runes were solid and sturdy, holding their shape no matter how much mana she slammed into them.

She twisted and wrestled the runes, but they didn't budge.

"What's wrong?" Blár asked when her breathing hitched.

Her hands curled into fists until the grooves of the boulder scraped her skin atop her fingers painfully. If she wasn't able to break these runes, didn't that mean she wasn't good at breaking runes? What if she was just terrible at rune magic?

Kolfinna quickly cast that thought away. She didn't have time for her insecurities. When she was alone and privy to her own feelings, she would allow herself to wallow. Now wasn't the time.

"It's not working. I-I'm trying—" She cringed at the hopelessness underscoring her words and tried to ignore the stinging in her eyes. The wind blew against them gently and she squeezed her eyes shut to keep the sand out of them—and the tears.

"Why don't we try breaking the rock?"

Kolfinna's eyes snapped open. "No! We have no idea

what would happen if we do that. What if we get stuck here forever?"

Blár studied the boulder expressionlessly, his winter-like eyes shifting to her. "You can't do it?"

A frown tugged at her lips. "It's not easy, you know."

"All right, then we just wait for the dreki and kill it ourselves." He struck his sword into the sand, where it tilted to the side. "We don't have much of a choice, do we?"

"I'll keep trying with the runes."

He either didn't hear her or he chose to ignore her because he didn't respond. A restlessness draped itself over Blár, so like the never-ending desert winds she had now come to expect. He paced back and forth. Sweat glossed his midnight hair and he kept pushing it back.

Kolfinna shifted her attention back to the runes, even as her mind wandered to the others. How were they doing out there? Were they even alive? Her heart trembled as she imagined Eyfura's and Mímir's bodies twisted grotesquely, fiendish monsters hovering over their corpses, and runes flying above their unsuspecting heads. They couldn't survive without understanding what to do. She was supposed to protect them, but she was stuck here— useless. And thanks to Revna's lies, she had wasted a whole precious day.

If Blár wasn't here, would she even be able to kill the dreki? He and the others had trained for years, while she was an amateur in every sense. Now that she was stripped of her powers, she could see just how weak she was.

She broke away from the boulder and instead kneeled on the ground, her mind racing. There had to be something she could do before the dreki showed up. Revna had told her runes came naturally to fae, and she had seen that herself when she had known the meaning of them immediately after seeing them.

Portal, she thought, whisking her hand over the sand. She ignored the heat of the sand as it burned her fingers. Swirls and shapes came to mind and she quickly mimicked them into the sand. She poured her mana into it with every flick of her wrist. *Portal out of here*, she emphasized, her fingers moving faster and carving the runes from her mind to the ground.

She heard the rustling of Blár's clothes as he moved to stand beside her, but she didn't dare break her concentration from the runes. She imbued the runes with her mana, bit by bit, but nothing happened. No tingling or swish of magic, no burning of the runes—nothing.

The runes were laid out in front of her, but they lacked the iridescent magic that clung to the runes in the castle. They were simply written words. She had failed.

"What is it supposed to be?"

"Runes," she said, her tone dropping low. "It didn't work."

"Why not?"

"I don't know." Kolfinna slapped the sand beside her rune writing—she couldn't bring herself to destroy it. "Maybe I'm not strong enough. Or maybe I don't have enough mana. Not everyone is like you, you know." She thrust a hand in his direction and her fingers twitched to claw at something. "With a freakin' vault of unlimited mana to use at their disposal."

"If you want to feel bad about yourself, do it when we're out of here," he snapped. His black hair shifted with the hot wind over his scowling face and he turned away from her. "Just give up and wait for it to show up."

He went back to circling his sword, his expression pulled tight. Kolfinna blew out some steam and tried to—unsuccessfully—clear her mind. She wasn't the only one with a lot to lose. If they weren't able to kill the dreki, they would likely die. They had packed food and water they had found at Revna's house, but that wouldn't last forever. What if blinding the dreki made it so that it wanted to stay in hiding?

Kolfinna pressed more of her mana into the runes like a helpless child throwing a bucket of water into a raging forest fire, hoping to make a difference. If only, she thought bitterly, her mana were as expansive as Blár's. Maybe then she would get somewhere. Maybe then, these runes would work.

She paused at that thought. Revna had been able to feel Blár's immense mana even though Kolfinna had never considered it possible. Fae were able to feel the life force of plants and nature, but could she also feel the mana and life force of other creatures? Of humans? Like Revna had?

Her gaze cut to Blár, who was peering into the sky impatiently, and she gently bit her bottom lip and exhaled while looking up at the sky. Was it possible? It sounded like something forbidden. Like something evil.

"Blár, do you ..." She licked her suddenly dry lips and her tongue caught the grains of sand. "Do you think I can borrow your mana?"

Blár stared at her like she had said something stupid, like she was joking, but her expression stilled him to seriousness. "Are fae"—he studied her, as if still wondering if she was joking—"able to do that?"

"I'm not sure." Kolfinna tugged at her braided hair, her fingers smoothing over her hair ribbon. "But I thought ... Maybe it's worth a try?"

"If it can get us out of here, sure," he said. "What should I do?"

Kolfinna released her braid and rubbed her hands over her uniform. "Um, I've never done anything like this, but can I hold your hand? I think that can help me channel it. I think. I'm not entirely sure."

He held his hand out to her and she paused to stare at the thick calluses on the ridge of his palm under his fingers and the sand beneath his nails. His hands spoke of years of training. Years of mana singing the skin of his palms. Years of fighting.

She slipped her hand into his lightly, careful not to squeeze or signal something romantic.

Kolfinna placed her other hand above the sandy runes. Her mana swished in her flesh, swarming her belly and chest, but she needed to look beyond her own mana. She tried focusing on Blár's hand. On the rough skin of his palms. She went beyond just his skin. She lulled her mana and focused on *his*. As if he were just another plant she was toying with. He would probably be a cactus if he were a plant. Rough and prickly and tough. Or maybe he was a rose; beautiful, but thorny.

Finally, she felt the prickle of his mana—she followed that prickle, and her breath caught in her throat at the enormity of it. The life force of plants was always fleeting and small beneath her fingertips, but this was on another level. His mana was like a vast ocean. It swept back and forth, unrelenting. She understood why Revna had been shocked when she first touched his hand and felt the immensity of it. It was unreal. She had never even known it was possible to harbor so much mana.

And what was even more shocking—his mana was *cold*.

Downright frigid, like icy shores and freezing glaciers.

He was truly winter epitomized.

Kolfinna drew forth from that unforgiving, cold ocean. She pulled a stream of his mana from deep within himself and trickled it from her hand to the runes splayed on the ground. Bit by bit, she spooled his mana like a ball of yarn. She tugged and tugged, and it was like pulling a ship by a piece of rope.

The runes on the sand glowed a golden hue as they came to life. Excitement bubbled in the pit of her stomach and she lurched to her feet, shifting her eyes to Blár, who stared at the ground in awe.

"It worked!" She released his hand. "It worked."

The runes continued to glow, but something wasn't right.

Her feet sank into the sand and the center of the runes fell into a gaping hole. She realized with a start that they were slowly being dragged into it, and that the gaping hole was widening, cracking farther into the sand. The sand licked her ankles hungrily, ready to pull her down.

Like lightning, Blár rolled to the side, away from the runes. She took a step in his direction, but the sand yanked her farther into it. A strangled scream escaped her lips and it pulled her waist deep. Her eyes widened and she clawed at the space surrounding her, her legs stuck in thickened mud. She tried to grab onto something, anything, but her hands slapped only sand. Until Blár's hand found hers.

She didn't think. She thrust her hands into his and trusted him. Trusted that he would pull her out. He yanked her toward him and her arm felt like it would pull from its socket, but the pain didn't register. Her fear was swallowing her the same way the sand was eating her. It took less than five seconds for Blár's hands to wrap around her forearms and for him to pull her out.

She flew forward and toppled on his chest as they tumbled on the ground. His arms tightened around her body. They both gasped for air, their limbs tangled together. She twisted her head and watched in horror as the runes were completely sucked into the black hole. The hole sewed itself together and sand bubbled up over it. In seconds, it didn't even look like something had been there.

Blár threw his head backward onto the sand. "What ... the ... hell ... was ... that?" he said between shaky breaths, his grip on her waist loosening.

Kolfinna slid off his chest and to the ground beside him. She didn't notice the hot sting of the sand or how close she was to Blár. Or the way his lean body had felt pressed against hers. She *definitely* didn't notice that.

What would've happened if they had been sucked into that? Nausea twisted her stomach into a tighter knot and shivers racked her body, despite the sickening heat.

Blár had saved her, again. How many times did that make it?

"I'm sorry." Tears pricked the corner of her eyes, but she wasn't sure if it was from emotions or the grittiness of the sand. "I didn't know that would happen."

He cursed loudly, pulling himself to his feet. "No need to apologize. Pick yourself up. We've got a guest."

Her forehead crinkled and she followed his gaze toward the sky. The dreki flew in their direction, wings flapping and mouth hanging ajar. Liquid fire dripped from its open mouth and it screamed into the sky, piercing her ears. The mana must've drawn it.

It roared again, shaking the sandy mountains and sending a shiver down her spine. She quickly scooped the long-forgotten sword and held it weakly in front of herself. Her gaze darted from the dreki to their surroundings. Where would it land? Her adrenaline pumping through her veins wasn't enough to mask the burning of her biceps from holding up the sword. Her breaths were shallow and quick. Beside her, Blár stood tall and icy, his own sword held high. They could do this. They could kill it.

The dreki opened its mouth and roared. It flapped its wings and dropped on the spot where the runes had been written. Its eyes were crusted and scabbed from when they last attacked it, and it twisted its head from side to side, unseeing, as it screeched loudly and breathed fire to their left. Kolfinna ran in the opposite direction of the fire, her heart racing.

As if it heard her, it craned its head in her direction and opened its mouth. The smell of decay and charcoal assaulted her nose and she watched in slow motion as it inhaled, its chest squeezing and halving in size before it swelled and a spring of fire shot in her direction. She rolled just in the nick of time, her hair whipping behind her.

Blár moved lithely like the Jötnar when it hunted its prey, his eyes narrowed and fixated on the dreki. Kolfinna dodged the dreki's fire breathing while Blár scaled the lizard-like body. He looked like he knew exactly what he was doing. Confidence oozed from his being.

The dreki kicked its head back, but Blár dug the sword into its shoulder and hung on as the dreki flailed, trying to shake him off. Kolfinna took her chance and ran to the dreki's legs. Scales adorned its body like armor, but there were tiny slits around the scales where she could slip her sword in. She angled her sword at the joint of the dreki's back leg and jammed it with all her might. It screamed louder, and she pushed harder, twisting the blade and then yanking it out. It stomped and roared, fire dripping from its mouth and onto the sizzling sandy ground.

Kolfinna rounded the beast, her gaze flicking to Blár, who was hacking away at the top of the dreki's neck, but he couldn't seem to get a clean cut. She moved without thinking, her leg tracing runes on the ground around the dreki. Fighting it wasn't working. No matter how much Blár swung at the neck, it wasn't budging. Maybe the dreki was a creature that had to be killed with magic? With runes?

Her mind was a blur as she circled the dreki and continued the runes with her feet, watching it carefully and dodging. It took minutes for her to circle the beast in a wide enough ring, but it felt like hours. Her thighs burned from exertion and she almost dropped her sword.

"Blár! Lend me your mana!" she screamed, waving her hands to catch his attention. The dreki turned in her direction sharply and opened its mouth to scream. She was already running to the side before it could blast her to a burnt crisp.

Blár jumped off its back, stumbled, and ran headlong to her. Sweat dampened his hair and a wildness shone from his eyes. She grasped his hand without thinking and dropped to the sand, her free hand searching the rune. She breathed out deeply and poured her mana into it, gripping onto Blár's mana and doing the same. The dreki imprinted the sand with its claws and screeched loudly, the holes in its eye sockets turning in their direction before flicking somewhere else. Kolfinna didn't have time to be gentle, so she yanked with all her might at Blár's mana pooling into her chest and her hand. She thrust it into the runes.

For a few seconds, she thought she failed. It was too big of a circle, too little mana for such a giant ring, and so unlike the small circle she had made earlier, but then the dreki's feet slithered into the sand, sinking deeper and deeper. It screamed, flapping its wings to lift its body up, but the sand was much quicker than when she had first made it. *Quickly portal out of here*, she had continuously etched into the sand around the dreki.

The dreki screamed as its body was consumed by the ground. A stream of pink silk flashed I front of her, catching in the swirl of sand and the thrashing lizard body. Her hair ribbon, she realized, reaching forward to grasp it, but it was too late. It warped with the rest of the dreki.

For an instant, the relief was palpable. Kolfinna's freed hair whipped around her face. "We did it." She sank into the sand. "It worked—"

They didn't have time to celebrate, because the world shook and spun, sputtering and careening into darkness. She barely had time to scream before being ripped away.

2 2

Kolfinna slammed into the cold, hard floor. Her head made an audible thump. The pain subsided when she sat up and rubbed it. Blár was crumpled in a similarly twisted position; he groaned and hissed, one hand pressed against his back. Crumbling and half-broken vases and statues sprayed the floor. Ripped paintings hanging by a thread were tilted on the walls and some were on the floor, the pictures unrecognizable with age and brown splatters. She realized they had been transported back into the room they had last been in.

Blár pulled himself into a sitting position with a sharp inhale. "How much mana did you drain out of me?" He flopped down on his back and cursed. Sweat beaded his forehead and his chest rose and fell with labored breaths. "Damn, I've never been so tired."

Kolfinna grimaced and fiddled with her hair. She hadn't realized she had used so much of his mana. Toward the end, she had thrown almost everything into the runes because it would've been impossible with her mana reserve. And she had grown desperate in the heat of battle. "Sorry, I didn't realize we would use so much … It was a bigger circle than the first time around, so we needed more mana."

"You don't look as tired as me." He narrowed his eyes at her, but she sensed no hostility.

"I channeled your mana into my body, and from my body into the runes. Um, but the leftover that I didn't end up using, well, it stayed with me … I guess," she trailed and cleared her throat. "But it's fine, because you'll replenish your mana in a day, so hopefully you'll be fine tomorrow."

He held his hand up, and tiny ice crystals formed on his fingertips. He brushed them away. "At least I can use my magic again," he breathed, pushing himself up. "Well, whatever, let's go look for the others."

A flash of pink caught her attention; it was her ribbon curled on top of a statue fragment. She brought a shaky hand to pick it up.

"What is it?" Blár must've seen the panic on her face because he was in front of her in seconds. "Kolfinna?"

She held up the ribbon, her face white. "My ribbon … It flew away with the dreki. If it's here, then the dreki must be"—her gaze roved over the torn rugs, the crumbling walls, and the ruined art pieces; it was too small of a space for the dreki to fit into and not break everything—" somewhere."

Bits of sand still clung to her ribbon and she slowly

brushed them away.

My portal didn't fail.

The coolness of the castle walls, so unlike the raging heat from the desert, brought a sense of relief over her. And something more—*pride.*

"So where is it?" Blár spun around the room with an unconvinced frown. "I'm pretty sure it would've busted this place down if it was let loose here."

"But what if, like Revna, its soul was trapped in that dimension? And once it's out of that dimension, it goes back to its body?"

"We'll deal with it when it happens." Ice crackled beneath his fingers and he ran a hand over his reddened forearms slowly, chilling the sunburns. Even from where she stood, she could feel the coolness of his magic. "If it was a trapped soul that's now back with its body, don't you think its body is long dead?"

"Unless it was preserved with runes," she pointed out. But she wasn't worried like earlier, because they had their magic back. Or, more importantly, Blár had his magic back. Because even if she couldn't fight the dreki on her own, he definitely could.

Kolfinna gathered her long, wavy hair in her hands and quickly redid her braid with her pink ribbon. In her peripheral vision, something shiny caught her eye. The trim of the wall was partially broken off, revealing tiny, golden inscriptions.

She inched closer to the wall, sidestepping a broken statue and dropping down so she could read the runes better. *Framework. Heat.* She tentatively touched the edge of the rotting, wooden trim, and snapped off another section. Symbols of a creature that looked hauntingly similar to the dreki flowed with the rune writings. Kolfinna continued breaking off pieces of the trim, her heart racing as the words swam over her mind. *Rune. Sand.*

"Help me take—" She barely got the words out, but she didn't need to, because Blár was already tearing off the trim on the other side of the room.

When they tore off the trim, it revealed a stream of rune codes lining the wall into an infinite loop. *Framework. Heat. Suns. Moons. Twice, thrice. Sand. Mountains. Hot. Dreki.*

She paused, eyebrows crinkling. Did each room have something similar?

Her gaze drifted to the next room and the blood rushed to her ears at the thought of what everyone else had endured. Were there any survivors? A chill settled in her bones and she hastened into the next room.

It was a hall of some sort, with a thick, matted, red carpet running down the center of the room and glass windows that covered most of the wall on either side of the hall. They appeared to be in a hall that served as a bridge that connected to another wing of the castle, she presumed from the deep, dark ravine she could see from the windows. Her steps clacked loudly in the empty room.

Just like in the other room, a myriad of words scored the bottom of the walls. But unlike the other room, someone had ripped off the trim. Pieces of rotten, wooden trim with rusty nails still attached to them scattered the hall. She inspected the runes circling the room. *Rune. Framework. Heat. Suns. Thrice. Trees. Leaves. Frames. Scythe. Demons.* She paused at the demons, her body growing cold and heavy. What did *that* mean?

"Do you think this room is linked with a dimension?" Blár peered out one of the windows. When she didn't answer immediately, he glanced over his shoulder at her. His sharp eyes perfectly matched the beauty of the skies behind him.

She found her voice again. "I'm not sure, but I think so, judging by the runes here. The gong sounded a few seconds after they entered the room, so if there is a dimension linked to this room, they should be in it. Unless they got out somehow."

"Maybe you can write something to bring them back?" He kneeled and turned over a moldering piece of wood. "If this truly was an area to train the fae, wouldn't it make sense that there would be a way to void the training and bring them back? I'm sure emergencies were a thing, don't you think?"

"Hm." She walked deeper into the room and leaned away from the glass windows. A niggling, intrusive thought told her she would fall into the ravine if she leaned against it. "I'll try that."

Kolfinna touched the stone wall beneath the windows and dipped into her mana, willing it to come out and do her bidding. Unlike in the desert, she didn't need to search deep inside herself to find a tendril of her mana. It hummed in her fingertips almost instantaneously, as it always did. Kolfinna imagined voiding the whole dimension in that room. Mana warmed her fingers and surged against the wall until gold runes fluttered on it in a single word: *void*.

The ceiling of the room ripped open into a black portal and four bodies dumped out of it, half-screaming. Eyfura slammed into the floor first, then Magni on top of her, and then Mímir, and lastly Truda. Blár lurched back in surprise, while Kolfinna was rooted in place—she hadn't thought it would work, much less *that* quickly.

All four moaned and twisted on the floor, blinking confusedly. Blood stained their uniforms and budding bruises littered their faces and hands. Truda pushed herself on her elbows. Twigs tangled her usually neat hair. Mímir jumped to his feet, his breathing labored and his eyes wild. He adorned a half healed black eye and a split lip. Magni pushed himself up on his arms and stared down at Eyfura like he didn't recognize her—and she looked just as stumped as he did.

Kolfinna waited for more bodies to drop through the gaping hole—because surely their numbers couldn't have dwindled down to only four survivors—but with an audible zipping sound, the ceiling closed back up.

"Kolfinna? Blár?" Mímir stumbled back, his knees wobbling together. He looked between the two of them. "You're alive. We thought ... we thought you died."

"How are we back here?" Truda hugged her elbows to

her chest. Her shifty eyes flicked from one corner to the next, as if something would attack at any second.

"I used the runes." Kolfinna's voice dropped to a whisper. There was nothing heroic about what she had done. People had died. If she had been quicker, if she hadn't trusted Revna, and instead focused more on getting out, they probably wouldn't have died. The realization hit her like a brick wall, and she staggered back, eyes stinging.

Mímir touched the runes she had written on the wall, turning toward her. "Did you create these?"

"Yes."

"Amazing." He kneeled beside them, his fingers skimming over the glowing words. "You've made a lot of progress ..." He pushed himself to his feet, and that seemed to be too much for him because he staggered and held the glass window to keep upright. "How is everyone?" He brought a shaky hand to smooth over his ripped, red cape. "Is this ... is this everyone who survived? I thought Eyjarr was holding on ..."

"No." Tears made clean streaks down Eyfura's dirt-smeared face, and her voice thickened with emotion. "He was with me, but ... but"—a strangled sob escaped her lips and she quickly covered her mouth—"that *thing* ate him."

Magni rested a hand on Eyfura's shoulder and she flinched from the contact, but then leaned into his touch. She buried her face into his shoulder, her body trembling with sobs.

Kolfinna wanted to comfort Eyfura like she had done every time Kolfinna needed it, but she couldn't move. Her guilt kept her frozen in place, and she feared they would blame her for not helping them sooner.

"What happened?" Blár finally asked.

Magni stroked Eyfura's hair as her cries subsided; a faraway, haunted look reflected in his emerald eyes. Gashes formed on the back of his hands in a claw-like formation. "We were in a forest and there were these—these *monsters*." There was a detached element to his voice, as if all emotions were depleted from him. Or perhaps he was tired—*very* tired. "They could fly and they were grotesque, and ... and they ate most of everyone. We had to hide from them and they kept chasing us down."

"I want to go home." Truda lurched to her feet and made her way toward the doorway Kolfinna had come from. She paused and turned to the other doorway at the end of the room. Tears shone in her eyes as she looked between the two doors. "Which way did we come from? Let's go, *now!*" When no one moved, her face crumpled further and she stomped her foot on the floor. "I don't care about the reward, and none of you should either! Screw the king, and screw this whole place! Let's go, *please!*"

Eyfura sniffled and wiped her tears with the back of her hand. "I agree. I think we should just forfeit this mission. What have we accomplished so far other than dying out? This is too dangerous for us to handle, even if we have a black rank on our side. We can't do anything if we can't use our magic."

Relief washed over Truda's tight expression and she

held her hand out to Eyfura. "Come on, let's—"

"No." Magni's voice was as sharp, jagged, and clear as shattered glass. "We've already come this far. Leaving now would just mean everything was in vain."

Eyfura ripped away from his touch, her lips twisting into a disgusted scowl. "Do you really care about the reward money *that* much?"

"It's not the reward money, but the fact that we haven't accomplished anything," Magni said. The wound on his hand dripped crimson blood onto the similarly colored carpet. "It's embarrassing. What will we do when the king confronts us? Say that we were too scared to move forward? All those people died, and for what? Nothing. We have nothing to show for what we did here. We would just be failures."

Mímir wrung his hands together and looked from person to person. "I agree with Magni. We can't abandon our mission."

"What?" Truda spun around to face Mímir, her fists balled together. "You agree—Oh." She huffed, rolling her eyes. "*Of course* you agree with him. Your rank will inevitably drop if we return empty-handed. You'll be seen as a failure for leading us all into failure. You're a selfish, inconsiderate, weak leader, Mímir. Fenris made a mistake choosing you."

Kolfinna cringed at the harsh words and she had to hand it to Mímir for keeping a straight face. She half-expected him to either look hurt or snap back at her. Instead, he did neither and held an air of calm. But the tension thickened between them all, and she noticed Magni's expression darken at the insult.

"Says the girl who wishes she were in his place," Magni scoffed, climbing up to his impressive height. Even with blood running down the side of his face, and the various red splatters on his sullied, white uniform, he was as intimidating as always as he looked down at her like she was dirt. "Captain Asulf doesn't make mistakes. There's not much Mímir could've done to change this situation. Who would've thought any of this would happen?"

"That's enough." Mímir raised his hands as if that could quell the group. "We're all tired—"

"Did those monsters knock a few screws loose in your heads?! If we stay, we *will* die!" Truda said. "I'd rather be a failure than be dead."

"You can go home then." Magni waved to the door. "If this mission means nothing to you, if your honor as a soldier means nothing—then walk out."

"Why do you care so much about this place? Does your pride as a Royal Guard mean more than your life? Or is it your honor?" Truda sneered. "Well, I definitely don't want to die because of your pride and arrogance!" She pointed between Magni and Mímir. "Both of you!"

Eyfura was crying, the tears mixing with the sweat and dirt on her cheeks. When she wiped her face, it smudged brown on her white sleeve. "I don't want to be here either. Please, let's just go back. I don't know if I can handle any more of this."

"We need to move forward." Mímir planted his feet

firmly on the floor and squared his shoulders. "We have to complete this mission."

Kolfinna watched them argue, and Blár did the same, his expression guarded. He was leaning against the glass window, the sunlight streaming around his tall frame and casting a shadow over the group. Their eyes met, and Kolfinna had to rip her gaze away. She was scared of what she would find there—if he wanted to stay or leave.

If they left right now, what position would Kolfinna be in? Would she still be able to become a Royal Guard? She had nothing to offer Fenris or the king if she couldn't complete this mission. Forget being a Royal Guard. Would they even let her live? Because why would they pardon her crimes if she couldn't make this mission a success? The thought of a noose around her neck made her inadvertently touch her throat.

"H-Hey, everyone, I think we can do it." Kolfinna's interjection sounded as flimsy as the deteriorated wooden trim piled on the floor, but it was enough to garner everyone's attention. "Um, I agree that we should continue this mission—"

"Unlike you, we have lives to get back to!" Truda threw her hands up, but then winced and touched her shoulder, where blood darkened the gray material of her uniform. "Some help you've been! Aren't you supposed to be deciphering all this stuff and making sure we don't die? Maybe you want us to die! How can we trust a fae anyway?!"

Kolfinna's face grew hot at the accusation, but she lost

her opportunity to defend herself because Truda was already arguing with Mímir and Magni again, all of their voices growing louder and more frustrated. Eyfura stood up to join Truda, her arguments blending in with Truda's.

"I'm better now!" Kolfinna suddenly shouted into the fray. She looked between everyone with pleading eyes. The noose around her neck seemed to tighten with their guarded expressions. "I learned a lot about runes while we were separated. I'm confident I can keep everyone alive unlike last time! Blár and I managed to get out of our dimension, and I got you guys out too, didn't I? Things are different now!"

Truda shrill laugh pierced whatever confidence Kolfinna had mustered. "What makes you think you can make this mission a success? Fenris thought you would help us succeed in this place, but look how far you've come! We started with twenty-four people on this mission, and we're down to *six*! Are we supposed to just die and wait for you to become experienced enough to know what to do? You don't know shit!"

"I—" Kolfinna's mouth felt as dry as the desert with two suns. Maybe if Truda's words didn't hold a semblance of truth, she would be able to retort. Kolfinna felt like she was on the ship with the draugrs again, but this time, the ship was sinking and there was no way out.

Truda continued her assault, "I'm not going to wait around for you to 'figure' things out! My life is not a guinea pig for you to—"

"Truda, you're embarrassing yourself." Blár continued

to watch from his place against the glass window. A cloud must've covered the sun because the sunlight waned and the room darkened, almost as if even the skies were scared of him. "We're soldiers. We don't desert our mission."

Truda averted her gaze from him and grabbed her injured shoulder with an angry look. "I-I know! But I don't want to die here."

"We won't die." Blár spoke as if he was making a promise, and even Kolfinna believed him.

Truda raised her head, and the light returned in the room, causing her brown eyes to look more like the color of trees than the blackness they had become in the shadowed room. "How can you say that with so much certainty?"

"Because I believe in my abilities." Blár's gaze dragged over to Kolfinna, and this time, she held it, her stomach warming despite the frigid color of his eyes. "And because I believe in Kolfinna."

Uncaged butterflies fluttered in the pit of her belly and she could feel the blush staining her cheeks.

Blár turned to look at the rest of the group and his voice held a note of authority that Mímir lacked. "When we're out here in this place—in these ruins—you all can rely on me to make sure you make it out alive. When we're in another dimension, put your trust in Kolfinna. She knows what she's doing, and she's trying her best to make sure we make it out."

Kolfinna no longer felt like she was on a sinking ship, and she used that confidence to speak up, her voice growing stronger, "Blár is right. I can get us out of here, but you need to trust me. Also, there's a lot that we learned while we were separated. When Blár and I were warped into another dimension ..." She then went into detail about what had transpired during their stay in the dimension.

"So there are dead bodies somewhere here?" Magni pinched the bridge of his nose as if he was being greatly inconvenienced. "Or are they preserved?"

"They should be preserved ... I think," Kolfinna explained. All I know is that their bodies are being used to fuel this place. The woman I met, Revna, said that—" She shifted on her feet and stared down at the matted carpet. To be honest, how could they believe anything Revna had said after she betrayed Kolfinna?

"So if we kill them—" Magni started.

"Why would you do such a thing?" Kolfinna's head shot up and she pinned him with a heavy look. "We can learn a lot from them. Don't you think that's valuable?"

He didn't look convinced and shrugged. "Powerful fae with unclear motives? I don't know about that."

"That's enough, Magni," Mímir said. "Let's find these fae. We can indeed find out a lot from them, like how this place works and what's valuable and what's not. Maybe there are secret passageways here that only they know about." He smoothed down the front of his uniform— blood, dirt, and other unidentifiable liquids stained the white material. "Or who knows. It would be invaluable to us to learn about this place and all it has to offer."

Eyfura swiped away the remnants of her tears and sniffed. "So we're going to continue?"

"Yes," Mímir said. "We'll continue."

As the tension in the room eased, Kolfinna released a shaky breath and her shoulders relaxed just the tiniest bit before the heavy hold of responsibility stiffened her spine. They would move forward, and it would be up to her to protect them all.

"Kolfinna." Mímir smiled through his strained, and clearly pained, expression. "Are you able to heal us like that lady did to you?"

"I'm sorry, I'm afraid that's too complex for me," Kolfinna answered.

"That's still amazing that runes are able to heal you," he said excitedly. "Your limp is completely gone! Maybe you can learn to heal too?"

"Maybe someday."

"Yes, someday." He turned to the rest of the party, all of whom sported injuries. "All right, let's bandage ourselves up and get going."

"Magni, you're bleeding." Eyfura motioned to his shoulder. Concern colored her tone. "Did they bite you?"

Magni brought a hand to his shoulder, as if he had forgotten he was injured. Red stained his fingers when he pulled them back. "One of them, yes," he muttered. "Just seconds before we got back here."

"I'll help you bandage," Eyfura said.

"I'm fine—"

Truda rolled her eyes. "Just take the help. How are you

going to explore this place if you're bleeding everywhere?"

Magni clamped his mouth shut as Eyfura helped him with his wound. Kolfinna watched the interaction silently. She couldn't relax even though they would move forward. Half of the remaining group didn't like her. Fenris had said he would take the party's words into consideration when making the decision to make her a Royal Guard, so what could she expect from Magni and Truda? She had to do better than her best.

Once everyone got patched up, it was time to move. The next room was another hall like the one they had just left, but this one was three times larger and reminded her of a ballroom. Studded tiles lay flatly on the floor in a patchwork of vibrant colors and dozens of glass chandeliers hung in the ceiling in a circular formation surrounding an enormous chandelier with different glittering teardrop gemstones. Although light streamed into the ballroom through clerestory windows, it was still dim.

"I didn't realize fae were so gaudy." Blár tapped one of the gem centered tiles with the toe of his boot. Some of the tiles were cracked, while others were missing gemstones.

Eyfura stuck close to Kolfinna as they stepped deeper into the empty ballroom. "How are you holding up?" Eyfura asked with a hesitant smile. She had cleaned the dirt off her face, but tiny smudges remained near her jawline and temples.

"I should be asking you that," Kolfinna said. Their footsteps echoed in the hall, and Kolfinna had to drop her voice so the others couldn't hear. "You look ..." She struggled to find an appropriate word, but came up with nothing.

"I know, I know. I probably look like crap." Eyfura gave a short, hollow laugh. "But I want to talk about something else. Or more like *someone* else." Eyfura's gaze flicked to Blár, who took the lead with Mímir, and she grinned conspiratorially. "So what's the scoop with you and Blár? You guys didn't sound or look like sworn enemies back in there—" She jerked a thumb to the doorway they had just come through. "What's between you two?"

"N-Nothing!" Kolfinna could feel the tips of her ears flush with heat. "We're just ... working together, that's all."

Eyfura cocked an eyebrow and gave her an unconvinced look. "That sounds very suspicious."

"And what about you and Magni?" Kolfinna raised her own eyebrow to mimic Eyfura. "You both seemed awfully close."

Eyfura snorted and shook her head; her purple earrings caught in the dim light and glimmered just like the glass chandeliers above them. "That's not even close to the same thing! We work together. That's it." Eyfura's gaze roved over Blár's tall frame, and she grinned. "I didn't think he'd be your type, but hey, I can't fault you. He *is* younger than Captain Asulf—"

"Eyfura, you're jumping to conclusions." Kolfinna's face grew hotter. "It's not like that."

"I don't believe you!" Eyfura laughed, and the strain around her eyes finally seemed to lessen. "What do you like about him the most?"

Before Kolfinna could answer, screeching at the side of the room caught their attention. Half a dozen cat-like creatures were moving toward them in slow motion across the ballroom. Gray, white, and red fur tufted around their bodies like thick manes, and their eyes glowed a vicious red. Fire danced at their paws and their tails were made of flames, whipping behind them in a swirl of sparking red and yellow. In unison, high-pitched screams emitted from their mouths.

Blár raised his hand and ice splintered from the floor by the creatures' feet, but they seemed to anticipate it because they lurched to the side, their movements lither than any of the other creatures they had seen in the ruins. One of them jumped in front of Eyfura and she hesitated, her face stilled into a shocked expression.

Kolfinna's magic moved like a whip. She forced the stones out of the floor with such speed that they whizzed forward and clipped the creature's head. The creature careened to the side, while the others charged at Kolfinna and Eyfura.

Ice erupted from the floor and captured two, encapsulating them in chunks of frost. The other two were impaled by a giant, sharp, ice spear. It happened so quickly that all it took was a few blinks and it was done. All the creatures lay on the floor dead—either frozen or speared.

Eyfura released a shuddered breath, a hand to her

chest. "I-I'm sorry. I froze and I couldn't think." She stared at the frozen creature, its tail no longer fire but instead a red, furry rope. "I must seem like such an incompetent guard. I'm sorry."

"You could've at least left some for the rest of us." Magni frowned and the fire on his fingers flickered to nothing.

"You moved too slow." Blár jammed a finger in Kolfinna's direction. "She managed to get one. Why couldn't you?"

Kolfinna hadn't killed the cat creature with her stones, but it definitely died when Blár impaled it with his ice spear. Truda noticed too, because she said, "You still ended up killing *all* of them."

"If you've got time to complain, then try to be quicker," Blár huffed.

They continued in silence after that.

Beyond the ballroom was a hallway, and beyond that were sets of doors that led to various different rooms: a breakroom, a mini kitchen, and empty rooms. Farther down the hallway were stairs that led down into a lobby, which extended into a dormitory. Rooms paralleled each other, all with the same things: a bed, a dresser, and a bookshelf. Some of the books were still intact, and all of them were written in rune writing.

"This can't be real," Kolfinna murmured as she picked up a book titled *Teachings of the Mer Folk*. The pages were thin and cracked when she opened it. An inky drawing of a half-fish woman filled the page.

Eyfura peeked over her shoulder. "What's wrong? What is that thing?"

Kolfinna placed the book back on the desk; half a dozen other books were stacked on the table haphazardly. She picked up another titled *The Great Elven Wars*.

"Come on, we have to move," Mímir called from the doorway, ushering them forward. "There's nothing in here."

Truda, who had been looking underneath the bed frame, straightened. Blár and Magni were already in the hallway, ready to move on to the next room.

"There are some interesting books—" Kolfinna started.

Mímir was already shaking his head. "We can take a look at them later."

"But these are also valuable things for the king and the country, aren't they?" Kolfinna wanted to take all the books in the room and bring them with her, but the look Mímir gave her stopped her.

"Kolfinna," he said, his voice stern, "the country needs powerful weapons. An artifact that can make us *stronger*. We don't need books. Although, I do agree that they're valuable, but that's not why we're here."

Kolfinna placed the book back down on the desk. She wanted to dive into the world of books and figure out the truth of where she came from. Because if these books were real and not some fantasy, there was more to her world than she thought.

As they continued down the hall, Magni halted in his steps and pointed inside one of the rooms. "What is *that*?"

Kolfinna hurried inside after everyone else filed in. It appeared to be an office of some sorts, a desk in the center and a map spanning the space of the wall behind it. The outline of their country, Rosain, was etched in familiar lines, but it didn't exactly look the same; there was more land in this version, and the borders were warped compared to current maps. But the strangest of them all, was the space *beside* the country.

There was the Forest of Great Divide that divided the country from the Mistlands, the uninhabitable, vicious land of shadows and mist, where monsters and evil creatures resided. Katla had told her the grounds erupted with lava there, the seas brushed poisonous gas onto the shores, and monsters hung on blood sucking trees, waiting to pluck the eyes of any strays. But what Kolfinna hadn't been told was that there were countries within the Mistlands.

The map showed lands beyond the Forest of Great Divide. The Ice Shores. The seas of Mer Folk. The High Court of Autumn. The High Court of Winter. The High Court of Summer. The High Court of Spring. The Elven Lands. The Deep Sea. The Blood Forest—

She stared at it in stunned silence.

Were there people still living there? Were her people thriving? But if it was as vast as it appeared, why did her people leave? Did they *all* leave?

"This is fascinating," Mímir murmured.

"Only monsters live beyond the Forest of Great Divide," Magni whispered, brushing away a string of cobwebs covering one corner of the map. "So what does any of this mean? Are there countries beyond the Great Divide?"

Truda pursed her lips. "Didn't you pay attention to your history classes? The fae abandoned their lands because it was uninhabitable due to the monsters and vicious nature of the climate and lands. They took over our lands, and then we defeated them. There's a reason why no one goes back there. So yeah, it kinda makes sense that there's a map of when they used to live there, right? It doesn't mean anything. This is over a thousand years old, isn't it?"

An uneasiness spread between them all; what if the fae were much vaster than Kolfinna thought? What if her people were out there? What if … She couldn't contain the thoughts swirling in her mind.

But if a land where her people could thrive and live comfortably existed, then every fae would have run to its borders. If she was able to flee to such a land, she wouldn't have to think about Royal Guards, proving herself, or being on the run.

Such a place didn't exist. At least, not anymore.

"Let's go," Mímir said. "We can look into it later once we've found something substantial."

"You think this isn't substantial?" Blár arched an eyebrow and jerked a thumb at the map. "There clearly was a complex society based on this map. What if there's a potential threat right next door and we have no idea? The military would be very interested in this."

"That's impossible." Kolfinna couldn't keep the edge out of her tone. "If there truly was an advanced civilization currently living there, every fae would run there! I've never heard rumors about that. Only stuff about how dangerous the Mistlands are. And if there was a whole other country—or by the looks of it, many countries— don't you think they would've tried to invade at some point? Or even trickle in? I've never heard of these places."

"It's probably from before your people migrated." Truda sighed as if she was wasting her time. "Come on, let's go. This doesn't prove anything."

"It does prove there's more to fae civilization than we know," Kolfinna whispered. "But if this place doesn't exist anymore ... what happened to it?"

And if what the map said was true, were there other races of beings other than fae and humans?

"We can find clues later, just like how you can decipher the books later." Mímir tapped his feet impatiently. "First, we need to find something substantial, like an ancient artifact or something of importance, before we can really dig down and figure out every detail of this place. Come on, let's go. We've got a lot to explore."

Kolfinna glanced back at the map, a multitude of emotions and questions surfacing ... But she couldn't dwell on it. She would have to figure it out later.

23

Kolfinna's head grew heavier with every step she took; she couldn't stop thinking about all the people who had died because of her. She didn't know most of their names, but she remembered their faces. There was Torsten, the Royal Guard with white-blond hair. Then there was Thyra, the brunette Royal Guard with a mole beneath her eye. Eyjarr, the middle-aged soldier with a family waiting for him. Embla, the soldier who lost her best friend, Brynhild. And so many others.

Her eyes strained with how much she had to pay attention to *everything*. Every upturned stone was a potential threat. Every wall had potentially dangerous runes written on them. Every corner they turned she had to have her guard raised. Halfway through their exploration, she felt like she hadn't slept in over a week. Her eyes felt gritty like there was still leftover sand in them. There was still so much of the ruins to explore.

To her left, Eyfura tripped over a cluster of bones. She cursed, and then muttered, "I'm not a fan of this place."

"Me neither." Kolfinna studied the decaying walls of the winding hallway. Matted, moldy carpet ground beneath her boots and she overstepped a pile of crushed bones.

That was one thing that was abundant in the ruins: bones. Whether human bones, animal bones, or indistinguishable magic beast bones—they cluttered the corners of the halls and rooms.

The hallway ended and they walked through an open archway into a spacious, brightly lit hall. One of the walls opened up to the outside. Pillars were erected at that wall and the only thing stopping anyone from falling was a rusty, peeling, metal railing. Cool air breezed across ten raised stone coffins at the opposite end of the room.

"What is this place?" Eyfura walked deeper inside.

"I can't use my powers," Magni growled, staring down at his hands. "Great. This is one of *those* rooms."

An ominous chill hung in the air and the shadows in the corners of the room seemed to darken, contrasting with the shimmering runes hanging on top of the archway that read *no magic*.

Something didn't feel right about the place. Like she shouldn't have been there. Like none of them should've been there.

Across the room, the railing creaked as Blár leaned onto it, trying to see into the ravine below. Eyfura gasped audibly. "How can you trust that rusty railing not to break? You'll die if you fall!"

He froze, blue eyes switching between her and the railing before he released it like it was on fire. He stepped away and held his hands up. "Ah, right. I forgot my powers don't work." He stared uneasily at the ravine. "And I'm not too fond of going *splat* that quickly."

Kolfinna remained rooted near the entrance, her instincts telling her to turn around and run. There was definitely something off about this room. Unlike the other rooms, it didn't lead anywhere, and the focus seemed to be on the coffins.

"Guys, help me here, would you?" Mímir voice was urgent as he tried pushing off the lid to one of the coffins.

"What are you doing?" Kolfinna asked slowly.

"What does it look like?" Mímir gritted his teeth and despite his injuries, he seemed adamant to push. "Come and help."

The wind ruffled Blár's hair, making his face appear even more still. "You shouldn't disturb the dead."

"There might be artifacts in here," he said impatiently, waving to the others. "Come on."

Magni muttered a curse under his breath but joined him. Truda shifted on her feet and stood near the entrance beside Kolfinna. She, too, seemed like she wanted to leave. "Is that really necessary? I don't really want to look at a decayed thousand-year-old body."

"Can you all stop complaining and just get over here? Is that really so much to ask for?" Mímir stopped pushing and looked at them with a twisted expression. He turned back and shoved the lid off the coffin. It crashed to the floor, snapping in half. He peered into the coffin, his eyes lighting up. "She's ... preserved."

That caught Kolfinna's attention and she rushed to his side to find a woman inside the coffin. Brown, wavy hair shot with gray streaks framed her face and long lashes brushed against her cheeks. A drab, ratted beige dress clung to her thin frame.

Kolfinna touched the woman's hand and yanked it back when she felt the familiar spark of mana. "She's alive," she whispered. "This must be one of the fae whose magic runs this place."

"This one looks the same," Magni called from another coffin.

Maybe Revna was in one of them? Kolfinna went to the next coffin and pushed the lid. It budged slowly and she was able to crack it open just enough to peek inside. Another woman lay dormant, but she was far older and frailer looking than Revna.

Blár shoved the lid off one of the coffins. "Hey, it's the hag!"

Kolfinna rushed to his side and grabbed the edge of the coffin. It was cool to the touch and sent a shiver down her spine. Like Blár had said, Revna's sleeping body was nestled in the coffin. Mana buzzed in the air.

Kolfinna was torn at the sight of Revna's peaceful face; on one hand, Revna had betrayed her and didn't deserve any sympathy. But on the other hand, she had healed Kolfinna's leg and taught her about runes.

"She's alive." She turned to the rest of the party. Eyfura and Truda stood near the entrance, not appearing keen to inspect the coffins. "They're all alive, but ... It seems like they have some sort of spell on them. Revna had mentioned that even if her soul escapes the dimension, it doesn't necessarily mean her physical body will be released as well."

"What should we—" But Magni froze when Mímir suddenly reached into his pocket and produced a dagger with a blade the size of his palm. He flipped the dagger in his hand and jammed it into the chest of the woman with wavy brown hair.

"What are you doing?" Kolfinna shouted, as he pulled the dagger out and frowned.

"Mímir!" Eyfura said, just as shocked. "What was that for?"

"Strange," Mímir murmured with furrowed brows. Mímir pushed Kolfinna out of the way to look at Revna.

"What are you doing?" Kolfinna grabbed his wrist. He tried to push away from her, but she held him firmly. She stole a glance at the fae he had just stabbed. Surprisingly, no blood pooled around her chest like she thought it would, and no blood stained the blade either.

Mímir wrenched his hand back with a glare. "Stop, Kolfinna."

"*You* stop," she snapped. "I don't know what's gotten into you, but this isn't right!"

"She's right." Magni looked at Mímir like he had lost his mind. "We can't just kill them if they're not doing anything. I'm sure the king will want to see them and see what we can do."

Blár grabbed Mímir by the collar of his shirt and shoved him a few feet away, where he stumbled backward and fell to the floor. Blár's eyes blazed with irritation. "How about you explain what the hell you're doing?"

"I thought it would be quicker to demonstrate." Mímir rose to his feet and dusted his pants. He shot Blár a dark look. "No need to get so violent."

"Says the guy with a dagger who just stabbed a"—Blár waved to the fae—"vegetable."

Mímir held up the dagger and the sharp edge of it glinted ominously in the sunlight. "This dagger is called the *Genfødsel Kniv*. It's an ancient artifact that dates back over a thousand years. It was crafted with the souls of countless innocent people, fae and human alike. Its sister is the *Død Sværd*. Sound familiar? The royal family owns that sword, but this one, in my opinion, is so much better. This blade is invaluable. Stab someone once, and they'll be put into an eternal slumber. The only way to awaken them is to stab them again with it. Useful, huh?"

Blár raised an eyebrow. "How is that possible? Magic isn't infinite."

Mímir nodded and twirled the knife again. "There is a tradeoff. Whoever stabs the person and puts them in a slumber, the blade takes years of your lifespan. Sometimes it's a few years, other times it's decades. You really don't know. It's been recorded in history that some people used it once and died straight away. The blade had taken their whole lifespan. It's dicey to use but useful."

"Useful?" Truda leaned against the moss-ridden door-frame and crossed her arms over her chest. Her eyes narrowed. "To who?"

"I've never used it for that." Mímir held his hands up. "But it's useful here, since they were likely stabbed with this in the first place."

"And you just so happened to have that on you?" Kolfinna asked, eyebrows raised. She was suddenly reminded of the night she had tried escaping the Royal Guards' headquarters and how, when she had poked a hole through the wall into the next room, she had found Mímir in the room with a dagger balanced on his thigh and a stack of papers in his hand. She shook that image away. There was nothing foreboding about that memory, even if it unsettled her.

"I figured it would be useful since we're in this place."

Magni peered at the lady Mímir had stabbed, an uneasy expression on his regal face. "You probably should have told us that before you stabbed her."

"I thought she would wake up." Mímir frowned again as he looked into her coffin. "But maybe it's because her soul is trapped in another dimension like Kolfinna said. Only this one"—he motioned to Revna—"was freed, correct?"

"Yes," Kolfinna said. "I freed her when we"—she glanced at Blár—"were in the desert dimension."

"Excellent. Now, if you don't mind ..." Mímir took his spot in front of Revna's coffin and positioned the blade over her body. Kolfinna cringed when the blade disappeared into Revna's chest. The instant he pulled the blade out, Revna's fingers started twitching, then she stirred, and then her eyes fluttered open.

They all watched in amazement as she pushed herself into a sitting position.

"Kolfinna?" Revna rubbed the side of her face. Her graying black hair spilled over her shoulders, and her bright lavender eyes flicked from person to person. "Oh my ..." She looked down at her withered hands, which now shook. "I'm ... back." Tears filled her eyes and she gave a soft, relieved sigh. "Thank you. Thank you."

Kolfinna couldn't rejoice in the moment like she would have if Revna hadn't lied to her and used her. Kolfinna would've been the first person to congratulate her and cry with her after her thousand-plus-year imprisonment, but when she looked at Revna now, the bitterness of being betrayed filled her mouth with an ashy taste.

Blár similarly appeared peeved.

"You—" he started.

Kolfinna cut in, "You used me. We made a deal, and you *used* me."

Revna reached over the edge of the coffin to touch Kolfinna's hand, but Kolfinna stepped away. "Kolfinna ..." Her hand hung in the air. "I didn't mean to hurt you."

"Then why did you not tell me how to use the runes properly to free everyone? We had to figure out by ourselves how to get everyone out of the other dimensions! If you hadn't wasted my time, I could've saved more people in our party." Kolfinna's voice caught in her throat.

"What was I supposed to do? Wait for someone else to come by and free me?" Revna smoothed out her scratchy, thinning dress with a huff. She waved a hand in Kolfinna's direction. "I don't like humans. They're partially the reason I was stuck here! So excuse me for not wanting to help them. But you have to understand, it wasn't about *you*."

Kolfinna was at a loss for words. Was she supposed to be grateful that Revna didn't dislike her? She couldn't believe that Revna was so dismissive about Kolfinna's feelings on the matter. But should she have really been surprised?

Before she could voice those thoughts, Revna was already speaking.

"Besides, I did help you, didn't I? I taught you about runes! That's far more important than anything else, isn't it? From what you told me, you had no other way to learn, so I did a huge favor for you." Revna dragged a finger over the edge of the coffin and inspected the dust between her fingers with disgust. "And, dear, let's not forget who fixed your leg. You should be grateful."

Kolfinna didn't even know what to say, but she could feel seedlings of unease growing in the pit of her stomach.

"Thank you, nonetheless." The corner of Revna's

mouth and eyes crinkled and she flicked her violet gaze over the party. Magni and Blár wore similarly blasé expressions, Truda and Eyfura appeared nervous, and Mímir kept close to the coffin and seemed to cling to Revna's every word with a look of awe.

"Mímir was the one to free you." Kolfinna's movements were stiff as she motioned to him. "He used the dagger."

Revna's gaze lingered on Mímir, her violet eyes flashing. "Oh, really? Thank you."

"Err, yes! Of course." He wiped the palms of his hands on his thighs and lowered his head. "My name is Mímir. I'm just ... I'm honored to be in your presence."

Revna swung her legs over the coffin and jumped onto the cool, cracked tiles. "Is this your whole party?" But even as she asked, she turned to the other coffins sadly. "My dear sisters are still trapped."

"Yes, this is our whole party," Mímir said after clearing his throat. "This is Eyfura, Truda, Magni, and you already know Blár."

"Ah, yes, how could I forget?" Sarcasm dripped from her words as she cast him a frosty look. Her feet padded across the floor lightly and she stopped in front of the runes arching over the doorway. "You can read this, correct, Kolfinna?"

"Yes, I can."

"Have you been using runes here?"

"A little," Kolfinna said. "I'm better at reading them, to be honest. I was able to get everyone out of the dimension by writing 'void,' so I did learn how to use it a bit."

"Splendid." Revna brushed her hands on the wall beside the door, mana sifting into the air before she spun around to face them. She pointed at the blade in Mímir's hand. "How did you get the *Genfødsel Kniv*?"

He lowered his head again, and Kolfinna had to wonder why he was showing her so much respect. He didn't even do that when Fenris walked into a room, and Fenris was the leader of the entire Royal Guards.

"It's been passed down in my Order," Mímir said with a hand over his heart. "My mentor gave it to me in order to free you."

"Your ... Order?" Revna's eyes lit with an unreadable emotion, while everyone else shifted on their feet— Kolfinna wasn't the only one confused by his words.

Eyfura eyed the exit and asked quietly, "What do you mean Order? Did Captain Asulf give it to you?"

"Yes, the Order." Mímir ignored Eyfura. "The Order of Queen Aesileif. We've been waiting for this for years."

Understanding dawned on Revna and her tone lightened. "*Ah*. You're one of us."

Blár stilled and asked slowly, "What are you talking about?"

"Perfect." Revna clapped her hands in delight. The sound echoed in the silent room. "You'll tell me everything, child. You'll also help me free my sisters now, won't you?"

"It would be my pleasure." Mímir bowed low for the third time.

"Mímir—" Truda said.

Mana pervaded the air as Revna held her hands up and flicked her wrists. Everything happened so fast that by the time Kolfinna finished blinking, stones had ripped from the wall and slammed into Truda, Eyfura, Magni, and Blár, pinning them into the wall so only their heads and tangled limbs stuck out. They gasped and struggled behind the weight of stones, their faces panicked.

"You bitch!" Blár growled.

"Now, now." Revna clucked her tongue as she approached him. "Language, dear. I don't know how much society has regressed since my time, but where I'm from, you speak to your elders with respect."

"Kiss my ass," he snarled.

"You really are dreadful to be around." Revna waved her hand and covered his mouth with stones, along with the other three. "There, better now. We won't have to deal with your useless drivel." She turned to Kolfinna, an apologetic smile gracing her lips. She no longer looked like a helpless, sweet, old damsel, but like a fierce, unforgiving force of nature. Like a title rising up to unleash its fury. "Do forgive me, dear. I know he's your lover, but he's human, and you really should be with another fae."

The words barely clicked in Kolfinna's mind and all the hairs on her body rose, telling her to run. She snapped her attention to the space above the doorway that read: *no magic.* But beside the doorway, it read: *clause: except for*

Revna. Kolfinna's stomach dropped. Revna had never taught her about clauses, but she now remembered seeing them in Revna's house.

What else had Revna kept from her?

"Revna, what are you doing?" Kolfinna wanted to bolt, but she remained fixed where she was, as if the stones in the room had also reined her in place. Mímir remained bowed, his lips twitching into a borderline leer. "Mímir? Why are you bowing?"

Mímir sighed. "Kolfinna, have you never heard of Queen Aesileif? I'm shocked you don't know your history."

"She was the last fae queen," Kolfinna said as she tried to remember the history of the last queen. She was the most hated person in Rosain history, since she was the biggest oppressor of humans. There were thousands of tales of her cruelty—how she used to eat the flesh of human babies, how she loved drinking wine from the skulls of her human enemies, that she killed a human slave every day for entertainment, and various other wicked tales. How much of that was true, and how much of it was anti-fae propaganda, Kolfinna wasn't entirely sure.

But where was he going with this? What did he mean Order of Queen Aesileif? And why was everyone pinned to the wall? Kolfinna didn't want the answer to all those questions, because it was already clear to her.

"What about that monster?" Kolfinna whispered. She willed herself to move forward, to run into the hallway where she could use magic, and maybe attack Revna and

Mímir, but her body refused to believe what her mind said was true.

"Monster?" He threw his head back and laughed, while Revna chuckled softly in the background as she inspected the coffins. "She was no monster! She was the last one to fight for your people's freedom! It's a shame that you don't even know that much about your own history."

Revna paused to stare into one of the coffins. "It's a shame those wretched traitors cut our beautiful wings off and trapped us here for so many centuries." Her tone softened and she reached into the coffin to touch the woman inside. "A shame indeed."

Blár tried shimmying his way out of the grip of the stones, but they didn't budge. Just like Kolfinna. Who couldn't think, or move.

Revna cleared her throat. "What's the status of Her Majesty?"

"The queen and her trusted inner circle are sealed away. The status of the commander and his army is unknown." Mímir straightened once more and placed a hand on his heart. "The Order is doing everything in their power to break the seal and free Her Majesty. It's ... a bit embarrassing to say, but freeing you is the biggest breakthrough we've had in centuries."

"You'll have to fill me in on all the details." Revna glanced at Kolfinna. "Dear, will you be joining us?"

"Joining you for what?" Kolfinna still couldn't move, and it was impossible to ignore the ever more frantic movements of Blár, Truda, Magni, and Eyfura against the stone bindings. "I still don't understand what's going on. What are you going to do with them? Why restrain them?"

"I told you not to trust humans, didn't I?"

"Revna, please tell me what's going on," Kolfinna begged. She didn't want to believe what was happening right now. This betrayal cut deeper, made worse by the fact that Kolfinna didn't know what to believe. Queen Aesileif was evil, but Kolfinna couldn't prove that. And neither could she disprove it.

"Revna is from the time when the humans and the fae fought," Mímir said with an eye roll. His voice was deeper, darker, and had a richer baritone. As if the light, easy way he had spoken had all been a lie—and maybe it was. He also stood taller, as if more confident, and every time he glanced at Revna, awe glittered in his eyes. It made Kolfinna sick to the stomach.

He continued, "There were also some traitorous fae who chose to side with the humans. The human side won, and Revna's side was either killed, sealed away like this, or sealed away with Queen Aesileif. The Order wishes to revive the old fae and the old world."

"W-Why? Mímir, you're not even a fae!" Kolfinna tried to draw forth the mana deep within her, but it only slightly fizzled at her fingertips.

"You don't need to be a fae to follow Ragnarök, but if you must know, my grandmother was a fae, and her parents before her, and their parents before them. But, as you can see, I wasn't blessed with strong fae blood and instead am mostly human. Blame that on my parents, I suppose." He raked a hand through his hair, and the black bruise on his eye stood out against the cuts on his hands. "But that's fine because it makes it easier to infiltrate when you're more human than fae because unlike you, who was blessed with mostly fae blood and who's gifted with fae abilities, all my attributes are human. You should join us, Kolfinna! We'll create a new world."

Mímir tucked the *Genfødsel Kniv* into the waistband of his pants, and the Royal Guard uniform suddenly looked wrong on him. The red of the cape reminded her of blood, and she wondered if he had knowingly marched everyone to their deaths this whole time.

Revna came to stand beside Mímir and put her hand on his shoulder. "Exactly! We will create a world where our kind can use magic freely. Why help the humans when they've done nothing but ruin you? Where you don't have to be persecuted for being who you are. Where you can be free. Think about it. *Imagine it.*" Revna waved at the mist and fog spread above the ravine, as if her mind too was traveling to her picture-perfect world. "In this world, this beautiful world we wish to create, Katla could've been alive. She wouldn't have had to die. That's the kind of world we want to create. A world where our people are safe. Isn't that everything you've wanted your whole life?"

That was exactly what Kolfinna had always wanted. It was the unattainable fantasy dream of every fae: to live normally. To not have to fear whether she would die tomorrow because someone found out who she was. To not have to be scared of what people would think of her. To be truly free.

Tears stung her eyes.

"But what's the price?" Kolfinna asked, voice wobbly. "That the humans are enslaved beneath us? How does that create a better world? It'll just reverse the roles. I want to live in a world"—her eyes met Blár's, and for a moment, she remembered back when they were in the desert and she had smiled and joked with him. And how her heart had raced being so close to him—"where we can live together freely. Where we can look past our differences."

Revna's smile faded. "How can you love the oppressors? Your sister would be so disappointed, as well as your parents."

Kolfinna thought of her parents, living happily in their countryside cottage deep in the woods. Her memories were foggy, and Katla had filled in the gaps for what she couldn't remember. But she remembered that they had been happy, always. Even if she couldn't remember everything, she had felt the warmth of their love.

She couldn't even remember if they had been fully fae or not, but it didn't matter.

"No," she said softly. "They would've wanted the same." Her voice grew stronger as she held onto the fragments she had left of them. "I want that world, Revna, but there are other ways we can achieve that. We can do it—"

"Humans are meant to be beneath us," Revna

snapped. "They're a pathetic race that's centuries behind us. They'll never catch up and they'll do everything to eradicate us. How can you side with them?"

"I can't do what they've done to us," she said.

"How disappointing."

Revna flicked her wrist and stones smashed into Kolfinna's chest, knocking the wind out of her. She fell backward, just as more stones wrapped around her body, keeping her stuck in place on the floor. The weight of the stones crushed her chest, sitting on her like a boulder.

"R-Revna, let me go!" Kolfinna tried pushing the stones to no avail. The stone embrace only tightened until breathing became difficult.

"I'm more worn out than I thought." Revna rubbed her trembling hands. "All my mana is wasted already."

Revna walked up to Eyfura and removed the stones around her mouth. She grasped her chin in her hands and turned her face. "What a pretty little thing," Revna said, inspecting her face from different angles. "I like the fire in your eyes."

"Get away from me—" Eyfura started, panic creeping into her tone.

Revna's hand covered Eyfura's forehead and part of her scalp. "It's a shame for such a pretty girl," Revna whispered, but a devilishly delighted smile curved her lips.

"What are you doing?" Eyfura stilled and then screamed. Her body convulsed and thrashed in every direction, trying with all her might to escape from Revna, but Revna kept her pinned in place.

Kolfinna realized with a start what Revna was doing; she was ... *consuming* Eyfura's mana.

But it didn't stop at just her mana—she was shriveling her life force. Kolfinna could feel the shifting of mana in the air. She was suddenly reminded of when she was younger and had depleted her mana, so she had decided to take the mana of a nearby sapling. She had been young, maybe six, and hadn't thought much of it. But as she took its mana, the sapling began wilting, and when Katla finally found her, she had been horrified. She had told her she was defying nature by stealing what didn't belong to her.

"It'll twist your soul," Katla had told her. *"You must never do that again!"*

Even when she was young, she had realized that what she was doing was *wrong*. But she could never imagine doing the same to a human or any living creature.

"Stop," Kolfinna cried and tried to free at least her hands from the rocks. She could feel the skin on her arms and hands scraping against the rough texture of the stones as she yanked at them. She shimmied her shoulders with a grunt and raised her head to where Revna was still draining Eyfura's mana. "S-Stop!" Kolfinna shouted. She tried popping her shoulders out from the restraints, but she was too cemented against the rocks. "Please! Revna, stop! You'll kill her!"

Her cries fell on deaf ears and it wasn't until Eyfura's screams were suddenly cut off and her body went limp against the stones holding her, that Revna released her.

Revna flexed her fingers. "Her mana was strong,

surprisingly, but not as strong as *yours*." She pointed to Blár, grinning. "I would love to devour it all, but I don't want to kill you, not just yet. I need your immense mana for my sisters."

Mímir's eyebrows came together. "We're not going to kill them?"

"No, not yet," she said. "When my sisters wake up, they'll be just as starved as I am, so we need to feed them with their mana. We'll keep them alive until then."

"Did you ..." The question hung in the air as he stared at Eyfura.

Revna made a throaty noise that sounded like a mix between a scoff and snort. "Heavens, boy, are you going to mourn over her? Are you greener than you're letting on?"

"N-No, of course not!" Mímir bowed his head. "I was just surprised."

Eyfura's head was lolled to the side, lifeless. Her blond hair framed her face like the iridescent glows of runes, and Kolfinna waited for signs of life—of her chest rising and falling, of her facial muscles twitching, or something—but she didn't move.

Kolfinna's heart dropped. "Why did you do that?"

"Dear, you can't really be that stupid."

"Mímir!" Kolfinna moved her head forward—it was the only movement she could do. "Why are you doing all of this? We're all part of the same team!"

"No," Mímir said. "We're not. I've always been a part of Ragnarök."

Ragnarök. She didn't know much about them, other

than what Eyfura had told her. That they wanted to change the country to how it used to be when the fae ruled.

"Kolfinna, Kolfinna," Mímir purred, stooping down until he was closer to her. "You have no idea how much of a disappointment you are to me. I was so excited to meet you and maybe recruit you, but you've been nothing but disgraceful. You did help me reach this place, so I suppose you're not *entirely* useless."

"Stop talking like you know me," Kolfinna spat.

"I know enough." He wove his fingers over her stray hairs. "You think I didn't notice how hard you were trying to become a Royal Guard? It's laughable since it's futile. You'll never become a Royal Guard."

"No, you're wrong."

"You think Fenris or King Leiknir planned to keep you alive after you fulfilled your purpose here?" Mímir threw his head back and laughed. "What an idiot! We were told to kill you as soon as we accomplished this mission. Eyfura was nice to you because she was ordered to stay close to you and kill you when the time came."

The words felt like a splash of ice water over her body. The pit of her stomach grew larger and larger. That couldn't be true. Eyfura had been by her side because she was her friend. Not because she wanted to *kill* her. Eyfura was too nice of a person to do such a thing. She was the light of the party. She couldn't ... *She couldn't.*

"You're lying." Kolfinna's words were but a whisper, and yet an ugly part of her wondered if he was telling the truth. If Kolfinna's actions had been in vain. If Eyfura truly was simply a Royal Guard meant to kill Kolfinna after she stopped being useful.

"She was the one who wanted to kill you herself," Mímir sneered, laughing as if he was telling the world the funniest joke. He rose up and planted a foot on the stones encasing her, slowly aiding in the crushing weight of the stones. Her chest felt like it would burst, and she wasn't entirely sure if the stones dug deeper, or his words. "Did you know that she hates your kind? Do you now see how futile your efforts were? How stupid you look?"

Tears pricked the corner of her eyes. "Let me go!"

She didn't have time to react because Mímir kicked her temple with his steel-toed boot. Pain exploded over her head and the room shifted in blurs of darkening grays and blacks. She opened her mouth to scream, to shout, but the world was slipping away.

"—take them into a room—"

"And Eyfura?"

"That one? Take her too, just in case—"

Her world flickered to complete darkness.

24

WHEN KOLFINNA WOKE UP, SHE REALIZED THEY had been moved into another room at some point. This room was much smaller, probably a former dormitory room, but it was bare of all furniture. Golden runes were carved into the wall that read *no magic is allowed* and the doorway was covered in a wall of stone. Their only light source was a single window, but escaping would be fatal since the area beside it on the outside was bare of any solid footing.

Blár, Truda, and Magni sat in silence. Eyfura's crumpled body lay in the center of the room. Her blond hair draped over her shoulders in loose curls, framing her face beautifully like a piece of art. So many artists would've loved to paint her face, Kolfinna thought with a strangled sob. But now she was a lifeless doll. Beautiful, but slowly rotting.

It felt wrong to have someone's life force sapped from

their being. When Kolfinna was younger and had tried taking the mana of the sapling, she had stopped when she realized she was killing it. Even then, as a young child, she had felt the wrongness of her actions. Manipulating and using a person's life force to boost your own mana was simply *wicked*.

The beauty of a fae's power came from nature. From nurturing and manipulating life—not human life, or animal life, but plant matter. Kolfinna had never met anyone else who used their power in a parasitic way.

Kolfinna didn't want to think about Eyfura's betrayal, but it was hard to ignore it when she was sprawled on the floor like that. Eyfura shouldn't have been twisted in such a way. Her white and silver uniform shouldn't have been so disheveled. Her laced silk gloves should've been immaculately clean and pulled tightly onto her fingers, not half-hanging on and half-torn from trying to rip away the rocks that had bound her. She should've been laughing and smiling and teasing. Not lifeless.

Kolfinna wanted answers. How could the same Eyfura who laughed cheerfully and smiled at everyone do such a thing? How could she befriend her with that motive? And why?

She should've never trusted humans, but Kolfinna definitely shouldn't have trusted a fae either. She had been so blinded by Revna and everything she represented. Her history, her people, her power—she had wanted to believe in her so badly. If she hadn't trusted her, if she had just left her alone, they wouldn't be here. They would've been continuing their journey through the ruins. Eyfura would've been alive.

How could Kolfinna let Revna betray her twice? Blár had shown his suspicions from the beginning, but she had just brushed it all away.

She was such a fool.

Tears ran down her face and she didn't care that they all saw it. They would all die anyway.

She started weeping loudly into her hands, her shoulders heaving. Her breaths came hitched and she couldn't control the torrent of tears. All her pent-up frustrations, her hopes, dreams, everything poured out in seconds. She had been so stupid to believe she could become a Royal Guard. That she could have friends and fit in like other people. She had been so foolish to think she could have what Katla couldn't have.

And she had been doubly stupid to trust Revna.

"Stop crying." Magni sighed, but his usually serrated words and cutting tone were missing their bite. He refused to look at Eyfura's corpse and instead stared at his hands intently, clenching and unclenching in silence. The stones had left a dusting of debris and powder on his white, crinkled uniform. He closed his red eyes, tone sharpening. "Why are you even crying?"

Kolfinna struggled to breathe between her sobs. Of all the ways she could've died, this was the least expected. It was also the type of most dishonorable death, because not only would she die because of her own ineptness, but everyone else here would die too. All because she had fallen for Revna's lies and freed her.

"You guys are a real piece of work." The back of Blár's head touched the wall and he clasped his hands together on his lap. His words were aimed at Magni. "Planning to kill your own kind? Really? I thought the Royal Guard were classier than that."

Magni didn't look like he wanted to engage in an argument, but he spoke nonetheless, "She's not a Royal Guard."

"She wanted to be," Blár countered. "And you guys were planning on killing her after you used her. I didn't think Fenris had it in him to be such a snake."

"I wasn't in on that plan." Magni sighed. "I had no idea they were planning that."

Truda curled into a ball and rested her chin on her knees. "Who cares? We're all going to die now."

"You've been working with Mímir for *years* now"—Blár's voice rose higher—"and you never noticed he was a member of Ragnarök?"

Magni's hands balled together tightly. "No. If I had noticed, I would've taken care of him. I wouldn't have let ..." The sentence hung in the air as he finally looked at Eyfura. He inhaled sharply and he looked down at his hands again. This time they trembled, but he tightened them again. Tight enough to leave marks on his ungloved hands, Kolfinna noticed.

"And maybe she wouldn't be dead then." Blár's voice cracked like a whip in the quiet room.

"And what about you?" Here, in the close-quartered dormitory, stripped of his bravado, Magni looked so much younger than he actually was. Or maybe he finally looked his age. Wide, guilt-driven eyes bored into Blár as if trying to pierce him with a glare, but Blár was harsher than him. Harsh, like winter. Magni's lips flattened into a straight line. "Didn't you say you would protect us all? Look where that got us."

Blár narrowed his eyes and even without his ice magic, Kolfinna could've sworn the room felt a tad bit chillier. "Neither of us could've predicted this."

"And that's your lousy excuse?" Magni laughed, but it sounded like a hollow sob. "I thought a black rank meant something. You're supposed to be the strongest person in the military! Couldn't you have prevented this?"

"That's enough fighting." Truda's voice held no substance, as if her will had already faded deep inside her. Pathetic and weak and so unlike her usual sharpness. She pulled herself into a tighter ball. "Come on ... I don't want to die with you both bickering in the background."

"We're not dead yet. That's something." Blár rose to his feet in one fluid motion. "And I'm not planning on dying yet. Kolfinna, you haven't given up yet, have you?"

All eyes turned to her, but she didn't have it in her to glare or hide her emotions. She probably looked every bit like the terrified, hopeless fae girl she was. Tears still clung to her lower lashes, and she made no move to wipe her damp cheeks. There was nothing left to do. Eyfura was dead, the door was blocked off with stones, and the runes didn't allow magic.

Truda took one look at Kolfinna and buried her face in her knees, hugging herself into an even smaller ball. Magni raked a hand through his hair, pushing himself deeper against the wall, but Blár simply stared at her. Unwavering, unblinking—he stared.

"Kolfinna," Blár said in a low voice, "you can't give up."

She swallowed the lump forming in her throat. "Why not?"

"Because we still have a lot to do."

"*You* have a lot to do. I don't." Her face crumpled as hot tears threatened to spill once more. It probably killed him to have to ask her for help, but there was nothing else for her to do. Nothing she could do. "All I've ever done is run, and even if we get out of this alive, that's all I'll be able to do. Run forever, because that's all fae can do in this world."

"If you really think that's all you can do, why didn't you join them?"

"I can't do that," she whispered. "I can't be the oppressor."

"You don't become the oppressor, not at first." Blár rounded the room, his hands pressing and searching over every crack lining the gray walls. "First, you're the rebel. Then, you're an oppressor. And then"—he stopped at the window and turned to her, the wind tousling his hair—

"you're in high society. You could be powerful. *If* they succeed."

"I can't be one of them. I just can't." Kolfinna hugged her knees to her chest like Truda was doing and tried to appear smaller—to disappear altogether. "I can't kill innocent people. I can't just ... destroy a society because I don't fit in it. I want to make room in that society. I want to change the way people think about fae. I don't want to do it like that—through violence, through killing, through *war*."

"Well then," he said, closing the distance between them, "it doesn't sound like you've given up to me." He held his hand out to her. "It sounds to me like you've got a lot of work to do. The first being to get us out of here."

Kolfinna leaned her back against the wall and closed her eyes to avoid his stare—and his outstretched hand. "It's impossible. The runes are too strong."

"You didn't even try."

"I don't have to." She motioned to the runes. "They're stronger than what I can do."

"You have to—"

"Stop!" She slapped his hand away, her voice shrill in the silent room. "I don't need to do anything! If you want to get out, then maybe you should try something?! I'm not able to do anything, all right? So just leave me alone." Her voice tapered off into a sob.

Blár scoffed. "Are you breaking down just because this girl"—he motioned to Eyfura like she wasn't important—"betrayed you?"

"Her name is Eyfura," Magni snapped. "She's not just some random girl. She's Eyfura, a Royal Guard who put her life on the line for this mission—"

"Was. Her name *was* Eyfura," Blár said. "And because of her betrayal, Kolfinna's giving up."

Kolfinna flinched. "I'm not breaking down or giving—"

"You are. Don't act like you're better off dead because someone wanted you dead. Isn't that supposed to be a normal occurrence for you anyway?"

"I trusted her." Her voice sounded small compared to the enormity of what he wanted out of her.

"Well, now she's dead, so she's not your problem anymore."

Magni slammed his fist on the floor. "Eyfura wouldn't have done that." His gaze slid over the Kolfinna. "She would never kill someone and definitely not *you*."

Kolfinna's breath caught in her throat, but she couldn't believe him.

"And why do you say that?" Kolfinna asked.

"Mímir's a traitor. You can't just believe anything he says." Magni looked at Eyfura, and Kolfinna didn't miss the way his lower lip trembled. "She liked you. She wouldn't have lied about that. She's not the type of person to be double-faced. Eyfura is a good person. She's not like me, or Truda, or Blár. She's a good person." He looked away from Eyfura, as if he couldn't bear to keep staring at her dead body. "She *was* a good person."

Kolfinna wanted to believe him more than anything,

but her brain was mush and she didn't know *what* to believe anymore.

Magni pointed to Eyfura's body. "Look inside her uniform."

Kolfinna froze at the request—she didn't want to touch Eyfura's cold body. She didn't want to be around her at all.

"She made something for you. Before we left for this mission." Magni's voice grew stronger—more confident. "She didn't betray you. *I know it.* Check her pockets."

She didn't want to face more disappointment and feel more of the sharp edge of betrayal, but curiosity got the best of her. Kolfinna inched closer to her body. Eyfura's uniform, which had been pristinely white, was now spotted with blood, dirt, and grime. Her naturally pink cheeks were pale and Kolfinna choked back another sob as she slipped her hand into her pocket. Her fingers met with something flat and she pulled out a makeshift wooden badge with a lion carving. For a second, she didn't know what it was. But then it hit her: it was a Hope Badge.

Kolfinna's sight blurred with tears, her heart sinking as it dawned on her. A Hope badge was given by friends and family to people trying to become a Royal Guard.

"She made it for you," Magni said. "She needed help with the carving, so she came to me, but I didn't want to help her because ... well, I just didn't. But she didn't give up. She tried to do it all ... She wrote your name on the back."

She flipped the badge and sure enough, *Kolfinna* was etched into the back with a tiny flower beside her name.

Her fingers curled around the badge and she cradled it close to her chest.

She let her tears fall freely down her cheeks. She hadn't trusted Eyfura in vain. There were a lot of things that didn't work out, but at least Eyfura hadn't betrayed her. She had made one friend at least.

"Okay, we can all cry sometime later," Blár interrupted. "We have to focus on getting out of here before they come back for us. You guys don't seem to realize we're on a time crunch."

Truda raised her head. "And what are we going to do once we get out of here?"

"Kill that hag and weasel pair," Blár said, as if it was that simple.

"Kill them?" Truda scoffed. "No way! Let's just get out of here! Who knows what that lady has up her sleeve?"

"That lady killed Eyfura," Magni said, and they all tried not to look at Eyfura's crumpled body again. He clambered up to his feet and dusted his pants. "There's no way we're not avenging her death."

"We're not going to run away," Blár said. He cracked his knuckles slowly. *Pop. Pop.* "Besides, if this lady is really part of this organization that's trying to enslave humans, I think it's our job to stop them. Imagine if this comes to bite us in our asses five years from now. How shitty would that make you feel?"

Truda pushed back her stringy, dirtied brown hair out of her eyes. "They won't succeed."

"They better not, and that's why we take care of this *now*," Blár said. "Not five, ten, or fifteen years from now."

"I don't like this," Truda said, and Kolfinna noticed the dried blood caking Truda's hair and neck.

Magni snorted. "I didn't think you were a coward."

Truda jumped to her feet, fire practically lashing from her tongue. "I can handle things that I understand, but I don't understand any of this. Rune magic? No magic in certain rooms? Being teleported into different dimensions? This stuff is just out of my realm, okay? And yeah, I'm scared of it all!" Truda waved to the runes in the room and turned her angry eyes to everyone. "But if we're going to fight, I'll fight."

Kolfinna rose to her feet alongside Truda. "I'll fight too."

"You don't have to. You're not human," Blár said. "This is our fight."

"I want to," Kolfinna said. "Because this is my fight too."

She didn't want to die here, and she couldn't continue to wallow in self-pity because she had thought Eyfura betrayed her. She had been momentarily blinded with guilt and treachery, but she couldn't just *give up*.

Kolfinna turned to the runes. They were too high up in the walls for her to reach on her own. But she was sure she wouldn't have been able to break it anyway. Maybe she could write a clause like Revna did?

Cracks lined the gray walls between the runes, but that didn't deter them. It was like the runes hovered *over* the walls. Chipping away at the physical wall would likely not do anything since it was the magic itself in the runes that made the runes work, rather than the physical form of the runes. This was all speculation, though, because Kolfinna didn't know much about runes in the first place.

She placed her hand over an empty space on the wall with the runes. In the room with the coffins, Revna's runes had worked even though she hadn't written them directly below or next to the existing runes. Did that mean the runes only needed a wall, or space, to be connected?

Kolfinna's mana spilled from her fingers. *Clause,* she narrowed her eyes at the gray wall, imbuing her magic with every thought. *Kolfinna can use her magic.* Her mana splayed against the walls, but it got absorbed and disappeared. She paused, waiting for the words to shimmer and glow against the gray stones, but nothing happened.

Again, she tried. She pushed her mana into the words and wrote in her mind, *clause, Kolfinna can use magic.* But once again, nothing happened.

Kolfinna deflated, pinching the bridge of her nose. It wasn't working.

"What's wrong?" Truda tapped her feet impatiently. "Why is it not working?"

Kolfinna spread her hands on the wall. "I'm trying."

"You do realize we're in a pinch for time, right?" Truda peeked out the window at the afternoon sun. "That lady said she was going to use us to feed her dead-faced sisters. I don't know about you, but I'm really not looking forward to being feasted on by a bunch of old ladies."

"If you want to try erasing these runes, be my guest." Kolfinna's fingers curled into a fist against the wall. "But unless you know how to do that, I'd like it if you shut up and let me work."

Truda huffed loudly but then screwed her mouth shut. She crossed her arms over her chest and leaned against the wall. "Fine, I'll stay quiet. I trust you to do your job."

Kolfinna's ears perked at that word. *Trust*. It was such a simple word and yet its weight could sink in an ocean. It felt so strange to have a human, especially someone like Truda, who seemingly hated her, trust her in anything.

As if sensing her surprise, Truda inspected her nails and continued, "It's not like we have a choice, you know. It's either trust you or die. I'd rather not die. I hate dying, actually. It's, like, the worst outcome."

"It *could* be worse," Blár said. "I'd rather die than be tortured."

"Okay, but what kind of torture are we talking about?"

Blár's eyebrow rose. "Is there a type of torture you like? I'd say all torture is worse than death."

Kolfinna stared at the runes, trying to block out their conversation. She breathed out deeply. In and out, in and out, in and out—

"But I think there's a level of torture that's maybe bearable," Truda said. "Like anything with fire is hands down terrible, we can all agree, I'm sure. But if I had to get my head dunked in water over and over, I think I can handle it."

Kolfinna's gaze flitted over to Blár, who was looking at Truda like she was crazy.

"I don't want to find out what I can or can't handle," he said. "I don't think I'd be a fan of getting eaten alive by a dozen thousand-year-old hags."

"*Guys.*" Kolfinna sighed and turned to them sharply. "I'm trying to focus."

"Sorry, sorry." Blár raised his hands. "Continue with your magic writing."

She turned her attention back to the wall and spread her mana into it, trying with all her might to swirl it into coherent words. *Clause, Kolfinna can use magic.* No matter how much mana she poured into it, or how much she focused, nothing made those words glow on the wall.

A frustrated growl escaped her lips and she pounded her fist on the wall. Pain pulsated in her hand, but she ignored it, the runes mocking her.

"What's wrong?" Magni came to stand beside her.

She waved at the runes. "It's not … it's not working."

"Why not?"

"I don't think I'm strong enough to add to it," Kolfinna said. She paced the room, making sure to avoid Eyfura's body. "I mean, it makes sense, doesn't it? Revna has years and years of experience with runes, and I have, like, what, four days of experience? I don't think the runes of these ruins are that strong compared to

Revna's. I think the ruins make it easier because it's supposed to teach fae warriors how to use runes ... But Revna isn't that forgiving. So, basically, it's not working."

"You've got to think of something," Magni said. "We can't just—"

"I know, I know." Kolfinna pressed her forehead against the rough, cool stone walls. "We can't just die here."

Writing new runes wasn't working, so what else could she do?

Then it hit her—why not try to break the runes like she had done at Revna's house in the desert?

"Maybe ..." She turned to peer at the glowing runes. "Maybe I can do something." She glanced at everyone in the room. "I'm going to need some help getting up there, though."

Blár exchanged glances with Magni. "You want his shoulders or mine?"

She hesitated between Blár and Magni. She didn't want to imagine hoisting herself up onto Blár, his face between her thighs and his hands gripping her thighs to keep her in place. Heat crept up her neck and cheeks and highlighted her ears with a blooming red. She didn't want that—she *definitely* didn't want that.

"I-I was thinking Truda—" Kolfinna started.

"No way." Truda raised an eyebrow like she was insane. "I can't do that. And besides, I don't think I'm tall enough either."

Blár looked amused, and Kolfinna's face grew redder. He jabbed a thumb at Magni. "Me or him, which is it?"

"I'll take"—she licked her lips, turning to the wall and then back at the two of them—"Magni."

Blár's eyebrow rose—and Kolfinna could've *sworn* she saw a hint of disappointment flickering in those intense blue eyes—but he didn't protest, while Magni did a double take. He didn't exactly look thrilled at the idea of it, but he kneeled to the floor nonetheless. Kolfinna hesitated before climbing over his back and sitting on his shoulders. The room shifted when he rose up and she gripped onto his shoulders tightly as they both swayed for a moment, but he found his balance and she loosened her talon-like grip on him.

When they reached the wall, Kolfinna placed her hands over the runes and closed her eyes. She imagined her mana constricting the words like a snake wrapping around its prey. She squeezed the life out of the runes, her mana pulsing with her thoughts. Her fingernails dug into the stones.

But nothing happened.

She tried again, with no results.

"It's not working," she growled.

"Try harder," Magni said. "We need you to succeed."

Her lips thinned into a flat line as she glanced down at Magni. He didn't say it out loud like Truda, but she could feel it. He trusted her. They all did. It was so bizarre to have humans trusting her. She should've been their enemy.

Kolfinna raised her chin and dug her nail into one of the runes. She didn't need to touch it, but she wanted to feel the rune and the wall it was inscribed on. She wanted to uproot it, make it disappear. She ran her hand over the stones, but even as she chipped away at the wall, the runes remained. It was as she thought: the runes would remain even if the wall crumbled.

Her hand paused on the single rune that read *no*. She wasn't able to break the whole sentence, but what if she just erased this single rune? It would take much less effort. At least she hoped so.

She placed her hands over the single rune and stared at it, imagining it disappearing beneath her fingers. Mana pooled out of her hands and covered the rune like a body of water before she honed it around the word, imagining her mana crashing into it like an angry, dangerous wave. It crashed against the rune, over and over like a relentless storm. She could feel her mana unspooling and draining faster than ever, but she didn't stop.

To her amazement, the rune crumbled beneath her hands. Kolfinna threw her arms up excitedly. "Yes—"

She swallowed a yelp when Magni stumbled forward. He cursed and almost smashed his face against the stone wall.

"Sorry!" she said after he found his balance again. She still swayed atop his shoulders and couldn't stop grinning from ear to ear.

The wall now read *magic*, instead of *no magic*.

She glanced down at the party, and her eyes met with

Blár's. Her breath stole away from her at the way he looked at her. Like he was so proud of her. And there was something *more* in his ice-blue eyes, something that told her *he* wanted to be the one holding her up.

The air between them felt like charged energy.

"Well?" Magni ripped her attention away. "Is it done?"

Kolfinna answered by flicking her wrist, forcing the stones in the doorway to break apart. The stones pulled away with ease, creating an open doorway.

"You did it!" Truda clapped her hands excitedly.

A grin broke out on Blár's face. "Good job," he said. "I knew you could do it."

Magni helped Kolfinna down to her feet and she didn't miss the relief on his face.

She stepped through the hole. "Now let's go."

"Do any of you actually know the way?" Kolfinna asked after they entered another dormitory wing in the ruins. They had been walking for over an hour, scouring the halls for Revna and Mímir, but they couldn't find them. And they were utterly lost.

"I was unconscious when we were brought into that room." Blár kicked down another door and peeked inside before moving to the next. "For all I know, we could be in a different castle altogether. I have no clue."

"I recognize that painting." Magni pointed to a shredded painting at the end of the hall. What was left of the painting revealed a young woman's face, an ornate crown glinting on her head. "We passed that before we got to that room with the coffins."

Kolfinna didn't recognize it, but all the paintings looked the same to her. "Are you sure? Because there are paintings like that at every level in this place."

"Yes, because this woman has a mole below her eyes." He looked at Kolfinna like it was obvious. "And she has red hair. The other paintings don't have that. Also, if you look closely, you can see the details of her dress show a different color scheme than most of the other paintings. Also, every painting tells a different story."

Kolfinna raised an eyebrow. "Color scheme? How is it any different?"

"The others followed a lighter theme to their colors. Beige, soft browns, pastels—they were lighter and more neutral. This one is more colorful and brighter. See the green in her dress? Of course, it could be the deterioration of time that pales the other paintings, but I digress." Magni frowned, as if realizing he was going on a tangent. "Anyway, I'm quite positive that's the painting we passed."

She tried to see what he saw—a woman in vibrant colors with a *story* to tell—but it didn't look as interesting as he made it out to be. It looked like any other old painting she would gloss over.

Truda squinted at the painting and gave it a once-over like Kolfinna had done. Whatever vulnerability she had shown in the prior room was now gone. She sniggered. "I didn't realize you were into painting. Sounds *very* Royal Guardsy if you ask me."

"What is that even supposed to mean?" Magni stepped on a pile of brittle, off-white bones that splintered beneath his boots. "I'm no artist. I just dabble."

"I didn't realize you were into painting," Kolfinna said.

"I dabble." He shrugged, walking to the end of the hall.

"So it's a hobby?" Truda used her air magic to brush away the scattering of debris out of her way and pointedly in front of Magni, who barreled through it like he didn't notice. "I shouldn't be surprised. Don't Royal Guard snobs like you *dabble* in all artistic avenues to diversify your hobbies? And, let's not forget, you love to rub it in people's faces that they're not classy enough to know what you're talking about. I mean, let's be honest. Us regular folks can't spend time on the arts when we're too focused on our next meal. Did your rich mommy and daddy put you in art classes?"

It wasn't like every Royal Guard was wealthy or came from an affluent family, but if what Truda was insinuating was right—that Magni came from a well-off family—she wouldn't have been surprised.

Kolfinna expected Magni to go off on Truda and snap at her with the same ferocity and pride he had shown just a week ago, but he remained calm.

He rolled his eyes. "No need to sound so bitter. Did I strike a nerve?"

"Oh you certainly did," Truda said as they reached the end of the hallway with the painting. "There was a kid in my class who was just like that. Acted like he was on top of the world because he had so many advantages over everyone else. But what pissed me off the most was that he acted like *he* was the reason he was there in the first place —not because he was born lucky."

Kolfinna glanced at Magni. "Are you a noble?"

"He comes from the Helvig family," Blár said. "They're pretty rich and influential. And snobby. Let's not forget snobby." He paused at the painting. The frame was rotting and split in various areas; at one point, it must've been painted a rich gold color, but now even the paint had peeled away. The painting itself was dull and ripped.

Magni narrowed his eyes at Blár, then at Truda. "You both sound awfully jealous."

"Are you kidding me?" Truda huffed. "I'm not jealous, just annoyed. I make enough money to be happy, so I'm not jealous."

"Soldiers don't make enough to be *happy*." Magni smirked, and he must've known how to get under Truda's skin because the look she gave him could skin grown men alive.

"Not true," Truda said hotly. "I probably make more than—"

"No, you certainly do *not* make more than me." He spoke so confidently that Kolfinna believed him, even though she knew nothing about the true finances of either the military or the Royal Guards.

The hallway split into two, one hall leading to the room with the coffins, and another leading elsewhere. Their group followed the former hallway, and Kolfinna couldn't stop the rise of goose bumps spreading over her body as they drew closer. The others, however, didn't seem as nervous, because they continued their banter.

"Hey, I'm pretty sure I make ten times more than all of you combined," Blár said with a laugh. "So no, not all soldiers make pennies."

"You don't count—" Magni started.

"Can we stay focused?" Kolfinna skidded to a stop and cast a wary glance at the three of them and then over her shoulder. Mímir and Revna weren't here, but who knew when they would show up? She cleared her throat. "We're about to have a big battle pretty soon, and you guys are talking about unimportant stuff. We need to focus."

To her surprise, Magni was the first to nod. "She's right."

"I'm surprised you agree with her. I thought your agenda was to go against everything she says and does," Blár said.

"You're really starting to piss me off," Magni said hotly.

"Guys! *Focus*," Kolfinna said. Straight ahead, at the end of the hallway, she could make out the open archway that led to the coffin room. "Revna is planning on freeing her sisters, so she'll have to go to that room at some point. I'm guessing she's jumping into different dimensions to free them. The others are probably locked away with runes like Revna was."

Blár blew out some air, and the temperature momentarily chilled. "We can either camp there or search this whole place for them. But this place is huge, and I'd hate for them to decide to run away once they realize we're gone. And you're right—they'll have to come to that room to physically free the others."

Magni seemed to consider those options. "I think we should wait in the room. That way we can prepare for them."

"How would we prepare?" Truda asked.

"By removing the runes that don't allow us to use magic," Kolfinna piped in.

Another set of bones, this time looking alarmingly similar to a human's, crunched beneath Blár's feet.

"They won't expect us, so we have the upper hand when it comes to that. And if we can use our magic, we have an even greater chance of winning," he said. "But I must ask." He gave Kolfinna a side look, and she didn't miss the hesitation that momentarily flashed over his face. "What makes this time different than in that room we were locked in?"

Kolfinna paused with the rest of the party when they reached the open doorway to the coffin room. Magni and Truda watched her as well, waiting for her answer. She knew the weight of those stares—if she wasn't able to break or modify those runes, their plan to sit tight in that room would be gone.

"There's one key difference in this room versus the other room," Kolfinna answered. "Revna was the one to write the runes in the previous room. I believe Revna's rune magic is stronger than the rune magic already set by this castle. I mean, it makes sense, doesn't it? This castle is meant to train fae warriors to become adept at rune magic.

They wouldn't make it impossibly difficult. I was unable to modify those runes simply because Revna made them. I'm not at her level of proficiency yet. But this room ..." She glanced inside the room—the stone coffins were exactly where they had left them, and the upturned stones from when Revna had attacked them were still there too. "This room has runes that I might be able to change, because I've proven that I *can* modify the runes in this castle."

That seemed enough affirmation for Magni, because he traipsed inside without a second thought. Truda followed after him. Blár lingered in the doorway, his icy-blue gaze regarding her carefully.

"You don't have to do this," he said quietly, searching her face for something—maybe apprehension, or maybe a hint that she didn't want to battle Revna?

Kolfinna kept her voice low. "I know, but I want to do this. I *need* to."

Blár reached forward and grasped a single lock of her hair that had come undone from her braid. He inspected it between his fingers, and for a moment, she forgot to breathe.

"You don't need to do anything." He released her hair, watching her intently. "If you're doing this because you think it might help you become a Royal Guard, then I'm telling you that you don't need to. You're basically an average civilian. You have no proper training, and no one will fault you for not fighting in this battle."

It would've been so easy to back out and tell him to

take care of the rest, but that couldn't be an option for her, because they needed her. They needed her to break the runes, and they needed her to fight alongside them. It wasn't just a human problem.

And even if it wasn't *her* problem, she couldn't let him and the others fight alone.

"I'm going to fight," she said.

He looked her over once more, and then nodded in Truda and Magni's direction. "If that's the case, you can count on us. Magni might act like an assmonkey from time to time, and Truda's got a stick up her ass, but they know how to fight, and they can fight well. Don't feel shy to rely on them."

Kolfinna didn't need to ask if she could rely on him, because she already knew the answer. She knew the answer back in the desert dimension, and she probably had an idea of it the first time he saved her life too.

A loud crashing sound jolted Kolfinna into a fighting position, but it was only Magni pushing one of the coffin lids off. Her heart was still thumping loudly as he called, "All the bodies are here."

"It doesn't look like they're awake," Truda said, inspecting one of the bodies. "They haven't come back here *yet*."

Kolfinna turned to the runes on the walls while Blár ventured deeper inside to also examine the bodies. *No magic. Clause: except for Revna.* Her fingers brushed over the clause runes Revna had written on the wall. She likely wouldn't be able to erase the runes, but it was worth a shot. She closed her eyes to better envision the runes crumbling beneath her mana. Her hands warmed with mana and she wrapped it around the runes securely, then tightened her grip on them. Tighter and tighter until she could imagine them cracking and becoming flecks of nothing.

Sweat broke out on her forehead, but nothing else happened.

"What do we do about the bodies?" Truda asked. "Killing them would end everything that's happening, wouldn't it? If their mana is running these ruins, then killing them would put a stop to everything. Isn't that what we want?"

"But if we kill them right now," Blár said, "that'll alert Revna and that backstabbing weasel that we killed them and there's no reason for them to stay here, and they'll run away then. Because aren't they just going to different dimensions right now and freeing their sisters? If we kill them, then poof, the sisters disappear and Revna realizes they're dead. Then she's on the run, and we're stuck here waiting and waiting until we realize they've already run away."

Kolfinna glanced at the bodies uneasily. There was no telling what these women were actually like and if they were truly 'evil,' but if they were all as proficient as Revna was at rune magic, they would be in trouble. "But what if Mímir stabs them when he comes back and then we have to fight all of them?"

"That's a possibility, yes," he said. "But remember

why Revna kept us alive? To feed our mana to these guys. I'm guessing when you wake up from the coma, or whatever it is, your mana is drained. Especially since these ruins are already sucking them dry every day. A lot of ancient artifacts have a give-and-take policy to make them work. That dagger Mímir used, for example, the *Genfødsel Kniv*, gives you the ability to put someone to sleep, but it takes years of your life, right? I'm guessing the same applies to when you stab them again to wake them. Maybe the dagger takes the mana of the sleeping person to activate it."

"That's a lot of maybes," Magni said, unconvinced. "Let's say you're wrong, and all these fae wake up with their mana and are ready to fight, there's a chance we might die. Especially if we can't use our magic."

"Also, I hate to poke holes into your theory," Truda added, "but Revna had used rune magic soon after she awoke."

"True."

"Alright, but they're probably pretty drained." Blár shrugged, and then pointed to Magni. "Worst-case scenario, when Mímir and Revna are here, you burn the bodies. That way, there's no possibility to wake them up. And then if they *do* manage to wake up, they'll be half-dead anyway."

"That's only *if* I can use my magic."

"Kolfinna will come up with something."

Kolfinna dragged her nails across the runes, as if scratching them away would work. She could destroy the "no" rune like she did in the previous room, but that had taken the majority of her mana. Would it be easier to just write clauses like Revna had done? Would that use the least amount of mana? She couldn't expect to fight Revna and Mímir if she didn't have a good supply of mana. She *could* use Blár's mana like she did in the desert dimension, but she had already depleted more than half of his mana, and he was their strongest fighter, so she couldn't afford to take more from him.

She hoped the clauses worked because if not, they would have to change their plan.

Kolfinna uncurled her fingers onto the wall and spread her mana on her fingertips. *Clause: except for Magni.* Mana heated her skin and the words glowed on the wall. It read: *No magic. Clause: except for Revna. Clause: except for Magni.*

She almost fell forward with how easy it was and quickly spun around to face Magni. "Can you use your magic?"

He held his hand out for everyone to see, and in seconds, fire flickered in the palm of his hand. A grin split his lips in half as the fire illuminated his emerald eyes.

"I still can't use mine." Truda held her hands up.

"Me neither." Blár frowned.

"I'm still writing it," she said with an exasperated sigh.

Her eyebrows came together as she focused her mana on the runes. *Clause: except for Kolfinna.* She breathed out, mana spilling from her and slowly seeping into the wall. Beneath that clause, she forced another one. *Clause: except for Truda.* The runes shimmered on the walls.

She spread her hands beneath the new runes. All that was left was to write Blár's clause. *Clause: except—*

Something smashed into her side and sent her hurtling toward one of the stone coffins. Her shoulder banged against the sharp corner and she bit back a scream as she fell to the floor in a heap. She blinked, feeling the warm blood pool on her arm.

"Color me surprised." Revna's cool voice whipped from behind her. "I didn't think you'd be able to break out of that room. I underestimate my teaching abilities."

Revna stood at the opening of the room on top of the creaky railing with a thick black sword in her hand. The mountain backdropped behind her. Massive skeletal wings hung on her back, making her appear even more sinister, and a glowing red beaded necklace hung on her neck.

Revna stepped down from the railing, the wings fanning out even wider. "You motley, inferior group of children are essentially blind in these ruins. You have no idea how much treasure is here." She held up the sword and motioned to the wings. "I doubt you humans have ever seen anything like it before. Fae society has always been so much more advanced than anything you humans can conjure up."

Even as Magni's mouth still hung open at the sight of the wings, he jumped into action. Fire shot from his hands at Revna. All Revna had to do was stare at the floor beneath her and stones rose to block the attack. Truda did the same, sending a wave of air slicing toward her. Revna flicked her wrist and another wall constructed itself in front of her like a shield before crumbling at the force of the blast.

Kolfinna scrambled to her feet, wincing at her throbbing shoulder. The bloody part of her uniform clung against the cut. Vivid red splotches painted her sleeve a darker shade of black. She quickly glanced at the wall, where Blár's name was missing, and then at the entrance of the room, where Mímir was now standing, dagger in hand. Blár still didn't have magic, but neither did Mímir.

They needed Blár in this fight. She had faced off against his impenetrable ice, and it had been monstrous. They needed that monstrosity right now and it was up to her to do that. If only, she thought darkly, running to the wall, if only she had written his name first. He would've been able to fight off Revna and Mímir easily. If only—

A wall of stones jabbed up in front of Kolfinna and she dove to the side to avoid getting crushed by the sudden attack.

"Where do you think you're going, fledgling?" Revna laughed and opened her mouth to say more, but fire narrowly burned her cheek. She flew forward a foot and swung her sword at Truda, who was closest to her. Truda ducked in time, sending a thrust of wind at Revna, who cast another stone wall to protect herself.

Kolfinna gritted her teeth together and poured mana into the floor quickly. She manipulated the stones, broke off a chunk of the floor, and hurtled it in Revna's direction. Revna's wings flapped and a gust of wind blew in their direction as she soared toward the ceiling, her wings looking alarmingly similar to the dreki's skeletal and leathery ones. She flew to the back of the room, away from the glow of the afternoon light. Truda gathered the air around Revna's wings to deter her movements, but a single flap of Revna's wings cast Truda's attempt away.

In the corner of Kolfinna's vision, Blár and Mímir exchanged blows with one another. Mana buzzed in the air and twitched beneath her skin as Kolfinna called forth the nature outside. But Revna was quicker. A makeshift stone spear rose from the floor and threw itself at Kolfinna. She barely had time to dodge, but another was already forming. And another.

Kolfinna jumped out of the way again, and then raised her own wall before the third could impale her. Stones collided against one another and she was thrown backward. She crashed into the railing and it bent beneath her weight. She hadn't even realized she had gotten so close to the railing, or that she was no longer close to the wall. Revna had successfully pushed her to the other side of the room with her spear assault, she realized with a start.

Just then, fire sputtered from Magni's hand and he shot another fireball at Revna, but Revna flew to the right, missing it, and swung her sword at the next one. The sword sliced it in half where it flashed and suddenly disappeared, as if absorbed by the black blade. Revna smiled a sinister smile and easily moved away when Truda sent pressurized air in her direction.

"Careful!" Magni shouted, running away from a hunk of the wall Revna sent in his direction. Blood dotted the floor with his movement. He cringed and sent a blast of fire at Revna, who swung her sword and waved her wings, sending gusts of wind to push away his fire toward Truda, who enveloped herself in a whirlwind to avoid the flames licking her skin.

"Careful," he started again. "That sword—don't—"

He cut off as another rock shot in his direction. This time, he wasn't able to dodge it and it smacked him right in the abdomen, sending him flying against the wall. Revna flicked her wrist and a stone spear shot from the other end of the room and flew toward him. Kolfinna lurched into action, her mana blazing with life as she slammed her palms on the floor, forcing the stone floor in front of Magni to open up. A wall jutted in the space in front of him, taking the brunt of Revna's attack before shattering.

"Don't get hit by the sword." Magni pushed away from the crumbled remnants of stone and with a flash of his hands, fire glinted off his palms. White debris and dust coated his eyebrows and hair. His lips curled into his signature scowl and he thrust his fire at Revna, who weaved through the air with her giant wings like the dreki had.

Kolfinna's mana beneath her skin stretched thinly and she pulled at it, drawing more of it from deep within herself. She had been using her mana all throughout the day, so she wasn't sure how much she had left. She already felt drained. Her bones creaked, her muscles screamed, and her wounds—old and new—ached.

Revna flew higher, dodging the fireballs and slices of air that cut lashes into the ceiling. Mímir and Blár wrangled on the floor, kicking and punching and rolling. Kolfinna couldn't keep track of them, Revna, and the runes.

"You traitor," Blár snarled, lunging for Mímir's throat.

Mímir jumped away.

"You're nothing without your magic," Mímir sneered. "Nothing but a spoiled, arrogant brat."

Kolfinna bolted toward the runes, but the world spun and she met the floor in seconds. Her jaw cracked against the floor and black dotted her vision. Her face throbbed and a metallic, salty taste filled her mouth. The crashes, booms, and crackling of fire faded for a few seconds and she struggled to lift her head. She tried pulling her leg forward but was met with resistance. Heavy, rough stones held her feet in a vice grip.

She felt the scorch of fire before she heard the hiss and crackle of it. A rock skidded to her left, and then another to her right. Another boom sounded behind her. She inhaled, and heat filled her throat. She blinked back rapidly and her vision came back. Magni stood in front of her, protecting her with a barrier of fire, while Revna pelted rocks at them.

In a split second, Kolfinna broke the stones binding

her feet and jumped up. Her vision swayed and she faltered on her feet.

Magni glanced back at her. "You okay?"

"I'm fine." Kolfinna rubbed her jaw and cringed. She hoped it wasn't broken.

Another rock narrowly missed their heads.

"Why can't Blár use his magic?" Magni asked, his fire barrier flickering away. Sweat and blood dampened his uniform collar.

"I couldn't write his name." Kolfinna erected a thin barrier in front of them while Revna threw more stones in their direction.

"None of my moves are reaching her," he said. "And her sword is absorbing my attacks when I do manage to get her. Truda doesn't have enough mana to fly, and even if she could, I don't think she can beat her in the air."

Their conversation was cut short when Revna created more stone spears from beneath their feet. Kolfinna jumped away, but the spear crashed into her chest, throwing her backward. Kolfinna slammed onto the floor, bits of broken rocks digging into her back. She bit back a scream and pushed herself to her knees, glaring up at Revna.

Revna was up high, moving her hands swiftly and maneuvering her attacks from her vantage point. They needed to bring her down to the floor so they could fight better. Most of their attacks weren't landing, and they were at a disadvantage since she could see everything.

"Magni!" Kolfinna shouted, running back to him as

another stone spear shot from the wall. She threw her hands up, creating her own spear to counter Revna's. The two spears cracked against each other in the air and the pieces flew in different directions. "Make the air uninhabitable for her! Just stream fire into the sky and have Truda create large gusts so the fire keeps fanning across the room!"

"We can't do that!" He rolled as a stone almost smashed his face. "She keeps attacking us."

"Try it!" she said. "I'll protect you both! We need to bring her down!"

"I'll try." He turned to Truda, who was dodging a myriad of stone balls Revna relentlessly shot at her. "Truda! Whirlwind! Now!"

Truda looked at him like he was crazy, but she must've seen something on his face because she gave a curt nod. Kolfinna readied her fast-depleting mana and widened her stance for any stray rocks that would inevitably be thrown her way. Truda raised her hands at the same time Magni did. A powerful gust of wind blew across the room, sending debris and bits of rocks swirling in the air. Magni's fire joined the swirls of wind and the temperature increased instantaneously. Thick heat waves blew in every direction, singeing the hairs on Kolfinna's arms.

Revna, predictably, ripped giant chunks of stone from the wall and threw it in Magni and Truda's direction, but Kolfinna was ready. She intercepted the attacks with quick barricades. They broke and she created another.

Revna's wings flapped in the powerful winds and she

faltered in the air as fire fanned in front of her. A half-scream strangled her throat when the fire licked her feet and spread to her body. She dove to the floor, where she pulled the rocks toward her body to cloak herself. The fire roared and finally sputtered as she tamped the rocks closer to herself.

Kolfinna was in front of Revna in seconds; she pulled her fist back and punched Revna across the face. A satisfying jolt ran up her arm when her fist connected with Revna's cheek. Revna skittered backward, swinging her sword in front of her to keep Kolfinna away. Kolfinna leapt away, but the sword nicked her chest. It couldn't have been more than a scratch, but she instantly fell to her knees as her mana drew to the sword. She sucked in a breath. It was such an off-putting, disgusting feeling to have her mana pulled like that—as if someone was yanking her vein like it was a loose thread.

Revna grinned in response. "My sword, *Magisk-æder*, loves eating mana." She lunged at her with the blade. "You'd know the history of this infamous sword if you grew up in my society, Kolfinna. Why side with these pathetic humans when they've done nothing but rip you away from your lineage and steal your history?"

A mixture of air and fire struck Revna's face and she fell backward, her wings pushing the floor to pull her back on her feet.

"How are you able to fly?" Kolfinna asked, pushing the stones from the floor to launch at Revna, whose footsteps pitter-pattered away.

"Elven artifacts," she said with a soft laugh. "Elves always envied our wings. I never thought I'd be using these, but what can I do after those traitorous bastards ripped my own off my back? Do you know how big of a disgrace it is to have your wings taken from you? The fae love to fly, and these humans *forced* you to cut your wings, your pride and history, off from you. Aren't you angry? Don't you want to take it back? Well, we can take that back, Kolfinna. If only you'd join us."

Elves. There it was again, something she was supposed to know but had no clue even existed. But she didn't linger on that—that was exactly what Revna wanted.

"Never," Kolfinna spat. "You don't want freedom for our people, you just want to be above everyone!"

"Pity. I had high hopes for you," Revna said, dodging another blast of fire. She flipped her hand and tall walls domed around her, shielding her from the fire blasts. Circular pieces of rocks the size of Kolfinna's palm suddenly carved out of the walls of Revna's dome and shot out in every direction.

Kolfinna erected her own shield and cloaked her hands with broken chunks of rocks while Revna continued attacking her shield. To her right, Magni was using a raised coffin as a barrier from Revna's attacks. Meanwhile, on her left, Truda was slicing the rocks in half with her air magic. When Revna's attacks slowed, Kolfinna emerged from her wall.

"You used me!" Kolfinna ducked from a sword attack.

"I helped you, and you helped me," Revna said. "You would've been stuck in that dimension without my help."

Kolfinna charged at her, intent on smashing her face with her fists of rocks, but at the last second, something snaked around her ankle. She barely had time to look down before the thick, green vine pulled her from under her feet. Her vision blurred and she yelped, flailing like a rag doll across the room. The smell of something burning assaulted her nose and she was released from its grip. She flew in the air and crashed into the wall.

Kolfinna doubled over, gnashing her teeth to keep from screaming. Her ankle felt like it would twist off her leg, and her back ached terribly. It was wet and sticky. Kolfinna struggled to sit up, her body groaning in protest. The vine Revna had used was half-burnt, she realized; Magni had helped her.

A movement to her right caught her attention. Mímir and Blár still fought each other; a sheen of sweat clinging to both of their faces. Time slowed as Mímir ducked from Blár's punch, flipped the dagger in his hand, and thrust it into Blár's stomach. Kolfinna's eyes widened just as Blár's did. He looked down, but it was too late. His eyelids fluttered shut and he collapsed in a split second.

Kolfinna gasped. Blár was out cold. Mímir stood over his body, breathing heavily, the *Genfødsel Kniv* in his hand. Kolfinna's mind whirled as she processed everything: Blár had been stabbed with the *Genfødsel Kniv*. If they weren't able to get the dagger from Mímir, Blár would be asleep *forever*. A chill settled in her bones. They needed Blár. If there was a war against the world as they knew it, they needed Blár on their side. Furthermore, she didn't *want* him to sleep forever.

Mímir's gaze drifted to the coffins and he took off running. Kolfinna's mind spun. He would awaken them all, and then they would have to face a horde of ancient fae bent on sucking their mana dry. That couldn't happen.

She picked up a nearby rock and threw it with all her force, not even bothering to feel for her mana. It whizzed past Mímir's head. He glanced over his shoulder at her, his eyes widening. In that split second, she forced a part of the floor to jut out in front of him. He tripped and skidded on the floor, the dagger flying out of his hand and clattering among the debris and rocks.

Kolfinna was in front of him in seconds. "You traitor!"

"Kolfinna—" He started rising to his feet slowly, his eyes flitting from the floor to her face.

She stomped a foot on the floor, pumping her mana into the stones surrounding her feet. In seconds, the stones launched at him from every direction. He didn't have time to react as half a dozen stones smashed into him and pinned him to the floor. She encircled him in another ring of stones, but this time, she clapped her hands together, forcing the stones to encase him until only his head stuck out from them. He wriggled against the rocks, but it was too solid.

"Kolfinna," he breathed, "stop—"

Kolfinna tightened her hold on him, but the stones suddenly released and he fell to the floor. Kolfinna's gaze darted to Revna, who had danced away from Magni's fire and Truda's wind attacks. Kolfinna's eyes narrowed. Revna was still watching.

Mímir searched the floor around him, but the dagger wasn't there. Kolfinna raised a stone beside her and shot it at him. He was so focused on his task that he didn't see it coming. It cracked against his temple and he fell forward, his body limp.

Kolfinna used her mana to pile stones around his wrists and feet, then melded the stones together until they became solid stone bindings. Once that was done, she returned her attention back to the fight. Truda and Magni were struggling against Revna. Their attacks, although hitting her occasionally, weren't doing much damage, if at all. Her sword leeched the brunt of most of the attacks, likely sucking the mana from them.

Kolfinna hesitated as she stood between the edge of two important decisions: she could either join the others to fight Revna, or she could search for the *Genfødsel Kniv* and wake Blár.

Her decision came quick.

Kolfinna dropped to her knees, her hands swimming across the floors. She kept glancing at Revna to make sure she didn't throw another attack or sneak vines over her body. As much as she wanted to fight, Blár was more important; if they had him in this fight—

"Kolfinna, we could really use your help!" Truda shouted just as she was hit in the chest with a large rock. She flew backward and tumbled like a doll.

Kolfinna cursed loudly as she looked between Truda and Blár, who remained still on the floor like a corpse. She wanted to help him, and a part of her knew it was more than just his powers that she needed him here. But they needed her right now.

Kolfinna ran to Truda and Magni. She would have to deal with Revna first.

She drew upon the mana deeply nestled in her body, feeling the nature in the ravine. She had been wary to use her nature powers in the ruins since she hadn't wanted to destroy the ruins, and simply because plant matter was far away, but she needed her powers more than ever.

She uprooted chunks of the walls and flung them at Revna, who attempted to dodge by jumping backward. Magni seemed to expect that because he sent a blaze of fire directly behind Revna. A scream ripped from Revna's throat and she flapped her wings and the *Magisk-æder* to free herself from it, but it continued to spread.

Revna tried to bolt up into the sky, but Kolfinna's vines were already spreading below her, hidden by the upturned stones she had thrown. They flung upward and grabbed her ankle, yanking her down. Revna grunted as she slammed onto the floor. Magni and Truda volleyed fire and air slices at her while Kolfinna continued to tangle her in vines. Revna swung her sword, trying to cut the vines. Kolfinna felt the tug of magic as Revna tried to take control of her vines with her mana, but Kolfinna didn't surrender. Her mana held tight over her vines, even as Revna tried again to take control of them.

Flecks of Magni's fire landed on the vines, but they didn't burn. Kolfinna's mana kept them from burning in the carnage in front of her. A realization dawned on Kolfinna: when Revna had tried attacking Kolfinna with vines earlier in the battle, Magni's fire had been able to burn them. But here, Magni's fire wasn't hurting Kolfinna's vines.

Revna might've been able to beat Kolfinna when it came to runes, but Kolfinna was better at manipulating nature.

She tightened the reins of her vines around Revna and squeezed tightly. Revna tried again to take over Kolfinna's vines, but her attempts were futile. Magni's fire roared over Revna's body and she thrashed against the vines holding her hostage and the unrelenting fire.

"Let me go! Let me go!" Revna twisted her wrist and she tried to cut the vines with the sword, but Truda kicked the hilt of the blade, where it skidded across the room.

Magni's fire finally calmed down and dissipated as he stood over Revna. He clutched his injured arm tightly and glowered at Revna. "You've lost."

"Kill her," Truda said. "It'll be better than—"

The floors began vibrating and the walls rattled. Pieces of stones bounced on the floors and skittered around the room with each vibration. A familiar, haunting roar resounded loudly below them.

A giant creature crashed through the floor, sending everyone tumbling back with its force. Kolfinna barely had time to scramble away as the dreki launched through the ceiling, sending chunks of stone to rain down on them. She quickly erected a thin barrier to protect herself, Truda, and Magni from the stones just as the dreki swooped back through the hole it had created in the ceiling and landed on the stone coffins. It opened its mouth and roared again.

It was even more monstrous here than it was in the desert dimension. It wasn't blind, either. Large, skeletal, leathery wings hung behind its spiky back. Black scales lined its body uniformly and giant, yellowed teeth poked from its mouth. Red eyes glowed sinisterly.

In the shock of it, Kolfinna suddenly realized she had relinquished control over her vines. Revna, now freed from Kolfinna's constraints, was running toward the open wall. Kolfinna stepped toward her, but something else caught her eye: Blár was lying a few feet away from the dreki, his body alarmingly close to being crushed if the dreki spun around at any moment. For a few haunting seconds, she froze. Save Blár, or capture Revna?

She needed to capture Revna.

But before she knew it, her feet pounded the floor toward Blár, and she nearly tripped over the littered wreckage of upturned stones, pieces of the ceiling and flooring, and remnants of their battle. The dreki opened its mouth and aimed a breath of fire in his direction.

She wouldn't make it, she thought in horror.

She definitely wouldn't make it.

Kolfinna spread her hand out and flared her mana into the floor, forcing a wall to stand around Blár; it would be a thin wall, since she didn't have time to solidify one, but it would be enough to protect him. The dreki spewed a breath of fire and blew her wall to bits. It inhaled again, ready to smoke Blár.

"Blár!" Kolfinna drew forth all the plant matter she could and thrust it around the dreki's tail, and then yanked at it so it would turn its attention away from Blár. It worked, and the dreki spun around to scream at the green vines and brown roots wrapped around its tail.

She skidded in front of Blár's body while simultaneously pulling the dreki's tail to keep its attention away from them. A quick glance at Blár's body revealed he was untouched by the flames, but he had gotten hit by small pieces of the ceiling, she reckoned by the new scratches and cuts on his face. But he was alive, and that was all that mattered.

Kolfinna tried to gather him in her arms, but he was too limp and heavy to carry. His head lolled to the side as she tried moving him. Seconds ticked by, and the dreki blasted the vines arounds its tail, and Kolfinna quickly lost sensation of the dead vegetation like a cord snapping in half.

Without thinking, she grabbed his arms and pulled. Her biceps screamed with exertion; he was heavy, almost too heavy for her to drag. Somehow, she managed to drag him across the floor, his back rolling over the rocks and fragmented stones.

The dreki roared again, blowing hot air into the room. Kolfinna threw up another wall between herself and the dreki, but it cracked under the heat of the dreki's fire breath, which fanned out in the room as the dreki swiveled its head in every direction. Magni and Truda were leaping away from its attacks, oblivious to Blár and Kolfinna.

"Find Revna!" Kolfinna shouted above the hiss of fire. She continued to drag Blár across the room, closer to the doorway. "We can't let her escape!"

"She's already gone!" Magni cursed and dove behind a coffin as the dreki shot fire at him.

There were so many things they could've done to prevent this—things they *should've* done, things *she* should've done—but she couldn't dwell on it, even as a bitter taste filled her mouth.

With the dreki breathing fire and demolishing the room and Blár's unconscious state, what could they even do against the dreki? All of them were practically running on fumes. They hadn't entered the battle with full mana in the first place, so she could only imagine how worn out everyone already was. The only thing she could think of was to wake up Blár so he could defeat it—because for Blár, the dreki was nothing. But where was the *Genfødsel Kniv*? It had to be somewhere on the floor. She prayed it hadn't fallen into the hole in the floor the dreki had created.

"Magni, Truda!" Kolfinna shouted as she erected another stone wall between herself and the dreki. "Distract the dreki for me! I have a plan!"

"Easier said—" Magni started, rolling away from the dreki's flames and sending a wave of his own.

"Please!"

The dreki's tail decimated a wall as it swung around to swipe Truda and Magni. Large chunks of the ceiling collapsed from above them, crashing into the floor and shattering upon impact. Kolfinna finally dragged Blár's body out of the room and into the hallway, pulling him farther and farther away from the fight. So long as Magni and Truda kept the dreki occupied, it wouldn't find Blár.

She spun around and sprinted back into the room, keeping close to the wall so the dreki wouldn't turn to her. She dropped to her knees among the debris, searching for the knife and throwing periodic glances at the dreki.

The dreki belted into the ceiling and flicked its blood-red gaze to her. Her breath caught in her throat and she rolled as it sent a wave of fire at her. Her clothes crisped in the heat and she fell behind one of the coffins as the dreki blasted at her relentlessly. The smell of smoke and ash assaulted her nose and she pressed her back against the warm coffin as fire sprayed around the edges of it. A glinting of metal caught the corner of her eye. Hidden beneath the rubble, the *Genfødsel Kniv* gleamed red with the fire.

Kolfinna infused her mana into the rubble and pushed the rocks aside, wrenching the blade free. It was light in her hands but heavy at the same time when she thought of all the souls that had been struck with it. Despite the inferno of heat in the room, she shivered, wrapping her fingers tighter on the hilt.

Something distracted the dreki—probably Magni or

Truda—and it stopped breathing fire against the coffins. Kolfinna poked her head around to see and sure enough, fire was streaming from Magni's hands and onto the dreki; it was pathetically small compared to the dreki's brilliant flames. But it was enough to distract the creature as Kolfinna slipped into the hallway, holding the blade far from her body to keep from accidentally nicking herself.

Kolfinna dropped to her knees in front of Blár. In this state, it almost looked like he was dead. His chest didn't rise or fall, and his eyelids didn't flitter like they were supposed to when someone was in a dreamlike state. Here, he was too still. Like a beautiful painting, or like a corpse.

The blade clattered to the floor, slipping from the blood coating her hand. Kolfinna hadn't even realized she was bleeding profusely from her shoulder, but now that she had a few seconds away from the battle, her hands shook.

She picked up the knife and placed it on Blár's chest. A thick rivulet of her blood marked the silver edge of the blade. She hesitated as red droplets stained the gray material of his uniform. What if the blade dug into his vital organs? She had seen Mímir use it on Revna's chest, and it didn't seem to damage her, but Kolfinna didn't want to take that risk. She instead pointed the tip of the blade at Blár's hand and pushed it into his skin. The dagger sliced the skin with ease.

In seconds, mana blazed at the blade and nearly scorched her skin off, and Blár's eyelids fluttered open. In seconds, the beautiful painting she had in mind came to life. He was no longer like a corpse as he sputtered, blinked, and gasped as if he hadn't breathed in years. His eyes flicked to her and recognition flashed through them.

All the tension in her body seemed to meld away in seconds—it was as if all the stress had been tied together by a ribbon, and Blár's awakening had unraveled it, allowing relief to pool over her. Tears formed in her eyes and she flung her arms around his neck. He grunted, trying to push himself to his elbows. He placed a hand on the small of her back.

"Blár!" she cried between sobs of relief. She buried her face in his shoulder, breathing in the scent of vanilla, sweat, and blood.

"Kolfinna?"

She pulled back to inspect his injuries; he was fine, but he appeared weak and slightly disoriented.

Blár brushed a tear off her cheek, his eyes searching her face. "What's wrong—why are you crying?"

"I thought you were—" She sniffled. A small part of her had believed he would sleep forever. She squeezed his hand and turned to the open doorway, where Magni and Truda were still fighting. "We need your help."

"Don't cry," he said. "What's happening? Where am I?"

"We're in the middle of the battle."

Kolfinna helped him into a sitting position. He groaned, his hand flying to his head. "I feel like shit."

The dreki's roar jolted him out of his bleary state and he stared past her, his forehead puckering. She followed his gaze to where Magni and Truda were keeping the dreki busy. But even from this distance, Kolfinna could tell that their attacks were either missing their mark or held no substance.

"You need to kill it," she said. "Magni and Truda are fighting it off, but they're exhausted. I don't have much mana left either—"

He was already shaking his head. "I can't freeze it." A cough shook him. "My mana is completely drained. I'm running on fumes right now. I think my theory is correct. That dagger uses the person's mana to wake them up because I don't think I can do much of anything for a few hours until my mana returns."

The color drained from her face. "Th-There has to be something—"

"I can maybe do one attack," he said. "Just an ice spear, maybe. But I'll need your help to keep me up on my feet. If I miss ... We need to run away."

"Okay, but you'll have to throw it from the doorway, you can't enter the room. I wasn't able to write your name with the runes."

"Help me to my feet."

His face turned white as he pulled himself into a standing position. Kolfinna placed the *Genfødsel Kniv* into the waistband of her uniform and slipped her arm underneath Blár to help steady him. She tugged him forward, her arm straining with his weight as he leaned against her.

The dreki spun around and swiped its claws at Truda,

who just barely dodged it. Her arm hung to her side limply, blood drenching the sleeve. Her breaths came in uneven gasps as she moved away from the creature. Magni moved like he was stuck in sludge. His fire barely had any spark to it. The smell of burning flesh and charcoal pervaded the air.

Blár stopped at the threshold of the door and breathed out heavily. The temperature in the room suddenly dropped quickly as ice crystals formed at the tips of his fingers. He held his hand up and ice crackled into a long, thin spear. A chill wafted over her from being so close and she shuddered as the icy grips clung to her body. The temperature continued to drop and the spear grew thicker and thicker.

"Block its attacks for me," Blár said. "It noticed."

The dreki craned its neck in their direction, its glowing eyes murderous as it stepped toward them. As if recognizing them both, it screamed and jumped toward them. Kolfinna drew forth more roots from the ravine and wrapped them around its legs with what little mana she had left. She tried to rein the dreki in with those roots, but they only slowed it down, the roots snapping with the dreki's forceful steps.

It rushed toward them, its feet stomping and vibrating the floor. Blár's breath came in white puffs from the cold and Kolfinna watched in horror as the dreki closed the distance between them. They only had a few seconds until it would be on them.

"Blár—" she started.

Mana burst from Blár's body in a split second. Kolfinna was flung to the side as Blár stepped forward, twisted his upper body, and thrust the ice spear directly at the dreki's face. It slammed right between its eyes, slicing through its skull until it was yanked backward. The dreki's body careened to the left where it crashed with a loud *thud*. Half the spear stuck out of its head, while the other half lay on the floor in a puddle of the dreki's blood and brain matter. The back of its skull was wide-open, spilling forth all types of liquids and fleshy material.

Blár fell to one knee, breathing heavily. Kolfinna reached forward to help him, but he waved her away.

"I'm fine," he said.

Kolfinna retracted, glancing at the dreki's decimated head. Even with the majority of his mana drained, Blár was on another level. If she had written his name in the runes, allowing him to use magic, how different would the outcome have been?

Truda fell to her knees with an audible sigh, all the fight draining out of her. Magni balanced against one of the broken pillars and leaned his head against it. The relief in the air was tangible.

"Truda, Magni—you both alive?" Blár asked.

"Barely holding on." Truda ran a hand over her face. Grime, tears, blood, and sweat caked her face. "But Revna ... escaped."

"She *what*?" Blár snapped his head up in her direction. "How?"

Kolfinna shifted on her feet. "Before we could defeat

her, the dreki destroyed the, um—" She motioned to the gaping holes in the floor and the ceiling. Bits of pebbles and dust still cracked off from them. "Um, well, she escaped when the dreki came here."

Blár cursed under his breath and opened his mouth like he would chew them out, but then he sighed and said, "Well, it's not like I can argue since I was asleep when all that went down. Anyway—Magni, how are you holding up?"

"I'm alive," he said, sliding down the pillar.

"Where's Mímir? Did he run off too?"

Kolfinna shifted her attention to the corner of the room, where Mímir lay on the floor in a crumpled position. His hands and feet were still encased in the stone bindings. By the looks of it, he was still unconscious.

"There," she said, pointing. "I don't know how he survived all of that."

"We'll take him back with us," Blár said. "As for the fae—are any of them alive?"

Magni pushed himself away from the pillar, and blood stained the once off-white stone material of it, and he dragged himself to the coffins. "By the looks of it, some are dead," he called out as he checked on each one. "The dreki's fire burnt some of them, but some of the others are still alive. We should take them to the king—"

"No," Blár said. "Kill them. Right now."

Magni froze. "But—"

"The king will want them alive so he can experiment and learn from them, but that's far too dangerous. You saw Revna. She was able to fly and use artifacts we have no knowledge of, and let's not even get started on her rune magic." His voice was hard. "The king won't care if any of them wake up and kill thousands of people. If any of them wake up, I'm sure it'll spell disaster for us all. Kill them. Immediately."

Truda nodded. "I'll take care of it."

"As for you." He turned to Kolfinna, and the harshness of his gaze softened. "You did pretty decent for your first real battle." He grinned, and her heart did a small somersault. Even though the heat of the battle was over, her whole body tingled with warmth. It was inappropriate for her to think he looked handsome in that moment, with blood, dirt, and sweat coating his body like a second skin, but she couldn't deny that he was wickedly handsome. With his tousled black hair and sharp wintery eyes —he was a dream.

She must've been going crazy to think that. Especially after the battle.

She averted her gaze. "Thanks," she muttered.

"Well, at least I think so," he said with a short laugh. "I can't say for sure since I was out of it for half of it, but you did well."

She was *definitely* crazy, but at least the battle was finally over. Even as she thought that, another voice told her it might've just been the beginning.

Kolfinna sat against a crumbling coffin; the crater in the ceiling cast a ring of moonlight onto the littered, torn floor. The smell of rot and decay lifted from the corpses, both the dreki and the fae, so strongly that Kolfinna's nose and eyes stung. Her eyelids drooped heavily and she rested her head on her knees, rocking gently. Now that the adrenaline rush of battle was over, Kolfinna felt empty and bone-weary. All her mistakes replayed in her mind—she should've lunged *this* way, not *that* way. She should've used *this* attack, not *that* attack.

She sighed, glancing over at the trio huddled in the center of the moonlight. Magni, Truda, and Blár had bandaged themselves up and were now discussing a plan moving forward. Their bounty was the *Genfødsel Kniv*, Revna's *Magisk-æder*, and Mímir—who was now awake and struggling to undo the stone bindings on his wrists.

She didn't want to join their conversation because she

was neither a part of the military nor the Royal Guards. Which left her wondering, where exactly did she stand? Did she even have a chance to become a Royal Guard?

Truda had said their mission was a success with that bounty and that it would be enough to pacify the king, but every time Kolfinna thought about the Royal Guards, Mímir's words replayed in her mind. What if the king and Fenris truly did plan to kill her after this mission? What if they deemed fae too dangerous and executed her? What if they didn't pardon her crimes? After all, most of the party was dead, so her usefulness was questionable.

She turned her attention to Eyfura's body; Magni had brought her to the room so she wasn't "alone" and "forgotten," but having her in the room reminded Kolfinna that she had failed her. It wasn't fair that Eyfura had to die here. Kolfinna had secretly hoped they could continue to be friends even after this mission. If Kolfinna had made different decisions, the outcome could've been better than this.

Her heart sank and she turned away from her. This mission wasn't a success. Too many had died.

"Now that this place isn't running anymore, we can have teams enter here and try to research as much as we can," Truda said. "We should regroup with the outside team."

Mímir continued to struggle against the stones. "Let me go," he said between grunts.

"You have the intelligence of a dead fish if you think we'll listen." Blár leaned forward and wove his fingers through Mímir's hair, jerking his head back so he could glare at him better. The moonlight made his blue eyes shine an ominous silver. "You're lucky I don't impale you right here and right now, Ragnarök scum."

Mímir's mouth trembled. "If you let me go, I can show you how to bring her back! She's not dead yet, but she will be if you don't free me."

Blár released him and he fell to the floor among the rubble. He wiped his hand on his thigh as if he had touched something rotten. "Keep talking nonsense and I'll freeze your mouth shut."

Magni narrowed his eyes. "Who are you talking about? You can't be talking about Eyfura."

"She's still alive! Revna didn't want to kill her just yet, since she wanted to use the rest of her mana to feed the others." Mímir shimmied his shoulders in an effort to free himself. "If you let me go, I'll show you how to bring her back."

Kolfinna slowly rose to her feet. Her foot brushed against one of the broken stone spears Revna had thrown at them in the battle, the sharp point of it dulled to a nub. The moonlight made Mímir's eyes look crazy, his face surrounded by the remnants of their battle, but she grasped onto his words anyway.

Eyfura wasn't dead? Now that he mentioned it, they hadn't checked her vitals. She had been so still that Kolfinna had assumed she was dead. But if Revna hadn't sucked all her mana and life force out, could she still be alive?

She ran to Eyfura and dropped to her knees. Even now, Eyfura looked too still to be alive. Her blond hair looked gray against the moonlight, and her pale skin was white and bloodless. Kolfinna pressed two trembling fingers against her throat and tried to feel a heartbeat.

Thump. Thump.

She gasped.

It was faint, but it was there.

Kolfinna placed both hands on Eyfura's chest so she could feel her mana more closely and more easily. For a moment, she couldn't feel anything, as if she was sifting through air, but then she caught a tiny dreg of energy.

Eyfura is alive.

"He's right," Kolfinna whispered, turning to the others. Tears pricked her eyes and she blinked away the tears. "She's still alive."

Truda looked unconvinced. "Are you ... sure?"

Magni violently grabbed Mímir by the hair and yanked him into a half-sitting position, eyes ablaze with rage. "How do we bring her back?"

"Free me—"

Fire sputtered from Magni's free hand and he brought it close to Mímir's face. "How do we bring her back?" he repeated. "You're not in any position to give us orders."

"Then kill me." Mímir body was shaking like a leaf, but his voice was resolute. "Because I'm not talking until you free me."

"He doesn't have to." Kolfinna clenched her hands to keep from quivering. "I think I know what I have to do."

Mímir gaped at her. "How could you possibly know what to do? You don't know anything!" He turned to the others wildly. "I can help her if you free me!"

Blár ignored him and kneeled beside Kolfinna in front of Eyfura. "What do you have to do?"

If Revna had been able to drain Eyfura's mana and life force, didn't that mean it was also possible for Kolfinna to do the same and *transfer* life force? She had been able to use Blár's mana, but maybe she could also manipulate life force like Revna did?

"I think ... I think I can manipulate her life force," she said as she turned to Blár. "Remember when I used your mana for those runes? Maybe I can do something similar, like transfer mana into her. Or ... I'm not sure, but I have to try."

"But none of us have any mana left," he said with an arched brow.

"One of us does," she said, just as everyone turned to Mímir.

Mímir gasped as the implication settled in; he shook his head and scooted away from them. "N-No! You can't do that to me!"

"We can do whatever we want, scum," Magni hissed, grabbing him by the hair and throwing him at Kolfinna's feet. His emerald eyes flashed with emotion at Kolfinna. "Bring her back. Please."

Life force and mana were practically interchangeable, but so different at the same time. Mana was energy, as was life force, but when mana became depleted, it didn't necessarily mean the body died. The body would replenish that mana with time. But life force was the energy that kept a person alive, and that couldn't replenish itself. Stripping away that mana was like peeling back skin to reveal flesh underneath. Could Kolfinna manipulate that life force from other people? Drain enough mana to tap into the life force? Or search for the life force beneath all that mana?

She had to try.

Mímir shouted at her to stop and tried kicking her, but it was no use. She placed her hand on Mímir's forehead and shoved it down to the floor, while placing her other hand on Eyfura's heart. She closed her eyes to concentrate and found Eyfura's tiny flake of life force. She then searched for Mímir's mana and found it easily; it was larger and like a calm, steady current of water. She pulled on that current, weaving it between her fingers.

His body went rigid when she took hold of his mana. "S-Stop!"

She paused, feeling the contrasting mana in her hands. She had never manipulated human life, and it felt wrong. She felt like if she did this, she would never be the same again and something within her would tarnish. She could hear Katla's voice in her ears. *"It'll twist your soul. You must never do that again!"*

She hesitated. What if it did twist her soul like Katla had said it would?

But then she remembered how kind Eyfura had been to her. How she was the only Royal Guard who made her feel welcome. She thought back to Nollar, Eyfura's younger brother, who was waiting for her to return.

She had to do it.

Kolfinna pulled at Mímir's mana and dug through it, trying to find the sliver of life force beneath it. She was so new to it that she couldn't distinguish between the mana and life force. She would have to drain the mana from him before tapping into his life force, she decided.

His body resisted, his mana refusing to meld in her hands, but she pulled harder, unspooling his mana until it dripped into her hands like a thread. A rush of exhilaration pumped through her veins when his mana poured into her. It was surprisingly warm, and that warmth spread over her body and curled her toes. But she didn't allow the feeling to remain, and instead poured it into Eyfura. Bit by bit, she poured Mímir's mana into her, until she felt *it*.

Whereas mana was warm, life force was *hot*.

It nearly burned her own mana as she wove it through her body and into Eyfura's. Despite the scorching feel of it, the rush of energy made her want to steal *all* of his life force. It was like a drug to her system, opening every pore in her body with bubbling heat. She wanted more, and a part of her didn't want to pour it into Eyfura's body, and instead wanted to keep it all for herself.

Blár touched her shoulder, and a jolt of cold snapped her from those thoughts.

"Is he ... dead?"

Mímir had stopped thrashing and his body had grown

weak, but he still had about a quarter of his life force in his body. She withdrew her hand from his forehead immediately.

"Um, no," she murmured.

She dripped the last dregs of the life force still on her hands into Eyfura's body and removed her hand from Eyfura as well. Horror filled her mind at the thoughts she had, but she quickly cast them aside as a rosy, healthy hue colored Eyfura's cheeks.

Kolfinna fell back onto her butt and released a shuddered breath. It was done. "She should wake up ... I think."

"You *think*? Is she alive or—" Magni started, but the words came out warbled to her ears. She rubbed her drooping eyelids; the weight of Mímir's life force leaving her body and going to Eyfura's felt like all her body's warmth had been snatched away.

"I'm going to sleep," she mumbled. "Take care of her, okay?"

Someone's calloused hands caught her shoulders, but she could barely keep her eyes open to see who it was.

"Hey—"

But sleep took her away without another second.

27

It had been two weeks since Kolfinna and the others left the Eventyrslot ruins, and she had remained in the Royal Guards' headquarters the past week, but now it was finally time to meet the king and hear his verdict.

Kolfinna fidgeted with the sleeve of her pink silk dress. It didn't fit her properly, as it should've been expected by now, but it was better than facing the king in any of the clothes she had. A Royal Guard had given it to her and she didn't know who it had belonged to, but it clung to her in all the wrong places. Her stomach looked frumpy and bulging, the sleeves were bunched together and made her shoulders look broad, and it was a few inches too long. She swore that once she had the money, she would invest in some proper clothes that didn't make her look like a fool.

Magni stood a few feet away from her, his pristine white and silver Royal Guard uniform cutting elegantly across his form. He ran a hand over his slicked back hair and inspected the large portrait that sat in the middle of the hallway leading to the throne room. Truda stared at her reflection on a metal vase and patted her hair, which curled at the ends and was tied together with a blue ribbon to match her military uniform. Both of them sported faded bruises and semi-healed cuts on their faces, and Truda even wore an arm sling.

Kolfinna felt out of place among them.

"Where's Blár?" Kolfinna asked quietly. The hallway of the royal palace felt like it had too many prying ears and eyes, even though only the three of them were there.

"Hmph. Who cares? He'll be here," Magni said.

"He's usually late to things like this." Truda fluffed her curls once more. "But—Oh, would you look that. He's here."

Kolfinna noticed his sharp, wintery eyes before anything else, and they were pinned on her, but the tightness around his mouth eased when he drew closer. Up close, she could see that his fur-lined military uniform was thicker and fancier than Truda's, and over it he wore a heavy fur-lined charcoal cloak.

Kolfinna tried not to look at the muscles rippling beneath his uniform. "You're here," she said when he came to stand in front of her. "I thought you wouldn't make it."

"And miss all those nobles ready to jump down your throat? I think not." He crossed his muscular arms over his broad chest. His icy gaze flicked over the hallway and then landed on her again. "You've never met the king, have you?"

"No." Kolfinna laughed; did he think she was important enough to meet the king casually? "Blár, most people don't ever meet the king."

"Not even during those stupid parades?" He raised an eyebrow.

"I never attended those things. Too many people." Kolfinna smoothed down the front of her dress with trembling fingers.

Blár must've noticed her fidgeting because he said, "There's no need to be nervous. The king has already gotten the reports of what happened back there. This is just a formality before he pardons your crimes."

"*Crime*. I didn't commit multiple crimes." She fiddled with the cuff of her sleeve. "But I still haven't talked to Fenris yet and given my side of what happened. What if they think I didn't do anything to help? What if they think I'm not useful and then they kill me like Mímir said they would?"

"I gave a good report on you." He shrugged and jerked a thumb at Magni, still critiquing the painting and Truda still fixing her hair. "I think my words weigh more than those two."

Kolfinna averted his gaze and focused on the plush, velvety, red and gold rug splayed over the white marble hallway. The rich red color reminded her of Fenris, and she found her mouth dry once more. "Fenris said he would be looking at what the other Royal Guards said about me." She shot a glance at Magni and lowered her voice. "He's the only Royal Guard who survived."

"And Eyfura."

"Yes, but she's still bedridden."

"You saved her life. That counts."

"I just ... I'm just nervous." Her frown deepened and she glanced at her stupid pink dress. Everything about the palace corridor looked elegant; from the vibrant painting of a beautiful queen that Magni admired silently, to the gold and glass chandeliers lining the ceilings, and the clear windows that streamed midday gold rays across the glittering marble floors—it was all too beautiful and too royal. She didn't fit in at all.

In contrast, she looked ridiculous in her stupid pink dress.

"It"—her voice came out thick—"it doesn't help that I look like a clown."

He tilted his head to the side, and the sunlight made his eyes gleam an electric blue as he slid his gaze over her figure. "You don't look bad and you definitely don't look like a clown."

"This dress is meant for someone tall and thin and beautiful." Tears threatening to spill. "I look like a clown and it doesn't compliment my figure at all. All those nobles will stare at me and think all these terrible things because I'm a fae, a commoner, a murderer, *and* I can't even find well-fitting clothes."

She expected him to comfort her, but he only looked amused. "They won't think that."

"Oh, they definitely will."

"Okay, they probably will," he said. "But I think you look great. And who cares what they think?"

"You wouldn't understand," she said. "And let's say the king *does* pardon me, but what if everyone retaliates at that decision? And Blár, it *does* matter what they think, because they're the ones who run society, aren't they? They have power, and I'm just a fae—"

"Hey, hey, calm down. You don't look like a clown. Let's just get that settled. What you do look like, is someone who's wearing clothes that don't belong to her. Like Agatha, from the children's stories. You remember Agatha, right?" When Kolfinna stared at him blankly, he elaborated, "She steals other people's clothes and eventually gets found out because none of the clothes she wears fits right, and she's sentenced to an eternity in the king's palace to serve as a seamstress for other people. You're basically Agatha."

Kolfinna's expression darkened. Not these stupid stories again. She wasn't sure if these children's stories originated only in his village up north, or if they were common stories in Rosain. "That's not funny." She frowned as he laughed softly. "And what is it with your stupid stories about stupid girls doing stupid stuff and getting punished for them? It's the same thing as the story about Gertrude you told me earlier."

"I don't make these stories up." He raised his hands as if absolving himself from the story's origin. "Take it up to whoever made them."

"But anyway ..." She was sure he was trying to distract her from the matter at hand, but nothing he could say would either comfort her or distract her enough. She had secretly hoped he would wipe her tears and tell her it would be all right, but that was the stupid part of her talking. Because she and Blár didn't have that kind of relationship. After today, they likely wouldn't see each other again.

Kolfinna ran a hand over her silk skirts. It was a pretty shade of pale pink, but that was the only good thing about the dress. The pit in her stomach grew as she imagined the people looking at her, pointing fingers, and chuckling behind bejeweled hand fans.

"Do I really look that ridiculous?" Her voice came out small enough to be swallowed up by the overwhelmingly embellished hallway.

"You look fine," Blár said.

She swallowed and stared down at her feet again.

"Hey now, don't look so dejected."

Kolfinna squeezed her eyes shut to keep from seeing the image of everyone giggling at her. Or the more pressing issue: her potential death if the king didn't think she deserved to live.

She snapped her eyes open when a weight fell around her shoulders. Her breath caught in her throat to find that Blár had draped his cloak over her shoulders and was now inches away from her. His fingers lightly brushed her collarbones as he fastened the clasp of his cloak on her.

"I shouldn't have said anything at all," he murmured as he finished clasping the cloak.

A chill settled in her bones at his nearness, and she unexpectedly found it soothing. It dissipated when he stepped back, and Kolfinna almost grabbed his hand to stop him, but her hand fell to her side.

"There," he said, inspecting the cloak. The backdrop of shimmering chandeliers looked cheap and dim in contrast to his smile. "Now no one can see your outfit. Or, well, they can't see all of it."

The cloak dragged to her feet, but it wasn't anything different than what the dress was already doing. But now she probably looked even more ridiculous, wearing a thick cloak that didn't fit her, that was *clearly* Blár's. She thumbed the material of the cloak and inhaled the scent of vanilla and cinnamon.

"They won't say anything too outlandish now." He continued to scrutinize her, and she suddenly felt hot under his gaze.

"Why do you always dress like ... like it's winter?" She pulled at the neckline of the cloak; the inside was lined with fur, and she was already sweating in it. "You do realize it's warm outside, right?"

"My powers make me cold pretty much all the time."

Kolfinna grabbed the clasp of the cloak and was about to unhook it, but Blár's hand snaked around her wrist. His eyes were sharp and he leaned in closer so only she could hear him. "Don't," he said. "Keep it on and everyone will know not to mess with you. Do you understand?"

She froze, unsure what to think of his words. To be under the protection of Blár Vilulf was an unexpected and surprising turn of events. Out of everyone who could've spread their wings over her, he was the last person she expected.

Kolfinna cleared her throat. "But why are you doing this?" Her voice was barely a whisper.

"You saved my life and I feel *kinda* bad for almost killing you a few times, so this'll make us even," he said half-jokingly. He straightened the front of his dark grayish blue uniform, his gaze flitting over to the gold-laced paneling between the tall windows. "I can't protect you all the time. I'm in the military and I go around all over the country, but if people know that you and I are friends, they'll be wary to do anything to you." He met her eyes once more. "And once you're a Royal Guard, you'll be under Fenris's protection. You'll have two black ranks on your side, so I think you'll be fine."

Kolfinna averted her gaze, suddenly feeling too hot— and it wasn't the cloak this time. "I had no idea I was upgraded from suspicious murderer to friend."

"*Friend* is a loose term," he said. "I'd say *acquaintance* fits us better. I don't know if we can be friends."

"Ouch." Her tone came out jovial, but it was only to hide the cold shock pulsing through her veins. She hadn't expected that. "You really know how to hurt someone's feelings. And why do you think we can't be friends?"

"Do you want to know the truth?"

"Yes."

He leaned forward, his breath tickling her ear. "You're far too pretty to be *just* a friend."

Blár's voice seemed to linger in her ear even as he pulled away, and when she looked up at him, he didn't look away. She almost forgot to breathe, completely lost in the intense blue of his gaze.

The door to the throne room suddenly wrenched open and their connection was severed. Kolfinna blinked back, feeling her cheeks redden with warmth. Blár turned toward the Royal Guard who appeared at the threshold. Kolfinna didn't have time to dwell on the moment because the guard motioned them forward.

"The king and Captain Asulf are waiting," the guard said.

Magni, Truda, and Blár went first, but Kolfinna hesitated where she stood; her fate would be sealed in that room. Whether she was branded as a murderer or a free woman would be decided today. She breathed out deeply and followed behind them, her heart racing.

The instant they walked through those doors, a wave of tension hit Kolfinna. It roiled and churned in the room with enough force to be an actual disaster. Eyes were on her in seconds, roving over her body and face in curiosity and animosity. She faltered in her steps, ready to spin around and run out of the room, but she kept moving forward. Heat spread over her cheeks and ears, her blood rushing to her face.

There was a carpeted path set in front of her, and on both sides of that carpet were dozens of seats, all of which were occupied. Some people wore military uniforms, while others wore fancy dresses with heavy jewelry. They watched her like vultures, ready to tear her body and pluck her innards. The sea of faces sent a wave of nausea over her; they all blended together into an angry storm. Everyone's attention was on her—not on Blár, or Truda, or Magni. Just her.

A murmur spread throughout the room slowly.

She wanted to throw up—the urge was so strong that she almost spun around to leave—but when she lowered her head, the fur collar of the cloak tickled her nose, and she breathed in Blár's scent clinging to the cloak. It soothed her, and she felt like she could breathe again. The nausea slowly ebbed away and she kept her gaze glued to the back of Blár's head and tried to ignore the pointed stares.

The hushed voices silenced when the room grew colder and colder, and Blár's footsteps resounded louder and heavier than anyone's voice.

Blár stopped in front of the throne and fell into a sweeping bow. Magni and Truda did the same, and Kolfinna scrambled to mimic them.

The king sat on his throne in the center of the room, his chin practically pointing up to the ceiling as he peered down at them all. He was more ordinary than Kolfinna could've ever imagined. She had expected a regal and handsome man, like in all the stories of princes and kings, but he was extremely plain-looking with ordinary gray-tinged russet hair, tawny eyes, and wrinkled skin around his mouth. If he hadn't been wearing all the fancy regalia of a king—the crown, the bushy cloak, the heavily adorned clothes—she wouldn't have remembered his face at all.

King Leiknir narrowed his cold eyes at Kolfinna, and a shiver ran down her spine. He might have looked like an ordinary person, but he held the gaze of a ruler. Fenris stood beside him stared at her as well, but his gaze wasn't as cold and lacked the revulsion she saw in the king's. He was garbed in his white and gold uniform, his red hair contrasting with the white, and his silver eyes boring into her. Or more specifically, at the cloak she wore.

"You may all rise." King Leiknir raised his hand.

Her attention was drawn to the midnight-black sword hanging on the wall behind the king. Sinister mana flowed from it and she was reminded of the power of the *Magiskæder* and the *Genfødsel Kniv*. Both of which had been handed to the Royal Guard, and then to the king. The sword above the throne felt similarly wicked, and she surmised it was another fae artifact. She vaguely remembered Mímir mentioning that the royal family had a fae artifact that was the sister of the *Genfødsel Kniv*. What had he called it? The *Død Sværd*? Was that the same sword he had been talking about?

King Leiknir's voice boomed in the quiet room. "Fenris has already filled me in about what happened, and I've read all of your reports." He motioned to Magni,

Truda, and Blár. "You all did an excellent job out there. Many lives were lost and you discovered a traitor. Nonetheless, we have much to learn from these ruins and I applaud you four for making these ruins accessible to us all. This is a great advancement for Rosain as a whole."

His eyes turned to Kolfinna and the weight of his stare felt heavier than the cloak on her shoulders, and if it weren't for Blár glancing over his shoulder at her, she would've shriveled within herself.

"Kolfinna the fae." King Leiknir leaned into his throne and regarded her coolly. Green and blue gemstones glinted on his crown and he twisted a heavy ruby ring around his forefinger. Kolfinna held her breath for his next words. "I've heard much about you and how you were able to read the runes. It is my request that you continue to serve our country by lending us your strength as a fae. We wouldn't have been able to do what we did without your help. It is my hope that you will continue to serve us as a Royal Guard."

A collective gasp filled the room, and even Kolfinna inhaled sharply.

A Royal Guard; she would finally become one.

She lowered herself to another bow. She couldn't hide the relief from her voice as she said, "That is also my wish, Your Highness."

His smile was thin and unnerving. "I'm happy to hear that. I have high expectations for you."

Kolfinna straightened her shoulders and tried to hide the grin twitching on her lips. From Blár's side profile, she saw a hint of a smile on his lips, and even Magni gave a short nod in her direction. The swarm of faces in the crowd almost didn't matter anymore with those words alone.

"That's all. You four are dismissed."

He didn't need to tell her twice to leave. She spun on her heels immediately, her gaze cutting straight to the doorway. All she had to do was leave and then she was free—

"Your Majesty," a strong, clipped voice resounded in the grand room. An older woman had her hand raised and she stared at Kolfinna like a hawk. Blond and gray hair framed her face, and laugh lines formed around her mouth, but there was no kindness in that gaze. "If I may interrupt—"

King Leiknir narrowed his eyes, and she noticed that even Fenris appeared peeved, his lips pursed into a firm line. "What is it, Hilda Helgadottir?"

Kolfinna bristled. Hilda Helgadottir was the third black rank in the country. She had also been the head of the Hunter's Association in her prime, so Kolfinna had a feeling that whatever she had to say wouldn't be in Kolfinna's favor.

"I've heard Kolfinna the fae is a murderer." She crossed her leg over the other and placed her hands on her knees. The chandelier lights glinted off the sparking, gems-studded rings adorning her fingers. "How can a murderer become a Royal Guard? If she is to be a Royal Guard, how can she uphold justice with such murky morals?"

"She's been absolved for her past in the same manner as you have, Hilda." Fenris's voice cracked like a whip, his tone piercing. "Just like how you were pardoned for your crimes of killing dozens of fae, some of whom actually weren't fae, Kolfinna has also been pardoned."

Hilda's smile remained frozen on her face, as if unaffected by his words. "Is that so?" she asked. "My duties as a hunter also saved countless people. I've never made a mistake, Captain Asulf, so I don't know what you're implying—"

"If you have any complaints about my judgment—" King Leiknir started.

"Oh, heavens, I would never dream of that!" She covered her mouth and chuckled. "I was simply curious about the morality of your newest Royal Guard, Your Highness. She will be in close proximity to you and the important people in this palace, so I was wondering if it's wise to have her here. I was only thinking about your safety, Your Highness."

"If you have further questions about Kolfinna, you're more than welcome to visit my office and we can discuss it further," Fenris said flatly. "But now is not the time, nor the place."

"Apologies, then," Hilda murmured, her smile absolutely villainous as she shifted her attention to Kolfinna. "I'll have to take you up on that offer, Captain Asulf."

"I'm not a threat." Kolfinna's voice rang across the room and it took her a moment to realize she had said it out loud. She glanced at Fenris, who gave her a reassuring nod. Blár smiled when their eyes met, as if urging her to continue. She gathered her confidence and turned to Hilda. "I plan to serve and protect this country and to help as many people as I can. I'm no more of a threat than you are, Hilda Helgadottir. I hope you can come to trust me. The fae are not your enemies."

Hilda's smile was sharp and unforgiving. "Is that so? I suppose we'll have to wait and see then."

Kolfinna couldn't say anymore because a Royal Guard motioned them toward the door.

She pulled the cloak tighter around herself. She was now a Royal Guard. She didn't have to fear the hunters anymore. Not even Hilda.

28

Kolfinna waited outside Eyfura's door
with bated breath; she had been in the Royal Guard
recovery wing ever since they returned from the ruins.
During that time, no one had been allowed to visit in
order to let her recuperate. Kolfinna had been relieved to
hear that—she was honestly too ashamed and nervous to
face her.

She hesitated another minute before gently rapping
her knuckles against the door and peeking inside. The
room was empty save for a bed, a stool, a couch, and a
nightstand. Nollar was curled up in a ball on the couch,
while Eyfura sat on the white bed with a handful of papers
in her hands. Her blond locks were pulled together
messily into a loose bun, and she wore a long, thin, fluttering nightdress that shifted against her body with the
breeze from the open window.

Eyfura's eyes lit up when she saw Kolfinna and she

placed the papers on the nightstand, a grin stretching across her lips. "Kolfinna!" she said. "Oh goodness, so good to see you! Come in, come in!"

Nollar shifted on the couch and mumbled something but was fast asleep the next second.

Kolfinna smiled at the sight of him. How many restless nights had Katla spent whenever Kolfinna had been sick or injured herself doing something reckless? She missed those days, but that feeling quickly passed.

"Come here, sit!" Eyfura ushered toward the stool. "Gosh, it's so good to see you walking without a limp! I know it was resolved in the ruins, but it's still amazing to see! Runes really are something else, aren't they?"

"Yeah, they really are." In the few weeks that had passed since her leg had been healed, Kolfinna had gotten used to having normal function of her leg once more, and not being in crippling pain all the time, but from time to time, she was amazed at how it had healed. It reaffirmed her belief that there was still so much she didn't know about runes and their capabilities.

Kolfinna sat beside the bed. "How are you doing?" she asked.

"Much better than before, but Nollar won't let me leave until I'm one hundred percent, so I've been a prisoner here." She laughed and reached forward to squeeze Kolfinna's hand. She suddenly became serious. "I heard what happened. Thank you, by the way. You saved my life."

"Oh, please don't thank me." She didn't know

whether to focus on Eyfura, Nollar, or the marbled white floor. "It's my fault that even happened. If I hadn't released Revna ..." The words lodged themselves in her throat and she found it hard to finish. "None of this would've happened."

Eyfura tightened her grip on her hand. "No, it was bound to happen. Mímir was a traitor all along. If he didn't betray us at that moment, he would've done it at another moment. Either at those ruins or on another mission. Things could've been *much* worse."

Kolfinna wasn't too convinced, but she nodded nonetheless. "I suppose ... I still would like to apolo—"

"No, no! Don't say the word." Eyfura grinned. A gentle breeze carried the smell of lavender throughout the room, rustling the starch-white curtains and filling the space between them. "You saved my life, so I don't want to hear anything other than you proudly saying that you saved me."

She had been so anxious to talk to Eyfura that she had almost forgotten how infectiously warm her personality was. Like the warmth and sweetness of honey on a summer day.

Kolfinna smiled. "All right."

"Great!" She clapped her hands together. "Now, have you talked to Captain Asulf at all?"

"I have," she said. "I gave him my side of what happened and we talked for a bit."

"About?"

Kolfinna shrugged and ran her hands over the thinning material of her brown dress. This one was actually hers; the Royal Guards had been gracious enough to go back to her old apartment and bring back her clothes.

When Eyfura continued drilling holes into her, Kolfinna sighed and answered, "Mímir, the next steps. That sort of thing. I didn't want you to worry, so I didn't want to bring it up."

Eyfura leaned forward. "Worry about what? Captain Asulf isn't telling me anything for the same reason, and because he wants me to focus on recovering."

"Unfortunately, Mímir was taken by the military," Kolfinna said. "They didn't think we would be able to be unbiased enough to get information out of him, and there was the fear that others within the Royal Guard sided with him and Ragnarök, so he's in military custody."

Eyfura's clenched the white sheets surrounding her thighs. "Seriously? That's not fair! He was one of our own, so it only makes sense that we figure out the extent of his treachery."

"That's what Captain Asulf said, but apparently the commander-in-chief insisted on taking him."

"Well, that's a bummer." Eyfura slumped against the wall and blew out air. "And what about the ruins? Will they be excavated?"

"Yes, they will be. I'm not sure who'll be on that mission. None of the details are exactly clear." Kolfinna laced her fingers together; there was still so much history inside the ruins she hadn't uncovered, like those books about Mer-folk and elves. She would love to explore the ruins further, sit down and research all the books, murals, and paintings—but it wasn't her call to make. Fenris had told her that he couldn't technically tell her any more than he already had until she was an official Royal Guard, which wouldn't be until the end of the summer.

"One thing we know for certain is that Revna and Ragnarök are planning for *something*, but who knows when and how it'll happen," Kolfinna said. "Captain Asulf isn't too concerned, because Ragnarök has been around for a while and they haven't done much, but ..."

"But it's still a worry." Eyfura reached for her nightstand and picked up a plate of peach slices. "Because they plan to take over this country, and we have no idea what we're up against." Eyfura ate one of the slices. "They've been silent for a while now, but this is the first big thing they've done in a while, isn't it?" She held out the plate to Kolfinna. "Want a peach?"

"Um, no, thanks ..." Kolfinna threaded her fingers together until they turned white.

"What's with that look?"

"Um, Mímir mentioned that they, Ragnarök, want to 'awaken' Queen Aesileif."

"Yeah, I remember him mentioning that ... Which is strange because she should be dead." Eyfura thought for a moment then shrugged. "But, well, considering how Revna should also be dead, I guess it's not *too* strange."

"We're just going to gather information and try to figure out as much as we can from Mímir," Kolfinna said.

"I'm sure they'll want me to do something about the research, since I'm the only fae in the Royal Guard now."

Eyfura's lips quirked up. "Oh, I heard about that! Are you excited about your instatement ceremony? You're lucky that it's coming soon, since the Royal Guards only have it once a year. Can you imagine having to wait a whole year to become a Royal Guard because the timing was off?" Eyfura pointed to Nollar, who was still in a deep slumber despite their conversation. "You'll have your ceremony with Nollar and his graduating class! Gosh, that's so exciting!"

"Yeah, I'm excited."

"I bet! The instatement ceremony is always so much fun! There's like a party, and food, and dancing! It's a blast. You'll love it, I promise."

"Speaking of ..." Kolfinna slipped her hand in the pocket of her dress and pulled out the Hope badge with her name carved on the back. "I got the badge you made me."

Eyfura's cheeks flushed at the sight of the crudely made lion. "I'm glad you got it. It's embarrassing that it looks so bad, though. I actually made a few of them, but they were terrible and I had to start over. I had asked Magni to help me with the lion's face, but he refused."

"I'm surprised he didn't help you, considering he seems to like you."

"What?" Eyfura looked at her like she had grown two heads. She laughed in disbelief. "Magni? No way!"

"He was devastated when he thought you died."

Eyfura tilted her head. "Really? But, well, he probably likes me as a friend, nothing more." But even as she said that, her gaze lingered on the vibrant purple assortment of lavender, petunias and amaranths in the vase on the nightstand.

"Did Magni get you those flowers?"

Eyfura's cheeks became pink.

Kolfinna continued, "And he seems to know that ... purple is your favorite color?" It was a wild guess, but she had noticed that Eyfura wore purple earrings. It probably didn't mean anything, but Eyfura nodded dumbly, affirming her suspicions.

"There's no way he likes me." Eyfura laughed again and she pushed a strand of hair behind her ear. "You're making me feel awkward about this now!" She shook her head, and her amethyst earrings caught in the light. "Anyway, what about you and Blár Vilulf? I thought he was your sworn enemy, and here you are, practically showing off to everyone that you have his favor. What was *that* about?"

Now it was Kolfinna's turn to blush. "How'd you hear about that?"

"*Everyone's* talking about it. Even *I* heard about it, and I'm stuck here."

"It's not like that. We're just ... acquaintances, I guess."

"I think I've got a lot to catch up on. And I guess it's a good thing I'm stuck here, so you better fill me in."

They both laughed. Even with the threat of Ragnarök,

of Revna, and of her position in the world hanging over her head—Kolfinna felt lighter to be talking to Eyfura in such a manner. All those worries seemed to melt away. She would take care of those issues later. For now, she would focus on this moment—laughing with her friend. It had been over a year since she had spoken to someone like this. Katla had been the last one she had ever been close to, but maybe there was room for others. And Kolfinna knew that this was what Katla had wanted all along. To belong somewhere.

ACKNOWLEDGMENTS

Thank you so much for reading *The Ruins of the Heartless Fae!* This book would not have been possible without the support and love of my family.

I want to thank my sister for being my number one fan since day one. My brothers and my mom for always believing in me and encouraging me. I especially want to thank my dad, who would've been so proud to see this moment. And of course, thank you to my husband for supporting me, pushing me forward when I really didn't think I could, and for giving me confidence in my words whenever I lost it. I love you all—greatly.

Last but not least, I want to thank my amazing developmental editor Dana for helping shape this story into what it is and for polishing up all the rough spots (and there were many), my cover designer Daqri for bringing my vague vision to life, and Emily for catching all those grammar mistakes.

Thank you all from the bottom of my heart!

ABOUT THE AUTHOR

Maham Fatemi is an avid reader, writer, and cat lover. When she's not obsessing over her cats, you can find her skimming a new cookbook, reading comics, or drinking an unhealthy number of oat-milk lattes. Maham lives in the Chicagoland area with her husband, son, and five cats. For new releases, visit her website at mahamfatemi.com

9 781961 171008